HAVEN

A TENNYSON BEND NOVEL

PT AMBLER

Warning

Intended for an 18+ audience only. This book contains material that is intended for a mature, adult audience. It contains graphic language, explicit sexual content, and adult situations.

Haven

A TENNYSON BEND NOVEL

PT AMBLER

HAVEN

All Dane wants is a stress-relieving weekend of salt spray, scotch, and sex. So, why does his PA think it's a good idea to send him to a hippy-trippy wellness retreat deep in the Australian tropical rainforest? The only thing that makes the place bearable is the hot-as-hell guy in the cabin next door, who may or may not be a lying, cheating hack.

Cayden's on a secret mission at the House of Glass Wellness Retreat to rescue his long-lost sister, Lucy, and repair his fractured family. It's not him that needs saving. Not until the possums attack and the pin-striped dude with his kill-me-now looks comes barrelling out of the cabin next door, ready to save the day.

Neither can deny the attraction that flares between them, but Cayden dare not dream of hearts and rainbows till he's unburdened by his mission, and Dane can't trust anyone with his truth, let alone his scarred heart. So, they resolve to keep things casual while they band together to find clues to Lucy's mysterious disappearance, dodge the retreat's zealous guru, and save each other from one too many kale smoothies.

Neither expect complications…like pesky emotions.

Haven *features forced proximity, digital detox, steamy nights between soft bamboo sheets, bugs the size of rhinoceroses, and enough organic fibre to keep everyone healthy and happy.*

NOTE FROM THE AUTHOR

Special thanks go to Rachael Herron and my 90 Day crew. Without you all, this novel wouldn't have been nearly so much of a joy to write or wrangle. And to lovely Maggie, Mel, and Marrije—my beta readers extraordinaire—thank you for your attentive eyes, kind words, and generous hearts.

To keep this novel authentic to its Aussie roots, the author has used Australian English spelling and grammar. Enjoy :)

CHAPTER ONE

DANE

Dane rubbed his eyes and straightened up, shivering when his back hit a cool spot on the leather car seat.

"Where are we?" Dane cleared his sleep-roughened throat. "Did roadworks divert the highway?"

The driver's eyes flashed up at him in the rear-view mirror. "Won't be long, sir. We're almost there."

Yes, but to where? he wanted to ask, exasperated.

Dane ignored the driver's surprised look, loosened the knot on his charcoal tie, and rubbed at the compressed spot on his forehead where he must have lain near-comatose for hours against the car's cool window.

The last thing he could remember was the dalump-dalump of the car's wheels hitting the highway lane markings as they sped north out of Brisbane, destined, he'd thought, for Noosa, where he planned to drown his exhaustion in salt spray and scotch.

But with Brisbane's city lights long gone on the southern horizon, all that remained of the highway was the metronomic flash of roadside safety markers—displaced by a steep, winding, potholed road, barely illuminated by the car's headlights.

Moments later, the dense canopy opened at the crest of a steep rise to reveal the wide starry arc of the Milky Way above and a small cluster of warmly lit buildings below.

The car plunged down to the base of the slope, where the cool white headlights illuminated a giant stone arch straddling the gravel road, carved with five ominous words:

House of Glass Wellness Retreat.

"What. The. Hell?"

Where was the sleek hotel overlooking the deep blue Pacific? The bars and cafés? The surf club serving grilled barramundi on endive, and ice-cold chardonnay?

Carol, his long-time PA, was usually reliable to book him somewhere appropriate whenever he wanted to extend a business trip for a night or two. But a hippy-trippy health retreat deep in the Queensland rainforest? What was she thinking?

Didn't she know hemp gave him hives?

Dane took his phone out of his trouser pocket and swiped the screen. Maybe he could book an ocean-view suite in Noosa for the weekend. It wasn't as though he'd planned to take an entire fortnight away from work, despite his GP's advice, Carol's insistence, and the exhaustion that sat like an anvil on his shoulders.

The critical tasks for Carter Medical Supplies' latest acquisition might be done, but that didn't mean he had nothing else to do—to rest was to fail.

He tried a travel app to book directly, but the working circle rotated around and around, going nowhere.

"Fuck." All he needed was one measly bar.

The car ground to a halt in front of a jasmine-laced pagoda where a blonde woman stood, dressed in a flowing white linen dress far more suitable for the summer heat than his three-piece suit.

She stepped down from the pagoda and pulled open his passenger door.

"Welcome to the House of Glass Wellness Retreat. I'm Bess." She smiled a serene smile that might as well have been fingernails on a chalkboard for all the serenity it inspired in Dane's cranky soul. "And you must be Mr Faulks. I greet you with joy and compassion."

Oh, hell, no.

He stepped out of the car, feeling the creak in every bone and muscle as he held his mobile phone high in search of a signal.

Any signal.

"Don't you have wi-fi?" he asked her.

"I'm sorry, Mr Faulks, but the House of Glass Wellness Retreat is a wi-fi-free zone. Inside the volcano's caldera, signals are erratic and thin."

Concrete lodged in his gut. The night was going from bad to worse. How was he supposed to get any work done without network access?

She smiled and directed the driver to set Dane's small suitcase in a wagon hitched to a golf cart.

"Don't worry about your belongings. They'll be taken directly to your haven."

"My…what?"

"Your haven," she repeated unhelpfully, as though he was supposed to know what the hell that was.

Sweat prickled his neck, but damn if he was going to take off his suit jacket before he could sort out Carol's mess. What had she gotten him into?

Doctor's orders, Carol's voice chided in his mind. *Exhaustion won't resolve without rest.*

His luck, she'd probably booked him in for the full two-week break his GP suggested he take away from work. As though he'd ever step away from his responsibilities for that long.

"If you'll follow me, I'll guide you to the hub where your fellow guests have gathered for Gordon's welcome and for dinner."

The driver's door shut, and the tell-tale sound of the car's motor started up. "Wait." He rounded the front of the car, holding his hand up in the universal 'halt' gesture. He'd be damned if he'd let the man leave him in a digital wasteland. The driver's window slowly rolled open.

"You can't leave me here."

Geez, Dane. Get a grip.

"This is a mistake. Coming here. Wherever here is." God, he was tired. "Can you drive me to the Sunshine Coast instead? Or, really, anywhere."

"I'm sorry, sir, but that won't be possible."

"Noosa can't be that far." Dane pulled out his wallet and offered a crisp one-hundred-dollar note. Cash always worked.

"I'm sorry, sir." The driver didn't sound sorry at all. "I have another booking tonight. Our service is stretched very thin over the Australia Day long weekend."

"You're heading back to Brisbane? Great. It's not all that much of a detour to take me home to Tennyson. Ten minutes, tops." He added another big note to the bribe, vowing to take it out of Carol's next Christmas bonus.

"I'm sorry, sir. That won't be possible." The driver shook his head, and the prickles at Dane's neck ramped up to rolling-in-cacti level. "I'll do my best to expedite another car and driver for you, but I doubt there'll be any available for at least twenty-four hours. Possibly longer. They always over-load bookings over holiday weekends."

Well, fuck.

Dane rolled his neck and heard the familiar crack-crack-crack of strained muscle, tendons, and bone.

Strategic retreat didn't come naturally, but he took a step back from the car and watched as it receded up the drive. The little red taillights split and shifted in his bleary-eyed vision before the car crested the rise and disappeared into the night.

He didn't want to do *wellness*, for fuck's sake. That meant mindfulness and air-dried kale and answering questions like, "How do you feel, Dane?"

God, no.

What he wanted—no, what he needed was a circuit breaker. To drink too much, fuck around with some choice guys, swim too far beyond the breakers, and sleep about twelve comatose hours.

Patience, Faulks. He took a slow, deep breath, then tucked his wallet back into his pocket. He might have had good reason to be tired and cranky—three months straight of twenty-four-seven work would do that—but a tantrum never got a man anywhere.

"What sort of scotch do you serve here, Bess? Any Talisker?"

"I'm sorry, Mr. Faulks. But the House of Glass Well—"

He held up his hand to stop whatever explanation she was about to give. Of course, the place didn't serve alcohol—it was a wellness retreat.

He followed Bess up into the pagoda and took a good look around the retreat.

Fairy lights lit up the sweet-smelling jasmine that laced the pagoda where he stood with Bess. Beyond that, a winding path swept around a garden to an old Queenslander-style cottage that glowed gold in the darkness. The place was nothing like the flash sort of beach resort he preferred, but it didn't look like the worst place to spend a night, either.

Time to buck up and make the best of it, Dane told himself. Tomorrow, he'd find a way out and return to plan A.

He straightened his spine and reached out to shake her hand.

"Please, call me Dane."

CHAPTER TWO

CAYDEN

Cayden's stomach growled at the tantalising aromas drifting from the kitchen door to the retreat's dining room, or hub… or whatever the fuck they called it.

Desperate for distraction, he opened his dossier labelled *Cayden Spicer: Pure Detox Wellness Plan* and flicked through to his fourteen-day personalised menu.

Day 1. Dinner: a forager's feast.

He imagined a plate full of nuts and berries.

"Hmm…odd, but edible."

Cayden cast his eyes further down the page.

Day 2. Breakfast: coconut oil shot and green smoothie; Lunch: green smoothie; Dinner: buttered bone broth.

"What the ever-loving fuck?"

"What was that, dear?" Edie leaned toward him. He'd dubbed her the *geriatric pixie* the minute he'd seen her tiny frame and spiky purple hair. She'd probably contest the geriatric part, but the more time he spent with the woman, the more he was convinced she'd wear the pixie moniker with pride. She and her equally geriatric but only slightly less pixie-like friend, Maxine, had a knack for speaking truth to whoever would listen.

"Nothing. Sorry. Just mouthing off."

"You mean about this piss-awful menu?"

He choked on a bit of ginger root floating in his water glass. "Jesus, Edie!"

"That's okay. You're allowed to say what you think. Better out than in, right?" She dabbed his hand, making him feel like a toddler with mucky fingers.

He grinned. "Everything on tomorrow's menu looks better out than in."

"Ha!" Her loud cackle drew the attention of the other guests.

"Shh, Edie." Maxine shushed her friend, but Edie paid her no mind.

She leaned toward him. "I'm still stuck on tonight. Forager's feast? That's got to be witchetty grubs and...and...."

"Crocodile meat?" Maxine guessed.

"Ugh." Cayden sniffed suspiciously at the aromas that *had* smelled delicious thirty seconds earlier. "Thanks for that, ladies."

He looked back down at his extended menu, hoping it might have magically changed in the five seconds since he'd last looked. No luck. Twenty-four hours of kale and he'd be shitting like Kermit, not to mention having serious cravings for one of Henrietta's delicious egg-and-bacon rolls. His boss's incredulous "you won't survive a day!" warning echoed in his mind as he scanned down to the second week's menu. Plenty of eggs, but no bacon, and not even a hint of carbs in sight.

Fuck.

So much for a font of health and happiness—how was anyone supposed to thrive on kale smoothies and bone broth? Whatever the hell that was.

His stomach growled another SOS.

Of course, he wasn't really there at the House of Glass Wellness Retreat for a detox. Or for any other brand of wellness Gordon-fucking-Fuller could offer. Not even Henrietta, his boss at the network, knew the true extent of his plan—and she'd approved funds for his investigation.

Henrietta, his boss and friend, had believed Cayden's claim that the retreat looked like a front for a cult enough to fund a preliminary investigation. What he hadn't told Henrietta was that he suspected his long-lost sister, Lucy, had fallen in with the alleged cult. Henrietta would eventually discover his subterfuge and probably fire him. It didn't sit right that he'd probably lose Henrietta's friendship over it, too, but he'd risk his job for his sister's life, any day.

If he was going to find Lucy, he'd have to be smart, and careful, and stay well under the radar—which meant he'd have to suck up the kale along with all the lies.

He did his best to not think about how much of his own life and happiness he'd put on hold to find Lucy.

In the days leading up to his fifteenth birthday, he'd mentally practiced his line—*I'm gay, I'm gay, I'm gay*—over and over. But that wasn't how the day had gone. He'd never gotten the words out. Instead, the crucial words became—*Lucy's gone, Lucy's gone, Lucy's gone.*

In one heartbeat, their lives had changed forever. His mission to *come out, come out, come out* had become *find Lucy, find Lucy, find Lucy.*

The tangle of words should have long ago lost their bite.

Everyone else knew. But around his parents he was stuck, like a fly in amber, as that fifteen-year-old kid in the closet.

Telling them felt like the last barrier. As soon as he found Lucy, alive and well, he could come out to his parents and get on with his life for real.

From the rickety cane chair in the back corner of the

dining hub, Cayden scanned the room for any kind of clue to kick-start his investigation. He'd chosen the position to get a good view of the staff, but some of the cane weave had come undone and was poking him in the arse.

If he had a partner in crime, he'd probably make some stupid wink-wink joke about it not being the sort of poking he usually got behind. Alas, at the rate Cayden's halfway-in-halfway-out sex life was going, there wasn't even the possibility of him having a partner in crime, let alone a partner in life. Not yet anyway.

For the moment, though, he had to go yet another layer deeper and pretend retreat life—the Zen-powered, kale-loving, data-detoxing life—was for him.

Of the dozen guests, his tablemates, Edie and Maxine, were by far his favourite. Bernice and Randall, empty-nesters who'd finally earned their 'me' time, came a close second, although florid-cheeked Randall's extreme-sport-level enthusiasm was going to get old real quick.

He glanced quickly at the six be-flowered book-club ladies—a few of whom were eyeing him like a tropical cocktail after a long hot day at the beach. Yeah, no. The afternoon meet-and-greet on the hub deck had been bad enough. They could stay on the other side of the room for dinner, thank you very much.

The twelfth guest was yet to show, though it must have been a man. Bess had been at pains to tell him he'd be sharing the deck to his split A-frame cabin, or *haven,* as the staff liked to call them, with a male version of the species. Thank gawd.

He sighed and lifted his glass for a cleansing drink, forgetting to use his front teeth as a strainer against the bobbing slivers of ginger, and just about choked as Gordon-fucking-Fuller strode through the dining-room door—a beaming grin stretched ear to ear.

Cayden's gorge rose, and instinct had him halfway to his

feet when his thighs bumped the table, Maxine and Edie shouted a warning, and he felt a rush of cold to his lap.

Iced ginger water doused his groin and his temper all in one.

"Shit."

"Never mind, dear." Edie tutted and went to sop up the mess with a woefully inadequate napkin.

Cayden caught her hand and gently pushed it away.

Hers was not a hand he wanted anywhere close to his junk.

He righted the glass, collapsed back into the cane torture device, and jerked his gaze back up.

Instead of Gordon, though, his eyes caught on another man who stood in the doorway.

The gorgeous specimen of a man had thick chocolaty hair turning to waves where it skimmed his open collar, heavy-lidded eyes under terse brows, and a slash of a mouth that screamed, *Get me the fuck out of here!*

Or maybe, possibly, that might have just been Cayden projecting. Straight out of *GQ*, the stranger at the door had the sort of presence only an insanely attractive man in a three-piece, pinstripe suit could achieve—graceful and gorgeous and goddamn impressive.

"Oh, look, Maxine, there's another bit of deliciousness." Edie giggled like she was eighty-going-on-eighteen. She patted his hand. "Don't worry, though, Cayden. You're still our favourite."

"Praise be." That earned him another pixie-giggle, but he didn't look their way—all he had eyes for was the tall drink of man at the door.

CHAPTER THREE

DANE

Dane tried hard not to waver on his feet as he crossed the wooden deck of the old Queenslander cottage.

What had Bess called it? The hub?

He followed a short, balding guy across the threshold into the blessed air conditioning of the dining hall, where his stomach roiled at the earthy aroma of food. When was the last time he'd enjoyed a proper, relaxed meal? Must have been Brady's New Year's Eve barbeque—a low-key night of thick, juicy steaks, and too many bottles of red, shared with Lachlan, Spencer, Malone, and Malone's new guy, Jet.

Dane had barely seen any of his mates since the start of summer, and they'd spent half the night berating him for his over-commitment to the office and under-commitment to their five-man tennis squad.

Four weeks and what felt like four-hundred hours at the office later, he'd happily take their ribbing as payment for another of those delicious steaks. But he was stuck two hundred kilometres away from Tennyson Bend and Brady's barbeque.

He sniffed the air appreciatively. Instead of a giant finger of scotch, a food coma would have to do the job of putting him under for the night.

First thing in the morning, he'd hitch a ride to Noosa Heads for a couple of nights' stay. No way would he last two weeks away from work. A few days of sun, sea, and sex were all he needed. Then he'd get back to normal life.

Tiredness tugged at Dane's bones. He shrugged off his jacket, lay it over his briefcase on the floor, and slid into a free seat at the table right next to the door, where the ease of escape suited him just fine.

He leaned back and let his heavy eyelids drop to avoid making eye contact with anyone, especially the floral-clad women at the same ta—

"Hi, I'm Michelle, and this is Lissa, and that's Anna beside you, and at the next table, there's—"

Dane stopped listening. The middle-aged woman with flicky nineties hair and a flirty smile looked set to introduce her entire cheer squad, and he just didn't want to know.

He thought about trading tables. Dane didn't care all that much what a bunch of unknown women thought of him, but it'd be an ungentlemanly move. Besides, his bones ached at the thought of getting up.

Michelle reached across and grabbed his arm. Her coral-painted fingernails were grotesque against his pale blue pinstriped shirt. "Can you even imagine this place? So amazing. I can't wait for my lymphatic massage, and—"

"Facial, and—" Lissa, beside her, chimed in.

"—sunrise yoga, and—"

"—oh my God, the seaweed wrap, and—"

Was it too late to beg for a pair of 'hear-no-evil' headphones?

"—steam room, and—" Anna quietly added over the top of her friends.

Dane blinked at that. A steam didn't sound too bad, in

different company. Before he could show any interest, though, the man Dane had followed into the room clapped his hands.

"Good evening! I'm Gordon Fuller, owner and manager of the House of Glass Wellness Retreat. I welcome you with joy and compassion. Congratulations on making your health your priority." The man beamed—a born salesman—but Dane wasn't buying. He let his eyes and his mind surreptitiously scan the other guests, who all listened to Gordon with rapt attention.

Only one person, half-obscured by a potted palm clear across the other side of the room, didn't seem to be hooked on Gordon's every word.

On first glance, the guy in the corner of the dining room looked at ease. He lounged back and slowly tapped a one-handed piano piece on the armrest of his cane chair.

Dane couldn't take his eyes off the man's loopy blonde curls. He was practically monochrome blonde, dressed in rumpled beige linen straight out of documentary filmmaker Sheridan Brown's *What to Wear on an Outback Safari* guide.

Dane wondered if the man's eyes fit the desert-dweller colour chart, too. Palm green, sandy hazel, or perhaps the clear azure of the sky over Marrakesh?

But then, something about the man's stillness made Dane reassess his opinion.

From his studiously blank expression, it looked like he was holding back rage, or pain, or revulsion.

It filled Dane with disquiet. He closed his eyes just to break the moment. When he opened them, the man was staring straight at him.

Hazel.

The man had hazel eyes.

Gone was the anger, and it was clear that the man felt anything but disgust as he surveyed Dane.

A lion stalking its prey.

Damn. Maybe an overnight stay wouldn't be so terrible after all.

The palm leaf in front of the stranger swayed in the night breeze, obscuring Dane's view and breaking their staring contest. He blinked as the moment was lost.

Something nudged at his elbow.

Dane glanced down to see Anna sliding two small cardboard boxes into his space at the table.

He picked up the smaller box and turned it over. The only marking on it was a stripe of rainbow colours. "What's this?"

"Ah—" A blush spread from her chest and up her neck.

Michelle came to her friend's rescue. "Didn't you hear Gordon? The big one's organic toothpaste—to help with detox. And that one's pH sticks—to test the acidity of your saliva, and your urine, and your—"

"Right. Got it." His left eyelid twitched.

In Dane's opinion, some things in life should remain a mystery.

Gordon's lecture on detox rose over the group's excited chatter. "Now, remember to test first thing in the morning, every day, mid-stream. Make sure you test your saliva before you eat or drink or brush your teeth. We've posted charts up here to record your individual results." He pointed to a corkboard on the wall behind him. "I always say there's no shame in acid wee, but the person most alkaline by the end of the retreat wins a grand prize. No cheating!" He beamed.

The phrases *acid wee* and *grand prize* burned in Dane's brain. He hoped never to hear them mentioned in the same sentence ever again.

Was the lion guy noticing the same brand of crazy?

Dane took another swift glance at those curls. Perfect loops to coil around his fingers, and hold, and…

Jesus. He really needed to get laid. Except he was so

exhausted he could barely keep his head up, let alone his dick. Which was pathetic, really. Thirty-two years old and craving a twelve-hour nap.

His gaze drifted to the man's mouth, seeing a flash of teeth as the man laughed with one of the elderly ladies at his table.

That smile was the stuff of fantasies.

In another place, and another time—at a club, for instance, where everyone knew the score—he'd be all over that guy. For the moment, though…

Dane stifled a yawn and blocked it all out—the lion guy, Gordon, the twittering women at his table—till a bunch of hippy-looking teenagers swarmed out of the kitchen carrying plates overflowing with colour.

The pageant didn't take long, but his impatient stomach grumbled, and when a salad ringed around a giant stuffed field mushroom arrived at his place, he dug in without ceremony, cutting out a wedge and forking it onto his tongue. Earthiness hit his palate nano-seconds before the surprising zing of feta, hid by the crunchy layer of toasted nuts and seeds. The hint of honey arrived last, and Dane moaned.

Total and utter bliss.

"Mmm." Add a bottle of smooth Cab Merlot, and the place might convince him to jettison his plan to escape to Noosa.

He opened his eyes to cut another piece of mushroom and found all three ladies' eyes on him.

"Wow." Michelle said. Lissa licked her lips. And Anna giggle-squeaked far too close to his ear.

"What?" he asked. "Have you never seen a man eat before?" He dug into the salad, forking an enormous chunk of avocado dripping with lemon juice, olive oil, and a hefty sprinkle of balsamic vinegar. He groaned again when the bold flavours swarmed his palate, and his stomach cheered for joy.

Lissa shook her head slowly, still staring at his mouth.

"Let us all pause," Gordon's voice rose, intoning far too sanctimoniously for Dane's liking, "and ask for wellness as we take in the bounty of the sun and the air and the water and the earth."

Dane shook his head and gave kudos where kudos were due.

"All hail the chef." He put his head down and loaded his fork again.

CHAPTER FOUR

CAYDEN

"Do you think he ever gets laid?" Maxine asked in a whisper so loud heads turned.

Edie either didn't notice, or didn't care, when she responded with the equally startling comment. "Not unless they make organic Viagra."

The pixies looked at each other and nodded sagely, then silently turned back to listen to Gordon with renewed interest.

God, Cayden hoped he was that terrifying when he was old.

The women had a point. If a man refused to brush his teeth with minty-fresh toothpaste, or give his pits a swipe with real deodorant, Cayden wouldn't be all that keen to get up close and personal. No matter how sexy. And Gordon the Organic Guru was far from sexy.

Cayden wasn't about to take chances with his own personal hygiene. Not that he was OCD about body fluids— he liked a good sweaty sex-fest—but Gordon seemed to have taken things to the extreme.

He did his best to listen to Gordon's impassioned speech

because reading between the lines was key to good investigative journalism, but the man's voice grated, and Cayden had to work hard not to show his rising antipathy. It wouldn't do to tip his hand so early.

As GOG wound up with an all-encompassing blessing to Gaia—as though Mother Earth cared to even notice such a flea of a man—Edie took over at their table.

"Oh, Lord, please let this not be our last supper," she monotoned.

"Amen," said Maxine.

"Amen," he heartily affirmed.

With that horror show finally over, they all tucked in to dinner.

By the time he'd hiked up to his haven, Cayden was a mass of wrinkles and fresh sweat. Mixed with the stale smell of airplane air and the fuming acid of his fury, he was close to pungent.

In the dozen steps it took him to cross his haven to the bathroom tucked in the back corner, he threw off every bit of clothing and swore never to put on another pair of socks in the steamy hellhole again.

He twisted the hot tap on full bore and stepped under the red-hot flow. It stung his skin, but he forced himself to breathe deeply, as he always did, amazed at how different shower steam felt compared to the humidity of the rainforest. Coming from the drier and more temperate south, the air seemed so thick it was practically drinkable.

Cayden washed with the sliver of goat soap the retreat supplied, enjoying the slip and slide around his happy nooks and crannies.

He gave his dick a friendly tug, but his heart wasn't really in it. After the long day, Cayden felt like a sweaty sock, turned inside out and worn twice.

Gordon would probably admonish him for washing the natural oils off his skin, which were no doubt full of essential thingamabobs and activated whatsits, but he couldn't care less what the nefarious bastard thought of his showering habits.

The hot water finally did its job—loosening his tight shoulders enough that he might sleep.

Maybe.

Cayden swiped the heel of his hand across the vanity mirror and saw Lucy's eyes look back at him.

His ribs clenched, welding his heart into a tight cage built of hurt and resentment and guilt.

Was he trying to find Lucy for her sake? Or for his own?

He stared at his reflection and found no answers.

Nothing about Lucy's disappearance indicated she'd been unwilling to go. Nothing except her uncharacteristic silence. She'd packed up her stuff, secretly sub-leased her room in a student share-house, and left.

A young woman off seeking adventure, the police said, not caring that Lucy couldn't hide a secret for anything. TMI just wasn't in her vocabulary.

No. She must have been coerced into leaving. Persuaded somehow.

Nothing else made sense.

Desperate, his parents searched in vain and spent a fortune they didn't have on private investigators. For six months, there was no activity on her mobile phone, bank accounts, or passport. Only then did the Victorian State Police concede that Lucy's 'adventure' may have actually been 'misadventure', and they handed the cold trail over to the Federal Police.

To fill the hole, finding answers became Cayden's life, and

a career in journalism gave him an excuse to ask questions. He'd searched obsessively until he'd started to wonder if the only way to find her was to stumble across her by accident.

Twelve long years later, he was still looking.

By the time the sliver-thin lead that linked nineteen-year-old Lucy to a bush commune high over Cunningham's Gap in Queensland's Main Range got to him, it was old news. But since it was all Cayden had to go on, he was determined to follow it.

Cayden traced the commune to land previously owned by a man by the name of Gordon Fuller. While Gordon—aka Gordon the fucking Organic Guru—may have moved on from one parcel of land to another, he was still the same man, and one thing Cayden had learned for sure was a leopard never lost his spots.

Cayden huffed out a tight breath, fogging the mirror all over again.

This time, he didn't bother wiping it off. He didn't need to see himself or her eyes to be certain of his path. But he was dead tired. The search would have to wait one more night.

After a cursory dry, he pulled on a fresh pair of briefs, then grabbed a random beer from his stash in the bathroom sink. He crossed the bedroom, switched off all the lights, and stepped out into the dark of night.

In the middle of the deck sat a double-wide yellow-and-white-striped banana lounge that was big enough for two. Cayden flopped down in the middle, not giving a flying fuck if his unknown new neighbour would willingly share the space or not.

A silky breeze with a hint of cool night filtered through the treetops, tossing his damp curls. The new moon just peaked over the eastern horizon, and the Milky Way shone bright above the pitch-black rainforest canopy. Familiar cicadas called into the night, harmonising with other unfamiliar swoops and squawks and scratching sounds. He hoped there weren't possums around. The evil creatures would make a racket at night on the corrugated roof.

Psst, his beer hissed as he twisted off the lid. Cayden gave an answering sigh, moaning around the head of the bottle at the first bitter-fresh taste of lager hit his palate. He swallowed three gulps. The bubbles cleaned away the last grunge of the day. He rested the glass to his chin and breathed into the mouth of the beer, turning it into a one-note pan flute—his kind of music.

A mozzie whined by his ear, but he couldn't bring himself to move. Woozy on food and booze, he drifted on the tropical evening air into oblivion.

CHAPTER FIVE

DANE

Slap!

Dane jerked up. All muscles fired in fight-or-flight mode. He blinked in the darkness.

Was he dreaming?

Slap!

Jesus.

The sure sound of breaking glass and an inhuman squeal had him vertical and racing to face whatever was raising havoc outside.

"Fucker. Get the freaking fuck off me!" The voice rose. "That's it! Run away!"

"What the hell is going on out here?" Dane wrenched open the screen door and flicked on the outside light, immediately regretting it as spots and streaks of light flashed in front of his eyes.

"Switch off the goddamn light!"

Blinking wildly, Dane saw the Sheridan-Brown-wannabe hanging half-on, half-off the enormous banana lounge, flapping his shirt around his head.

What the hell?

"I said switch off the fucking light!"

Everything went midnight black.

Dane flicked his inside light on instead, slid shut his screen door, and took a wide path around the shattered brown glass beside the lounge. He held his hands out like a horse whisperer, calming a mad steed. "Hold still."

The man stilled. Warm light cast from inside gleamed in his curls. He looked like some kind of grown-up, sexy cupid. A leonine cupid.

Jesus, he's so beautiful.

"Did you get it?" The man sifted his fingers roughly through his hair. Then he jerked his head around to look for God knew what. "Is it gone?"

"There's nothing here but you and me."

"Thank fuck for that."

The blonde blinked in that slow, dreamy way that made Dane wonder if he, in fact, was the one dreaming. The moment was sure mad enough.

"It was huge. Fucking massive." The guy held his hands out wide as if to demonstrate the size of a giant flying fish that had evaded his grasp. "Naked."

"Uh…" He mirrored the slow blink as the adrenaline dissipated and exhaustion returned to his body. He assessed the puddle of spilled beer on the deck. Just how much had the man drunk? "You were attacked by a huge, naked—?"

"No, dude. You're naked."

Dane looked down.

Well, fuck.

"Right. I'm just gonna…" He hooked his thumb in the vague direction of his room. Then he retreated to pull on a pair of boxers and searched for anything useful to sweep up the glass shards.

His latest unread copy of *The Financial Review* would have to do.

When he returned to the deck, the golden man had disappeared. Dane kneeled to collect the bigger pieces of glass and brush the smaller shards down between the planks of the old wooden deck.

"You won't get it all."

Dane looked up and was struck dumb.

The guy wasn't a muscled Adonis, but he was outrageously beautiful.

"Thanks." Grateful for the distraction, Dane took the glass of water and sloshed it around to get rid of the worst of the spilled beer.

"It should be me thanking you. Let's just move the banana lounge over to cover the glass. We can do a better job in the morning. I'm Cayden, by the way."

"Dane." Dane didn't know when *he'd* become part of a *we*, but he was too tired to make anything of it. He helped haul the yellow-striped banana lounge across the puddle and didn't protest when the guy switched off the outside light and returned with two beers.

"Take a load off." Cayden flopped down on the far side of the banana lounge and tapped the empty spot beside him. "Fighting off murderous possums is thirsty work."

With a jolt, Dane realised he was still on his knees.

It was a novel experience.

Cayden held his hands up in mock-surrender and chuckled. "I promise I'm not crazy."

"Uh-ha, certifiable," Dane disagreed. For lack of a better idea, he shifted up to sit on the banana lounge and accepted the proffered drink.

"Ha! Wouldn't be much use to you if I'm crazy."

"To me?"

"When you need rescuing from hellish possums," Cayden explained with not even an ounce of humour in his tone.

"Right." Definitely certifiable.

Cayden held his long neck out to clink. "Cheers, neighbour."

"Cheers." Dane stared out into the moonlit rainforest—a far safer place to rest his eyes than the blond stretched out close beside him—and listened to the night-time chorus.

He took another swig. Bitter, tepid lager slaked Dane's dry throat. It wasn't even in the realm of his favourite drink, but on a hot, steamy night, after fighting off invisible demons, it went down, damn fine.

Dane let out a deep breath and settled deeper into the softness of the banana lounge.

Nothing about the night had gone to plan, but he let himself relax and drift on the star-drenched night.

CHAPTER SIX

CAYDEN

Sans the pinstriped suit, Dane lost none of his presence.

Cayden wanted to climb into the man's lap and say, *thank you for saving me from the big, bad beastie*. He restrained himself, though, because he wasn't some kind of gothic romance damsel-in-distress.

To distract himself, he examined Dane.

Clouds drifted across the three-quarter moon, leaving only a hint of moon-glow on the gorgeous man's chin and nose and sharp cheekbones. Cayden wasn't ashamed to admit he wished he'd packed a pair of night-vision glasses in his suitcase to see Dane better.

Cayden could happily watch Dane settle into his bones any time, day or night.

Cayden envied Dane's don't-give-a-shit-what-anyone-thinks-of-me vibe. He could never achieve it in a million years. Hell, even his blue-and-white boxer shorts matched his suit—pinstripes, sharp creases, and all.

"Do you seriously iron your underwear?"

Dane shifted his weight and moved his beer bottle to cover his groin.

Note to self—do not stare at the dude's tackle.

Why he'd gone there, he had no idea. Well, maybe one idea…

Distract! Distract!

"What are you doing here, dude?" The man's presence at a health retreat made no sense.

"Carol," Dane huffed into his bottle, as though that explained everything.

Wife? Girlfriend?

Shit. Any hope of getting into the guy's pinstriped boxers disappeared in an instant.

He took another slug.

After a long, still silence, Dane turned his head toward Cayden and said, "I've been stressed, I guess. Tired. Don't tell Carol I admitted it. She'd never let me live it down."

"Got you by the balls, eh?"

"No." Dane grimaced. "She probably thinks so, though, since she booked me blind into this retreat. Didn't tell me any details."

"Seriously?"

Dane nodded, then shrugged. "According to Carol, I've been insufferable lately."

"Maybe she has a point," he teased. "Ironing your boxers is kind of insufferable."

Dane started nodding, then shook his head instead. "No. She's wrong."

Cayden pressed his lips together tight, but he couldn't contain a loud snort, setting off hundreds of shrieking bats from the surrounding fig trees.

Instinct made Cayden ducked for cover—protecting his head as their leather wings whop-whop-whopped the air.

Eventually, the night stilled enough that he could feel the banana lounge shuddering with Dane's unsuppressed laughter.

"Bastard," he muttered.

"They're fruit bats, Cayden. I don't think you're on their desired menu."

He lounged back, pretending he'd never hidden like a little kid afraid of monsters in the night.

"What about you?" Dane asked.

"Huh?"

"Why are you here?"

Cayden thought of the wild cover stories he'd made up on the flight from Melbourne—chronic fatigue, insomnia, a fascination for wellness and the uber-natural restoration of body and mind.

Any of those lies would suit.

If he'd learned anything as an investigative journalist, though, it was that keeping a false story straight was incredibly difficult. The liar and the lie were almost always exposed, and always at the worst possible moment.

This time, however, telling the truth wasn't an option.

"My sister dared me." That felt sort of almost true.

"Dared you? Seriously? That's twisted."

"Yeah." Cayden glared out into the night. Twisted was a good word for it.

"Didn't figure you for the hippy-trippy sort."

"Yeah, no. This place is a crock of shit." The scathing words were out of his mouth before he could remember that he was supposed to stay under the radar.

"If you're so unconvinced by its merits, why are you here?"

"I told you, my sister—"

"Dared you. Mm-hmm. Sure. Keep your secrets."

Well, fuck. If he wasn't careful, Dane would see right through him.

Hiding his truth grated, but something about the dark of

the night, and Dane's sexy-as-fuck don't-give-a-shit vibe, made him want to be real.

Perhaps it was just the tongue-loosening booze.

He eyed Dane.

The dude could do with a few wrinkles in his pinstriped boxers.

"As a reward for your bravery, you can have another beer from the mini-bar."

Dane lifted an eyebrow. "Generous of you."

"Don't get too excited. There are limits. Bringers, keepers and all that."

"Isn't the line finders keepers?"

He ignored that. "Besides, I'm already sharing my banana lounge with you."

"I think you'll find that this is *our* banana lounge." Dane tilted his way and raised one sexy-as-hell eyebrow.

Cayden rolled the word *our* around in his mouth. It sounded awfully cosy.

Dane went on. "Just like this is our deck, our view, our—"

"Your delusion." Cayden blew a note into his bottle, enjoying himself immensely. "You're just lucky I'm feeling magnanimous tonight."

That sexy eyebrow rose again.

"Speaking of magnanimous." Dane shook his near empty bottle. "I believe you promised to share."

Cayden chuckled and swung his legs off the banana lounge. He wobbled a bit when he stood and made a beeline for the bathroom sink, returning to Dane with the last two bottles of the six-pack.

"I once saw a documentary on exotic parasites where this dude drank copious amounts of beer to get rid of an enormous intestinal worm. I mean, that fucker was over a metre long. He held it up for the camera like it was some sort of beast he'd caught on a deep-sea fishing expedition—proud of his mighty fine catch." Cayden held a fist up high, doing his best *holding a fish by the tail* impression, and grinned. "Like a kid doing show and tell."

Dane looked at him as though he'd grown another head, but Cayden was just warming up.

"To beer therapy." Cayden raised his bottle for another toast. "Can't get pissed on a few, but might as well enjoy the buzz. My luck the rest will get confiscated by housekeeping." He took another swig. "Speaking of piss, what the hell was all that about the pH of spit and urine? Next thing you know, we'll be expected to test our blood, and sweat, and tears, and seme..."

"Body fluids."

"Yeah, yeah, right, body fluids. Nice one." He took another sneaky peek up through his eyelashes. Take away the pinstripes and the guy looked like he'd be a fantastic fuck. The thought made him drool. "Pavlov," he blurted.

"What?"

"You know, the dog and the bell and the drool and…"

"I've heard of it."

"Jus' saying." He tried not to slur. "With all the testing of body fluids, we'll need bells ringing morning, noon, and night." He paused. "It'd be like jingaling—take a piss, jangalang—hock up spit, jongolong—whack out a—"

"TMI, mate."

"Nah. Or, you know, I could just stay near you. Don't need a bell." The man was seriously drool-worthy.

"If you're about to claim my presence makes you need to take a leak, you can go find another banana lounge."

Cayden didn't like the sound of that. He was comfy, and the company was hot. Besides, that wasn't really what he meant. "Not a leak, per se."

"It's all just mumbo-jumbo pseudoscience. In the eighteenth century, doctors used to let blood by cutting or leeching." Dane waved his fresh bottle out to the stars. "In the twenty-second century, we'll probably be shuttling up to the stratosphere to suck on ozone for a cure."

Cayden rolled over onto his back and looked out into the starry universe. It made a beautiful sort of sense. "Like oxygen therapy, but not."

"Quick trip to Saturn for gravity therapy to improve bone density."

Cayden squinted to look for the planet's rings.

No luck.

"Cold out there. Do you reckon you'd sweat on Saturn? Getting a good sweat up is thera... therapeutic." He tried flexing his abdominals. They weren't cooperating, but the view down his torso gave Cayden a better idea, anyway. He played with the waistband of his briefs. "Not to mention—"

"Please don't."

"—no really. We should both tug one out and compare pH. Nothing weird about it."

"I think your idea of weird and my idea of weird live on different planets."

Cayden shrugged. "Didn't take you for a prude."

"It's hardly prudish to say no to a mutual masturbation session purely to test the relative acidity of our cum. Besides, I hardly think you know me well enough to take me for anything."

Smart aleck.

"I wasn't actually proposing we jerk off together, but since you suggest it..." He let the words hang in the air. "There's nothing better for a good night's sleep. Very—"

"Therapeutic." Dane finished for him.

Cayden couldn't tell if Dane was grumpy or amused.

"You know, I was fast asleep until you woke me with your hollering."

He'd go with amused. "You're welcome."

"That's not…no, I won't rise."

Cayden eyed his crotch. "Pity."

Dane groaned. "Are you always so…so…"

"Clever? Wonderful? Sexy?"

"…so much of a wise-arse?"

"Hmph."

Dane's grin gleamed in the soft moonlight. "Did your sister dare you to come here to fix you? Or get rid of you? It must be one or the other."

Cayden's gut dropped.

Well, shit. There goes the party.

It took all his willpower to muster a fake smile.

"You can't fix perfection, my friend."

"Says the man afraid of a marsupial."

That wasn't fair. "It was a dragon-sized marsupial, and I've got the scratches to prove it." Cayden angled his left knee out to show the long scratch turned red welt on his inner thigh. "I'll die from tetanus, and then who'll be sorry?"

"You're avoiding the question."

Yes, he was, but Cayden wasn't about to admit it. "Do you always pester people like this?"

Arrogance had never done it for him, but sheesh, Dane's arched eyebrow was sexy as fuck. The man didn't need to say a thing to make his thoughts known.

"Did I, or did I not, provide beer?"

Dane nodded. "You did."

"Well then, I rest my case."

"Your case, my arse."

That sounded like an invitation, so he lecherously perused Dane's amazing body.

Dane groaned, and Cayden's dick throbbed in response. Thoughts of his sister faded as rapidly as his rising heartbeat.

CHAPTER SEVEN

CAYDEN

Cayden woke spread-eagled on the banana lounge to the grey light of dawn and a kookaburra's wild laugh echoing across the valley.

A mosquito whined near his left ear, and he lazily swatted it.

Then he felt the itch.

Not just one itch. Dozens of fiery-hot welts screamed *Alert! Alert! Alert!*

Cayden twisted and leaped off the banana lounge in a move worthy of a stuntman, then dashed to the safety and security of his haven.

He slid the mosquito screen shut with an emphatic clonk and made a beeline for the shower, flipping the cold tap on full. He doused himself under the summer-warm flow till the subterranean water cooled and the many bites became one giant goose bump.

Shivering, he shut off the tap and let the clinging water droplets air dry. No way was he rubbing with a towel.

He needed antihistamines and a time machine, stat.

What a night.

For the first time since waking, he thought of Dane—the moonlit curve of the man's silhouette and how much he'd wanted to reach out and touch it.

Cayden couldn't remember falling asleep, but, at some point, Dane must have woken and seen Cayden lying there beside him.

Had he thought, *get me some of that peach-ripe deliciousness?*

Or, had he thought, *it's nice to be reminded that I'm seriously super sexy, but best let the poor gay dude ogle me from a safe distance?*

The first was optimal.

The second more likely.

Dane hadn't encouraged Cayden's clunky, half-arsed attempts at seduction. But he hadn't socked him in the nose, or mocked him, or run over the hills and far, far away. The only thing Cayden knew for certain was the guy had woken through the night and left Cayden to the mercy of the local wildlife.

That desertion burned almost as much as the bites.

"Bastard."

He was itchy, grumpy, and felt far from sexy.

That was good, because getting laid wasn't his mission at the House of Glass Wellness Retreat. He just needed to put aside his wants and keep his need to find Lucy in the forefront of his mind—to remember the stakes.

"Lucy's freedom is way more important than your libido," he reminded his reflection.

If he were a saint, it might have been enough.

The problem was, he wasn't a saint. That one percent of him was very influential. He looked down. Maybe two percent.

He tried another tack.

"A fuck is for a night. Family is for life."

Better.

That pep-talk done, Cayden pulled on a pair of board shorts and a wafer-thin tank. Then he grabbed his phone off the charger and pressed the contact for Henrietta.

His boss would kick his arse when she discovered his true motivation for investigating Gordon Fuller and his House of Glass, but she was far away in Melbourne. Cayden wanted support from the non-boss side of her—his closest confidant. No, he needed that.

Silence.

No dial tone.

He pulled it from his ear and inspected the screen. Not even a fleck of a signal bar.

He waved it above his head.

Nada.

He groaned. "Can nothing be easy?"

Since he saw no alternative, Cayden yanked on his dorky trek sandals and ventured out into the big, bad world of wellness, in search of higher ground.

Away from his and Dane's haven, the path continued up the near-vertical inside curve of the ancient volcano crater. The rough circular rim would draw rain and protect the valley from salty on-shore winds, encouraging dense rainforest to grow in the rich volcanic soils. Ordinarily, Cayden would be eager to explore the landscape. It'd been ages since he'd gone camping, and he missed connection with nature.

Like everything else, though, that would have to wait.

Blinkers on, he climbed the loamy, leaf-littered path to where the rich rainforest petered out and scrub took over. The soft path, cast in shade by the early morning light, transitioned to dusty rubble, then raw rock, split and bound by sinewy, exposed roots.

Cayden tripped and scrambled up the path. Sweat gushed from every pore, and grit filled his shoes. His temples pounded with the beat of his pulse, and the wretched, full-body itch felt like vengeance on his very soul.

"Death by Queensland," he gasped, then paused for the millionth time to wave his phone high. The light on the screen was nothing but a tease. "Definition of madness."

Above, the track curved ever steeper through the thinning trees to where he could trace angel-fire flaring between the grey scale, craggy rim and the pink arched light of sunrise.

He ducked his head and powered up the last of the treacherous slope on nothing but stubborn determination. When the first rays hit his face, he flinched from the brightness.

Breath heaving, he looked up from his shoes and forgot for a long, happy moment the sweat, the grit, and the bites that flared as hot as his raging heartbeat. He scrambled up onto a giant granite boulder and gaped in utter wonder at the incredible view.

To the east, the Pacific Ocean glimmered red and pink, gold and mauve, and every blue imaginable, spreading uninterrupted to the wide horizon.

Balancing with his arms stretched out, Cayden turned to the north and then the south, where the Great Dividing Range split the land from the sea with thousands of kilometres of ribboning mountains.

To the west, early shards of light struck the green hinterland that rippled into the distant darkness.

He couldn't see beyond the hills, but Cayden knew they would eventually give way to an equal-opposite horizon of arid red.

The immense curve of the Earth took his breath away. It left Cayden feeling like if he didn't grip tight to the land, he might just float away. He let gravity pull him down to lie like a starfish on the night-cool boulder and enjoy the rough texture of the stone beneath his fingertips. And, in the sky above, he searched the stars as dawn gradually faded into day.

"Gorgeous," he sighed.

"I know," came a voice out of nowhere.

Dane.

"Holy shit!" Cayden's heart tripped, and he twisted around so fast he could probably add gravel rash to his woes. He shaded his eyes from the glare of the sunrise.

"What the hell, man?"

"Sorry. Didn't mean to startle you."

Dane stood perfectly upright and perfectly balanced on sure runner's legs, his wide chest expanding and contracting as though he'd just run up a mountain. Which he probably had.

"Where did you come from?" Cayden asked.

Dane pointed to the south where the barely there path continued between sharp boulders before it disappeared into a dip.

"There's a platform over the second hump along the ridge," he said, as if that explained everything.

"You ran up here?"

"Yeah. Gorgeous, isn't it?"

Cayden looked him over—navy runner's shorts and a thin white tank made near-transparent by sweat that sheened his glorious skin.

"Yeah." Cayden chuckled. The view was to die for, and the landscape wasn't bad either. What wasn't to like? "You'll never convince me to run up that fucking hill, though." He shook his head and lay back down on the cool stone. "Talk about signs of madness."

"Each to their own." Dane shrugged. "The endorphin rush is worth it, and the view is the cherry on top." His voice came closer, and Cayden felt the air move close by his side.

"Each to their own," he shot back, and was rewarded with a thwack to the hip. "Hey!"

"Shove over, would you?"

It was tempting to tell him to get his own boulder to laze on, but sharing tight quarters with Dane wasn't exactly a hardship. Trying not to be as obvious as a teenager with a crush, Cayden shuffled across just enough to let the taller man wedge a hip onto the boulder. His nerves twitched where their hips connected, which made his blood hot, which made his bites flare back to life.

Fuck.

"Have you got fleas or something?" Dane asked the third time Cayden wriggled on their shared granite bed like a bear scratching against rough bark.

Cayden lifted his shirt to show Dane the red welts raised red hot right across his abdomen.

"Holy shit!"

"Death by mozzies." He raised his shirt higher to draw Dane's attention north to the bites behind his light dusting of chest hair. "Just one more bloodsucker and I reckon I'd have been a goner."

"Geez." Dane's gaze stroked his chest. Cayden shuddered at the thought of Dane's long, lean fingers touching him—soothing his bare skin.

"Go on. Find a constellation. I dare you." Could his ploy to get the man to touch him be any more shamefully obvious?

Probably.

Did he care?

Fuck, no.

CHAPTER EIGHT

CAYDEN

"Serves you right for sleeping on the deck."

That was rich. "Serves *me* right? You're the heartless deserter. Why didn't you wake me?"

"I nudged you. Hard."

If the dude had nudged him hard, he'd have been a whole lot happier right about then. No doubt about that.

He lay back down and stared up at the pastel sky.

"You were comatose. I doubt anything but another killer possum could have woken you."

Cayden shuddered. "So much for being my saviour."

"Knight-in-shining-armour duty does not include tucking you into bed at night. Someone else can fluff your pillow."

Well, now, there was an idea that wouldn't disappear in a hurry.

He got out his mobile phone and typed *fluff your pillow* into the search bar, hoping the Urban Dictionary might translate it as *give amazing head.*

The *working* symbol turned around and around, and

Cayden suddenly remembered why he'd originally climbed up to the crater rim.

"Shit!"

He waved his hand in the air like a tween at a Bieber concert.

This high, and still no signal?

"What's wrong?" Dane asked.

"Looking for a signal. I need to talk to my producer."

"Producer?"

"Yeah."

"You work in film?"

"Nah. News television."

"Seriously?"

"Sort of. Well, not really."

"That's clear."

Was it his imagination, or had Dane's tone cooled?

"Technically, I'm a production assistant. I do research for an investigative news program."

"So, your job is to make sure everything reported is correct?"

Definitely cooler.

"That's me—glorified fact-checker. Except there's not much glory involved."

An awkward silence bloomed, and Dane surveyed him with serious, forensic intent.

The change in mood puzzled Cayden, so he pointed at his mozzie-ravaged face, grinned stupidly, and threw out his most-reliable, self-deprecating joke. "This ugly mug does not do screen time."

Dane did not laugh. The silence lengthened. And Cayden started his bear-scratching-slash-Bieber-concert-waving again. He didn't get excited about his job, either.

Eventually, Dane nodded shortly. "I see what you mean."

"Hey!"

"No, really. If your disaster of a face came on screen, I'd change the channel."

"That's it!" He shoved Dane away, jumped off the boulder, and took off.

Dane's mocking laughter followed hot on his tail. "I'm only trying to help."

"Go away. We're not friends anymore." Cayden waved his arm around again. At the rate he was going, his battery would be dead before he found a signal.

"It's six in the morning."

"Thank you very much for the chronological update. You can go now."

"Six o'clock is way too early…"

"Not in Melbourne. Daylight saving, dude."

"Seven, then. What's so desperate that you're going to bother him so early on a Saturday morning?"

"Her—don't be sexist."

Cayden could practically hear Dane's eyes rolling behind him.

"Why do you need to bother her so early? Surely you're not on the job now?"

"Actually, I am." He see-sawed his hand. "Sort of."

Shit, he shouldn't have said that. What happened to staying under the radar? Was he going to spill all his secrets?

"This place is hardly newsworthy. What could you be fact-checking here?"

"I can't really say."

"You can't really say?"

"No. Not yet." Not till he found Lucy.

If Dane screwed with his investigation, he might lose his sister forever. That wasn't a risk he was willing to take.

For so many years, he'd trailed after threadbare leads: this person heard that person say they'd seen a twenty-something woman who looked just like Lucy on the ferry crossing to Tasmania; or saw her sing back up at the Byron Bay Beach Pub, even though Lucy couldn't sing to save her life; or, and this was Cayden's very favourite, Lucy's high-school boyfriend claimed he'd heard her voice on the CB radio while trucking Adelaide to Alice Springs, only he couldn't write down the details because what would his wife think about him obsessing over some woman's voice? Right?

Yeah, right.

Jerk.

False leads wore his heart thin. But the one that led him to the House of Glass was different.

This time, he had almost solid evidence leading him almost directly to Gordon fucking Fuller's door.

Almost.

The *almosts* warned Cayden to be careful—to not risk complete exposure—but the temptation to blurt out the truth burned acid in his gut. How would it feel to have someone else's active support? To have someone else on his side?

His parents knew he was searching for Lucy. Of course, they did. How could he not tell them? But they were too heartsore to want to know about every failure, every disappointment. Which left him searching alone. Again.

Except here was a guy—a smart guy—wanting to know his story…maybe even wanting to help.

The scuff and crunch of steps silenced behind him. Cayden paused and turned.

Dane stood, feet slightly spread, fists to his hips, eyebrow raised.

"What?" Offence was the greatest defence, right?

"Oh, nothing. I'm just wondering what to believe." Dane raised a pointer finger. "You're here because your sister dared you." He lifted his middle finger. "Or to conduct some sort of hush-hush news investigation. Is that it, or do I get a third option?"

Cayden kept a straight face and flipped up his ring finger. "I came to the retreat for hypnosis to cure me of an addiction to subcutaneous ball-bearing implants." Then he flipped up his pinkie. "I have a three-foot-long intestinal worm that nobody but GOG can cure."

"GOG?"

"Gordon the Organic Guru. GOG for short."

Dane snorted. "Can he cure your warped sense of humour while he's at it?"

Cayden didn't even need a nanosecond to think about that.

"Hope not."

"Hope so."

He dragged in a huge breath. Relieved.

Dane's teasing meant they were okay.

About some things Cayden was sure—Dane was easy on the eye, had energy to burn, and had a healthy disrespect for the kale revolution, all good reasons why he'd be perfect to help Cayden ferret out the truth.

But was the risk worth it? Of that, he wasn't so sure.

Cayden eyed him as Dane dropped into a deep squat, grabbed his toes, and lifted his arse up till he was folded in half, head down, legs straight, the alignment of his spine all grace and symmetry. As his chest slowly expanded and contracted, Cayden saw the subtle clench of Dane's glutes before he uncurled, ever so slowly, one vertebra at a time.

It took all of Cayden's resistance not to reach out and touch. "Actually," he blurted, "they're both true."

Fuck. What had he done?

"The ball-bearings and the worm?"

"What? No. I'm here to investigate. My sister dared me... sort of..." *Make a mess, why don't you, Cayden?* "I'm looking for..." Shit, why was it so hard to spit out the word *her*? "... the truth. You can't tell anyone. If Gordon gets a whiff of my true purpose, he'll throw me out. And then..." He couldn't finish that thought.

"The truth about...?" Dane's eyebrow went up.

Shit. That eyebrow.

"Cults."

Both of Dane's eyebrows rose.

"Sort of. Maybe." He tried to explain.

"You think the retreat is part of a cult?"

"A cult is an exclusive group whose leader has a destructive influence over its members."

"Thank you, Mr. Dictionary. You seriously think this place is a cult?" Dane repeated.

Cayden flipped his hand back and forth. "Maybe. Maybe not. I found historical ties to a suspicious commune. Serious red flags."

Dane didn't look convinced.

"I can't say much more, not without risking the investigation."

"Cryptic, Cayden."

"Yeah, well, with good reason."

Dane leaped up on another giant boulder, turned his back on the Pacific, and leaned out over the shadowy crater.

"What are you doing?" He followed Dane's gaze down to the retreat.

"I'm looking for pentagrams, or crop circles, or..."

"Oh, for fuck's sake, I didn't say they were aliens. Or witches." He felt exposed, raw, and inexplicably desperate to convince Dane that he wasn't some shifty hack inventing a story. "Maybe it's just a godawful hippy-dippy retreat. But if it *is* a cult, then a lot of people could be in danger. That's what I'm here to discover."

Just as Dane turned away, the first rays of sunrise streaked across the ocean and caught him high on his pedestal. Head to heel, the light licked every square inch of exposed flesh and turned it to gold.

"Dude, you're glowing like a fucking Oscar."

Yeah, Cayden couldn't really claim suave as his middle name, but he didn't care because his idiotic words caused the golden god to turn and look at him, which gave the sun's rays a chance to lick his front as well.

Bonus.

The man was like some final cosmic test, a test he figured he was failing miserably, until Dane quirked his lips and said, "Where do we start then?"

The question took him completely by surprise.

"We?"

"You want definitive proof that the House of Glass Wellness Retreat is a front for a cult? One way or another, we'll find it." He pointed down toward the retreat. "Besides, if I'm stuck here for goodness knows how long, I'll need something more than Zen and the power of lentils to think about."

Cayden wanted to say *me, you can think about me*, but what came out was, "I think lentils are banned here, dude."

"Not the point, dude."

Which was fair.

"I just have one stipulation."

"Stipulation?" Cayden parroted back.

What the hell, Spicer? Get your head in the game.

"Just one." Dane held up a finger, then pointed down into the crater valley. "We need to plant a temperature-monitoring device in the veggie patch. If the devil rises from the depths of that volcano, I want prior warning."

Had he heard that correctly? "You want a devil detector in the veggie patch?"

"Correct." Dane *sounded* deadly serious. Except, when the man folded himself into another one of those arse-up teases, Cayden saw his mouth twist.

Well, fuck. Not only was Dane gorgeous, he was funny, too.

"Hilarious." He made a show of rolling his eyes, even though Dane couldn't see. "Wait, I thought you were leaving."

Dane tugged an earpiece out of the small pocket in his waistband. "Tried that. There's not enough of a signal up here to do a web search, but I got through to Carol. She says there's nothing going till after the long weekend. Said it's a miracle she could book me a place here. As though anything about this place is miraculous."

Cayden couldn't help smiling at Dane's indignation. He was clearly a man used to getting his own way. "Read you the riot act, eh?"

Dane sighed. "Pretty much."

If he truly wanted to leave, Cayden had no doubt Dane could find a way. If he flashed those gorgeous blue eyes, he'd have a dozen people jangling their car keys to do the honours. Which meant something was keeping Dane at the retreat. Cayden didn't care what it was. He'd happily accept the man's presence and gladly call it fate—just one more reason why sharing his story with Dane felt right.

He knew it was risky to let Dane help him investigate Gordon and the House of Glass Wellness Retreat.

What if Dane gave the game away, and he lost Lucy altogether?

But what if accepting Dane's help meant he found Lucy faster?

What if? What if? What if?

Cayden was sick and tired of *what ifs*.

"Okay. You can be my wingman." He pointed a finger at Dane. "But follow my lead. And don't fuck it up."

Dane nodded, but his lips twisted.

"I'm serious, dude."

Dane schooled his expression. "All right." He held up his palm. "Do we need to spit before we shake?"

CHAPTER NINE

DANE

Dane pressed his foot to the hub deck railing and set the rocker rocking, slow and easy. He didn't give a fuck if The House of Glass Wellness Retreat was a front for a cult or simply the brainchild of a hyper-hippy on organic speed. He didn't believe Cayden's can't-lie-for-shit story, but some of the man's crazy must have rubbed off on him because what else could Dane blame for his flip-flop decision to stay?

Maybe it was the delicious dinner that had lulled him into acquiescence.

Perhaps it was the deep, deep sleep he'd risen from that morning feeling refreshed and raring to go.

Quite possibly, it was bonding with Cayden over killer possums and beer that had him eager for more.

"Cryptic Cayden." He held his glass up to the bright morning light and searched in vain for clarity.

He found none.

The drink—and he was being very generous to call it such —was so thick that each swallow slimed down his throat like a very un-sexy oyster. Its only saving grace was that it helped wash down the coconut oil shot the chef tricked him into taking as a starter.

Dane needed eggs, preferably with smoked salmon, capers, and hollandaise sauce, on a neat slice of toasted sourdough. Just the thought had him salivating…which made him think of Pavlov…which made him think of Cayden…which made him think of sex.

Again.

Shit.

Eager to get away from Cayden before he could promise more help, Dane had left the man on the crater rim. He'd half run, half slid on his arse, down the rough trail, collecting what felt like half the loose stones off the trail into his shoes and shorts.

A cold shower improved his equilibrium, but even that was short-lived. One glance at his personalised menu in his Vital Serenity Wellness Plan had him questioning every choice he'd ever made—including employing Carol.

Again.

Gastronomic torture wasn't too harsh a claim. Who did he have to pay to start the day with something he could bite, and chew, and keep in his stomach long enough to feel full?

For a short while, he could forgo luxury, the club scene, and his nightly scotch, but giving up decent food was a line he wasn't willing to cross.

And Carol knew it.

He touched the camera app on his mobile, pulled his best cranky-boss expression, and snapped a selfie of him and his horror breakfast.

His text message wouldn't get through to Carol till the next time he ran up to the platform on the crater's rim, but he thumbed the words "Extraction Team. Stat!" and pressed send. Why wait to begin his campaign for retribution?

From his rocking chair on the hub deck, Dane gave a

noncommittal return wave to a middle-aged couple. They approached the hole-in-the-wall service window to the kitchen and came away with identical clear, silky shots and thick, yellow smoothies, but far from identical expressions.

With a happy, lip-smacking sigh, the man downed the shot like it was some kind of life-giving elixir.

The woman took a sip, grimaced, and returned the near-full shot glass to the kitchen. Then she escaped down the steps to the garden, her flowing kaftan camouflage against the giant red-flowered poinciana tree.

The paunchy man strode over with his smoothie, hand outstretched. "Randall Paige. Call me Randy."

Yeah, that wasn't happening.

"Dane." He shook the man's hand.

"Pleasure to meet ya, Dane. And this is my wife, Bernice." He waved behind him, not aware of her defection to the garden. "How about this juice stuff, eh?" He patted the waistband of his shorts that looked like they were about to lose their battle with gravity. "I feel like a new man already."

While Randall-call-me-Randy amused himself waxing lyrical about the health-giving ingredients of his liquid breakfast, Dane saw Bernice dig a little hole in the flower bed, pour her smoothie in, and then cover the evidence.

The move reminded him of his sister, Alice, and the many times she'd poured the remainder of their shared drink into a faux planter pot at whatever club or pub they'd tried that Friday night. "Fifty percent spit," his twin would always say as she'd reject the last mouthful.

It didn't matter that they'd shared DNA. Alice refused to share his saliva.

Dane ignored the wrench in his fifty-percent-empty heart, tipped his glass up, and chugged the last of the smoothie. When grit hit his tongue, he wished he'd heeded her memory.

"Ugh."

If he complained, the staff would probably just congratulate him on upping his mineral intake and offer to make more.

Ten seconds later, he wondered how long it would take to walk to the nearest café for a morning espresso.

Not that he was dependent.

He just liked the bitter kick.

And idle was just not his natural state.

Dane craned his neck to look up the drive, to freedom.

He could hear the cheer squad ladies before they appeared.

"Hector is so sweet."

"I'd take him home."

"That tush!"

"Mmhmm."

"Magnificent view."

"I know, right!"

Giggle, giggle.

All decked out in fluoro Lycra, they swarmed the beehive-shaped ceramic water-filter on the deck behind him.

Don't ask. Don't ask.

"Who?"

Shit! Suckered in by a notable tush.

In his defence, that sort of thing was right up his alley. Though the sweet bit he could do without—Dane was more into tight, and hard, and available.

"Hector, the wellness consultant," one woman cooed.

"So sweet."

"Not as sweet as you, though, Dane." Michelle patted his shoulder, and the other women took that as permission to close ranks around him.

Damn.

He set the rocker off into faster movements so they'd have to back away or risk their toes getting squashed.

"Or Cayden," one lady on his left chirped.

His rocker stuttered.

"He's gorgeous."

"So young."

"Those curls."

"He'd make a great pool boy."

"Yeah." They sighed together like a flock of cartoon birds on Snow White's windowsill. Actually, cougar was probably the more apt analogy.

What's the collective noun for cougars?

He didn't know.

What Dane did know was that while Cayden's cupid curls made him look young, they were deceptive. There was history in those lion eyes.

"You should have come walking with us, Dane."

"Hector is such a great guide. And a great guy. Apparently, he does Ashtanga yoga, and Iyengar yoga, and tai chi, and…"

And Dane stopped listening because the gorgeous cupid in question stood over one of those Lycra-clad shoulders, staring straight at him, tonguing a goddamn straw.

The tease.

Dane shoved his foot extra hard against the railing, sending the rocking chair back, spooking the ladies and turning their twittering giggles into henhouse squawks.

As Cayden walked into the melee, his cheeks hollowed around the straw. Then his face contorted with revulsion.

Dane couldn't help smiling. "It wasn't that bad," he lied.

Cayden shoved the tall glass into Dane's face. "You have it then."

"What's in it?" one lady asked.

"Mine was yellower, so I suspect they're individually tailored smoothies with unique health benefits," Dane said.

That sales pitch had them hurrying away to the kitchen hatch, leaving him with Cayden, who looked more like a toddler about to have a tantrum than a grown man.

He took another sip. "Gah! So gross."

"What are you, twelve?"

"It's disgusting, Dane."

"The colour probably comes from blueberries, or beetroot, or cacao. This time tomorrow, you'll be cranking with natural antioxidants."

Cayden pursed lips around his metal straw and mumbled something that sounded suspiciously like *I'd rather crank something else*.

Dane rocked harder.

"What did you discover? Anything helpful?" Cayden asked. "I didn't get anything useful out of them." He threw a thumb over his shoulder at the kitchen.

It took Dane an embarrassingly long moment to figure out what Cayden was on about.

The investigation.

Right.

Unfortunately, he had nothing.

Well, almost nothing.

"Hector has a sweet arse."

Cayden stared at him, myriad expressions flashing across his face.

Entranced, Dane barely noticed that he'd slowed the rocking chair.

Cayden licked his lower lip, then leaned down and teasingly whispered, "Is that code for 'we're going to do something I'm really, really, really going to enjoy later on tonight?'"

"No." Dane fought to keep a straight face. "It's code for

'drink your smoothie, or the locals will notice you're a seditious rebel in disguise.'"

"Fine." Cayden dragged across another rocking chair over from the far corner and slung his feet up on the railing beside Dane's. "But I'm never having one of those coconut oil shots again. At this rate, my taste buds are going to jump straight off my tongue and run far away. I'll never get to taste cronuts again, and it'll be all your fault."

"What the hell's a cronut?"

Cayden's rocker stopped. "Serious? You've never had a cronut? Dude, divinity on a plate. It's a mongrel pastry combo of doughnut and croissant."

"Sweet tooth, eh?"

"Don't judge. My mother says, *sweets for the sweet.* My father says, *you're a walking heart attack, Cayden,* right before he tucks in to the salted caramel version. It's his favourite."

"Which is your mother's favourite?"

"Oh, that's easy. Boston cream. You should see how it oozes out." Cayden made a deep, rumbly sound. "It's orgasmic."

"You're making that up."

Cayden grinned. "You'll never know."

"Jesus." The man would test his self-control. They needed to fuck before Dane started thinking of hearts and flowers and love—a sure trap he wanted nothing to do with. Ever.

They rocked for a bit, side by side, and Dane wracked his memory for the last sane thing either of them had said.

"What did you expect them to know?"

"My parents?"

"God, no." He hooked a thumb over his shoulder. "The breakfast staff."

Cayden shrugged. "The answers to all my questions, of course."

"You think the kid who makes the smoothies will have answers?"

"I live in hope."

He could tell Cayden was half-joking, but still. "Your optimism astounds me."

"Why?"

"Because you're a journalist. Hard news doesn't jibe with a happy worldview."

"Doesn't mean I can't see the positive." He shrugged. "Last year, I researched a story about teens doing the Duke of Edinburgh Award. They volunteered up on one of the islands on the Great Barrier Reef to help turtle hatchlings reach the sea alive. If not for them, most of the poor turtles would be eaten by birds, or their innards ripped out by rocks or sharp coral in the shallows."

"That's...nice." The word *random* sprang to Dane's mind.

"And, over Christmas, I interviewed a couple of guys on a remote weather station way, way out on an island in the Coral Sea. Total strangers, they got trapped there during that freak early summer cyclone and fell in love." He smiled and winked. "Now that's what I call a whirlwind romance."

Dane stopped rocking, and his feet thudded to the wooden plank floor.

Two men getting together on an island in the Coral Sea? Was the man serious? Malone and Jet?

Could Cayden's question be a coincidence? Or was he fishing for answers?

Even if Malone wasn't one of his closest friends, there was no way Dane would share his and Jet's story with a journalist.

"How did you know I'd be here?" he snapped out.

More to the point—*how had Cayden so easily drawn him in?*

CHAPTER TEN

DANE

Malone and Jet might have met and fallen for each other on an island owned and operated by the public purse, but their relationship was not for public consumption. That didn't stop the media swarming the minute Malone brought Jet home to Tennyson Bend.

No way would Dane reveal private information about his friend. Not to some cock-arse reporter, reeling him in with underhand stories about cults and sisters and…

No.

"How did you even know I'd be here? And to pretend that your sister…" Dane couldn't finish that thought.

Hell, the man probably wasn't even gay.

Shithead.

"What? Here? At breakfast?" Cayden looked down at his smoothie and frowned. "You all right, Dane?"

Oh, Cayden was good. Really good. "I take it back—you're a natural hack. Just the right amount of cynicism." Dane could barely speak past the cannonball-sized lead weight lodged high in his chest. He stood up in a rush. The chair rocked wildly and skidded across the deck.

"Jet and Malone are my friends. I will not sell them out. They deserve to be left alone. No public grilling."

Cayden's eyes bugged out, but he didn't cower under Dane's fierce glare. In fact, he was looking at Dane as though he'd grown a second head. He stood up slowly. "What the fuck are you on about?"

The innocent ploy wasn't going to work. Not this time.

What made it worse was Cayden had co-opted Dane into helping him destroy Gordon. All for a story?

Heinous man.

Dane tried to get the shakes under control.

Cayden opened his mouth. Probably to give some ridiculously thin explanation. But nothing came out.

"Speak now, or I will march into Gordon's office and spill your sad little conspiracy cult theory. I bet he'd love to know how you're spreading malicious tales about him and his retreat. All to get private information from his guests."

"What the fuck, dude?" Cayden squared up close, his voice low.

"Don't dude me." He poked at Cayden's chest. "I see through you."

But he hadn't seen through him. He hadn't seen that Cayden was false. He hadn't seen that Cayden didn't have a moral bone in his body.

The lie caught at his gut, and acid boiled. How gullible could he be?

Nobody had to tell Dane that it was dangerous to trust others. That was a given. But Cayden had drawn him in, made him believe, made him change plans, for fuck's sake. All because he thought he was needed.

"You lied to me." The words came out menacing and low. Hurt.

"No." Cayden grabbed his elbow, but Dane shook him off.

Cayden's intent stare turned cautious, then fluttered

away. "Well, yes, maybe, about some things. What do you expect?" He looked around and pulled Dane by the wrist to the far corner of the deck, where they were less likely to be overheard. "But I didn't lie about that."

"It doesn't matter." He stepped back from Cayden, shoring up his defences.

"Clearly it does matter, or you wouldn't be so angry," he said in a hushed voice. "You seriously know Malone and Jet? That's crazy. How do you know them?"

If the bastard thought he'd tell him anything about his friends, he was seriously mistaken. "God, you're a leech. Private is private for a reason, Cayden." People like him didn't care about the damage they caused.

"A leech? What the fuck are you talking about?" Cayden stopped at Dane's mutinous glare. "Hey, hey." He held his hands up. "I don't know what you think you know, but—"

"Good morning, retreaters!" Gordon's voice bellowed.

Dane twirled around to see everyone on the deck. When had that happened?

"Ready for some beautiful detoxing?"

"Hell, yeah!" Randall called out.

The collective groan was loud and clear, punctuated by a few nervous giggles.

None of them seemed to notice the drama unfolding in the back corner.

Dane moved toward Gordon.

He didn't give a shit about detox or whatever else Gordon was peddling, but the man didn't deserve some hack reporter flinging around salacious accusations.

"What are you doing?" Cayden grabbed his wrist again.

Dane pointed to Gordon. "He deserves to know that you're setting him up to face a public firing squad."

"What the hell? Where did that come from?"

"Dragging people's lives through the mud is disgusting, Cayden."

"Don't you dare!" Cayden grabbed his elbow with two hands and jerked him to a stop, then stepped up uncomfortably close.

Dane couldn't look away from those horribly beautiful golden eyes.

"I'm not here for a story, Dane." His nostrils flared, and Dane could practically hear Cayden's teeth grinding together. "I am not here for a story," he repeated, slowly, insistently.

More lies. "You told me you came here to—"

"I know what I told you." His deceiving eyes shifted over Dane's shoulder.

"You lied to me."

"Yes. I think we've already established that."

"You're still lying to me."

Cayden's lips pressed tightly together. "Yes."

Dane wanted to roar. He didn't know why he didn't just step away.

Before he could spit out a word, Cayden leaped in.

"Why are you so fucking angry? This isn't about you or Jet or Malone, who I did not know you knew, by the way. I championed those guys' right to privacy. But whatever. They're so far from this situation, they may as well be on Pluto."

"You told me you wanted to discover the truth, but all you want to do is ruin Gordon and his business. He might be delusional, but he's hardly evil, and nobody, not even him, deserves a viper in their ranks."

"Now I'm a viper?" One of Cayden's eyebrows went up. "I thought I was a leech."

"This isn't funny."

"You're right. It's so far from funny it's fucking frightful."

"You're a flea."

Cayden poked his chest. "Don't you dare play alliteration games with me, arsehole. Because I'll win. I'm here for one reason, and that's discovering the truth. You got that, buster?"

Dane opened his mouth to protest.

"No. You let me talk." Cayden grabbed his shirt with both hands. "We might have bonded over beer on a banana lounge, but I don't know you, and you sure as hell don't know me. I don't owe you anything. Including my truth. Whether you believe my intentions are honourable or not, I really don't care, but you'd better not get in my way." Cayden squeezed his eyes shut and heaved in a breath.

When he opened them, Dane could see the raw pain in the man's eyes.

That pain looked real.

His stomached flipped, and acid rose to his throat.

He swallowed thickly.

He breathed out.

Nobody was that good an actor.

Perhaps this was about more than a journalist chasing a story.

Perhaps it was personal—as personal as the source of his own anger.

Dane didn't make it a practice to second-guess himself, but maybe, this time, he had it wrong.

Problem was, if he couldn't trust his instincts, what could he trust?

Gravel-voiced, Cayden continued. "People's lives are at risk."

Lives? Was the man serious? Or was this just more subterfuge?

Dane tracked his Adam's apple as he swallowed.

"This is about someone I care about." Cayden's cheeks turned pale. "My sister."

Holy shit. "Your sister?" Dane felt the shard drive painfully deep.

More lies?

Would Cayden descend that low? Dane didn't know what to believe.

Anger warred with remembered pain, and his mind shuttled back to that day when Alice so bravely spilled her guts on live television. His crazy, wonderful, colourful twin sat there, stick-thin but rightfully proud of the progress she'd made, explaining to the nation the psychological struggle of anorexia nervosa.

In return for her courage, the presenters spouted prejudice and ignorance.

No true empathy, no genuine compassion.

They'd questioned her rationality. They'd questioned her willpower. They'd questioned her beauty. And, most unforgivably, they'd questioned her worthiness. They'd shamed her in front of the entire nation.

Mere hours later, she was gone.

Their words silenced Alice for good and left him a husk of a man.

A lump lodged in his throat, and he saw his pain mirrored in Cayden's swimming eyes.

Cayden's fists twisted in his shirt.

Dare he believe Cayden was speaking truth?

Dane brought his hands up to cover them. He squeezed hesitantly. "Your sister?"

"Lucy." Cayden's fists gentled a bit, but Dane could still feel the tension. "My older sister. I came here to save her from that man." He pointed over Dane's shoulder. "To bring her home." He jabbed at Dane's chest. "To my parents," *jab,* "whose hearts have not rested," *jab*, "for fifteen," *jab*, "fucking," *jab*, "years."

Dane grabbed Cayden's staccato finger.

Rationality and control had always been Dane's friends. He searched for them with slow, purposeful breaths. "All right."

"What?"

"I said all right. The proof of your claim is in finding your sister. Correct?"

Cayden nodded sharply.

"Then we look for her."

"Just like that?"

No. Not just like that. Stoicism took determination. And guts. But without it, he'd fly apart at the seams.

"Cult or no cult, if we find her, then maybe—" He maintained eye contact with Cayden, to make sure the man understood how close to the guarded edge he was teetering. "—maybe I'll trust you."

He'd wait, and he'd watch and figure out for himself where truth and innocence lay—and be there to protect it.

Dane's neck prickled with sweat. He took a deep breath and twisted his neck to look out across the flat, green lawn to where the pool rippled silver in the morning light.

"Fancy a swim?" he asked.

"What?"

"A swim. Don't think I could stomach a steam in this heat, but the pool looks good."

"What?" Cayden sounded confused.

Dane didn't blame him. If he did one more flip-flop around the guy, they'd both be spinning.

Something one of the Lycra-ladies had said tickled his memory. "If we're lucky, there might be a pool boy we can question."

"Dude. Do you have a split personality or something?"

"Or something." Dane shrugged and turned again to look directly at Cayden. "You're a liar, but if there's even one grain of truth to your story, then the place warrants an investigation. I'll help you find your sister. But that's it. Then we go our separate ways."

Cayden's lips twisted. "Allies for a cause?"

Dane thought about that. They weren't friends. They weren't partners. They didn't have a special bond. But he didn't need any of that to justify his decision. "I'd call us cautious allies."

Dane thought about spitting on his palm and offering it again, but Cayden's curt nod seemed to be all the acknowledgement he was going to get. "A swim sounds good. I'll fill you in while we float."

CHAPTER ELEVEN

CAYDEN

Cayden's day wasn't going to plan.

He was tired, itchy, hungry, and feeling damn sorry for himself.

Not to mention confused.

Not knowing what had set off Dane's weird spike in temper pissed Cayden off. And being pissed off stupidly pissed him off even more because anger took energy that by rights belonged to finding Lucy.

He didn't need anger right then. He needed cool-headed, action-stations, on-fucking-point, Special-Agent-Dale-Cooper-worthy investigative prowess.

Ugh.

"Fuck it." Cayden ran across the sun-hot bricks and cannon balled into the pool, then came up spouting like a dolphin.

He flicked his hair off his face and turned to watch Dane strip down to a pair of fire-engine-red, painted-on swim-mers, walk slow and steady to the deep end, curl his toes over the pool edge, and do an elegant dive with perfect form and minimal splash.

The bastard.

Three breast-strokes later, Dane reached the shallow end where he tumble-turned and pushed off again. The water barely rippled as he surfaced for a quick breath, then butter-fly-kicked to the deep end, turned again, and then dived deep to the pearlescent tile floor. Refracted sunlight danced on his skin as he merman-undulated his way back to the shallows and Cayden.

It was the most graceful tantrum he'd ever seen.

When Dane finally breached the surface, he wasn't even puffing. Just blinked water out of his eyes, slicked his hair back, and turned to Cayden. "Right, then. Tell me the story."

The silence lengthened.

Dane frowned. "*A swim sounds good*, he says. *I'll fill you in while we float.*"

In other words, Spicer, time's up.

"Fine." Cayden slung his arms wide on the lip of pool and did his best to look like it wasn't a gut punch to talk about his sister. "When I was fifteen, my sister disappeared."

Dane's frown deepened. "As in disappeared-disappeared? She was taken?"

The doubt in Dane's voice grated. Cayden understood, though. It was a question he'd asked himself so many times. He didn't answer, just continued with the story—or what he knew of it.

"She was nineteen. It looked like she'd left of her own accord. She dropped out of all her university courses. Her stuff was gone. And she'd given written notice to her land-lord." Cayden's simmering anger rose with every inane detail.

Nothing to see here, folks.

"All above board, right?" He didn't wait for Dane's reply. "Except it wasn't. The landlord aside, nobody knew she was leaving the city. The state. Hell, maybe even the country. Not one soul. And that just wasn't what Lucy was like. She couldn't keep a secret to save herself. You know? It made no sense."

He remembered the day so clearly.

His fifteenth birthday. Family tradition said they'd go together for Yum Cha. Only, when he and his folks had gone to pick Lucy up from her student share-house, all they'd found in her room was a bare bed, a paint-stained desk, and dozens of oily putty spots where her sketches, watercolours, and charcoal pictures had wallpapered the walls.

All of it—gone.

"It pissed her housemates off. None of them had any idea she'd planned to leave, but they all subleased their rooms individually, so, legally, she was only obliged to give notice to her landlord. None of them cared about Lucy. They just didn't want the hassle of finding a new housemate."

"My parents reported her missing to the police, but the fuckers just waved them away. 'No sign of harm,' they said, 'just a young woman spreading her wings.' Which might be true for some, but that wasn't Lucy. They didn't know my sister. 'My imagination gives me wings,' she always said. She loved me huge—even when she was a bratty teenager, and I was just a snotty little kid."

He felt the prick of tears.

God. Every time. Every. Bloody. Time.

Cayden dunked his head down under the surface, drowning the inevitable tears.

Blended with the tepid pool water, his tears flowed like silky fingers through his hair—a tender, healing hand. Not ready to rise, he opened his eyes underwater and saw Dane's lower half. The white waist tie on the man's fire-engine-red swimmers dangled loose, dancing in the water as Dane stepped closer and closer, then squatted, thighs wide, their knees nearly, but not quite, touching.

He didn't want to rise.

He didn't want to talk.

And he sure didn't want to see Dane's reaction to his sob story.

Cayden let out his last bubble of breath and closed his eyes. Wallowing wouldn't solve anything, but he desperately wanted to stay there in that floaty, serene nothingness.

Even more than oxygen, he needed one more moment for himself before he had to face the world, and Dane.

Something scratched him high on the sensitive inside of his right thigh, and he reflexively clamped his legs shut, tucked his hips down into the foetal position, and accidentally sucked in a choking mouthful of pool water.

A vice clamped to his left elbow and hauled him up.

"Hey!" Dane cried.

Cayden could only answer with coughs and splutters, hacking out a soggy mess.

Dane didn't let go. He squeezed Cayden's elbow tighter, fingertips pressing almost painfully into the joint. And Dane hadn't just pulled him up. He'd plastered Cayden to his chest —so close they were practically crocheted together.

Doily, anyone? Cayden wanted to ask.

And he would...just as soon as he got his breath back. Instead, he wrapped his arms around Dane's middle, hooked his chin over Dane's left shoulder, and chose for a moment to just give in and feel.

Aggravation aside, Dane was perfect to lean against. Perfect height. Perfect solidity. Perfectly fucking perfect.

The only imperfect thing about him was he was straight.

And taken, Cayden reminded himself.

The man was probably just trying to be sensitive, or brotherly, or heroic, or some shit like that.

God, he was tired.

He reached up to pat Dane's shoulder blade with one hand and wipe his own face with the other. The man might have a misplaced hero complex, but he didn't deserve to be snot on.

Dane didn't return the embrace, but the vice-like grip on his elbow softened, and the shoulder under his chin dropped ever so slightly.

"Future reference," Cayden murmured into the man's sun-kissed skin, "knights in shining armour aren't supposed to drown their damsons before they save them."

"Damsons?"

"Mm-hmm. Male damsel," he explained, playing up the *isn't-it-obvious* tone. "Lucky for you, I live to be saved another day."

"Lucky me," Dane grumbled into his ear, and the little puffs of air stoked an unwelcome fire. Holy hell, the man could sell him a snow cone in Antarctica.

Carol, Carol, Carol.

The mantra helped him break away. He spun around in the water and tried to get a grip on everything, including his priorities.

Mission number one—find Lucy.

Mission number two—preserve sanity.

Yeah. Good luck with that, Spicer.

CHAPTER TWELVE

DANE

Clear across the other side of the pool, Dane watched Cayden plough his arms through the water, forward and back till waves lapped messily at the tile walls.

Dane already missed the contact.

He ducked lower to his shoulders and swished the water, too.

"Have you ever heard of a place called Home?" Cayden asked.

Was that a trick question? "Umm…"

"The only clue I've found to where Lucy went that's checked out so far is the quasi-hippy-free-love-secret-commune Gordon Fuller called Home. Emphasis on the quasi, because there was nothing *free* about it." When he met Dane's eyes again, the sadness was gone—replaced with fierce anger.

"I'm a fan of Gaia—I mean, you go, girl, for creating nature, and I wish you well in saving the planet humans have screwed up so badly, but the call of nature shouldn't result in kids being born with six fingers, if you get my drift."

Dane got it. He considered interrupting Cayden's diatribe

because reliving the trauma was obviously causing more hurt, but he needed more information—some kind of basis for trust. So, he let Cayden ramble on.

"The local authorities were 'watching' them." Cayden curled his air-quote fingers and rolled his eyes. "Because none of the kids were signed up for school. But nobody thought to report on a string of young women who arrived out of nowhere. As though it wasn't clear as glass why they were there."

"And you think Lucy joined the commune?"

"Cult. That's what it was. Calling it a commune takes it off the hook. And I don't just think it—I know it."

"But how do you know it?"

Cayden shook his head and looked away. For a while, Dane thought Cayden wouldn't answer, but then he rolled his eyes and shrugged. "There are anonymous forums where people from all around the world talk about escaping abusive families, religious groups, and cults. Even conversion therapies. Horrible places. Scary stuff. Things you don't want to know. Things I never wanted to know. But I had a feeling." He shrugged. "Just a gut thing, I guess."

Cayden stopped working his arms, probably too caught up in memories to move.

Dane knew how that felt.

"I put my sister's picture up on all the forums." He looked up again, directly at Dane. "From one, I got a response."

Those lion eyes.

"You found her?" God, he couldn't even imagine.

But Cayden shook his head.

Dane's gut clenched. He might not trust the guy, but he wasn't a total bastard. Cayden was hurting, and he felt compelled to help. He needed to help.

"No. Not exactly. I found someone who recognised her. Maybe. From way back then. Another young woman.

'Elise,' she called herself, although I doubt that's her real name. She'd run away from home and found Home. Yeah, yeah, I know. Confusing, right? But that's what they called it."

"Jesus. That's screwed up."

"Yeah. Elise couldn't tell me how long she'd been there. Weeks. Maybe a month or two. She got away. Got a lift from a trucker on the highway coming over Cunningham's Gap to the Gold Coast. Idiot. But, you know, hitchhiking was probably less risky than staying. And she was scared. Even online, years later, and with nothing to trace her identity except a name that probably wasn't even hers, I could tell. She was truly scared."

Dane had no words. Sometimes imagination truly was a bitch. He felt clunky in his skin, useless to help, and supremely aware of how not half an hour ago he'd been at the man's throat.

Metaphorically.

He stepped closer and made a noise that meant *I hear you; I feel for you; I share your pain.*

Cayden didn't seem to notice.

"Anyway, about a decade ago, the commune-slash-cult went underground, or disbanded, or whatever. Gone. Leaving only council records that traced the land to Gordon." His voice dripped with tension. "A year or so later, good old Gordon founded this place." Cayden's inference was crystal clear.

"Did you follow the money?" Dane asked. "People's finances can reveal all sorts of secrets and motivations. I'm no investigative reporter, but logic tells me it's a wise path to take."

The gold in Cayden's eyes flashed molten. "I don't need to raid Gordon's piggy bank to know he was involved in Lucy's disappearance." He stepped closer and dropped his voice. "All that time, he probably knew where she was. He might even know where she is now."

Dane nodded, recognising the thin sliver of hope for what it was—blind desperation, the last piece of the puzzle Dane needed to accept Cayden's word.

Cayden hadn't given him any concrete information. Nothing he could trust. But Dane wasn't so cold a bastard that he could ignore the man's heartfelt need.

It wouldn't help to insist that Cayden share every detail of his story. It wouldn't dilute the hurt or bring Cayden's sister back. Dane knew that for sure. Because, just like Cayden, he'd had a fluorescent neon light flashing above his head, yelling *SISTER AT RISK*, too. And he'd been too late to heed the call.

The only way he could truly help Cayden was to help save his Lucy.

"Maybe she's still here," Dane ventured to hope.

Cayden let out a shuddery sigh, and Dane could practically feel the seismic shift tremble through the water.

"So," Dane said, "where do we start?"

CHAPTER THIRTEEN

CAYDEN

First up on his morning schedule, Cayden spent a gruelling hour he would never get back with Herbert the psychologist.

Herbert tried to get to his "core issue" so that he could "make the most" of his Pure Detox Wellness experience.

Yeah. Good luck with that, Herbie.

His issues weren't the sort that could be fixed with spinach.

In return, Cayden asked probing, behind-the-scenes questions about the retreat. Turned out Herbert's only beef was that his colleagues tended to flitter in and out, rarely staying longer than a year.

It didn't surprise Cayden.

Gordon would likely share his dodgy philosophy, then send his followers out into the world to spread the word—like a sticky spiderweb that caught flies unawares. Cayden imagined in the middle of that web a message in spider-script—*The Word of GOG*.

After surviving Herbert, Cayden visited Fern, the phlebotomist.

The vampire-red door ought to have clued him in, but it

instead triggered inappropriate fantasies about Dane's hot-red swimmers, which meant Cayden walked into her den blind to the danger, hastily adjusting his shorts.

She'd pinched and flicked and sucked his arm dry—all with a breezy smile—then waved him off down the hill to the next dose of torture on his hard-core Pure Detox Wellness Plan schedule.

After losing about a litre of precious blood to Fern, a visit to the nutritionist seemed moot. But he found his way to the blue wooden door anyway, because the first rule of under-cover journalism was to blend in. "Stay under the radar," he'd instructed Dane the night before—which meant following their respective wellness plans, worse luck.

Would it have killed Henrietta to approve the funds for the same indulgent Vital Serenity Wellness Plan that Dane's Carol booked for him?

"For Lucy," he affirmed his mission and knocked on the door.

The nutritionist would probably tell him his new diet should comprise three celery sticks and a litre of unpas-teurised yak's milk per day. If he was lucky, he might get to sprinkle that joyful brew with purple, Madagascan, guano-infused rock salt, or whatever the hell was the latest wellness trend, before being forced to chug it down with a smile.

"Under the radar," he reminded himself again.

On the positive side, if he screwed up the investigation, lost his job, and was disowned by his parents for failing as a son, he could open up a Bloody Mary beverage stand down Melbourne's St. Kilda shore, add the drink to the virgin menu, call it Pure-as-the-Driven-Snow Mary, and make a fortune with all the hipsters.

As a life-slash-business plan, it wasn't too bad…well, all except having to make nice with the hipsters. That was a radar he had no interest in getting under.

Meanwhile, Dane was probably off getting a facial, or a pedicure, or whatever other froufrou thing was scheduled on his plan.

Cayden, meet Envy; Envy, meet Cayden. Fucking awful to meet you, Envy.

He wasn't super jealous. Not really. But he wouldn't have minded a massage. Just to work out the kinks.

"Ugh." He rolled his shoulders, feeling about one hundred and twelve years old. "Shoot me now."

"What was that?"

"Shit." Cayden leaped and lifted his gaze to see a small, shiny-headed, well-preserved man standing in the doorway. He had that feather-light, sun-polished, endorphin-lover look—like he ran a marathon before breakfast every single day. "Shit. Oh, fuck. Sorry." Yeah, his mouth could probably do with a detox too.

"No worries, mate." The bald man smiled toothily. "You must be Cayden. Call me Shiloh. You're just in time. Come on in." Shiloh directed him to sit on a zebra-patterned beanbag and gave him the friendliest, most demoralizing roasting of his life.

"But it's the Mediterranean diet," Cayden protested three-quarters of the way through Shiloh's exhaustive narration of his self-reported Pre-detox Dietary Food Journal. "Lots of olives, and gelato, and—"

"I can see that." Shiloh's toothy smile turned eviscerating. "Going forward, though, how about we cut the pizza back to one a week? A slice now and then won't hurt, especially if you pair it with a nice raw salad. No need to skint yourself, eh?"

One slice?

Fuck that.

The minute he was out of the House of Glass, he'd be

mainlining a pint of ale with a side order of meat lovers deluxe. His stomach rumbled at the thought.

Why on earth had he been honest? He was smart. He was savvy. Why hadn't he thought to fictionalize his journal with fresh grilled fish and olive oil-drizzled asparagus, instead of pizza?

Could he really be any more of an idiot?

Food-shaming really wasn't his jam, so, midway through the nutritionist's ode to roast beetroot, Cayden lost patience and redirected the conversation. "That's really interesting, Shiloh. So…how do you like working here?"

Subtle might not have been his strong suit. But who didn't enjoy talking about themselves?

Aside from people with secrets.

True to form, Shiloh was a walkover.

"Mate, I've been here for years." Over a decade, it turned out. He'd seen many artistic young women come and go. Nobody named Lucy, but Cayden was painfully aware that his sister could have changed her name and her appearance.

Anything was possible.

Cayden started taking detailed mental notes. The most innocuous piece of information could be the nugget that turned an account into the last piece of the puzzle. But as Shiloh talked, and Cayden listened, Cayden's wild hope that Lucy might be hiding in plain sight gradually faded.

CHAPTER FOURTEEN

DANE

Dane was clear on Cayden's instructions.

If you think someone's trying to draw you into GOG's cult, don't be like, 'Thanks for the offer, dude, but cult living just isn't for me.' Act like you don't know what they're on about. Draw out the conversation. Just don't be too obvious, you know? Ask simple questions. Act like you're interested.

Too easy.

He tried not to be obvious about it—as per Cayden's dictate—but to Dane's intense disappointment, offers to join Gordon's cult proved elusive.

Jade, the pint-sized massage ninja, was unfailingly circumspect. This was a good thing, given that she had a special knack for making him sound like a bad porn star.

"Oh, yeah...right...no...mmm, right there...ahh...yeah... there," he'd moaned as she pummelled and pressed him to his limit.

Jade had some kind of special mojo-magic going on with her thumbs, and her elbows, and her heels, and... "Oh, fu—" He jerked back as she found yet another pressure point and dug in. "Sorry, Jade." He apologised for the fiftieth time that hour.

"No worries, Dane."

Turned out being tenderised like a hunk of cheap, gristly beef made *interested* and *simple* about as challenging as brain surgery. He'd be useless for pretty much anything besides lazing by the pool for the rest of the day.

Carol would be pleased.

Cayden, not so much.

The staff's professionalism was admirable, Dane supposed, given that they were privy to guests' personal information. Prospective clients would shun the place if they thought their personal details were being flung around like confetti to anyone inquisitive enough to ask questions.

But that did nothing to help Dane discover anything juicy about the retreat.

When he met up with Cayden for lunch under the shade of the giant poinciana tree, the look on Dane's face must have betrayed his failure to discover anything useful.

"Nothing?" Cayden asked.

"Sorry." He shook his head. "You?"

"Nada." Cayden's lips twisted.

Dane didn't know him well enough to be sure if it meant disappointment or frustration, or both. Not being able to read the man caught him out. Which was idiotic. They barely knew each other. Why did he think he ought to be able to read the man's emotions, let alone his mind?

Dane leaned his shoulder beside Cayden against the rough bark of the tree and sipped at his smoothie. The cool, crisp taste of green apple and celery soothed his palate in the midday heat. It wasn't terrible, but it wasn't satisfying either.

"I'd kill for a four-cheese pizza." Cayden channelled his very thought. "Hell, a cube of Gouda would be enough to get me hot and bothered right about now."

"Hot and bothered, eh?" The image that came to mind had nothing to do with the summer heat.

"Don't mock my appetite for creamy goodness. This is serious. How are we supposed to investigate if our brains are starved? Deprivation in pursuit of wellness is a total scam. I mean, think about it—we pay them to not feed us. Who the hell thought of that bit of fuckery?" Cayden rolled a bit to the left, and Dane felt their shoulders press lightly together. It was the barest touch, but Dane felt it down to his toes.

Cayden gestured to the hub deck. "And all those brain-washed idiots up there are bragging about all their delightful deprivations."

Dane got it. "Sounds like a tagline. You fishing for fresh stories already?" He regretted his words the minute they came out. How were they supposed to work together if he was riding Cayden's arse about being an ambulance-chasing reporter every five seconds?

Cayden stepped away from the tree trunk, back stiff and straight. "I'm just saying it's a status quo that ought to be questioned."

"I know. Sorry." Dane felt immediately chastened, which grated. All he'd done that day was try to help. And where had it gotten him?

Nowhere.

He turned away from Cayden and the hub and searched through the trees for a tell-tale glimpse of the road that led away from the retreat. He grappled with the instinct to run far, far away—back to his comfortable, normal, familiar life.

"I'm starving," Cayden said, abruptly. "Let's go get a refill. Wouldn't hurt to mingle with the masses for a bit. Someone might have noticed something helpful. The kitchen staff, too. They're notorious gossips. Maybe I can coerce them into feeding us a little under-the-table treat while I'm at it. Then, while you're off questioning the professional pamperers, I'll interrogate whoever's running the gym. We can meet up before dinner in the steam room. Compare notes. Sound good?" Cayden's voice was all professional—impersonal.

Inexplicably, Dane felt like he'd lost something. "Sure."

"Five o'clock?" Cayden didn't wait for his answer, just turned and walked a direct path across the grass back to the hub.

"Sounds like a plan," Dane said to the rustle of the summer wind in the poinciana tree.

CHAPTER FIFTEEN

CAYDEN

While he waited for his five o'clock date with Dane to roll around, Cayden rocked in one of the hub rockers and watched Shorty, the aged gardener, pick weeds out of the lawn.

Cayden couldn't see any weeds, but the gardener insisted they were there.

"Gotta get rid of the buggers before they take hold," Shorty said, which Cayden thought was good advice in many circumstances.

"Too true." He scratched at his bites. Bloody mosquitos.

"O' course, not all weeds are bad. Some are mighty fine, if you know what I mean." Shorty winked, then ducked his head back under his massive wide-brimmed hat. "Herbs and such." He backtracked, but Cayden's attention was piqued.

"Herbs?"

"Ya-hum."

"Are we talking special herbs? Not garden-variety herbs? Parsley and such?"

Shorty winced. "Not 'sposed to say nothin' about the pantry. Gordon would have my goat."

Gordon was involved?

The rocker silenced as Cayden stopped and straightened up. "I won't say anything. Promise."

Shorty looked him over, slowly.

Was the man checking him out?

"You seem a cool sort," Shorty concluded.

"Yeah. Yeah. I'm cool." Sort of. That very second, Cayden was feeling pretty hot under the collar. Was Gordon into drugs? It shouldn't have come as a big surprise. GOG looked high pretty much every time he saw him. "So, herbs in a...did you say a pantry? Is Gordon keen on gardening too?"

"He enjoys planting. Harvesting, not so much." Shorty stepped up to the deck railing. "I can sort you out...if you like."

"Sort me out?" What did the man—? "Oh!" Jesus. He'd done plenty of deceitful things in his search for Lucy, but he'd done nothing outright illegal. Was he really willing to step over that line?

As a last resort, maybe. But there were other ways to discover people's secrets. Better ways. Legal ways. And Shorty wasn't going anywhere. If it turned out he needed the information to press Gordon about her whereabouts, he knew who to ask.

Cayden twisted his wrist to see his watch. Nearly time for a steam. Plus, he didn't want to keep Dane waiting.

He eased out of the rocker. "Maybe. I'll let you know. Good to speak to you, Shorty. I've got to get to a thing." He pointed his thumb toward absolutely nowhere specific at all and made tracks for the pool terrace and the steam room.

With any luck, Dane would have something solid to report.

"Every single day, dude. We need to do this every…single…day." Cayden drew the words out, thick as the eucalyptus-scented air swirling in the therapeutic steam room. If not for the mosquito bites arrayed across his chest and arms, he'd be in heaven. They were a minor discomfort and would probably be gone by morning, but in the steamy heat, they itched and flamed angry red. He felt like he'd rolled around in a prickle patch.

He slouched low as he could go on the oyster-shell tiled bench, lifted one leg up to rest his arm on his knee, and slicked away the river of sweat that seemed determined to pour from his forehead into his eyes.

Edie and Maxine sat cosy together on the adjacent bench. They wore colourful geometric swimsuits with frills around the bust that did little to hide the effects of gravity on their well-worn and, he hoped, well-loved bodies.

Across the other side of the steam room, Dane looked like a swimwear model from *GQ's* Best Bods of Summer edition. He sat upright in the classic captain-of-the-swim-team pose —feet firmly planted, fists pressed to each knee—all lanky strength and commanding vibe.

Eyes sealed shut, Dane tilted his head back to lean against the wall, fully exposing the smooth hollow at his throat. His sharp Adam's apple bobbed up and down at slow, mesmerising intervals. Cayden fancied he could see the man's pulse, and he wanted to plant his lips right over it and feel it thrum against his tongue.

That or sink himself into the man's hair that curled and whirled like a silky-sweet ocean of Spanish hot chocolate—sweet, molten goodness.

Fuck.

Cayden shifted again in his seat to relieve the building pressure.

It didn't work.

He averted his gaze and tried his best not to think about Dane in *that* way.

That didn't work either.

It made him sort-of, maybe, not-really glad that Edie and Maxine had crashed their steam room debrief.

Ogling wouldn't hurt, but leaping on the man would probably be too much.

Especially given that Dane was straight.

And already taken.

By a woman named Carol.

Ugh.

Cayden tried to look away, but his eyes kept boomeranging back to Dane.

Eventually, he decided to just give in to temptation. If the man didn't want to be ogled, he really ought to wear more clothes. He should put on a shirt or maybe one of those enveloping kaftans Dane's cheer squad women all seemed to wear when they weren't wearing skin-tight Lycra.

Cayden's eyes dropped.

And socks. The man really should cover those high arches and the ridges of bone and sinew that led down to his toenails which were painted…was that green nail polish?

The colour shimmered like fucking merman scales.

It was so disgustingly cute Cayden thought he could probably forgive how badly the colour clashed with Dane's red-hot swimsuit.

Might as well just give in to the lust, he decided. "Strike that. We need to come in here multiple times a day, every single day."

"Mm-hmm," Dane rumbled from his side of the steam room, not even bothering to open his eyes. As though he had no interest in ogling Cayden in return.

The bastard.

"Morning, noon, and night, dude. Morning, noon, and night." Cayden pressed the point—hoping to get a reaction.

"TMI, young man," Maxine said, her voice dry as dust.

Cayden went still.

He saw the gleam when Dane's eyes slitted open and threw a micro-glance Cayden's way.

A long beat of silence went by before Cayden's stumbling mind caught up.

"Maxine!"

"Don't 'Maxine' me, young man. I see you taking photographs with those honey eyes of yours, and they're not of me or my darling Edie, despite our magnificent figures."

Cayden couldn't think of a single thing to say to that, and Dane went back to his silent, captain-of-the-team pose, with only a slight twist of his glorious lips to show that maybe, just maybe, the man wasn't horrified by Cayden's blatant interest.

Down, boy.

"Don't embarrass the boys too much, Maxine. Or they'll stop providing such wonderful entertainment." Edie chided her friend. "Come on. It's getting hot in here—in more ways than one." She slow-winked at him. "Let's leave the boys to their…activities."

"No need to leave on our account." Dane said.

The words banished any fresh hope that Dane might leap over the sexual fence for him.

Jesus, Cayden. Why would you even think of that?

Dane was a no-go zone.

He averted his eyes and took a long drink of tepid water to stop the words *please leave, you octogenarian mistresses of embarrassment* from popping out his mouth.

They waved cheekily before swishing out through the cedar door.

And then it was just him and Dane.

Alone.

Do not think of activities.

Think of Carol.

Carol. Carol. Carol.

Yeah. Basically, Cayden *was screwed*.

Certain his cheeks must be flaming redder than the man's swimming trunks, Cayden surreptitiously shuffled closer to the corner of the bench, turned so he wasn't looking directly at Dane, and stretched his legs out.

The silence was agony.

Ignore, ignore, ignore.

He closed his eyes and tried to fry his brain by sucking as much hot steam up his nostrils as he could manage.

It didn't work.

Mysteriously, Dane rose from his side of the steam room, strode over to Cayden's side, lifted Cayden's legs up by the ankle, sat down, then dropped Cayden's heels down onto his very warm, very firm lap.

Had Cayden fallen asleep?

Was this all a dream?

Since every dude had a six-pack in his dreams, Cayden did a surreptitious pinch test to the love handle bunched at his waist.

Nope, not dreaming.

Which meant Dane was actually touching him.

On purpose.

What did it mean?

What could it mean?

He cleared his throat intending to blurt out something supremely sexy, like *take me, take me now*, but Dane beat him to the punch.

"Spill before we get interrupted again. What did you discover?"

His words brought Cayden down with a thud.

Lucy.

Shit.

Worst brother ever.

He was there to save Lucy, not to dive into some guy's pants. Even if they were sexy as fuck.

Dane jostled his feet. "Did you learn anything useful?"

Cayden breathed in the heat. "Nope. Eight hours of my life I will never get back." He shook his head.

"Nothing?"

"Not unless you want to know how to milk a nut."

Dane's brows went up, and when Cayden realised just exactly what he'd said, he rushed on.

"Or the chemical composition of beetroot? That was a good bit of info. Might come in handy after the zombie apocalypse…" *Jesus, stop rambling, Cayden.* "Or something."

Oh, and, while you're at it, you might want to stop drooling too.

"It can't have been that bad. Nothing about the retreat? Or Gordon?" Dane scritch-scratched his fingernails through the leg hairs just above Cayden's ankles. It tickled.

He didn't pull his legs away.

"You said yourself—any piece of information might help find her, no matter how minute," Dane said.

Cayden tensed, and Dane's fingertips suddenly felt like cheese graters scouring his skin. Cayden knew the needle-in-a-haystack theory all too well.

"Nothing else?" Dane pressed. "Nothing that helps us find Lucy?"

Us.

Shit. Cayden liked that *us*.

The rapid switch from horny to pissed to warm-fuzzy felt like whiplash.

He liked that *us* too much.

Shifting his feet off Dane's lap, he leaned forward to rest

his elbows on his knees and let the sweat and the steam roll down his nose.

"What about you? Anything?" he asked.

"No. I've used the word *home* more often today than an agent at a real-estate convention. Got nothing. And Lucy's a common enough name, but nobody I've asked could think of anyone." Dane's voice dropped a smidgen lower. "Sorry."

"Yeah." That was pretty much his story, too. "That's okay." It wasn't, but what else could he say?

Cayden reached down for his water bottle and saw Dane's goddamn merman toenails sparkling on the floor.

Dane and whimsy weren't an obvious match, but Cayden couldn't look away.

Dane must have noticed his attention. "Tessa called it clam," he said.

"What?"

"Tessa, the pedicurist. She called the colour of the nail polish clam. What do you think?" Dane flared his toes out on the oyster-shell tiled floor. The spaces between were just wide enough to fit Cayden's tongue.

Oh, sweet Jesus. "Save Lucy, save Lucy, save Lucy…"

"What?"

"Nothing." He may as well have substituted *Lucy* with *pickles* for all the use the mantra had at dampening his revving engine.

"Who did you talk to through the afternoon?" Dane asked.

Cayden sighed with relief at the simple question. Reporting his findings was as easy and familiar a task as pulling on his socks. All he had to do was imagine he was facing Henrietta instead.

He jammed his water bottle between his knees and freed his fingers to count.

"Gladioli, the chef, and Jamie, her offsider. Bess and Sam

and Dwight, the admin team." He changed hands. "And Shorty, the gardener, who said he doesn't know anyone named Lucy, but he sure knows a lot about a *special herb pantry*—translation, *weed*—that GOG planted just over yonder." He pointed through the wall, not knowing if it was the right direction or not. "That info might come in handy if I need to press GOG for Lucy's whereabouts."

"Translation, blackmail." Dane smirked.

Was that judgement Cayden heard? Not that he gave a fig —blackmail paled as a sin compared to kidnapping.

He raised his ring finger. "Fraser, the gym dude. He was busy leading a hula-hoop session with your cheer squad ladies, so we didn't get to chat much."

"Who?"

"The cheer squad ladies." Cayden waved a hand around. "You know, the women you were making nice with at dinner last night." For the life of him, he couldn't remember their names.

"Michelle, and Anna, and Lissa—"

"Lucy?" A vice clamped his lungs.

"Fuck no, sorry... *Li-ssa*." Dane slowly articulated the name. "Not Lucy."

Shit. Deep breath.

"You must have come across others. Maybe not here, but...sorry, man." Dane pinched his mouth shut.

Lucy. Cayden swallowed thickly. "You're right. It is a common enough name. I should be used to it by now."

Since Cayden arrived at the House of Glass, he'd finally felt closer to his sister—every step he'd taken at the retreat was on a patch of ground where she might have walked; every flower he smelled she might've sniffed; every view he'd seen she might have gazed upon mere moments, days, or months before.

Dane's hand cupped his shoulder. He squeezed once, warm and solid. Friendly.

Reassuring.

Distracting.

Lucy should be his front and centre, his here and now, his one-hundred percent of everything.

He was finally closer to her, and yet it was a man's touch that brought him comfort.

In the thick moment, Dane's hand slid down Cayden's arm.

Disarmed, Cayden loosened his vice grip on the curved edge of the tile bench. Dane's fingers wove between his and flexed ever so gently, then stayed laced through his, as though that was where his hand belonged.

With that one simple, unexpected move, the man took him to swoon-ville.

Cayden didn't know what to do. He was so fucking confused. Was it a come on? Did straight dudes even do that? Or was Dane simply being caring? Human?

He swivelled back to Dane to look for some kind of sign of how to proceed, but his focus didn't land on the man's face. Instead, it fell south to Dane's chest—so strong and sculpted and...speaking.

Shit.

What had they been talking about?

"...least of all me, should expect you to get used to it, or get over it, or whatever the hell people say. Nobody ever knows what it's like to lose a..." Dane tapered off with a shake of his head. It left Cayden even more confused because the man's words and actions did not match the chill in his eyes. Instead of friendly affection, or—God help him—liquid heat, he saw cold turmoil, a place Cayden instinctively didn't care to go.

It certainly wasn't for a stroll through the warm town of swoon-ville.

Cayden straightened up, using his own strength to press each vertebra firmly against the hard tile wall, reluctant to even peer into the mysterious rabbit hole of Dane's mind. He had enough burdens without adopting more drama.

Which probably made him a dick.

He looked down.

Mm-hmm.

That particular one percent of his anatomy was already one hundred percent attentive to the man.

The ghost of Dane's hand returned and made him shiver, despite the ratcheting heat.

They'd already breached the do-not-touch barrier. Maybe it was time to test those waters for real. Take away some of the confusion.

Not wanting to spook Dane, he slowly unhitched their fingers and turned his hand over, palm to palm. He flexed a little and felt the kiss of moisture. Dane didn't seem to react, but when Cayden looked up, the man was frowning, fierce.

"Shit." He pulled away. "Sorry, dude."

Fuck.

Not a come on.

Bile rose.

Cayden leaped off the bench. "Idiot." He drove his fingers into his wet hair and yanked hard.

Epic fail!

In dire need of a rock to hide under, Cayden wished he was anywhere but stuck in a tiny, fucking steam box.

He didn't know which was worse—death by embarrassment or death by sous-vide.

"It's okay," Dane said, voice gruff.

Cayden sucked in a lungful of thick steam. "Nah, dude.

That's not cool. You were just being nice, and it's so not okay to get touchy-feely with a straight guy."

Not quite able to bring himself to meet the man's gaze, Cayden's stupid eyes drifted south and latched onto Dane's seriously gorgeous lips that quirked and softened and....spoke.

Shit. Not again.

He really needed to practice fucking listening. "I'm sorry. What?"

Dane quirked a smile. "I said bathhouses aren't really my scene. But I'm not opposed to a taste or two when the urge strikes."

Mmm, a taste.

"Wait, what?"

Did Dane mean…?

Cayden tried to focus. He really did. But that one word —*taste*—had his inner-Pavlov's dog drooling.

A fresh bead of steam gathered high on Dane's temple, rolled around his brow, and caught on his eyelash. He blinked, and the bead dripped to the curls on his chest, joining every other lucky drip that had obeyed the same course of gravity.

Cayden sighed, wanting quite desperately to obey gravity too.

"Hey." A hand ghosted past his vision.

"Huh?"

Dane pointed squarely at his own chest. "Not straight."

His one percent went supernova. "Fuck me."

Dane's eyes sparked fire, and he reached his hand out.

Like he was caught in some kind of tractor-beam, Cayden went to him, not stopping till his shins butted up against the solid side of the bench between Dane's spread knees. His vision filled with slick, creamy skin and thick, wavy hair. The man was like the most decadent hot chocolate—molten silk.

He wanted to taste and touch and smell and…

Dane grabbed for his reaching hand just as…

Thud!

The door crashed open, and a wave of icy air cut between them.

No time to think, let alone react. Cayden stood stock still, intimately close to Dane as Randall barged in, then came to an abrupt halt.

"Whoops! Sorry, mate…and, um…mate."

Dammit!

"Hurry, Randy. You're letting the hot air out." Bernice pushed her husband through the doorway.

Jesus. Could he not catch a fucking break?

Cayden wanted to stamp his foot. Throw a goddamn tantrum. But seeing the couple reminded him of one very sticky, very unfortunate, very aggravating fact—Dane might not be straight, but he wasn't single either.

He didn't know if Carol was Dane's wife, or his girlfriend, or one-fifth of a polyamorous relationship, but the facts remained—Dane wasn't free, and Cayden didn't do sexy times with dudes who were taken.

Head still high in the cloud of steam and desire, he slowly drew his hand from Dane's, returned to his original place on the bench, set his focus on the gleaming tile wall across from them, and pretended Dane hadn't rocked his world.

CHAPTER SIXTEEN

DANE

Dane dialled the ceiling fan up to hurricane level to battle the stillness of the sultry night. He stripped off his sweaty clothes and draped them over the lone chair, then padded naked into the rain shower in his haven's bathroom.

Hours had passed since Randall and Bernice interrupted him and Cayden in the steam room, but his blood still hummed. He felt like a teenager in heat.

Must be the exhaustion.

If anyone cared to ask, he would have said *making good on his promise to Cayden* was next on his agenda. But Cayden had elected to stay in the hub for Gordon's post-dinner lecture on The Mother—whatever the fuck that was.

Left to his own devices, Dane planted his forearm flat on the tile wall and leaned in. The water pummelled his neck and shoulders. He rounded his back and watched his dominant left hand pull rhythmically at his soap-slick cock.

He didn't bother to play—fucking artistry could wait till Cayden joined him.

For the moment, he just planted his feet and stroked. His

heartbeat raced in time with his fist, hell bent on bringing efficient, perfunctory relief.

Dane felt the tepid water course like an intrepid tongue around the lean globes of his butt and down his crack. It dripped off his nose and cheeks, and he sucked it in, nearly choking as he latched his mouth tight to his left bicep.

Jaw wide, he tongued the giving flesh, panting on humid air that smelled of rainforest and precum. He tasted the tang of sweat and the lingering slick of butter.

Tightening his fist, Dane stroked faster, not letting up till his vision wavered, and every bit of him clenched tight on the precipice.

All it took was one sweep of his thumb across his sensitive head, and he shot an arc of cum across the tile.

"Holy fuck." His chest heaved and his knees buckled. He slid sideways into the corner of the shower, not trusting a single bone in his body.

Eventually, Dane shut off the shower and dried off. He padded out of the bathroom, pulled on a fresh pair of boxers, and stood in the middle of the simple room, aimless.

It was a truly novel experience.

Dane always had a plan. He was never idle. Never bored. Never purposeless. Never gave in to lassitude.

Exhaustion shimmered grey on the edges of his vision, but he wasn't ready for sleep. Not yet. He was keyed up. Ready for…something. He didn't know what.

"Haven," he scoffed, not sure which he was more annoyed with—himself or the place. He paced, feeling the cool wooden planks underfoot. The intense whip of fanned air muffled the cicadas' chorus to a dull whine but did little to temper the prickling heat.

He rolled his neck and heard the crack-crack-crack of his neck. A dozen deep tissue massages and he might begin to feel human. Add a few bouts of yogic sex and he'd probably feel loose-limbed and ten feet tall.

His mind returned to that moment in the steam room when Cayden finally realised that he wasn't the only gay man in the room. Dane could have leaped on him right then and there.

Dane couldn't seem to stay away from the man. And not just physically. Which was weird. Dane didn't do relationships. He didn't do romance. He wasn't boyfriend-partner-husband material. Hell, he didn't even do friends with benefits. Love was a trap he had no intention of falling into. Dane did convenient, fly-by-night, forgotten-by-morning sex.

Scratch the itch and be on his merry way.

Cayden wasn't exactly convenient. He was messy, and awkward, and bothersome.

And gorgeous.

But their time together at the House of Glass was finite. He could open that door, scratch the itch, then just as easily shut the door at the end. Clean and simple.

All he had to do was keep his head. Help the man, fuck the man, then move on. That shouldn't be too hard. He could control himself.

So long as Cayden wasn't looking for more.

Decision affirmed, he shoved on his reading glasses, wedged his knees beneath the low desk, grabbed his laptop from his briefcase, and fired it up.

If he was going to help find Cayden's sister without resorting to hot-water strategies like blackmail, they needed to systematize their investigation.

He pulled up a fresh spreadsheet and typed *HOG* into the banner.

Against dates and times, he inputted all the details from his Vital Serenity Wellness Plan into the *Dane* column, coding events as *meal*, *treatment*, *lecture*, or *pH test*—ignoring for the moment that he had no intention of ever testing the pH of his spit, let alone his piss. In the next column, he inputted everything he could remember from Cayden's schedule, which wasn't a lot. In their free blocks he allocated *pool*, *gym*, and *steam*, and cut and pasted *rim* to every morning, for a daily run along the crater's edge, and after a second's hesitation, he copied and pasted *screw* to every night.

No sense using coy euphemisms about that.

The only other person who had remote access to his digital cloud was Carol, but he wasn't worried she'd inadvertently see his work since his tech wouldn't sync while he and his laptop were stuck in the crater's digital wasteland. If she invaded his privacy, she deserved every bit of that minor embarrassment for sending him to the retreat in the first place. As far as Dane was concerned, she could suffer right along with him.

Further to the right, he created a column generously labelled *clues* and filled in what little he knew. Then he made another column called *results*. With any luck, that blank field would fill with time.

It was only when he sat back to take in the full picture that he realised he'd actually officially committed himself—not just to helping Cayden find Lucy, but to his dubious wellness plan, too.

Shit. What had he done?

He pressed ctrl A, hovered over the X for a long second, and then ground his teeth and diverted to the S key, saving his work to the hard drive. He shut the laptop lid and slipped it back inside his briefcase.

Out of sight, out of mind.

Yeah, right.

Exhaustion beat a drum at his temples, but there was no way he would sleep with every nerve-ending twitching.

Screw; read; sleep—that was the plan. Now he just needed Cayden to come to the party.

He switched the overhead fan from a manic hurricane speed to gentle whirligig, and the sounds of the rainforest flooded in—the squawks of fruit bats, the chittering of a trillion cicadas, and the constant rustle of the canopy shifting in the wind.

He slogged a tall glass of ceramic-filtered water and brushed his teeth with his own spearmint toothpaste. It was probably full of carcinogens, but Dane didn't care. Towelling his mouth, he glanced at himself in the bathroom mirror.

Nobody would call him a silver fox for a few years yet, but his cheeks were looking hollower than usual, his cheekbones sharper, and the skin beneath his eyes had taken on a purple tinge—as though the need to sleep was sucking at his bones.

Finally, run out of distractions, and well over waiting for Cayden, Dane fished from his suitcase Alice's battered copy of Mervyn Peake's *Titus Groan* and thumbed to his bookmark —the plastic coating yellowed and brittle and the bright pink tassel faded with age.

Dane recalled the very moment when Alice had presented him with a plain white envelope marked only with the number 16, written in thick, black ink.

Since he expected a voucher, he'd ripped it open ready to gloat to his friends, then nearly died when out fell a bookmark covered in sparkly rainbows. She might as well have hung a fluoro pink sign above his head, flashing 'GAYBOY!'

It wasn't till hours later that he'd quietly taken a second look at the gift and saw what she'd written on the back.

"Welcome to the club, bro-mine :) xoxoxox."

"Ex oh ex oh." He smoothed his finger over the sparkles, still bright behind the aged plastic.

The shock-horror of embarrassment had long ago worn

off, overshadowed by the horror of her death and the grisly discovery that she'd left to him her precious collection of musty, second-hand books.

For years, Alice's library remained in boxes. Just the thought of cracking those seals and delving in had torn the breath from his chest.

Years later, when he bought his Tennyson Bend apartment, Dane had shelves purpose-built, finally unpacked the books, and lined them up in alphabetical order. He'd resolved to read a chapter per night—reopening his heart to the pain and the joy and the sheer craziness that was his twin. Then and there, he'd taken her ragged, paperback copy of *Aesop's Fables* down from the top left corner of the shelf and opened to page one.

Each book felt like connecting to a small part of her. He smelled the same musty old smell Alice had smelled, read the same words Alice had read, and fell in love with the same stories Alice had loved.

Dane turned off the main overhead light and let the warm glow of the bedside lamp bleed into the crisp white of the sheets. Naked, he slipped between the bedsheets, knuckled the pillows at the concave of his spine, opened to chapter one, and read.

CHAPTER SEVENTEEN

CAYDEN

"Are you seriously serious?" Cayden briefly contemplated violence, but Gladioli was safely ensconced behind the two-foot deep, tuck-shop hole in the wall.

She pointed at the collection of glass jugs along the wall of the hub deck. Each was par-filled with an inch of clear liquid that shone in the early morning sunshine. "Just fill to the line with tap water and you're on your way to a new you."

Sweet Jesus. He was doomed.

He'd done hours upon hours of research about Gordon and his House of Glass retreat. But, somehow, he'd never realised that a saltwater flush was not a super-salty, super-floaty, Dead Sea-like bath.

Cayden shook his head. "Is this really necessary, Gladioli?"

The chef's smile turned into an evil grin. "The trick is to take it real slow. Just go with the flow."

"Ugh," he grunted, not remotely convinced, but the words *under the radar* spun in his mind on repeat. He hefted the bottle tagged with his name, cosy beside Dane's, then dragged his feet back up the path to his haven.

He tiptoed past Dane's shut-tight door, careful not to disturb. There wasn't much in life less sexy that purposely giving yourself the shits.

Safely ensconced in his own haven, Cayden dutifully followed Gladioli's instructions. He diluted the clear brine to the thin angel's halo line close to the top of the bottle, gave it a quick shake, and poured a glass.

The salt was still wretched, but Cayden kept chugging. He gagged on every mouthful till the first glass was empty.

Gut roiling, Cayden raced to the bathroom sink, sure that he was going to lose it.

He had to brace his knees to stop from collapsing in a puddle. Shuddering, he broke out in a cold, clammy sweat that rolled up his spine and lifted every last hair.

"Holy fuck in a fucking henhouse." Cayden didn't know which was worse—the taste of salt or the taste of bile. He cupped his hand under the faucet, slurped up a fresh mouthful, and then swallowed to clear his throat, worried that if he gargled, he'd bring the whole thing back up.

He ran a head-to-toe assessment. Not exactly good, but better.

What had Gladioli said? Something about going with the flow. "God. The worst pun award goes to the chef."

Cayden eyed his wan reflection in the mirror. "Note to self—don't chug."

The next hour he didn't really want to commit to memory.

He'd taken to refilling the glass after every few sips because leaning his head back to drink the bottom half of the glass triggered his gag reflex. But that wasn't even the worst of it. After five hundred sips, the gig had gotten loud, and he really, really, really hoped Dane wasn't on the other side of their shared bathroom wall.

One thousand, three hundred and seventy-six sips in, Cayden could take no more.

He stood naked in his fifth shower of the day, arms braced against the steamy tiles, barely feeling the rivulets of hot water as they streamed down his back and into every raw nook and cranny. Any other day, that might've felt good with a capital G, but, in that moment, he felt about as good as goose guano.

Exhausted too.

Cayden put his forehead to the cool tile and reached down to flip off the shower knob. All he wanted was to collapse in bed and sleep for a fucking century and never, ever, drink another fucking glass of fucking saltwater ever fucking again.

In fact, he'd banish salt from his diet…

Seasoning on your delicious juicy steak, sir?

Nope.

Salt crystals edging your margarita glass, mate?

Hell, no.

A swim in the ocean, dude?

Not on your fucking life.

Cayden bypassed the many-times-used towels that hung like wet fish on the rail, shuffled to his bed, and flopped down on the mess of sweaty sheets. His stomach still gurgled, but there was nothing left in him to come up or go down, so he closed his eyes and allowed himself to be still for a quiet moment.

Through his one open eye, Cayden saw dappled light on the lush green tree outside his side window, but the streaks of morning sunlight that had bathed his haven were gone. Which meant it was past noon.

He flopped a hand over his face and wiped at the drool crusting his face to his pillow. "Jesus, mouth like marmoset."

The pillow felt damp beneath his cheek, and the sweaty sheets tangled around his legs.

Stuck fast and desperate for water.

Fresh water.

If he ever even saw a fucking salt shaker, it'd be too soon.

He imagined a tall glass of iced water with a wedge of fresh, zingy lime bobbing around. It sat just out of reach, saying, "Nah-ne-nah, you can't have me!" Or it would, if inanimate objects could talk.

"Sign of madness," he mumbled into the gooey pillowcase, but extreme thirst was motivation enough to at least give moving a try.

Leading with his left arse-cheek, Cayden rolled over onto his back. Every muscle protested, and a wave of death-warmed-over sloshed over him. "Isn't this detox thing supposed to make you feel great?" he asked the universe.

The universe said nothing.

Or, at least, nothing helpful.

Some kind of bird warbled just outside his window. Probably mocking him in bird speak. Which was fair, because what kind of idiot thought drinking half the ocean was a good idea?

"Show of hands. Who's the biggest idiot in the room?"

Cayden half raised his left arm, then let it drop. Limp.

The fan spun overhead, flicking a bit of hair across his nose. It tickled, but not enough for Cayden to do anything about it. Then he started getting dizzy watching the fan spin, so he closed his eyes.

Better.

Except bright flashes of light burst behind his eyelids, and he wondered if maybe he might be allergic to salt. Clearly, the detox lifestyle was unhealthy, and he needed to get away from GOG's world as soon as possible. At the very least, his shitty under-the-radar plan needed adjusting.

If only he had a partner, someone who loved him enough to bring him a drink, give him a sponge bath, erase history… useful things like that.

It seemed like a good idea to holler to Dane for help, but they probably weren't close enough yet for the dude to see him bare-arse naked, lying in his own drool. Which begged the question—how close did a man have to be to be okay with that?

"Hypothetically, of course," Cayden asked the whirling fan, because, in reality, he'd never tied himself close enough to a man for that. And he never would if he stayed in his current, seriously unsexy condition.

He sighed.

None of those domino thoughts would bring him a drink or a shower.

No, not just a shower. He needed a sixth shower.

The thought of all that fresh water raining down on his head was enough incentive to kick the sheets off and haul his arse upright. His head spun in one direction and his stomach in the other.

Anyone who called detox a treat seriously needed their head read.

He bypassed the sink to step straight into the shower and flipped on the cold tap. Under the drenching rain shower, he opened his parched mouth for a blessed drink.

Holy hell, it was like a cold beer after running ten k's on a hot summer day. Cayden could practically feel his flesh absorbing the water, rehydrating every vein and muscle—a flooding creek after drought—and he drank and drank and drank.

How long did he stand there? Cayden had no idea. Long enough to start feeling human again and guilty over the indulgent amount of water he was using. Eventually, he finished and grabbed one of the many towels he'd hung up to dry before he'd crashed. It should have been wet. Or damp, at the very least. But it was bone dry. Which meant he'd been asleep longer than he realised.

"Shit!"

Dripping wet, he flung the towel over his shoulder and raced out into the main room.

He rifled through the clothes he'd strewn across the floor for his mobile phone. He'd not had mobile reception for days, but the habit of carrying it was hard to kick.

Dead.

"Stupid thing." He threw it on the bed.

Cayden spun around again. Searching.

The haven was not your typical hotel room. No bedside clock. No television. No espresso machine. The miracle, he supposed, was that it had electricity at all.

My watch!

He rifled through his clothes again.

"Where the hell is—"

3:59

"—fuck!" How'd he lost half a day?

Not bothering to dry off or take the time to think, he donned a pair of cotton shorts and shoved his feet into his thongs. Then he scrambled out the sliding door and slip-slid down the slope to the hub.

Dane's ladies waved at him from the rocking chairs on the hub deck, Shorty snapped his secateurs at him from the other side of the pool hedge, and Shiloh hollered, "Mate!" at him from a golf cart zipping by.

Cayden didn't stop for anyone, just kept going, past the pool and up past the first few treatment huts. He rounded a corner and paused to catch his breath and figure out where he needed to be. Heart thumping, lungs imploding, the world tilting off its access, Cayden doubled over to rest his hands on his knees and haul in precious air. It came with the bonus of ninety-nine percent humidity, but that was the least of his problems.

He opened his fist to check the watch-face.

4:03 pm.

"Shit a brick!"

He hated being late.

Between each hut was about ten feet of verdant rainforest that grew up and arched over each roof, all but cloaking them from the bright afternoon sun. Despite the deep shade, the brightly coloured doors of the treatment rooms stood out.

Red, blue, green, orange, yellow, pink, purple, or brown?

Which one was the right one?

"Hmm." Every bit of him protested at the thought. "What are the chances it's—"

The brown door swung open.

Ugh.

"Under the radar." It wasn't the best suck-it-up-princess pep-talk he'd ever given himself, but it'd have to do. And so, for the second time that day, Cayden took a willing step toward his doom.

CHAPTER EIGHTEEN

DANE

Dane hadn't seen Cayden for a full thirty-six hours.

He'd left Cayden in the dining room with the rest of the guests, anticipating the man would knock on his door for a friendly fuck the minute the evening education session ended.

Only that knock hadn't happened.

First thing Sunday morning, hungry after his usual early morning run, Dane had arrived at Gladioli's kitchen window for breakfast, only to find no breakfast and a neat row of glass bottles, each with a guest's nametag tied neatly around its neck.

"Saltwater flush," Gladioli had said, waving gaily at the glass bottles like a hippy-dippy game-show starlet on 'shrooms.

At the end of the row, two bottles sat side by side with his and Cayden's names scribed beautifully on little tags.

Dane instantly connected the dots.

Detox.

Fuck.

No wonder the place felt deserted.

The only flushing he needed was from his balls, and he could take care of that for himself, thanks very much.

"You bottle—" she'd started, and he'd stopped her with a rude-as-hell talk-to-the-hand followed by a not-on-your-fucking-life-lady look.

"Thanks, but I don't think so. What other delicious creation do we have for breakfast today?" he'd asked. Nobody would ever characterise him as charming. He was too serious for that. But Dane knew the value of the metaphorical carrot. He could be sweetness and light if the situation demanded it.

Gladioli hadn't looked all that convinced by his charm, but she'd retreated into her kitchen domain, made a lot of noise, and returned with a palatable macadamia nut, almond milk, maple syrup, and cinnamon smoothie. As far as breakfasts went, it hadn't been half bad. Way better than drinking half the ocean.

The smoothie had powered him through a few hours while he roamed the retreat, asking questions, doing his best to fulfil his side of the bargain. He'd chit-chatted with Shorty in his garden, flirted with the admin crew, did a workout under Fraser's avid eye, and discovered nothing at all helpful about Cayden's sister or her fate.

Short on answers, he itched to read the retreat's annual business reports and cross-check those numbers with on-the-ground data. But in the digital wasteland that was the House of Glass Wellness Retreat, deep-dive research just wasn't possible.

Even if he wanted to climb to the rim of the crater in the heat of the day, internet reception up there was still thin. And no way could he ask Carol to dig on his behalf. He'd do what he could to help Cayden, but roping in his PA was a professional boundary he wasn't willing to cross.

Twenty-four hours after he'd last seen Cayden, he was cursing the man.

For twenty-four hours there'd been no sly innuendo, no flirtation on the banana lounge, no copping a feel in the steam room, not even a cheesy wink in the pool to let Dane know Cayden was up for it.

Not once had they crossed paths.

Since there was no way Cayden would have submitted himself to the saltwater flush, the best explanation Dane could come up with was that Cayden had found his sister, hadn't thought to let Dane know, and was caught up with her somewhere off-site.

Not that that was likely.

By the next morning—a full thirty-six hours after he'd last seen Cayden—Dane's curses had turned to concern.

He cupped his hands to Cayden's glass haven door.

All he could see in the dim haven was half of a rumpled bed, clothes strewn about, and a towel carelessly dropped on the hardwood floor. Either Cayden was a messy fucker, he'd left in a rush, or someone had tossed his room.

"Where the hell are you?"

The possibility that Gordon might be a kidnapper sounded more and more plausible.

Despite his worry, Dane's body seemed to have finally got with the Vital Serenity Wellness Plan because he'd slept like the dead and woke well after the pre-dawn chorus.

Despite the gathering heat of the day. He thought about going for a run because it helped him feel steady and right. But his need to know what had happened to Cayden over-rode all of that.

Instead of tracking all the way around the path to the hub, he took the more direct route under the shade of the red-flowering poinciana tree. As he passed by, he held his hand out to press his palm for a second to the solid grey trunk—to feel the ripples that made it look so much like the skin of an elephant. Strong and wise.

"Holy shit, dude!"

Dane jerked his head up so fast he almost head-butted the tree.

Cayden was leaning over the hub deck railing, a manic grin plastered across his face. "You've got to try this!"

Behind Cayden, a few other early risers stood sipping shots or smoothies, but Dane paid them no mind. All of Dane's attention was on Cayden as he continued his path across the lawn and into the mulched flower bed by Cayden's bare legs, and he had to exercise an inordinate amount of self-control to not reach through the white pickets to touch the man's leg—to be sure he was real.

"Where have you been? Are you okay?" His voice was possibly too harsh, but Cayden didn't seem to notice his tension.

"Try this. I swear, dude. Nectar of the gods. Practically orgasmic." Cayden leaned over the railing with a highball glass filled with a drink the colour of burnt oranges.

Dane leaned in and sniffed the drink. Had Shorty's weed made its way into the morning smoothie? "Are you high?"

Cayden grinned. "Nah, worse luck. Here." He pushed the glass into Dane's hand.

"What's in it?"

"God knows. I was so famished. Just grabbed it and drank. That's my second glass. Go on…drink."

Dane wrapped his lips around the straw and sucked.

Tang and spice and sweet flooded his palate. He moaned, closed his eyes, and swallowed.

"What is that?"

"I know, right?" Cayden slapped him on the shoulder, then grabbed the empty glass. "We need another."

Not you; not I; *we*.

As though they came as a pair. No doubt in his voice.

Dane watched Cayden's sweet arse jive across to the kitchen window, returning with a fresh juice and two shots of something cloudy.

"Bottoms up," Cayden called.

Dane tossed his shot back, the sharp ginger tonic hitting his palate at exactly the same moment he saw Cayden tip his shot over the railing and into the flower bed at Dane's feet.

Growling, he hotfooted away from the mess, grabbed the fresh glass of juice, yanked out the straw, and slugged it down.

Better.

"Awesome, right? It wouldn't go too well with pizza, but nothing's perfect."

Dane peered up for divine inspiration. The morning sun that sliced in below the roofline caught the right half of Cayden's face. Half-cupid, half-demon—Dane wasn't sure which half he preferred—both were gorgeous.

Hell.

"You're a menace," he grumbled weakly.

Cayden ignored him. "Carrot, tangerine, and turmeric. Let's add it to the beverage stand. We can call it Freshly Squeezed Camel and make another fortune."

Wary of being drawn into the vortex of Cayden's future, Dane stayed mute, leaving that *we* well and truly alone.

He leaned against the railing and licked the last of the delicious juice off his lips, imagining a line of camels waiting for Cayden to give them a squeeze. Cute didn't even begin to describe it.

Damnit.

The man threw him off-kilter, lopsided, cockeyed, askew. Which just wasn't okay.

"Fancy a steam?" Dane asked. It was a hair-split choice between that and asking if he fancied a fuck, but he needed to get back on level ground, and *they* needed to get back on task. A debrief in the steam room would be a good start.

Cayden rocked back on his feet. "Sure, dude. Yeah. Where've you been? I've hardly seen you." A blush rushed across his cheeks, and he rushed on. "I mean, not that I was super keen to hang out through all that." He waved his arm around in the kitchen's direction. "No shame. We're all just animals with, you know, innards, right? But I don't think I can ever look into that Elvis dude's eyes again. I mean never, ever, ever again. What did you think? Not that we need to discuss it, because it's so not a cool topic of conversation between friends. But..."

Cayden's verbal diarrhoea was kind of cute.

Shit. When had he become someone who appreciated cute?

Never. That's when.

He liked his men on the manly end of the scale. They didn't have to be beefcakes, but he liked less-than-gentle handling and a deep-timbered voice. Cayden was not...that. Add a fruit-juice sugar high, and the guy practically channelled his inner tween.

Cayden rambled on.

Dane was so distracted by Cayden's ramble that it took an embarrassing length of time to realise what he was on about.

"Cayden." He grabbed Cayden's hands. Cayden jerked reflexively, but Dane held firm. "You didn't do the saltwater flush yesterday, did you?"

That stopped the endless flow of words.

"Uh, yeeeaah." Cayden drew out.

Oh, God. Dane didn't know which to feel more—amusement or horror.

Cayden's eyes went wide. "Didn't you?"

Dane dropped his head down on their gathered hands, then looked back up, shoulders shaking. "Fuck, no."

"But…"

Dane shook his head. "Detoxing may be all the rage, but it's never been on my bucket list."

"But…"

He loosened his grip and patted Cayden's hands. "It's called free will, Mister Spicer."

"Bastard." Cayden pushed him away from the railing. "There I was, thinking you were suffering just like me."

"You're not going to whine and say it's not fair, are you?"

"No," Cayden whined.

Oh, God. So cute.

"Next time, just say no."

Cayden sniffed and held out his palm flat. "I need Carol's number."

"Why?"

"Oh, nothing. I just need to call her and explain that you didn't bother following the Vital Serenity Wellness Plan that she chose so carefully for you, just because it wasn't on your pinstriped bucket list. Wonder what she'll think about that rationale, eh?"

Dane shook his head. Cheeky bastard. "It hardly matters what Carol thinks of what I do. She has ideas. Some good. Some not so good. And this idea is of the 'not so good' variety. I respect her, but it's not as though we're married or anything."

Cayden blinked. "You're not together?"

"Together?" Where on earth had he got that idea? "With whom?"

"Carol."

Seriously? "God, no. She's my PA."

Cayden's face went blank. "Your PA?"

"Yes," Dane said slowly.

"As in your personal assistant?"

"Yes," he repeated. Maybe there really had been 'special herbs' in the smoothie.

"So, just to be clear. She's not your girlfriend? Or your partner? Or your…"

"No." He thumbed his chest, just like he'd done then. "Not straight. Remember?"

"Yeah." Cayden looked over Dane's head. "I just thought you meant, well…that you're bi or…something." He grabbed at a red flower. "And…I guess I just, um, stopped thinking clearly right about then." His voice rose like he was asking a question.

"I'm gay." Dane couldn't be any clearer than that.

Cayden's eyes dashed sideways, and down, and back up high—anywhere but directly at Dane, and he worked his mouth like he was fussing over an olive with a big-arse pip.

After a drawn-out moment of silence, Dane thought it best to just move on. "Okay. Now that we've gotten that straight, let's—"

"Bad pun alert." Cayden finally met his eyes.

"—move on."

"Let's not. I don't forgive you. Not even remotely."

"For not being clear that Carol isn't my plus-one?"

"No…well, yes. I did feel terribly guilty for lusting after you. But that's not what I'm talking about. I don't forgive you for avoiding the saltwater flush. The whole time, my only consolation was that you were undergoing the same torture as me."

"Can't we just move on?"

"No. Your punishment is to hear every shitty detail."

He winced. Time to try a new tack. "You look great. Buzzing with energy."

"Don't care."

Hmm…maybe a newer tack. "Don't you want to hear

what I learned while I spent my day investigating instead of detoxing?"

"Shh!" Cayden swivelled his head like a manic bobble-head.

Nobody was close enough to overhear.

"I thought the mission to find Lucy was everything," Dane pressed.

"It is, but…"

"Well, then." Time for a third tack. With his now-free hand, Dane reached forward and skimmed a finger along the waistband of the man's shorts. Over the button, he hooked his finger and pulled.

The move couldn't be misconstrued as anything but a come-on.

Cayden hips jerked forward. His eyes opened wider still, and that delicious lower lip dropped open.

"Here." He took Cayden's hand and wrapped it around the empty juice glass. "Go do something useful and take this back. And then…"

"Then?" Cayden took the bait.

"Then we steam."

CHAPTER NINETEEN

CAYDEN

Cayden hotfooted it into the steam room complex, whipped off his shirt, and took an arresting douse under the cold shower. He could still feel Dane's hands squeezing his tight.

As touches went, it had been pretty tame, but his dick didn't get the memo, and his wet shorts clung like a magnet to his semi.

Just in case anyone but Dane was in the steam room, Cayden strategically held his cold-water bucket where the sun rarely shone, hefted open the cedar door, and stepped into swirling steam.

"Glorious privacy. Thank the ever-loving fuck."

"Mm-hmm," Dane responded, barely shifting from his Zen swim-captain pose. "Doubt we'll have it to ourselves for long, though."

"Pity." Minimizing temptation, he sat well away from Dane.

"Yeah. I'm a convert."

"Have you ever done an improv class?" Cayden asked. "You know—one person says 'we went to the museum and stole a unicorn horn,' and you have to start your response with 'yes, and…' You've got no option but to go with what-ever you're given."

"Why are we talking about acting classes?"

"Not acting. Improv."

"I stand corrected. Why are we talking about improv?"

"Because this place has that effect on me. I keep saying 'yes, and.' As though I have no choice—no free will. 'Drink this,' Gladioli says, and I drink it. 'Do this,' Fraser says, and I do it. The colonic was like that. Stupid."

"You didn't have to do it," Dane protested.

"But that's just it, Dane—the retreat has totally screwed with my rational sense. It's like the House of Glass has converted me into GOG's new cult." He shudders. "Besides, if I hadn't picked up that bottle, they would have asked too many questions. Questions I can't answer. Staying under the radar is key. Remember?"

Dane dropped the Zen. "You didn't think to take the bottle, empty the saltwater down the loo, and return it to Gladioli a few hours later? Nobody had to know if you did the flush or not."

That stumped him.

Shit. Why hadn't he thought of that? Maybe he had really been converted.

"Gordon is not the all-powerful wizard. He won't know if you're full of shit or not."

"Gross pun."

Dane grimaced. "Did you at least learn anything helpful yesterday?" He held up his hand and clarified, "Regarding Lucy?" Dane probably did need to add that clarification because, yes, Cayden had learned lots of helpful things about his body. Most notably, what it did not enjoy.

Cayden shook his head. "The saltwater flush totally wiped me out. I woke in a daze. A parallel universe kind of thing. I raced up to the treatment room, through the brown doorway, and it was happening before I could even think. Just like that." He snapped his fingers.

"The brown doorway?" was Dane's only question, because of course it was.

"Don't get me started on the brown doorway. It was bizarre. The colonic technician looked like an Elvis wannabee in navy whites. Skin like shea butter. Hair swooped high. Buff. Total shoo-in at wet t-shirt competitions. He stood there in the brown doorway, more Zen than you are right now, and said, 'come into my sanctum'—"

"He did not."

"He sang, 'Come into my sanctum, I have a gift for you.'" Cayden laughed.

It was that or cry.

"Creepy Elvis."

"Very." Cayden agreed. "Then he patted his examining table and said, 'Take off your shorts and climb on up.' And like all good Elvis wannabes, he sounded reasonable."

"I don't think reasonable is a factor here."

"Hush. There's a first time for everything. Now, are you going to let me tell my tale?"

"Are you sure this guy was a professional? He doesn't sound like the sort of person who should give a colonic."

"Tell me about it. Remember, we're dealing with a warped cultish universe here."

"Of course." Dane waved his hand to urge Cayden to get on with it.

"So, I got naked and lay down on his table."

"This is getting worse."

"Shh. I got on his table, and, get this, he said, 'Just lie back and think of England.'"

"What? He did not."

Cayden snorted and scooted closer. "He might as well

have. No, wait…this is what he actually said. And, I swear, I could not make this up. Listen."

"I'm not listening to a single word."

"He had this tube thing hooked up to a tank of fluid. He said, and I quote, 'A smidge of lube and it'll slip right in, no worries.'"

"No. You made that up."

"I swear, I did not. 'Relax Cayden,' he said, 'just go with the flow.' I half expected him to offer a post-coital spliff."

Dane groaned and dropped his head into his hands.

"But wait, that's not even the best bit."

"Please, no." Dane shuddered.

"Just as he was about to pop my arse cherry, he said, 'You look familiar.'"

"Cherry? What?"

Glad that he'd finally won Dane's full attention, he said, "I kid you not. I had no idea what to say. I mean. How do you respond to someone who recognises you from your arse cheeks with a honking big tube inserted between them? Is there some etiquette I'm not aware of? I couldn't think of a single thing to say except to straight out ask, 'You recognise my hole?' And what do you reckon was his answer?"

"Jesus."

"He said, 'No, your face.'"

"You're an anal virgin?"

Cayden straightened. "An anal virgin? Seriously? That's what you got from that story?"

"Do you just not like it, or—"

"No. Dane. Focus. I'd never seen that man before, but he recognised my face." Cayden pointed directly at his offending visage. "What does that tell you?"

"Ahh?"

Cayden rushed on, eager to get to the good bit. "It tells us he's seen someone who looks very similar to me. Which means he might know Lucy."

"Lucy?"

"Yeah. We're siblings. It's not outrageous that we'd look similar, even though she's female and I'm—"

"Male," Dane finished for him, and Cayden leaned back against the tile, glad to have finally gotten through. "So, what did he say when you asked him who you look like?"

"I didn't ask him."

"What?" Dane shuffled forward. "Why not?"

"Because I'd just come out of a saltwater-induced coma and I had a honking big tube up my arse. I wasn't exactly thinking clearly."

"Yeah, okay. So…?"

"So, after all that trauma, I slept like the dead. Again. It wasn't till I woke up this morning that I realised I'd landed on a crucial piece of intel."

"Okay, so, we just have to find this Elvis guy and question him."

"Already sorted. I've booked you in."

"Booked me in? For what?" Dane asked. Then he must have twigged. "No." He stood and crossed the steamy divide and crowded into Cayden's side. "Absolutely not."

"What's the big deal? I'll go with you for moral support. He needs to see my face, anyway. It's perfect."

"No, it's not. It's so far from perfect, it's practically on… on…" He paced the small room, head in the misty steam.

"Uranus?" Cayden's lips twisted.

"What are you, twelve? No." He held up a hand. "Don't answer that. How did you even book me in? That's a breach in privacy, for sure."

"Easy. Forged a note. Bess, the office chick, said it was no problem. Ten o'clock. I have a confirmation note here. See?

Ta-da!" Cayden pulled from his board shorts pocket a soggy piece of paper, torn and smeared. "Oops."

"That's not happening. Also, we need to discuss boundaries."

He waved Dane's protest off. The man could weather a little embarrassment for the cause. "It's not that uncomfortable. Seriously. It's just anatomy. No big deal."

"Cayden, you are the worst liar I have ever met. And the worst investigator."

That stung. "I'm an excellent investigator. Just ask Henrietta," he protested, ignoring the liar-liar-pants-on-fire accusation because that was mostly true.

"Who the hell's Henrietta?" Dane paced by, giving Cayden an excellent opportunity to perv on the long taper of his back—all that slick skin.

"My boss."

Dane turned to face him, giving Cayden an even better view.

As Dane passed him again, Cayden itched to reach forward and hook into Dane's fiery-red swimmers, just as Dane had done to him. Only he wouldn't stop there. Since he was a gentleman, he'd go north first. He'd trace his finger through those grooves, between his pecs, then up, up, up to those lips. He'd slip inside his mouth to tussle with that wet, warm tongue, and—

Dane's lips were moving.

Jesus. He really needed to focus better. "What?"

"I asked, does Henrietta know how 'method' you go?"

"What?"

Dane stepped closer, just as Cayden had wanted him to do, and hooked his fingertips around Cayden's jaw, thumbs caressing his cheekbones. "Why are you so…" Dane started in a softer voice, then paused. He took a deep breath, dropped his hands, and turned away.

"What?" Cayden asked.

"Nothing."

"It's clearly not nothing."

"Doesn't matter. We need to get back on track."

Cayden's guilt-o-meter ratcheted up at the reminder. Never mind *think of England*, he ought to be thinking of Lucy. "What about you, then? Did you discover anything useful while I was *method acting*?" He totally failed at keeping the irritation out of his voice.

"Nothing useful. But I have some ideas. I spent yesterday watching the staff. The rhythms of the place. That sort of thing. The gardener, Shorty? Seems he's not so much a weed-fan as a Cayden-fan. I'm sure he'd probably give you more information if you asked."

Cayden blushed.

"Don't be cute," Dane said, and his serious brows flattened.

Cayden thought *that* was cute, but it was probably wise to keep that to himself. "I may have lingered longer with him than I ought to have. And I *may* have not protested when he checked me out. Sort of. Maybe."

"More improv?"

"Something like that." Even in the steamy heat, he could feel his cheeks rage hotter.

Luckily, Dane gave him an out. "Have you looked at the retreat's finances? Any unexplained holes in the business records? Nefarious activities usually leave a money trail."

"Finances aren't really my forte." Cayden bit his lip, embarrassed that he hadn't thought of that.

Dane nodded. His seriousness was sexy as hell. "Open-source company records might help, but tax records would be best. They're a little trickier to find. I'd ask Carol to help, but I don't want her made culpable if what we're doing is discovered. Besides, she'd ream my arse for working when I'm supposed to be on a break."

"This isn't work, exactly."

"True, but you don't know Carol."

And you never will, was the unspoken addition to Dane's oh-so-transparent statement.

It left Cayden feeling deflated. Which was so incredibly stupid. They may have intersected at the retreat, but that was it. Their lives were separate. He never *would* know Carol.

Dane paced by again, a tiger trapped in a cage. "If you're up for it, there's an art class this morning. The teacher's not on staff, but she might have some useful information."

"What? Holy fuck, dude, why didn't you mention that earlier?" Art was Lucy's life. She could be there. Hell, she could be the teacher.

Have to get there.

Now.

Cayden threw aside the hurt and leaped up so fast he just about slid into splits.

His arms windmilled, and Dane grabbed for him.

He tried to shake the man loose, but Dane wasn't compliant.

"Back up, Sherlock." Dane's hands went to his waist, stabilizing him before they both went down.

"What time's the class?" He reached for the bulky watch on Dane's wrist.

"Nine-thirty. Plenty of time to finish the steam, then shower and change."

This could be it, Cayden thought—the crucial moment; the point of no return; the line in the proverbial sand. "Come on." Heart tripping, he grabbed their buckets and hustled out the door.

Cayden didn't bother showering. With a towel flung over his shoulder, he raced out the main door.

"Hold up, Cayden," he heard Dane call, but didn't stop.

On mission, Cayden made a beeline for their haven, slapping at palm fronds, dragonflies, and anything else that got in his way.

"What's the rush?" Dane huffed close behind him. "It's only an art class."

"Only an art class?" Cayden stopped and turned.

Momentum slammed Dane into him, and Cayden reflexively braced for impact, palms perfectly positioned to catch Dane's solid chest as they clashed.

The steep path gave Cayden the extra inch needed to put them eye to eye, lip to lip, and they locked for a stunned moment—breath for breath—so close he couldn't even focus as Dane's head tilted a miniscule degree.

Cayden's heart hammered in his ears.

"What about Elvis?" Dane asked.

"What?"

"The fraudulent appointment you made for me."

"Oh." That Elvis. "Fuck Elvis. This is more important."

"It's just art. Are you going to tell me what the big deal is, or do I have to guess?"

"It's not just anything. Don't you remember? My sister's an artist. It was her..." he swallowed, then tried again, "...*is* her thing."

He reached up to hold Dane's face right where he needed him, then drilled home his point. "Don't you get it, Dane? The art teacher could know Lucy. Could even *be* Lucy."

CHAPTER TWENTY

DANE

Since Cayden was desperate to learn if he'd found his sister at last, they arrived at the art studio early. But the woman who opened to Cayden's rapid knock missed the mark by at least a generation. "Come in, come in." The woman held the door open, her waist-long medusa braids chimed with silver bells.

Cayden went up on his tippy-toes, looking over the woman's shoulder into the bright-lit space.

"Hi. Are you the art teacher?" Dane asked.

"Yes. I'm Celeste. Please come in."

Dane gripped Cayden's tense shoulders. The woman was too old to be Lucy, but that didn't mean she was a dead end.

"Pleased to meet you, Celeste. I'm Dane, and this is Cayden."

Cayden interrupted. "Do you know Lucy? Lucy Spicer?"

She flinched at his clipped tone, which made her bells jangle. "Ah..."

Dane squeezed the tense muscles again. The man needed to cool it, or they'd learn nothing. "We heard there was an amazing artist up this way by that name. Maybe working near here, or…?" He left the question hanging and smiled, turning on the charm.

Celeste smiled back. "The only Lucy I know is Lucille Nantwich. She does silk printing. Could that be who you're thinking of?"

"Maybe. How old is she?"

"Hmm…maybe forty, forty-five at most."

Cayden wilted, clearly disappointed, and his curls jostled with the harsh shake of his head. "Damn."

Dane squeezed again and steered him to one of the trestle tables on the far side of the studio.

Celeste twirled her way between the tables and placed lumps of red-brown clay on waxed paper at every spot. Her matching silver bangles stacked halfway up each arm tinkled with each movement. "Here you are, dears. This'll help you work out those stubborn worries." She chimed and tinkled and sashayed her way back to the door.

While they waited for everyone else to arrive, Dane mindlessly worked his clay, turning it into a near-perfect sphere, while Cayden, sitting opposite, stabbed a punishing finger into his lump over and over and over again.

Dane sighed.

A welcome breeze coasted through the rippled glass louvers that lined walls of the cavernous art studio. They warped the lush greenery that surrounded the building, flooded the space with dappled green-gold light that refracted and cast tiny rainbows here and there, including on Cayden's left cheek.

Dane pursed his lips and elected not to tell Cayden that he was blessed by the Mardi Gras gods. The man was clearly not in the mood for that.

Above their heads, thousands of painted leaves stuck to the ceiling only emphasised the feeling of being in a treehouse—a purple, pink, blue, green, yellow, orange, and red tree.

Dane didn't say anything about that, either.

"Patience," he said instead. "We'll find her."

"Welcome, welcome, everyone," Celeste sing-songed, her bells and bangles providing backup harmony as she ushered newcomers into the class. "Find a spot. Spread out. Get comfy."

Once the small group of fellow guests at the retreat finally settled, she turned on the spot in the centre of the room, bangled arms spread wide. "Blessings to you all. My name is Celeste. Today is a magical day. Today you'll rediscover, or perhaps even discover for the first time, the part of your spirit that shines with creativity."

Cayden groaned and stabbed his clay again.

"Now, I'd like all of you to take off your shoes and stand up." Celeste spread her arms, hands up. "That's it. Twenty-first century life has a habit of squashing it down, but it's there. I promise."

"If she talks about the blossom within, I'm out," Cayden griped, but he followed Celeste's direction.

Dane toed off his runners and rolled his neck.

Mentally, he added to Carol's debt. She owed him big time for forcing the place on him.

"Stand tall. Full and strong. I want you to breathe deep. Take in the air. The moisture in the clouds. The scent of the trees. The foetid breath of the animals. Take in everything. Feel how you are part of it. Flow with it." Head thrown back, Celeste spun around, arms stretched high and wide. Then she slowed. "Now be the trees. Close your eyes and let the wind move you. Stretch tall. Reach those green fingers to the light. Feel the life-giving energy of the sun." She gave a breathy exhalation. "Wonderful. Now, plant your feet. Extend your toes into the soil. Grow those roots deep. Draw in the moisture. Let it feed every bit of you. Delve deeper. Sink into the oozy mud. Shift with it. Feel the fine grain of the sand and the great heft of the rocks, the soft loam of the soil and the slick slide of the clay. Curl yourself around the stones. Shimmy into the cracks in the rocks. Embrace it. Now bind and become one with it. Be the Earth."

Something in Celeste's fervour must have rubbed off because Dane felt his toes flex against the wooden floor. His breath slowed, and his shoulders dropped. Not so much that anyone else would notice, but Dane did. He opened his eyes to see Cayden staring straight at him.

"Have transcended to another plane?" Cayden asked with a smirk.

"Hell, no," he scoffed, then rolled his eyes because Cayden clearly wasn't buying it. Besides, since when did he care what anyone thought of him?

He busied himself sitting down. "Buried myself in the ground, more like."

Cayden nodded, sombre. "So long as it's a metaphorical grounding, I think you'll be fine."

"You're a dick."

Cayden made a seesaw motion, but there wasn't any vacillation in Dane's assessment.

"No, you really are a dick," he asserted.

Cayden's laughter was the last ingredient Dane needed to really, truly relax.

He kicked the man's ankle under their table, then left his foot there—his arch spooning the prominent bone at Cayden's ankle—and returned his attention to Celeste.

"Today, we'll be coiling ceramic pots. As you build your pot, remember that feeling of being one with the earth. First, you need to draw your desired shape on your piece of waxed paper, then you need to fill that shape with tight coils of clay…" Dane avidly watched Celeste's nimble fingers coil the clay into a blunt-ended canoe shape. "That's it. Roll those snakes." Her voice rose and fell as she wound between the trestles. "Become one with the clay. Draw on its power. Let it hold you, just as you hold it. Be the vessel."

The cool clay gave just enough in his warm hands to do his bidding as he rolled it into a long snake and started forming the base of his pot.

Cayden took a different approach—squeezing his clay like he was giving it the world's worst hand job. Watching him manipulate it was a special kind of torture.

"Ever heard the phrase 'choke the chicken'?" he asked with as straight a face as he could manage. "That, or, 'get a room'?"

Cayden grunted, but Dane could see the small smile and counted it a win.

Cayden switched up his technique to twirl the clay like he was trying to spark fire with two sticks. The bottom of the clay flew in all directions, but he didn't seem to care.

A kid plonked down on a stool beside Cayden. He looked like a young surfer kid with shaggy, beach-bleached hair spouting off in all directions and inch-wide stripes shaved over each ear. Within a minute, he'd turned his lump of clay into four long uniform snakes.

"Looks like you've done this before," Dane said, earning a grin.

"Yep. Heaps of times."

Dane lay his clay snakes and gradually coiled them till they reached his precise pencil outline. Cayden's pencil design was circular, too, but his clay snakes were more like frankfurter chains, and it didn't take long for his circle to become an unidentifiable, lumpy shape.

Dane itched to fix it. "Interesting design."

"Thanks. Not sure if I'd give it such a highfalutin' name as 'design', though."

"I like it," the kid said.

"Thanks, dude."

"My name's not Dude. It's Leif."

Cayden paused his coiling. "As in a tree leaf?"

"Nope." The kid squished one of his beautifully smooth snakes flat and used a wooden spatula to write *LEIF* in the clay. "Mum spelled my name like that when I was born."

"Dude—I mean, Leif—sorry, dude. That's a cool name."

"Thanks. I like leaves. They're my motif." He pointed to the ceiling.

Dane mouthed the word *motif* to Cayden, then looked up. "You did that?"

"Yep."

"That's amazing. You're really talented."

The kid preened. "What's your name?"

"I'm Dane. And he's Cayden."

"Hi." Leif collected up the flattened clay and squelched it in his hands, laughing when fat clay worms squeezed out from between his fingers. Then he rolled it into a ball and mimicked Cayden's fire starter twirl. With sure movements, he coiled his base, then started on the walls.

Dane watched Leif and Cayden shift with suppressed energy on the bench. Leif bit his lip, and Cayden muttered to himself. Both totally focused on their tasks. The two of them were so cute together.

He blinked, wondering where the hell that thought had come from.

"Do you live here, Leif?" He searched for a distraction.

"Nope. I just come to do art. Aunt Celly doesn't mind."

"Aunt Celly?" Cayden asked.

"Yep." He twisted all the way around and waved at Celeste. "She lets me help clean up after."

"Wow. She lets you clean up, huh?" Cayden grinned. "Lucky you."

"Yep."

"Everyone." Celeste clapped her hands, setting off the bells and bangles. "Once you've shaped your base, you'll need to smooth it out. Make sure there're no holes in the bottom. Gravity is a powerful force. Wouldn't want anything to get through."

"Wouldn't want that." Dane muttered, but he took her words to heart. If he was going to put this much effort into something, he'd do a quality job.

"Once you're happy you have no holes, wet your fingers and smooth the bottom."

"Oh, lord." Cayden's shoulders shook.

"You okay over there, Cayden?"

"Perfectly fine, thank you Dane."

"Excellent."

Celeste chose that moment to swing by their trestle table. "Well done, boys." She winked at Dane. "Once your bottom's happy, you can start coiling the top of your vessel."

Did she think they were a couple?

The thought was...not terrible.

He got caught watching Cayden's fingers manipulating his clay. He must have forgotten to draw in oxygen because his vision blurred, and he had to haul in a quick breath.

But then Leif asked, all earnest innocence, "Are you happy with your bottom, Cayden?"

Dane's breath turned into a cough, turned into a choke, turned into a very unfortunate snort-laugh.

It felt surprisingly good.

"What's so funny?" Leif asked.

"Never mind him. Too much sugar for breakfast." Cayden's explanation was ridiculous, but the kid seemed to buy it.

Leif rolled another sausage. "Make sure you squeeze out the bubbles because they burst in the kiln."

Cayden returned, "It's just like making a pizza, only with no salami."

"What's pizza?" Leif asked.

"Seriously, little dude? Which planet did you come from?"

"My name's not—"

"Sorry, Leif. Seriously? You don't know pizza? Did you hear him, Dane? Leif's never had pizza."

"Amazing."

"No, not amazing. It's a travesty. We have to fix it."

"Talk to Gladioli," said Dane. "I bet she'd cook you a pizza. If you ask nicely. Yesterday she made me meatloaf."

"Actual meatloaf?" Cayden reached sideways, put his hands over Leif's ears, and whispered incredulously, "As in, real beef from a cow?"

"Well, no. She called it nut-meat-loaf. But it was tasty."

Dane could tell the instant it dawned on Cayden that Gladioli had fed him real, solid food at the exact same time that he'd suffered the saltwater flush.

"You a-hole."

Dane wasn't about to take that admonishment. "Own your choices, mate." Then he turned his attention to Leif. "You must know the retreat pretty well. And everyone that works here."

"Yep." Leif sat up straight, eager to please. "I know everyone."

Cayden stiffened, catching on quick. "Do you know a girl called Lucy?"

"Lucy?"

"Yeah." Cayden nodded jaggedly.

"Not a girl. A grownup," Dane corrected, then looked to Cayden. "Thirty-ish?"

He nodded. "Yeah. Yeah, that's right."

Leif's head swivelled between them. "Umm. I don't think so."

"That's okay. Take your time, Leif." Dane tried to bring the moment down a bit.

"Anybody called Lucy," Cayden pressed.

Leif shook his head. "Nope, don't think so."

"Somebody here at the retreat, or that you've heard about, or…"

The kid couldn't be much over eleven or a lanky ten years old. His shoulders started curling in, and Dane felt bad. He wished he could turn back the clock thirty seconds.

"Enough, Cayden."

"But…"

Dane reached out and touched Cayden's hand, softening the grip that squeezed a clay snake into a misshapen mess. "He doesn't know her, Cayden."

"But…" His voice was raw.

"We'll find her another way. I promise."

I promise.

The worst thing he could possibly have said.

How could he promise Cayden anything?

Not only did he have no control over Lucy's whereabouts, their time at the retreat together would end—sooner rather than later. He had no business promising anything.

He pulled back his hand and returned to the very real texture of the clay—for strength? Perhaps.

Or grounding?

Leif and Cayden must have felt the heaviness too because neither made a sound. They quietly got on with building up the walls of their pots.

A while later, Leif asked a tentative, "Cayden?"

"Mm-hmm?" Cayden hummed back.

"Would you like it?" Leif slid his complete pot on the waxed paper along the table, into Cayden's workspace. "I made it for you."

"For me?" Cayden blinked.

"Yep." Leif gave a hopeful half smile.

"But..." Cayden pointed at his own wobbly pot.

Leif's smile wobbled a bit too, but he rallied. "It's a four-leaf clover. See? For luck." Leif had pinched together four points on the rim of his pot to create four lobes radiating out from a central point—just like a four-leaf clover. "It might help you find your Lucy."

Cayden blinked and gently touched the smooth clay edge. "It's..." Cayden's voice dropped roughly, barely forming the word.

"Impressive," Dane tried, his throat thick at the kid's kind gesture.

Leif shrugged and bit his lip.

"It's amazing." Cayden's voice was low and serious. "Thank you, Leif."

"You're welcome." Leif grinned, swivelled out of his seat, and ran off toward Celeste.

When he looked up from the table, he saw Cayden's eyes glistening. It took all his strength not to rush around the table to lift the man up in a crushing hug.

He braced his feet around Cayden's under the table and said, "We'll find her," because he couldn't bear to take away all the man's hope.

CHAPTER TWENTY-ONE

CAYDEN

Cayden batted a sun-drenched palm frond away. The steep path really wasn't wide enough for both of them to walk side by side, but he liked the feel of Dane's presence beside him. Dane had a steadying effect. Like gravity.

Their shoulders and elbows and knuckles brushed on every arm swing. Dane's pinkie finger hooked and then dropped his pinkie; hooked and then dropped; hooked and then caught. Cayden held his breath for a few moments, sure Dane's move must have been accidental, circumstantial, happenstantial. But Dane's pinkie didn't drop away. If anything, Dane hooked them together a little more strongly.

Dane might have been just trying to make him feel better after a crap-house morning. Trying to lend his support or something. But it didn't feel platonic. It felt like a nine on the sappy romance scale.

"You ever seen a John Hughes film?" Cayden asked as they neared their haven. "*Sweet Sixteen, The Breakfast Club, Pretty in Pink*? Super huge in the eighties. My sister loved them."

Dane frowned a little, which Cayden recognised as his thinking face. "Vaguely. Maybe. What about them?"

"Nothing. Just, this…us…" He squeezed Dane's pinkie, unsure how to even say what he meant, "We feel a bit like that."

"Like a ridiculous teen movie?"

Were he and Dane ridiculous? He didn't think so. "No. Like a classic." He left off the romance qualifier because he didn't want to sound like a total sap. He squeezed Dane's pinkie again. "We could call it *Pretty in Pinkie.*"

Dane dropped his finger. "Fuck off," he said. His voice was gruff, but the blush crossing his cheeks told Cayden the man doth protest too much.

"No! Come back." He grabbed Dane's hand and wrangled their pinkies back together. "Better." Cayden whistled up into the trees.

Dane snorted, but he didn't let go. "Why aren't you all sad and frustrated and pissed off?"

"Do you want me to be?"

"No, but…" Dane pressed their shoulders together, and Cayden felt the consoling warmth.

"You think I should be livid?"

"It'd make rational sense. Celeste was no Lucy. And your Elvis-wannabe won't be back to question till next week. They're both blows to your mission."

Cayden understood his incredulity, but Dane hadn't witnessed the many promising leads that'd fizzled out. Once a man experienced that kind of disappointment a few dozen times, he learned to buck up and move on. No point wallowing.

"Now, there's an idea." Still linked, Cayden turned to walk backward, risking falling flat on his arse to see Dane's reaction to his words.

"What?"

"It's okay. I get it. You're angry for me, and you want to provide comfort."

Keeping a straight face was hard work.

"Ah-um…" Dane's thoughtful frown deepened.

"And you know a blowjob will help me feel better," Cayden stated, matter-of-fact.

"For me to give you…?" Dane stopped, making their linked arms stretch apart as Cayden continued up the hill.

"Well, yeah." Cayden tilted his head. "If the whole point is to console me, then it wouldn't be appropriate the other way around." He moved back down the hill, well into Dane's personal space. "Do you need me to sell it better? It's cool. I'm a method actor, remember? I can do anger. Just give me a moment to channel my inner—"

"You're really not angry?"

"No." For a moment, he let himself be serious. "I'm disappointed, but it's not the end of the line. I know she's here. Somewhere. We just have to look in the right place."

"I had some ideas—" Dane started, but Cayden wasn't ready to go down another rabbit hole of disappointment just yet.

"They can keep." He dragged Dane a smidgen closer. "You wanna know what I'm thinking about?"

There went that sexy brow again.

"I'm thinking it's been far too many hours since this very pinkie was thinking dastardly thoughts." He held their linked fingers up like Exhibit A in a court trial.

"What sort of dastardly thoughts?"

"The dastardliest of dastardly thoughts. Practically rabid."

"Hmm." Dane played along. "That's pretty bad."

Cayden nodded and stepped a half inch closer. "Yep."

It wasn't till the word popped out of his mouth that Cayden realised he'd picked up Leif's vocabulary. Dane's pursed mouth told Cayden he'd heard it, too. A too-long beat of silence later, their eyes met, and Cayden cracked up.

"Are you done yet?" Dane asked. Not looking at all impressed.

But nothing could wipe the smile from Cayden's face, especially when Dane grabbed his hand and pulled him determinedly uphill toward, Cayden hoped, the promised BJ.

Cayden's skin prickled with acute awareness. The moment their feet stepped onto the rough planks of their haven deck, he crowded Dane against the deck post, ducked his nose up under Dane's ear, and breathed him in. Hand-warmed clay, and salt, and sweet vanilla.

Leaving Dane's ear, he mouthed softly along the sharp jawline. He loved the catch and release of his lips on Dane's stubble. He could have played a lot longer, but when Dane's long fingers dropped from his lower back to his arse and clutched on tight, Cayden knew playtime was over.

He coasted back up to Dane's ear, nipped at the soft lobe, and whispered his desire. "Wanna start with that blowjob?" Because suddenly he wanted to give more than receive.

"Start?" Dane's voice rumbled, low.

"Mmm-hmm."

"And then?"

Cayden pulled slightly back to look Dane directly in the eyes. "Then you get to taste me."

Dane blinked, then barked a laugh. "That was the corniest come-on ever."

"Ah, there it is."

"There's what?" Dane wrapped one arm around Cayden's upper back, then pressed firmly between his shoulder blades to draw their chests together.

It felt a whole lot like affection.

How had they arrived there so fast?

"That smile." He brought a fingertip up to run along the plush curve of Dane's lower lip. "It's seriously sexy."

Cayden pressed closer, grazing Dane's scratchy chin with

the tip of his nose.

Dane's arms tightened. "Seriously, huh? Talking about sex…"

The word shot straight to Cayden's dick. He gripped the wooden railing on either side of Dane's hips and ground his firming cock hard into Dane's thigh.

Making room for him, Dane shuffled his legs a little wider.

As their heights aligned, his nose butterfly-kissed Dane's. Cayden shivered. Tiny sparks zipped between them, running to ground.

"Are you a banana-lounge kind of guy?" Dane planted a soft kiss in the left corner of his mouth. "A shower kind of guy?" He skipped to the right. "A white-bamboo-sheet kind of guy?" The next kiss landed halfway along his jawline. "Or…?" His words dangled, leaving Cayden's imagination dangerously free to fill in the blank, and Dane's lips oodles of time to reach the thrumming pulse at his temple.

All of the above, he wanted to say.

But Dane hadn't offered that.

"I see where you're going with this," Cayden teased, buying a bit of time because he didn't really know what kind of guy he was with Dane. This wasn't his usual Friday night horndog session. Dane was different.

"The real question is—where are we going with this?" Dane asked.

Cayden pulled back just enough to focus on Dane's face. "Oh, that was good. Nice wordplay."

Dane's lips twitched. "You approve?"

"Mm-hmm." Cayden moved back in.

"Do you approve of this as well?" Dane rolled his hips. The rough material between them rasped, but all Cayden could feel was the hot throb of Dane's cock. The time to prevaricate was over.

CHAPTER TWENTY-TWO

DANE

"What the fuck is bone broth?" Cayden scrunched up the personalised menu page from his Pure Detox Wellness Plan with noisy contempt, then lobbed it all the way from Dane's bed to the wastepaper basket in the corner.

"Buttered bone broth," Dane corrected, then turned his head a minute degree and gnawed at Cayden's tight nipple.

"Ugh. Sounds disgusting."

Dane felt Cayden's fingers thread through his hair, holding him in place. Cayden scratched idly at his scalp, making Dane want to purr. He was far too comfortable to move.

"We could just stay here," Cayden suggested.

"In bed?"

"Mmm…" He licked the tight nub. "Horizontal."

Loving Cayden's cream-caramel skin, Dane stroked his right hand down the man's sweaty side and across the pale crease of his hip where dilated veins threaded blue, just below the surface.

A shudder rippled through Cayden's whole body. The

man's involuntary response only made Dane want to touch more.

"Your bites have mostly faded." Dane traced between a few fine marks left behind.

"Mm-hmm…most of them were gone by morning."

Just like most of his partners, Dane thought. One and done—gone before dawn.

Spreadeagled in the centre of the mussed bed, Cayden looked debauched. Dane lay part way over him, perfectly positioned for torment. He hooked a foot over Cayden's left ankle and rubbed at the light hair with the sensitive arch of his foot. It tickled a bit, but he didn't care.

"I think you have a foot fetish."

Dane snorted. The point of contact felt right. "Would you care if I did?"

"God no." Cayden ran his fingertips lightly up Dane's spine, then down. "So long as it also comes with a mouth fetish, and a dick fetish, and an arse fetish." He pinched Dane's arse. "And a—"

"Nipple fetish?" Dane retaliated, diving in for another bite.

Cayden moaned again, and Dane chuckled, mouth softening against the tight flesh.

"You're so easy." He flattened his tongue and licked full across the man's nipple, earning another shudder and a breathy moan.

"Get up here," Cayden demanded.

Dane didn't comply. He firmed his tongue and speared the nub over and over, tasting only the barest hint of sweat after his repeated lashings.

Hand splayed for purchase across Dane's shoulder blade, Cayden tried to make him shift again. "Ugh. Get your arse up here. I'm hungry."

Right on schedule, Cayden's stomach rumbled. Loud.

"See? I'm starving," he mock-whined. "You wouldn't want me to starve, would you?"

Dane dropped his chin to Cayden's chest. "And your solution is to eat me? I don't think Gladioli would approve of that dietary supplement."

"Vitamin C, dude. Pure protein."

"Mm-hmm."

"Purer than fucking bone broth, that's for sure." Cayden pressed the point.

If Cayden wanted to blow him and drink his come, Dane wasn't about to deprive the man. But it wouldn't do to let him get the last word in. "It's buttered bone broth."

A sharp smack landed on Dane's butt cheek, and he choked on his laugh.

"Get your arse up here, and I'll show you how I butter a—"

Dane slapped his hand across Cayden's mouth. "Don't say it," he said with as much authority as he could muster while naked, lying half-on, half-off the man. "Or neither of us will be able to drink the stuff with a straight face."

Cayden nipped at his palm, but Dane refused to let go. "Nod if you understand me," he instructed.

Cayden nodded slowly, heat in his eyes.

Oh, Dane liked that.

"Well done." He shuffled north a few inches, slipped his knee between Cayden's thighs, and thrust once against the firm ridge of Cayden's hip. "I think you deserve a big reward."

Cayden snorted, right into Dane's hand.

"Eww!" He pulled away, but not far enough to stop the slap Cayden landed on his arse-cheek.

"Oi!" Dane protested, slipping south out of reach. "What was that for?"

"Too much cheese."

That was rich. "Gotta have something to go with your corn."

Cayden cracked up, and Dane felt the rippling shudders to his toes.

God. Had sex ever been like this before?

He didn't have to ponder that question for long.

Short answer? No.

Long answer? Fuck, no.

Sex wasn't about warmth, or affection, or lingering touch.

It was hot, anonymous, and finished the second he came.

Usually.

But with Cayden, Dane didn't want to rush.

He skirted the edges of Cayden's pecs, twisting and tugging gently at the whirls of golden hair.

Cayden latched on to his shoulders and tried to hasten Dane's return north, but Dane was stubborn about that, too.

He lapped at the hollow of Cayden's throat and the thrust of his Adam's apple, then nipped at Cayden's chin. He loved the tease of bristles on his lips.

"Finally," Cayden grumbled as Dane aligned them chest to chest, hip to hip, and claimed Cayden's lips for plunder.

Who knew making out could be so much fun?

He stroked deeper to search for Cayden's true taste.

He ploughed his fingers into Cayden's hair, just as the man had done to him, scouring through the curls for purchase.

In turn, Cayden wrapped his legs around Dane's thighs and pulled Dane tighter into his musky heat.

It was all Dane could do not to come.

Sharp nails dug into his shoulder blades, giving him little warning before Cayden rolled to get the upper hand.

"Oi!" Dane cried again.

But Cayden just hustled south—man on a mission.

"We don't have time for another post-come coma," Dane warned.

"Don't care," Cayden muttered against his treasure trail. His hands shifted south, too, and skimmed every inch his mouth didn't touch.

In truth, Dane didn't care either. If Cayden wanted to suck him off, he wouldn't protest too hard. He threaded his fingers through Cayden's delicious curls and directed his head to the main event.

Cayden licked from root to tip, then blew on the wet strip.

It felt an awful lot like a tease, but Dane knew Cayden meant it as a promise.

He angled out his right knee, exposing himself just a little, and Cayden took the not-so-subtle hint to play with his balls. He wasn't rough. Just palmed them softly and skittered his fingertips, like a blind man learning his terrain.

He'd had his dick in many a hot mouth, but when Cayden gripped Dane's shaft and circled his sensitive head with his talented, dexterous tongue, Dane felt an intense rush of physical and emotional warmth.

It wasn't just some stranger performing a trick of seduction. It was Cayden—Cayden's mouth, Cayden's hands, Cayden's eyes boring back into his own.

He wanted to run a finger down the side of the man's face, but that'd be too sappy. Too much like affection. He clenched his fist at his side and said nothing, silent but for the porn-worthy sounds Cayden summoned from his throat.

Not that Cayden seemed to mind. He just went to his task with more gusto, firming his hand and sealing his lips around Dane's head.

The move made Dane reflexively jerk and shove his cock deeper into the man's mouth.

Accepting the invasion, Cayden moaned, and the sound

wave reverberated clear down to his toes. Cayden drew off to lap greedily at his slit and take a taste of what was to come before plunging back down.

Hot and wet—it was all just too good.

The entire performance had Dane's balls cheering like a pair of fucking pompoms, but his flavour on Cayden's tongue must have triggered a different sort of hunger, because the man's stomach chose that moment to roar.

Loudly.

Cayden ploughed on through the unbidden symphony, but Dane couldn't help laughing as the rumbles continued. Every chuckle inadvertently micro-pulsed his cock deeper into Cayden's mouth.

"Fuck, fuck, fuck." Sweet, sweet torture.

It killed him, but Dane dove his fingers into those delicious curls and dragged Cayden off.

"No!" Cayden wailed and grabbed for Dane's cock. But Dane was quicker and stronger. He rushed the man, flipped him onto his back on the mattress, and landed in a plank with Cayden's wrists held firm in his fists.

"First, let's get you fed." He dropped to peck Cayden's lips in thanks for their fine, fine efforts at seduction.

"No," Cayden protested, but when the rumbling continued, Dane folded back onto his knees, nipped playfully at the offending stomach, and rolled off of both Cayden and the bed.

He pulled on his abandoned swimming trunks and t-shirt —they'd do for a quick jaunt to the hub for dinner.

"And then?" Cayden asked, still splayed across the mess of sheets. His hard cock waved in the evening breeze.

Dane grinned.

"Then we play."

CHAPTER TWENTY-THREE

CAYDEN

"Dane! Over here!" Bernice hollered from across the other side of the dining room.

Beside her, Randy waved, as though there was any way they could have missed hearing his wife.

Cayden leaned toward Dane. "We're barely twenty feet away, for fuck's sake."

Dane shoved a mug of bone broth into his hand. "What was it you said about going under the radar?"

"But that wasn't how our night was supposed to go. Seriously, dude, where are your priorities?" The plan was to fill up, run back to their haven, strip, and then get dirty. They weren't supposed to get all social and shit.

But Dane had already made a beeline for Bernice and Randy.

Translation—suck it up, princess.

Cayden looked down into his mug and sighed. Floating on top of the broth was the most enormous butter-burg known to man.

Out of better options, he traipsed after Dane.

"Thank goodness. Dane, you're on my team." Bernice

vice-gripped Dane's elbow and dragged him into the seat beside her, which left the hard wooden bench seat for Cayden.

With all the subtlety of a two-by-four, he plonked his mug of broth on the four-seater table and slid his arse in. "What're we playing?"

"Healthy Hangman. It's the same as a regular game of hangman, but we can only use words of healthy things," Randy answered, oozing eagerness from every florid, fleshy pore. He dropped a heavy hand on Cayden's shoulder. "Seems we're partners."

Cayden shot Dane a glare, because while sometimes in life a man had no choice but to eat the brussels sprouts first, he didn't have to like it. "Not so fast, Randy. Before we tie the knot, let's decide if we're compatible or not. I'm partial to classic rock and long walks on the beach. How about you?"

The noise of the others in the room filled the momentary silence at their table. Then Bernice snort-giggled, Randy turned an even brighter shade of pink, and Dane raised his hands in surrender.

Cayden took that as a win—especially since the man was finally paying him some attention. "Needy, much," he muttered to himself.

"What was that?" Randy asked.

"Nothing."

Dane leaned forward. "Have you talked to Randall, Cayden? He knows everything about the retreat. Right, Randall? Tell him what you know about the place. Cayden has a curiosity streak a mile wide that I just cannot appease."

The meaningful look Dane sent his way half-mollified his irritation. But Bernice ruined it with a sly, "Bet you can."

Dane choked on a sip of broth, and Cayden's cheeks took on the same pink streak Randy was rocking.

Team colours. Excellent.

Bernice snickered.

Dane coughed.

Randy said, "What?"

And Cayden realised any hope of ending the night a winner was doomed. "All right, all right. You've all had your fun. Let's get on with it. Who's going first?"

"I've got one," Randy said, then had to explain that L.O.V.E was in fact a healthy-hangman-worthy word, "because love heals everything."

Which was ridiculous. In Cayden's life, love had proven to be a burden, not a cure.

In his wildest, most wondrous dreams, Cayden thought romance would be nice. But from the distance where he sat, day after day, dreams of love felt ethereal, intangible, unattainable.

Down the track, Cayden thought he might hunt for true love and a family of his own—the works—but all of that would have to wait till his heart was out from under the yoke of Spicer family drama.

A half hour later, when his mind was full to the brim with worthless facts and figures about the retreat, the only question left he could think to ask Randy was, *do you know where GOG holds his secret cult gatherings?* But that was probably going a bit too far. Cayden decided it was time to leave off the interrogation and refocus on the game at hand. If he and Dane were ever going to get dirty, it looked like Cayden would have to play dirty first.

Cayden leaned toward Dane and whispered, voice low, "This isn't what I thought you meant when you said we'd play."

"Shh, I've almost got it. It's on the tip of my tongue."

"I know what I'd like to put on the tip of your tongue."

Quick as a whip, Dane backhanded his chest. "Stop distracting me."

Cayden had to smile at the man's unconscious familiarity. "So serious."

Satisfied he'd levelled the playing field, Cayden sat back in his hard seat and watched Bernice and Dane scramble for answers.

The guy might look like *GQ*, but his brain was pure *Nerd Quarterly*. Secretly, Cayden found the man's intensity endearing, but he wasn't about to give away any advantage by telling him that.

He took another sip of his now-lukewarm buttered bone broth, gagged on the slimy texture of the dishwater brew, and winced again when Dane and Bernice solved Randy's far-too-easy R.E.T.R.E.A.T in two minutes flat.

Whoever invented Healthy Hangman didn't understand the meaning of irony. Cayden sourly quelled the urge to strangle his partner.

"Come on, Randall. This time, we have to win. S," he guessed.

"Why so pissy? It's just a game." Dane turned the screw.

"I'm not pissy." Pissiness dripped from his voice as Bernice gleefully added a head to their noose.

"Uh-hmm." Dane side-eyed him.

"It's fine for you, Mister Lymphatic."

"No worries, Mister Colonic," Dane laughed, and the lazy sod lounged back, sipping his fucking buttered bone broth.

"Behave, boys," Bernice the word-slayer warned, amusement clear in her voice.

Randall hmm-ed and haw-ed and finally came up with the letter "M."

And that's how their stick-man got a long-arse body.

"Shit," Cayden grumbled.

In truth, he didn't give a flying fuck if he and Randall lost. What he really wanted was to win with Dane, with his butter-slick lips, and chocolaty thick hair, and gorgeous cut abs that Cayden couldn't see because they were under way too many layers that wouldn't have been there if they'd stayed horizontal in bed. Naked.

Ugh.

"E," he tried, with no success.

Randall followed on with "X," earning Cayden's suppressed wrath and Bernice's not-so-suppressed giggles—because, really?

"D" got them either a very short leg or a very long dick. Cayden thought it best not to ask for clarification.

The death knell came with Randall's only slightly more reasonable "F", and Dane's gleeful grin matched Bernice's as she filled in O.R.G.A.N.I.C.

"Dude. How did we not guess that?"

Randall shrugged. "Not clever enough, I s'pose." A fact Cayden could hardly refute.

The word, however, gave him the perfect idea.

He grabbed the mini whiteboard, erased Dane and Bernice's travesty, and drew four short dashes.

Time for a win.

Ten minutes later, with no dashes filled, one very hung stick figure, and two very puzzled opponents, he high-fived Randy and did a happy dance in his seat. "Good job, partner."

"On ya, mate. But what's the word?"

With as much fanfare as he could summon, he filled in G.U.R.U.

Bernice and Randall tilted their heads in unison, but Dane twigged straight away. He kept a straight face, but just barely.

"I don't get it. What's healthy about a guru?" Bernice asked.

"Not a goddamn thing," Cayden answered. "Unless you're a GOG."

"Agog?" She frowned.

"No. A GOG. Tell them, Dane."

"Nope." His nostrils flared. "This one's all yours."

Cayden huffed. "Gordon the Organic Guru, also known as GOG. It's what we call him."

"*You* call him," Dane said.

Cayden side-eyed him. "Fine. It's what *I* call him."

Smiling, Bernice shook her tut-tut finger at them. "You two are so cute together."

Randy leaned forward. "Dane and Cayden are just neighbours, Bernice. They didn't even come to the retreat together."

"Mm-hmm, sure they are," she said, and Cayden wondered when they'd slipped from veiled to visible. Not that there was really anything to see. At most, he and Dane were a holiday fling. Nothing more. Not now.

Cayden had other priorities.

Dane grabbed the mini-whiteboard marker. "This one's for you, babe," he said, winking saucily. "Seven letters."

The wink was probably intended for Bernice's benefit, but Cayden felt like he'd been claimed. Was the man playing it up for show? Or was his teasing affection real?

"O," he threw out before his partner could do damage with his love of fucking X's and Y's.

Then Randy got lucky with "T".

Cayden blinked, studying the mini whiteboard. It didn't take long, however, before the answer came to him, and he resolved to get Dane somewhere private, ASAP.

"P. R," he called out, not bothering to stop between letters to know if he'd hung or if he'd won. This one he was sure of. "E. I. N."

"Nice," Bernice approved. Dane bit his lip, obviously trying not to laugh. And Randy rubbed his genie-bottle stomach. "Could do with a hunk-o-meat right about now."

"Truer words have never been spoken," Cayden concurred.

A dash of pink flashed across Dane's cheeks, and he muttered something that sounded suspiciously like, "Oh, God. Kill me now."

Desperate to get out of there, Cayden tossed down the last of his slimy broth, tapped the table, and stood up from his seat. "Right, everyone, that's us done. Time for—"

"A swim." Dane interrupted.

"What? No! Why?" Had Dane forgotten their agenda? Eat, then play. That's what he'd promised.

But Cayden couldn't protest again because at that very moment, Gordon fucking Fuller traipsed through the door, greeting his new acolytes with a rousing, "Good evening, detoxers!"

Randy surged to his feet, and pronounced, "Hey, it's the organic guru!"

Already standing, Cayden ducked for cover behind the same helpful potted palm he'd used for the same purpose on day one.

He did not want to be on GOG's radar.

Not yet.

While the crew applauded GOG for showing up, as though that were a good thing, Dane stepped to lean against the wall beside Cayden and brushed their hands together in a way that nobody else would ever notice. It was just for him. It said, *I'm here for you.* Cayden knew it was temporary, but a tiny flame began to glow in his heart.

"Look at you all—clear-eyed, shiny-skinned, open-heart-ed." GOG's bald scalp shone almost as bright as his grin.

Randy let out a "whoop!" before Bernice could shush him, and Cayden shifted closer to Dane's solid side.

"Love it! But, you know, detox is only one part of our mission here at The House of Glass Wellness Retreat." GOG beamed. "Some of you may have noticed that on Wednesday there are no scheduled massages, treatments, classes, yoga, or…" he lowered his voice, "…colonics."

That got a rousing applause.

"Now, some of you word-nerds might know that Wednesday is derived from the Old English name for the Norse god Woden—or Odin, for those of you partial to a certain cinema franchise—and Woden was a man of action. So, this Wednesday, your challenge is to get active." He grinned toothily. "To cater to the varying fitness levels and interests of the group, there are four different activities on offer." He picked up a small pile of papers and separated out the first sheet.

"The first option is a pre-dawn climb up Mount Coolum. It's a steep ascent, but the view over the Pacific at sunrise is life-changing. You'll be back in time for breakfast and have free rein of the retreat for the bulk of the day. Second is a mid-morning trip to nearby Eumundi Markets. This is a fantastic chance to shop local—practicing the mindful-living ethos we espouse here at the House of Glass. The third option is early morning beach yoga and an ocean swim on Noosa's north shore. It's exposed out there, so Hector will provide a sunshade, and Gladioli will make you a delicious picnic brunch. And the fourth option is a full-day, pairs-only canoe trip up the pristine Upper Noosa River Everglades. There won't be a guide, but you'll have a map to self-navigate, and Gladioli will supply a simple picnic to enjoy along the way." GOG turned to the corkboard and pinned four sheets of paper beside the dreaded pH graphs. "All you have to do is sign up for your chosen activity."

Cayden leaned a tiny bit to the right and pressed into Dane's shoulder. "Canoe?"

"Canoe," Dane said, at the very same time.

It was that easy.

Too easy?

Cayden angled his body toward Dane. "Glad to hear we're on the same page."

"Same boat," Dane corrected, a tiny smile feathering his lip.

Cayden rolled his eyes. "All right, smarty-pants."

Dane's answering chuckle was barely an exhaled breath, but it was enough to fan the fire within.

CHAPTER TWENTY-FOUR

DANE

Damnit.

He'd assessed the mood of the room so wrong.

It was supposed to be just him and Cayden getting up close and personal in the pool. Instead, half a dozen others had agreed that yes, indeed, a swim did sound like the perfect post-healthy-hangman plan.

Dane let his legs waver like seagrass as he sunk down into the depths where silver moonlight danced on every solid surface, and tried to ignore the chatter that warped through the water.

In the distant shallows, Cayden's arms and legs and beautiful arse no doubt churned with the rest of them, but Dane didn't look for him. He needed to get his head in gear. They'd already spent way too much time together—even Bernice had commented that they seemed joined at the hip. Not that he gave a shit what anyone else thought about who he took to bed, but he didn't want his actions to give Cayden the wrong idea.

Dane was just scratching an itch.

Nothing more.

As soon as Cayden's mystery was resolved, he'd be gone—back to his normal life at Tennyson Bend.

Trouble was, there might not be a mystery to solve.

The only signs of anything dodgy going on were Shorty's hints of illicit weed production and Gordon's hyperbolic views on the healing power of coconut oil.

Dane still thought they ought to follow the money, but there was no sign of anything illicit going on, let alone a cult. Nobody he'd met had been coerced into working at the retreat, physically held there against their will, or—as Cayden was determined to keep on the table—brainwashed to stay.

Likelier was the possibility that he was the one being brainwashed—by Cayden's touch and taste and…and every other fucking thing about him that made Dane want to curl around him and growl at anyone else who came close.

The urge had to be temporary, though, because he was just scratching an itch.

Dane closed his eyes, drew all of his attention into his core, and let himself drift. He didn't care which way was up or down as he enjoyed a few blessed moments of freedom until his human need for oxygen would demand he re-join the world.

Lungs straining, he held on, controlling the craving, feeling the buzz of denial, revelling in mind over body.

He released the last bubble of air and opened his eyes.

Looking back at him was a single, staring eye.

Shit.

He couldn't stop the reflex to jerk his head back and water rushed in. Choking, he thrashed for purchase in the shifting water, broaching the surface with spluttery coughs.

Great thwacks landed on his back and just about pushed

him back underwater. He kicked out, swiping at his water-blurred vision, desperate for the safety of the pool edge.

Disembodied shouts of, "Get help!" and, "Is he drowning?" and, "You right, mate?" jammed his ears—but one voice won through them all.

"You're okay," Cayden's familiar tenor murmured, right by his ear. "Everything's okay." His voice soothed with a hand at the small of Dane's back.

Gripping the pool edge tight, Dane dropped his forehead onto the back of his hands, closed his eyes, and arched his spine out into that far-too-welcome touch.

That hand told him a story. It said *I'm here*, and *I care*.

It felt so good.

So right.

Why did it feel so right?

Dane let himself stay, just for a moment, and then he opened his eyes, blinked away the droplets that caught in his eyelashes, and straightened away from the touch.

The hand didn't travel with him, but he could still feel the ghost of it, so he dropped a little lower in the cool water to submerge the want and the need.

"I'm okay," he said.

Gruff.

Dismissive.

Needy.

Excitement over, the others drifted back to the shallow end, but he could still feel Cayden's presence.

So much for the pool offering respite.

"I don't need babysitting," he asserted with a last throat-clearing cough.

"Course not."

Dane schooled his expression and twisted to face Cayden. So close, Cayden's two eyes again became one.

"Gonna have to call you Cyclops from now on."

"Why?" Cayden asked.

"One-eyed wonder." Dane huffed the barest of a laugh and rolled to float on his back and stared up at the Milky Way splayed out in one enormous arc across the night sky.

On the southern horizon, the distinctive kite shape of the Southern Cross shone brightly, its starry-bright tail pointed to the South Pole. If he followed that star for a couple hundred kilometres, he'd soon be home in Tennyson Bend, safely ensconced in his simple, sleek apartment. Safe from sexy cupids who cared.

What he needed was a distraction.

He dove deep and swam breaststroke along the floor of the pool to the shallow end, where he surfaced a few feet from the rest of the group.

All eyes went to him.

"Anyone had a body wrap yet? I'm supposed to choose between an avocado-nut-butter wrap and a chocolate-mud wrap. Avocado's healthier, but it's hard to go past chocolate."

"Don't be an idiot, Dane. You don't eat it," Bernice said in her usual succinct way.

Randal contradicted his wife. "Not while you're in it, maybe, but afterward..." He made the worst telegraphed 'O' face Dane had ever seen.

The other ladies ignored them both with louder and ever more enthusiastic calls of "Avo!" and "Choc!"

"You suck," Cayden said, telegraphing too, and Dane wanted to kick him, hard.

Bernice shook her head at her husband. "Body wraps draw out toxins. Why would you eat something that's just sucked out all the pus and sludge and dead cells from your skin?"

They all fell silent at that image. But Anna raised her hand like a schoolchild and Bernice said, "Yes, Anna?"

"I have an avocado body scrub at home. It's nice."

"Thanks, Anna. Good tip."

"If it was a coffee bean scrub instead of chocolate, I'd have that," offered Lissa.

Michelle rolled her eyes. "Yes, but Lissa, it's not coffee."

And they were all off because one reliable facet of the retreat was that everyone had opinions on the value of treatments. Hell, he'd overheard two of them debate the relative merits of celery versus cucumber as though they weren't both ninety-nine-point-nine percent water.

What had his life become? If anyone had foretold that he'd be wallowing at a fucking wellness retreat, living on everyone's timetable but his own, he'd have told them to buy a clue. Give up control over his daily life? Hell, no.

Yet there he was, following Carol's dictate, Cayden's mission, and GOG's rules.

Days had passed, and he'd barely thought of real life—his work, or his friends. Of one thing, he was certain—when he saw Carol again, they would have words.

The others all huddled together in the other shallow corner of the pool, whispering heatedly, while Cayden treaded water in the deep end.

Dane was just getting used to being left blissfully alone, when Michelle turned from the group and announced, "We've decided Cayden should give you a chocolate mud wrap."

"But I'm not—"

"But he's not—" Dane and Cayden said in perfect synchrony.

Michelle overrode their objections. "Or you could get wrapped together."

He'd put the *what* on the menu, not the *who*.

Beep, beep, beep, Dane wanted to say. *Back it up, folks.* "I don't think the guests are supposed to be put to work here."

He licked his lips and slid further along the pool edge

toward the deep end, but no distance was far enough to be safe from the image in Dane's mind—of him and Cayden, wrapped together, separated by nothing but slick chocolate...

Jesus. Now he really needed life support. Stat.

CHAPTER TWENTY-FIVE

CAYDEN

"Didn't think we'd ever get out of there." Cayden followed Dane up the path to their havens. The position was no hardship since he got to watch Dane's tight arse in his red swimsuit.

It took him a few seconds to realise Dane hadn't responded.

Surprised, Cayden hopped a quick step to catch up and lay his palm flat on Dane's lower back. Not to cop a feel, but to connect, because something wasn't quite right.

He tried again. "And where'd they get the idea that we're boyfriends?"

Still, Dane said nothing, but his increased pace up the stairs gave Cayden hope.

Sort of.

Maybe.

God, he was sick of being unsure.

All evening Dane had yo-yoed hot and cold.

Present and absent.

Supportive and standoffish.

At first, he'd thought it might have been Dane's way of

compartmentalising his public and private self. But, when they arrived at the last step to their haven deck and Dane still held his shoulders stiff, Cayden wasn't so sure anymore.

Round and around, the doubt twirled. He paused on the last step and let Dane shift away from his hand.

It had felt so natural to place it there. Warm and intimate and right.

And confusing. When had he gone from casual fuck to chivalrous boyfriend?

Never. That's when.

That's not what they were about.

All they'd done was share a drink, some disarmingly candid chats, idle flirtation, the hottest kisses known to man, some horizontal mambo, and a blowjob.

That was it.

In some circles, that was the tame half of a first date.

Hell, maybe to Dane they were no more than an anecdote to entertain his friends.

I met this idiot. We fucked. End of story.

Which was fine by Cayden—sort of—so long as they got to the fucking part.

Since the man's face was cast in shadow, Cayden tried reading Dane's tight posture, with little success. The man was a closed book.

"I'm kind of wiped," Dane said to his screen door. "I think, tonight…" He paused, and in the empty moment, the usual cacophony of the rainforest rushed back in. "I think we need to take a break."

A break? What the hell?

"You think we need to take a break?" Cayden parroted. Surely, he'd heard wrong. "Did I miss something?" To take a break, they needed to be together. When had they decided that?

Still with his back to Cayden, Dane rubbed his neck. "Yeah, I mean, no, I mean…"

"Well, that's clear."

"I just think," Dane started, again, and then stopped, again, and Cayden decided being pissed off was a legit response to the bewildering situation.

Cayden grabbed Dane's upper arm and pulled to turn him around. "Back up a minute. I'm confused. Boyfriends, part-ners, lovers—they take breaks. Newsflash—we," Cayden waved a hand between them, "are none of those." Hell, anything more than friends who fuck was a stretch. And they hadn't even gotten to that.

Dane lifted that bitch of an eyebrow. "Fine. Pick another phrase. I don't care."

He didn't care? That stung, but he pushed it aside. "If you don't want to fuck, just say 'Cayden, I don't want to fuck. Please be on your merry way.'"

If they weren't going to fuck, he wanted to know so he could get some sleep.

Why was he so angry?

More to the point, where had their easy alliance gone? It was as though their friendly vibe had suddenly split into two entirely different wavelengths.

Had Earth's magnetic poles flipped?

Was their magnet now pushing them apart rather than together?

Perhaps the error was his own presumption.

He'd already served Dane's purpose—one and done—and it was time to move on.

Except he couldn't help re-hearing the words Dane had left him with earlier that evening—*then we play*. He'd assumed it was a promise—a promise Dane had yet to deliver.

The dude lit his fire, for sure, but no matter how much

Cayden might want to jump his bones and snuggle afterward, he would not be the one that clung. If Dane didn't want to continue where they'd left off, that was entirely up to him.

Cayden trod heavily across the wooden deck to his haven and slid open the mosquito screen door. "If you change your mind, you know where to find me."

"I just think…" the bastard repeated, then trailed off.

The rejection absolutely, for real, did not sting.

Not a single bit.

"Nah. It's cool, dude. You do you."

What choice did he have, anyway? It wasn't like they'd made some great promise to each other.

"It's cool," he repeated. "No harm, no foul." He pointed into the dark of his own, separate, private haven. "I'll see you in the morning. Or, you know, whenever."

Fuck.

Leave Cayden.

Now.

Cheeks hot, he stepped inside and slid his door shut behind him. Blind in the dark, he shuffled through to the bathroom, grabbed onto the hard edge of the vanity, and leaned his forehead against the blessed cool of the mirror glass.

"Shit. It's official," Cayden berated himself. "I'm a clinger."

CHAPTER TWENTY-SIX

DANE

"Shit. It's official," Dane berated himself. "I'm a bastard."

Dane didn't want to hurt the guy, but how else was he supposed to maintain an emotional distance when Cayden was like fucking fairy floss on his fingers—sweet, and irresistible, and maddening as hell?

He'd be far easier to ignore if he didn't look, touch, or smell so good.

Or exist.

It should have been easy to fob him off. He'd done it to many a man before. But the task had taken a level of willpower Dane hadn't had to exercise in years. And he still wasn't entirely successful.

The man's touch screamed affection, and intimacy, and promises—things Dane never usually had to guard against, but which had started to fray his control. Cayden got under his skin. What next? If they continued on the same trajectory, would they soon be swapping secrets along with sweet nothings?

Desire was one thing. A quick fuck dealt with that.

True intimacy, though, that was a slippery slope into love—

the worst of all the four-letter words. No way was Dane interested in going down that path. Not when every single person he'd ever truly loved had died. Love wasn't hearts and roses and comfort. Love was a death spiral down into pain and despair and heartbreaking loneliness. No way did he want to go there.

Not again.

With every step Cayden had trailed him up the path, Dane's mind yelled, *stay away, stay away, stay away.*

Then, when that warm touch at the small of his back fell away, his heart cried, *come back, come back, come back.*

The discordance had him spooked.

The only thing Dane could think to do was to put space and time between them. It was that or give his feelings free rein…and he already knew that wasn't safe. Dane needed to shore up his defences.

If he was going to let himself enjoy the man, he'd have to make his limits clear.

They could fuck, but…

No lingering.

No snuggling.

No confiding.

Nothing intimate or personal.

That had to be the deal.

No harm, no foul, Cayden had said before retreating to his own haven, except Dane had seen the confusion, the disappointment, and the hurt in his eyes. And the wrench that pulled at Dane's gut tested his resolve.

No way did he love the guy. There wasn't much risk of that. But he liked Cayden. He liked him a lot.

And when he slid shut the door of his own haven, he thought for a fleeting moment that he might just have fallen into his own trap of self-delusion.

Safe in his own haven, Dane shucked off his wet swimming trunks and showered, then let his body air-dry as he brushed his teeth with his own store-bought, non-organic, mint-flavoured toothpaste.

He spat and swished into the porcelain sink and ran his fingers roughly through his damp hair.

Bare-arsed, Dane settled down between his cool bamboo sheets and flipped open *Titus Groan* to where his ragtag rainbow bookmark held his place.

Why Alice had loved the book, Dane didn't know. It was full of grey men living grey lives in high grey-walled isolation. Still, he dutifully read the nightly chapter because that was the task that he'd set himself, then closed the book and switched off his bedside light.

Restless and irritated, his eyes kept popping open and tracking the streaks of cool moonlight that travelled slowly across the room. Hours passed, unable to sleep. When the celestial white light hit on his and Cayden's shared haven wall like a fucking spotlight of destiny, or some crap like that, Dane gave up.

Fuck it.

Naked, he threw off the sweaty sheet and crossed outside to the edge of the deck.

Under the starry sky, the rainforest canopy looked like a wild, dark, tempestuous ocean, surging across the land. He squeezed the timber railing, squared his shoulders, and breathed in the scents of living green, and earthy brown, and the latent yellow heat of the day.

A tiny breeze blew, lifting the sweat-damp hair off his brow. He was glad to get that tease of relief, but Dane suspected the only thing that would bring genuine relief was through the door of Haven fourteen.

As much as he'd tried to put Cayden out of sight, out of mind, it hadn't worked.

Twenty feet wasn't far enough—he'd need a state line between them to keep the man completely out of mind.

Stuck in the same boat, Cayden had said. Which was true enough, for the time being.

Might as well enjoy the ride.

But he had to be careful.

Dane tapped the rough wooden railing with one staccato reminder for each new ground-rule:

No lingering.

No confiding.

And no more fucking soul-searching.

He took another breath of the rich, thick air, then turned.

He re-crossed the moon-raked deck and slid open the screen door, stepped inside, and quietly shut the door behind him.

Cayden lay on his side. One arm raised like he was climbing a ladder, hugging the edge of a feather-soft pillow to his face, and the other arm cocked behind, pointing to his bare arse.

For long minutes, Dane watched Cayden breathe, deep and even.

Still.

Peaceful.

Luminous.

Light years from the irritating restlessness that had plagued Dane.

Want was one thing—that he could quash—but need was entirely different.

Naked as all the beasts of the rainforest, Dane crawled up the bed to lie spooned a whisker's distance from Cayden's back. He rested his head on the empty half of Cayden's pillow, breathed in the retreat's proffered coconut shampoo, and melted into sleep.

CHAPTER TWENTY-SEVEN

CAYDEN

Cayden woke to morning wood, a cold back, and a spooky feeling that he wasn't entirely alone.

He rolled onto his back and looked around. Nothing. Nobody was there.

He reached out to feel the other pillow. Just like the sheets, it was wrinkled and cool from damp sweat. Had he rolled all the way over there?

He traced a fingertip along the most suspicious fold in the sheet, and, feeling like a bit of a paranoid idiot, he leaned down to sniff. Other than a slightly tangy hint of dried sweat, the sheet smelled no different than usual.

"Idiot." He flopped back, spread-eagled on the bed, and let his hand stray south to give his old friend a quick welcome-to-the-day tug. But the persistent feeling that he wasn't alone undid any smidgen of pleasure or comfort.

He gave up, swung out of bed, swiped two pH sticks from the pack on the bathroom vanity, and padded to the bathroom. He stuck one in his mouth to slather with saliva and held the other strategically in front of him while he did his business. That done, he noted their colour change against the codes on the box, threw the strips in the bin, and then took an extra-long minute to wash his hands.

Check and check, Cayden ticked off the first two things on his mental to-do list.

He splashed his face with sun-warmed tap water and brushed his teeth using the gritty organic toothpaste the retreat supplied. "Method acting is for shit," he told his reflection, spraying flecks of toothpaste onto the mirror in a constellation of foamy-white stars.

Cayden quickly dressed and headed down to the hub for his daily dose of disgusting.

"What's the sludge of the day, Gladioli?" he asked through the kitchen hatch window.

"Guess." She winked.

"Coffee?" he guessed, hoping the world had tilted enough on its axis to make that a possibility.

"Ha!"

"But if it's organic?" he pressed.

She shook her head.

"Chocolate?"

Maxine stepped up to his side. "Don't bother trying to guess, Cayden. Gladioli refuses to tell us what's for breakfast. Says it's special." She rolled her eyes. "I'd kill for a banana smoothie. Mmm, with honey, and cinnamon, and ice cream."

"Get a room, Maxine," Edie butted in, poking her tongue out at her pixie friend. "And stop trying to sweet-talk Gladioli, Cayden. Come check this out." She grabbed his hand and hauled him through the dining-room door. Inside, the usual late breakfasters crowded around the cork noticeboard.

"What is it?" He couldn't keep the cranky from his voice. "My tank's running dangerously low, Edie. I'm in serious need of breakfast."

As one, the women all turned to him. He shuddered. Creepy.

"What?" he repeated.

"You're going to need a lot of energy tomorrow, Cayden." Michelle winked.

He shuddered again. "Tomorrow?"

Lissa pointed at the corkboard, and he bravely waded through the women to see what they were all on about.

In an elegant cursive script, written under Activity 4: Canoe the Everglades, were their names, Cayden & Dane.

"Well, that clears the murky waters a smidgen, not."

"Pardon, Cayden?"

Fortunately, none of the women heard him, because Gladioli chose that moment to holler, "Come and get it!"

Half a second later, he was alone.

Cayden stared at their names for a long second, his finger twitching to trace the sharp slice of the handwritten letters and the perfectly formed ampersand between. All that was missing was the *4 Eva* to take him truly into teenaged fantasyland.

Finally, the lure of breakfast won, and he wrenched his gaze away.

"Gah!" was the consensus on the noxious apple cider vinegar shot, but the frothy, khaki-coloured smoothie riddled with tiny black flecks wasn't too bad.

"Mmm." Cayden hummed around his re-usable straw. "Kiwi and banana, and—"

"Good head," came a voice by his shoulder.

Startled, Cayden rammed the straw into the back of his mouth.

He sputtered at the liquid that tried to go down the wrong channel. "Geez! Warn a guy!"

It wasn't his only cause of protest. Cayden had to do his best to not gape at Dane's bare torso, fully on display above what must be the skimpiest pair of running shorts on the planet. "Do you not own a shirt?"

Because, really.

Dane stood tall with his hands rested on his hips. Glistening sweat emphasised the grooves around his abs, and his pecs, and his triceps, and his tight calves, and his…

"When you're done perving…"

Cayden's snapped his attention up, and a few women behind him snickered. He didn't bother to find out who.

"…we need to go do a thing," Dane said.

That sounded promising.

"A thing. Right. Sure. I'll just—"

Cayden slogged his mystery green drink, taking special joy in slurping up the frothy head as it reached the bottom of the glass.

He plonked the empty glass down with an emphatic clonk. "Done."

Dane grabbed him by the hand and tugged him along the path that led toward their havens.

Maybe he ought to have been pissed at Dane's radical backflip, but Cayden decided it'd be better to fuck first and ask questions later.

Once they were out of sight of the hub, however, Dane diverted off the main path.

"Where the hell are you going, Dane?"

"Here," Dane said, as though that answered anything. Then he bush-bashed between two giant frangipanis, their lush yellow-and-white flowers heady with scent.

On the other side of the floral jungle, Dane stopped and dropped Cayden's hand. "Look." He pointed.

Annoyed, Cayden huffed, but he followed where Dane pointed to see an old picket fence, white paint peeling and half covered in moss. Beyond it was a time-wild, gone-to-seed, kitchen garden, rampant with weeds. Beyond that was a dilapidated old Queenslander-style wooden cottage, built high on stilts.

The whole thing looked like it was being slowly but surely swallowed by the rainforest.

"So-o." Cayden drew out the vowel, at a complete loss to account for Dane's caveman mode. "I guess this isn't a booty call, after all."

"What?"

"Booty call. You know—grab a guy, drag him back to your cave, use him for wild sex. Booty call." He shrugged. "Unless this is your idea of a cave."

Dane's lips pinched, but Cayden couldn't tell if it was with amusement or anger.

"If it is," Cayden continued, "please know I'm judging you right now. And finding you wanting."

"I found it," Dane said.

Cryptic. "Found what?"

Dane pointed at the cottage.

And Dane called *him* cryptic? "An old cottage? I don't get it."

"Look at the windows. What do you see?"

Okay. He'd play.

Cayden inspected the old cottage. "I see four old sash windows, all closed, and all…"

Oh, God.

"See?"

"…clean, Dane. Everything else is a mess, but the windows are squeaky clean." He reached for the rusty latch. "What's inside?"

"Weed." Dane drawled, right behind him. "Lots and lots and lots of weed. It's an amazing setup."

"Are you serious? Holy mother of shit! Dane. It's GOG's weed pantry!"

Cayden gave up on the latch and scissored his legs over the waist-high fence, then waded through the sea of green. Dane followed.

"This side is a front for anyone who stumbles across it. Like us."

"Only less suspicious people. We know better."

"Exactly. The three other sides of the cottage are panelled in glass. It's a three-sided glasshouse."

"Wow. Do you know what this means?"

"Yep."

"Real leverage against GOG," Cayden burst out.

"The public won't care about an operation like this. But marijuana is still technically illegal. Gordon won't like this coming to light. It could shut the retreat down."

"Blackmail."

"Yep."

"Stop saying yep," Cayden complained. "I can't plan blackmail while thinking of Leif."

"Because Leif is innocent, while blackmail is illegal," Dane helpfully summed up.

"Thank you, Captain Obvious. But so is kidnapping, and imprisonment, and…"

"I thought you said Lucy disappeared?"

"Yeah. No sign."

"So, you don't know if any of that actually happened. Right?"

Cayden refused to answer that.

Technically, all his suspicions were conjecture, but he knew in his gut that Lucy hadn't just run away. There was more to it than a whim. There had to be. Or why would she have stayed away?

As he reached for the door handle to look inside, Dane grabbed his arm and wrenched it away.

"Don't touch it," Dane rushed out. "You'll leave fingerprints."

"But—" he protested, but Dane yanked Cayden flush to his chest, and all thoughts of Lucy and Gordon and illicit fucking weed rushed from his mind, replaced by pure, hot Dane.

Did you sleep wrapped around me last night?

Bidden by ghostly sensation, the question flared hot in his mind. But before he could ask it, Dane grabbed his hand and tugged him back toward the retreat proper through a blur of white and yellow and green. "Come on. Nefarious deeds can wait, but my chocolate mud wrap can't."

"Dane, wait!" Cayden protested.

But Dane didn't wait. "Come on," he called back, flashing an enigmatic smile. "Don't want to be late."

CHAPTER TWENTY-EIGHT

DANE

"You're like a human sausage roll. Except with chocolate for a condiment instead of tomato sauce." This was Cayden's not remotely helpful assessment of Dane's state of incapacitation.

Dressed in nothing but a thin, disposable thong, the gooey, brown, chocolaty mud oozed around every bit of him —between his toes, around his legs, inside his belly button, under his arms—hell, the warm ooze had even crept up his arse crack. If Jade hadn't cocooned him tight in the blanket, a slight breeze could have slid him straight off the narrow treatment table, through the floor-to-ceiling windows, and down the steep crater slope. The heat lamps Jade positioned over his prostrate body just made the oozy feeling that much more intense.

"You know, Jade, if you ever want to torture someone, wrapping them up like that'd be a brilliant method to get them to stay put." Cayden reached across from the other treatment table to flick Dane's earlobe.

"Behave." Jade stole the words straight out of Dane's mouth.

Jade leaned over Cayden, flexed her arms, and pressed her pointy elbows into the two hollows on either side of the base of his spine.

Cayden groaned, long and deep, and Dane grinned with satisfaction. He couldn't mete out justice himself, but Jade's expert massage-ninja ministrations were a fine substitute.

He remembered well how Jade had jammed his knots with her thumbs, and knuckles, and elbows, and heels, and... yeah, the woman had Cayden firmly in her control.

Sweet justice.

"What was that about torture?" Dane asked and whistled a few notes as though he had not a care in the world. Cayden deserved it after all his teasing.

"Just you wait," Cayden menaced. "As soon as your man-sized sausage roll finishes baking, I'm gonna—" He groaned again, the low-pitched sound taking a direct path to Dane's groin.

Nice work, Jade, he thought. Not at all sarcastic.

Cayden could threaten all he liked, so long as he made good on the implied promise.

Later.

Sometime while Dane had slept secretly curved around Cayden's gorgeous back, his subconscious must have finally embraced Carol's plan to get him to relax. He'd woken in the pre-dawn grey feeling curiously light and loose-limbed. He'd levered his knee out from between Cayden's oh-so-warm thighs, slipped back into his haven to dress, and headed out for a run up the crater side.

High on the rim, overlooking the grand Pacific, Dane had greeted the morning and resolved to enjoy the craziness between him and Cayden. He decided to break his "one and done, gone before dawn" rule, and enjoy the man for as long as their orbits merged. Which included giving the man shit when he deserved it. "My man-sized sausage roll is up for whatever you—"

"Boys!" Jade snapped.

"Sorry, Jade." Dane tried his best to hide his smile. Unsuccessfully.

"Sorry, Jade." Cayden hid his face back in the doughnut hole of the massage table.

"Dane is a caterpillar. Not a sausage roll," she said, with absolute conviction.

"Yes, Jade," Cayden said.

"He will emerge a butterfly."

"Yes, Jade," Cayden mumble-snorted.

"He will fly."

"Not from a tall building, I hope." Dane couldn't move his head very much, but he had a fine view of the wide-open sky and the steep rainforest that tapered out of view. It'd be all right to fly over that—with the right apparatus.

"Flutter just like a butterfly." Jade linked her thumbs together and waggled her fingers *just* like a butterfly.

Okay.

"Or a bat," Cayden offered.

Hmm.

"Or a gnat."

"Not helpful, Cayden."

"A butterfly," Jade insisted.

"Thank you, Jade." That'll be all, Dane thought.

She leaned over him, smiled upside down, and then covered his eyes with a wide strip of dark blue silk. The lights went out, and his other four senses rushed to the fore, highlighting the fact that his dick had risen to the occasion, too.

Shit.

Carol had meant for his wellness plan to put a spring in his step, not in his goddamn dick.

Poor Jade didn't need to face an erection when she unwrapped him. "How much longer do I have wrapped in here?" he asked.

"About fifteen minutes."

Fifteen minutes to temper the beast…

Or convince Cayden to do the unwrapping.

"Fifteen minutes till you spread your glorious new butterfly wings," Cayden joked. "What colour do you think they'll be, Jade? I vote for fuchsia."

"Shove off." Dane wished he had use of his arms to thwack him or strangle him.

Or silence Cayden with a scolding kiss.

He heard a finger-snap by his ear. "I've got it. Turquoise, to match your merman toenails."

Yeah, no. "Find me a trident, and I'll put my merman toenails somewhere you'll—"

"Dane," Jade rebuked.

"Sorry, Jade," he grumbled again.

Cayden's chuckle was low and intimate and did nothing to reverse Dane's other, far more pressing issue.

Still, Dane thought as he heard Cayden not-so-subtly quiz Jade about the retreat, he didn't want to be anywhere else.

Determined to relax, Dane closed his eyes, lashes brushing against the warm silk, and breathed deep. He let all his muscles relax, and he floated, calm in his chocolate wrap, like a beast in the primordial ooze.

Dane penned a quick mental memo to his PA.

Dear Carol, thank you.

CHAPTER TWENTY-NINE

CAYDEN

As they trailed back up the path for Dane's afternoon facial, Cayden decided he was onto a good thing. "Vicarious enjoyment rocks," he said.

"I think you're misunderstanding the meaning of vicarious." Dane's arm brushed his, and every single nerve in his body zinged.

"What have I misunderstood? I'm enjoying what you're getting."

"Mm-hmm." Dane nodded. "I get it. But people usually experience vicarious enjoyment from a distance."

"You want me to leave?" he asked, unable to keep the slight hurt from his voice.

Cayden never intended to get into anything with Dane beyond a glorious screw or two, but hanging out together, whether or not they were in bed, felt light and easy. Dane was hot. No doubt about that. But now and then, beneath the molten hot chocolate, Cayden saw hints of soft chocolate mousse. He didn't want to want more. Cayden had other priorities. But he could feel his heart developing other ideas

—dreamy ideas about the future, about having and holding, till death do us part.

Which was just plain ridiculous. He wasn't in a position to ask for a date, let alone a ring.

A long, silent beat passed, and for probably the thirty-seventh time that day, Cayden wondered if he was reading Dane properly.

"No," Dane finally said.

Cayden waited for the rest of the explanation, but Dane didn't expand.

Ugh! It was maddening. Were they, or were they not, a thing?

Before Cayden could ask that question outright, though, he needed to know what answer he wanted in return.

A thing or not a thing?

Pesky problem, that.

"Well, stop being the word police. It's unattractive." Cayden brushed their knuckles together as they walked, just because he could, and did his best to keep pace with Dane's longer stride.

"The word you're looking for is *mooching*," Dane corrected him. "As in, 'Cayden is mooching off of Dane.'"

"Yes. Yes, I am," Cayden readily agreed. "Because my boss didn't shell out for the Vital Serenity Wellness Plan, like yours did."

"Carol's not my boss. I'm hers."

Cayden pointedly ignored that. It was clear from the way Dane spoke about his PA that they had a close and highly dependent relationship. If Dane thought he was the boss, he was deluded. "The more people I get to question, the better chance I have of finding a helpful clue. And since you're meeting staff who I won't get to meet, I'd say going with you is the most efficient arrangement." The quicker he could find his sister, restore his family, and put the mission behind him, the faster he could get on with life. Then he could ask questions. Questions like—fancy going on a date, Dane?

Not that it was about him. Not at all.

"Why don't you take the facial, then? I don't need it. And you don't need me there."

"Gawd, no. These pores are pure, dude." And he liked having Dane there.

Out of the corner of his eye, he saw Dane shake his head.

Dane's presence was a distraction, but so long as hanging together didn't undermine the investigation, he figured he could afford to be a little selfish.

Was a bit of fun too much to ask for?

Once he found Lucy, he could truly indulge his desires. All of his desires. Things like finding a career that actually suited him and making a true home, with a partner, and a…a pet—a pet that said *I'm here to stay.*

He eyed Dane again, impatience welling. "We need to step up the search."

"I agree," Dane said slowly, carefully. "At some point though, we might need to concede that Lucy's not here."

Cayden grabbed Dane's arm, pulling him to a stop. "What? No. What are you talking about?"

"Cayden. It's—"

He zeroed in on Dane's winter-blue eyes. "She's here. Somewhere. I know it. You found the weed. That's something."

"We can use the weed. Information is power, after all. But where's the connection between that and Lucy? Weed does not a sister make."

"Not specifically, but it's a sign that—"

"All I'm saying is—"

"I know what you're saying, Dane. Believe me. I know. But I can't not look. Not looking means giving up. And giving up means…" His voice trailed off, unable to finish the thought, let alone the sentence.

Cayden turned again to face the path, slicked a drip of sweat from his temple, and resumed his steady pace up the hill. He hoped Dane would follow.

A few seconds later, he heard Dane move, but Cayden didn't say anything. What could he say?

The scratch and scrape of loose gravel beneath their feet added to the snaps and whips and whirs of birds and insects calling to each other in the muggy heat. Cayden fancied the animals were bickering, too—over territory, or worms, or sweet fruits of the rainforest. Or maybe they were flirting—performing mating dances, declaring their intentions, making forever promises.

Were they as clueless as Cayden felt?

Probably not.

"How many false leads have you followed over the years?" Dane asked.

Hadn't they covered this already? "None…or…maybe a few."

Dane's silence spoke volumes.

"Fine." He huffed, feeling the heat of the summer sun blast down on his bare head. "Too many, all right? Are you happy now? Jesus Christ, dude, why such a downer?"

Dane pulled him to a stop once more. His eyes were so intent, Cayden felt like a bug under a microscope. "All I'm saying is, you need to prepare for disappointment."

What the fuck? Wasn't Dane supposed to be on his side?

"No, I don't," he snapped.

A golf ball-sized lump caught in his throat. He tried swallowing, but that thing was fucking huge, and it stuck fast. He tipped his head back and caught the liquid heat of the mid-afternoon sun. Flares and flashes blitzed his vision, and he blinked the telling moisture away.

Who the hell was Dane to tell him when a lead was dead? He was the fucking journalist. Not Dane.

Preparing for disappointment meant giving up. "I refuse."

The afterimages of the sun gradually scattered back up into outer space where they belonged, and he stared at Dane till, eventually, he, too, shied away.

"Yeah. Okay. I get it," Dane said, voice gruff.

And Cayden thought just maybe he did.

Maybe they could be on the same page after all.

CHAPTER THIRTY

DANE

"Welcome, you must be Dane. My name's Shelley." The thirty-something woman pointed to her name tag clipped neatly to her white scrubs top.

"Good to meet you." Dane threw a thumb over his shoulder. "That's Cayden."

He didn't bother explaining Cayden's presence. Why create roadblocks before they existed?

Shelley checked her clipboard with a light, worried frown. "I'm sorry. I didn't realise this was booked as a couple's beauty treatment."

"Oh, no." Cayden jumped in. "I'm just along for the ride. Make sure he behaves himself."

Which wasn't exactly a denial of their relationship status.

The presumption that they were together would normally irritate Dane, but he let it go. Having Cayden there beside him felt weirdly normal.

"Please come in." Shelley waved them inside.

The yellow-doored treatment hut looked much like all the others—whitewashed wooden slat walls, high peaked roof, and a wide picture window along the back wall, framing a beautiful north-westerly view.

Still hours before the sun would drop over the western horizon, every leaf flared flat to the sun's rays, shimmering in the muggy heat.

Cayden nudged his elbow. "Funny how you can almost see photosynthesis happening, eh?"

"Mmm," Dane agreed. "Storm's coming, too."

"What? It's blue skies."

"Nah. I can feel it. The air's charged."

"So now you're the storm whisperer?"

"Dane's right," Shelley said.

They both turned to her, and Dane grinned. "I like you."

"Charmer." She blushed. "Please have a seat."

In the centre of the room sat a moulded tan leather monstrosity that looked like a cross between a race car bucket seat and a dentist's chair. Dane didn't know if he ought to feel excited or worried as he inserted himself into the seat.

"Dude, cool chair." He stroked the pleather by Dane's shoulder. "All that's missing is a steering wheel, and we'd be safely far from here in sixty-seconds flat. What else does it do?"

"Hands off," said Shelley in an if-I-have-to-tell-you-one-more-time mum voice.

It didn't dissuade Cayden at all. "Where's the eject button?"

"It's the red one. Don't press it."

"Ha! Good one, Shelley."

"Do you mind?" Dane complained. "I'm trying to relax here."

"Yeah, yeah. Keep your knickers on." There was a silent pause, and then they both sniggered.

"Are you boys done yet?"

Dane cleared his throat. "Sorry."

"Sorry," Cayden apologised, too, but he didn't look remotely contrite.

"All righty, then. Let's get to it." Shelley draped a light blanket over Dane's body, then dragged a dinky wooden stool out from under one of the display shelves and patted it. "Here you go, Cayden. I think this is about perfect for you."

"Sweet."

She rolled over another wheelie saddle chair for her to sit on and pulled out a large round magnifying glass.

"Now, Dane, let's have a look at your skin."

Slowly, her magnified eye inspected every square inch of his face.

"Are you going to dust for fingerprints, too?" Cayden asked.

"Worried I'll find someone's prints other than yours?" she shot back, amused.

That shut Cayden up.

Next, she brought her fingers close to his face. "May I?" She waited for his nod of approval before smoothing her fingertips along his jawline. Out of the corner of his eye, he saw Cayden's mouth firm. The man's jealousy felt ridiculously good, even if it was totally misplaced.

"Your dermal layers are showing signs of tension and dehydration. Probably from overexposure to air conditioning. Do you work in an office, Dane?"

He felt like a chided kid. "Yes, but—"

"And I bet your home is air-conditioned, too?" At his nod, she went on, "It's not good for you to be inside so much. You must get out more. Your skin is the most wonderful organ. You need to take care of it."

Cayden snickered. "Hear that, Dane? Your most wonderful organ."

They both ignored him.

"Gordon and Gladioli and Shiloh will teach you how to take care of it from the inside, but you need to take care of it from the outside, too. I recommend you expose your skin to natural humidity and hyper-oxygenated places like forests."

Cayden nodded. "Forest bathing. It's a thing."

"Absolutely. And spend regular time at the ocean where you'll absorb sea salts and the minerals suspended in the water and the air. A salt crystal in your home would help, too, but you need to dwell in the biosphere—that's the only way."

"Mm-hmm. Sure." Could he sound less convinced?

"There's no goddamn way I'd have a salt crystal in my home," Cayden grumbled. "I've had more than enough salt to last me a lifetime. Hell, I don't think I'll even want it on fish and chips anymore. A squeeze of lemon maybe, some tartar sauce, but no salt. No way. No how. Never again."

Dane raised an eyebrow. "Good thing we don't live together, then."

"Too right," Cayden snapped back.

The words shouldn't have pinched.

Dane turned to Shelley. "He's not a fan of salt."

"I, ah…so I gather."

"Right, so…" He prompted Shelley to get on with it. He needed the distraction.

"Sorry, yes, for your skin, I recommend the rejuvenation facial. First, an herbal scrub to break down your dead skin cells; a coal-and-aloe peel to help draw out the impurities; a rehydration mask that'll delve deep into the tissue layers, repairing and restoring; and last, an essential oil massage that'll leave your skin feeling relaxed and protected."

He blinked.

"Sound good?" she asked.

"Sounds divine." Cayden's sigh dripped with barefaced envy, and Dane had to laugh at the one-eighty-degree turn.

"Thanks for the assist."

"No worries." Cayden patted his arm. "Glad to help."

"Right, then. Let's get to it." She pressed or pulled some kind of lever tucked under the chair that laid him out flat, then wrapped his face and neck in a hot moist towel that smelled fresh and zingy.

"What is that? I can't quite place the aroma."

"Lemon myrtle. It's lovely for your skin. Tastes great in yogurt, too."

Cayden leaned in for a sniff. "Mmm…good to know."

"Breathe deep." Shelley instructed. "In through your nose and out through your mouth. Let your body lie loose and light. Relaxed."

Inhaling the lemon myrtle scent, Dane's lungs soon felt broad and open and fresh.

Pan flutes and a water feature sounded gently in the background, not quite covering the excitable birds outside, but weaved around the sounds of their breaths and the occasional scuff of chair wheels as they rolled across the wooden floor.

After the hot towel came a scrub of Himalayan pink salt, crushed rosemary, and lavender essential oil.

"That smells so good. Remind me to take some home, Dane. It'd be great seasoning for a rack of lamb."

"What about the salt?" Dane tried to ask without moving his lips or jaw. But he was no ventriloquist, and Shelley hushed him.

Next came the charcoal-and-aloe face peel. As Shelley was smoothing it on, Cayden asked, "What's your opinion on finger painting, Shelly?"

"Great way to get in touch with your inner child. I once walked into the retreat's art studio to find a dozen people body painting on an enormous canvas."

"Anyone called Lucy?" asked Cayden, his voice deceptively light.

Shelley stared up at the ceiling for a moment, then shook her head. "No. I don't think so. I wonder what happened to that mural."

"You're sure?"

She nodded and pursed her lips with amusement. "Persistent, aren't you? You remind me so much of a woman I met at the last staff Christmas party."

"Really?"

Shelley nodded, but didn't elaborate, and Dane could practically feel Cayden's restless energy pulsing by his side.

"What was her name?" Cayden asked.

"Gosh, I don't know. Hold still, Dane." She laid a gauzy mask-shaped cloth over his face with strategic cut-outs for him to see and breathe through and dabbed it down to the oozy mask beneath.

"Was her name Lucy?"

Shelley laughed. "See. I told you. Persistent. Hmm, Lucy… let me think. No. I don't think so. June, maybe? Something like that. She wore these amazing dangly earrings that she'd made herself. They had beautiful stones set in them that matched her eyes. Just like yours. Amber, I think."

"Hazel," Dane corrected. Even though that wasn't a stone.

Lion eyes.

After she removed the charcoal-and-aloe face peel, Shelley smoothed on a light antibacterial treatment of lemongrass suspended in macadamia nut oil. "Let's leave that to sit for a few minutes for it to have its full medicinal effect."

The hydrating mask came next. She draped some kind of full facecloth over the top and a warm pack across his eyes, and she and Cayden chatted on.

Their voices gradually blended into the tinkling sounds of the water feature, the wild birdsong heralding a storm, and the bass growl of distant thunder, leaving Dane to drift in gentle comfort.

He didn't even need to tell his muscles to settle. The last bit of tension sighed out on Dane's breath, and he felt both heavy as lead and light as a feather, and the soft darkness took him into sleep.

Dane didn't know what brought him back.

A voice? Or the weight of a hand on his shoulder?

"What do you think, Cayden? Which would Dane's natural aroma team best with—native finger lime or ti-tree oil? That's native too."

"Ooh, that's nice. Finger lime, for sure."

"Thought you'd like that."

"Hey." Dane's protest sounded like he was talking underwater. He cleared his throat. "What about what I'd like? It's my skin."

"Sorry, Dane. I just thought…" Shelley's words petered out. "Sorry. Here. Smell this."

Still blinded by the towel, he sniffed.

A sharp aroma powered up his nose. "Holy crap! What is that?"

"Ti-tree. Now try this one."

Hesitantly, he inhaled again.

"Mmm…better."

"Native finger lime it is."

Well, fuck. Cayden was right. "Go on then."

Dane shivered as she lifted the blanket to expose his left arm, then smoothed oil over his shoulder and spread it around and down to his hand and fingers, stroking smooth and firm the entire length.

As his body heat warmed the oil, the tangy aroma came in subtle waves.

"Why's everything you're putting on Dane's face edible, Shelley?" Cayden asked. "You're such a tease." From the rustle and soft thud beside his ear, Dane figured Cayden clutched his grumbling stomach.

Another low rumble chased her laughter.

"That wasn't me."

"Mm-hmm."

"It wasn't! Although it could have been. I'm withering away here."

"Don't think you could wither if you tried." Dane threw out.

"Oi!"

Dane chuckled. The man was so easy to get a rise out of.

"Shush, the both of you," Shelley admonished. "How's that kind of pressure, Dane? Do you prefer a lighter or a firmer touch?"

"Firm."

A rumbly sound came from Cayden, and it wasn't his stomach.

Dane had to contain himself not to crack the drying mask with a smile.

Continuing the smooth movements, Shelley's hands glided around and along his muscles, all the way to his fingertips, over and over. Easing down his arm, she focused on his hands, separating and pulling on each finger, spreading the oil, working it into his knuckles. The warm, citrus scent cleared his mind, lulling him again.

Then he felt cool air on his right arm, and tentative, less-practiced hands started stroking.

Cayden.

Dane consciously slowed his breathing.

Mimicking Shelley's more certain hands, Cayden's oiled fingertips swept down the sensitive inside of his right arm to his palm, where Dane's nerves fluttered and jerked.

If Shelley on her own, or Cayden on his own, had taken point on the massage, his body would have known how to react. Instead, their out-of-sync touch was a confusing battering of comfort and ease versus heat and desire.

Eventually, they aligned in a sustained synchronous pull on his middle fingers. Each side of him hummed—only for entirely different reasons.

Shivering, Dane felt the shift in air pressure before a crack of thunder charged across the sky.

Cayden leaped, pulling Dane's finger, hard.

"Ow! I kinda need that finger, you know."

"Shut up," Cayden grumbled, and Dane smiled.

Dane didn't care if Shelley could hear him when he turned his head like a sunflower to the sun and whispered, "that finger has plans tonight."

Light flashed at the edges of the eye mask, chased by a sharp crack of thunder, and Cayden made a cough-squeak sound that Dane interpreted as proposal accepted.

Impatient, Dane pulled his hand from Shelley's hold and nudged the blackout mask from his eyes. The bright glare of day flared across his vision. He blinked away the afterimages and sat up to get a better view out of the hut's wide picture window.

Heavy, grey-green clouds loomed overhead from the east and cast bilious gloom across the wide crater valley. Squalling wind stirred the dense rainforest canopy. And a flock of white cockatoos took off with a squawk in protest as they rushed to escape the fast-approaching storm.

"Jesus." Cayden brushed the shivers from his bare arms. "It's like Armageddon."

Cayden's words seemed to trigger the gladiatorial battle— rain roared on the corrugated iron roof and the wild green canopy danced to the beat of its wild drum.

CHAPTER THIRTY-ONE

CAYDEN

Dane's face loomed in the stormy darkness.

Cayden's breath hitched. "Dane?" His voice rose, questioning, though he wasn't too sure what he was asking. *Are we gonna fuck?* Sounded brash, even for him.

They stood in no-man's-land between their two haven doors, shivering, rain running from their hair in rivulets.

"You're steaming," Dane whispered.

"You're hot, too," Cayden whispered back.

A tiny smile flickered on Dane's lips before he took Cayden's jaw in both hands and leaned in.

The first kiss was gentle—a soft brush of lips and a slow sweep of the tip of his tongue.

Then Dane speared his fingers into Cayden's dripping wet hair, tilted his head ever so slightly, pressed a bit firmer, and swooped in a bit deeper—all tongue and teeth and bristled cheeks. Dane growled into the kiss. His fingers gripped and tugged at Cayden's hair, and the soggy world stripped away. All Cayden knew was Dane's taste and touch and heat.

He smoothed his oil-slicked hands over Dane's bare back, trying to feel every bit of skin at once. The man's defined muscles bunched and eased, and his delving tongue loved and left in teasing synchrony.

Cayden wanted more.

He felt a tug at his waist and realised Dane pulled at his soaked shirt.

Dane didn't bother to unbutton the cotton, just pulled it up and over his head, catching Cayden's ear as he yanked in haste. The offending cotton landed with a wet slap on the wooden deck.

Dane must have noticed his flinch because he closed the gap and laved Cayden's lobe, doing nothing to soothe and everything to evoke desire.

"That's it," Dane growled huskily into his ear, and Cayden felt the button on his shorts give.

Locked together, Cayden could feel their heartbeats thrum in rapid concert as Dane manoeuvred them through Dane's door and into his haven. They shuffled across the wooden floor with singular focus till Cayden felt Dane's mattress behind his knees.

With barely a bounce, the soft bed cushioned their landing, and it was no longer just warm hands and strong lips and that all-consuming tongue that had Cayden flying. The weight of Dane's body, rough hair, slick skin, and, best of all, the hot, naked cord of his rock-hard cock, made Cayden feel like he was going to shoot off like a rocket.

Dane arched and ground down hard. Once. Twice.

"Fuck, fuck, fuck!" Cayden cried, racing far too quickly to the edge.

Overwhelmed, he tapped desperately at Dane's shoulder, not even knowing if he was asking the man to *stop, stop, stop,* or to *go, go, go,* and his mind screamed *NO!* when Dane slowed his hips to a barely perceptible grind.

Dane clearly wasn't able to read Cayden's mind because instead of speeding up he eased down to cover Cayden, he married their chests together and licked sweetly at each corner of Cayden's mouth, left, then right.

One gigantic tease of a move.

Cayden would have complained if the care Dane took wasn't such a fucking turn-on.

He instinctively chased the heat, jerking up into the groove at Dane's hip, slick with shared precum.

"Yeah," Dane encouraged breathily, and manhandled him up the bed till they were again plastered together.

Torrential summer rain beat down on their shared haven roof—a constant battering that swamped the air, enveloping them in heavy, intoxicating heat.

Cayden shoved his heels into the mattress and thrust up, declaring in no uncertain terms exactly what he wanted.

In response, Dane hooked a hand under Cayden's left knee and pressed his abdomen firm into the sensitive skin on the inside of Cayden's thigh.

When Dane eased away, Cayden couldn't stop himself from whining in protest, and he scrambled madly to hold them together.

Dane didn't disappear. He just eased south, dropping wet kisses in an agonizingly slow, meandering path from clavicle to cock. His wicked fingers randomly touched and rubbed and smoothed and squeezed till every square inch of Cayden's skin thrummed.

"Best fucking organ," he groaned, and his body, undecided if it wanted to sprawl open or clench shut, shuddered and shifted in search of more.

Dane reached to cover Cayden's mouth. "Hush," he said.

Having none of that, Cayden nipped the pad of his middle finger. "Fuck hush." He drew Dane's fingertip inside his mouth.

Dane seemed to ignore Cayden's sharp teeth and the twisting fingers in his hair as his tongue continued on its merry way down Cayden's happy trail and traced between drips of precum like some kind of twisted dot-to-dot game. Dane's regrowth mercilessly sandpapered Cayden's aching cockhead, and all Cayden could do was groan under the onslaught.

By the time Dane's tongue made it down to his sack, Cayden felt flayed alive. The man could draw and quarter him and he'd have no defence.

Did he care?

Fuck, no.

He tried one last time to position Dane's mouth right where he wanted him—hot and tight around his cock—but Dane resisted.

Cayden sucked and lashed Dane's finger in a blatant demonstration of what he wanted the man to do for his cock, but Dane didn't seem to get that memo, either.

"Fo' fug' sa'," he garbled, before Dane pulled the finger out of his mouth, gleaming wet. "Don't be an arse—"

The term *swallowed whole* didn't do the moment justice. Cayden's hips bucked, once, twice, three times, totally out of his control, as he discovered just where that wet finger had gone.

"—hole!"

Yep. Right there.

Not knowing which he preferred—the hot vacuum on his dick or the firm drill in his hole—Cayden's hips jack hammered between the two, till electricity fired deep in his core and there was no holding back.

Whole body straining for release, he tapped Dane's shoulder in warning, but it was far too late. He came, quaking, deep into Dane's throat.

Cayden couldn't see Dane swallow. Next time, he promised himself as his chin thrust up to the ceiling and he jerked with the final payment, he'd lay his palm flat on the man's throat and feel it go down.

Dane released his hold on the back of Cayden's thigh to stroke himself off, but that wicked finger maintained its ministrations, still massaging deep to urge the last spurt of seed out and onto his hungry tongue.

Cayden lay sprawled on his back, legs and arms askew, eyes riveted to Dane's left shoulder as it flexed rapid-fire. He thought he should probably help the guy out, but the tidal wave of lethargy crashed over him, and he lay, unable to do anything but watch.

Dane stared back. Blue eyes, winter fierce. Neck flared red. Chest heaving with desperate need. His movements stuttered, then lurched, and he came with a deep growl, and collapsed on top of Cayden in a sweaty, gorgeous heap.

The sight and feel of Dane undone made Cayden's gut curl—his want for the man suddenly so close to need that it scared him.

So, of course, instead of saying something sexy, or clever, or even sweet, he patted Dane on the head, like a fucking puppy, and uttered the stellar phrase, "Gotta love the two-pronged approach."

Yeah. Good one, Cayden.

Dane breathed heavily as he rolled off and onto his back, arm slack across his eyes as though he couldn't bear to look.

To be fair, Cayden couldn't really blame him.

Infinite minutes later, Dane stirred. He lazily turned his head and raised his evil eyebrow. "Two-pronged." Dane snorted, and Cayden caught a flash of teeth. "Good one."

Was he in a dream? Cayden wondered.

Dane yawned and rolled toward him. He pulled one pillow down to scrunch under his head and lay his right arm over Cayden's waist.

Not holding tight, but solid.

Real.

Dane's fingertips idly stroked Cayden's soft skin on his other side. It tickled a bit, but Cayden didn't protest. He just grasped the searching hand, held on, and, like Dane, he closed his eyes and slept.

CHAPTER THIRTY-TWO

DANE

Cayden was channelling Sheridan Brown again. Low on the deep wooden steps of the visitor's centre, he sat dressed in half of his beige safari outfit, sans shirt. With his canteen full of ceramic-filtered water in one hand and a bag of raw cashews in the other, he gazed off into the distance.

"You look like you're waiting for a hippopotamus to appear," Dane said.

"Don't be silly, Dane. Hippopotami aren't endemic to Australia."

"Crocodile, then."

With a teasing grin, Cayden pulled his feet a half inch further from the water's edge.

According to their cartoonish paper map, the Upper Noosa River everglades followed a narrow and windy path, north of Lake Cootharaba, into the wild dunes of the Great Sandy National Park.

Dane held the edge of the canoe firm against the stepped wooden jetty, waiting for Cayden to finish his snack and get settled in the front. After nearly an hour on the water, they were finally getting the hang of the thing. Crossing the shallow lake had been straightforward, with hardly any breeze to throw them off their north-easterly course toward the northern edge of Fig Tree Lake.

Paddling was easy, but Dane knew he'd be feeling the repetitive motion later in the day. He already felt a twinge between his shoulder blades. Not sore enough to warrant a ninja-level massage from Jade, but he could probably convince Cayden to reciprocate with a soothing rubdown.

An occasional light breeze fluttered the low, scrappy tree-tops and rippled the tea-coloured lake water before all settled once again into perfect stillness.

Birds and frogs and insects sang their songs in pops and coos and whips and warbles. The sounds echoed eerily across the water.

Cayden capped his water bottle, zip-locked his bag of nuts, and grabbed for the edge of the canoe. "I feel like we're playing hooky from our girlfriends."

"Speak for yourself. I never had a girlfriend."

"What?" One foot in the canoe, one foot out, Cayden twisted, sending the boat careening. "Never?"

"Cayden! Sit the fuck down, would you?" Dane grabbed the jetty edge.

"Oops, sorry." He sat and waited for the canoe to stabilize before he looked back over his shoulder. "No, but seriously? You never did the girlfriend thing?"

Dane let go of the jetty and unthreaded his paddle from the canoe struts. "No. Didn't see the point since, you know, I'm gay."

"Right."

Cayden's strangled laugh-huff could have meant anything, but Dane didn't bother trying to interpret it. He dug his paddle into the tea-coloured water and pulled.

"You didn't just pretend? Never?"

"No. Now, are we done with the twenty questions yet? Ready to paddle?"

"Aye, aye, Captain."

Just as Dane was beginning to feel the serenity of the water and the reflections and the wide blue open sky, Cayden returned to his interrogation.

"Okay, so, no girlfriends, but you know what I mean— this feels like nicking off with a school camp crush."

"You saying you have a crush on me, Mr. Spicer?"

"No." It might have been Dane's imagination, but Cayden's neck looked a little pinker. "But, just, like..." He waved his paddle around his head, drips flying everywhere, explaining nothing at all.

"Reliving my teen years isn't in my top five list of favourite activities." Truth be told, it wasn't even in Dane's top fifty list of favourite activities. Being a teenager was crap. Why would he want to relive it?

"It's a fantasy, Dane. Go with it."

"Fine," he grumbled. "I'm imagining a younger, shaggier, hornier Cayden." Yeah, if he was totally honest, that probably would've inspired a teenage crush.

"So…"

Dane groaned.

"I was just wondering…if…like…you know…"

"For fuck's sake. Spit it out." Cayden was right. It was like being back in high school.

"…the other night…"

Dane knew in an instant what other night Cayden meant.

Not last night, no…Cayden meant the night Dane had secretly plastered himself to the man's back like human glue, then left in the morning without saying a word.

Yeah, he knew that night.

Dane just paddled. What could he say?

Cayden did a quarter-head turn—not enough to make

eye contact—then squared his shoulders and dug deeper into the water. "When I woke up, I could have sworn someone had been there. Slept there. With me, I mean. Did you…?"

Dane opened his mouth to answer, but nothing came out. How could he explain the drive to sleep with the man? To seek comfort and peace in his arms?

Jesus. He sounded like a romance novel.

What next?

Poetry?

A fucking sonnet?

Hell, no.

With no answer he was willing to give, Dane tried to duck the question with a jest. "Have you been leading Edie on again, Cayden? Shame on you for making her walk the steep path to your haven instead of you going to hers. Have you no respect for your elders?"

His joke fell like a lead sinker.

"It's okay if it was you. I mean. Always welcome. But maybe stick around next time. Wake me up. Let me know you're there. A good sleep is great. Very restorative. But I'm not opposed to a bit of nookie, you know?"

Dane did know, but he didn't know what to say.

"If you weren't there, then…" Cayden's ears flushed pink.

Still corralling his thoughts, Dane concentrated on steering the canoe. He dipped his paddle in the water and pulled long and hard, then knocked the paddle snug against the rim of the wooden canoe with the flat of his right hand, turning the paddle into a keel to keep them on course.

Three paddles later, Dane was still no closer to being able to explain his actions—his presence in Cayden's bed or his stealthy departure. How could he own up to it when he didn't even know what *it* was?

"Just tell me, for fuck's sake." Cayden gave Dane a half-beat to answer, then said, "Here. I'll help. Repeat after me—I, Dane…ah, what's your last name again?"

Yeah. That pissed him off. Though why that was, Dane didn't know. It wasn't like he'd ever swapped surname with any of his previous bed partners. Sometimes not even first names. The true outlier was him knowing Cayden's surname.

He cleared his throat. "Faulks."

Cayden's shoulders dropped, and he rolled his neck. Dane could practically feel the crick, crick, crick from two meters away in the back of the canoe.

"Okay then, repeat after me—I, Dane Faulks…"

He snorted.

"Oh, come on… what will it hurt?" Cayden asked. "Your pride?"

Touché.

"Fine. I, Dane Faulks."

Cayden nodded with approval and gave the second line, "…admit that I…"

"Admit that I."

"…snuggled Cayden Spicer, the most gorgeous, most scin-tillating man in all of creation."

That was going too far. "You're not that clever."

"Good thing I never claimed to be most clever, then."

"No. Just the most gorgeous and most scintillating."

"Now you've got it. Good boy, Dane. And the rest?"

Cute he could just about cope with. Condescending, he could not. "'Good boy, Dane'? I swear, if you pat me on the head…"

"That would never happen," Cayden said. "Although it's heartening to hear you use the future tense. God. Just imagine the future if we stuck together, eh? Weird."

Weird, indeed. "Your immediate future looks very soggy to me."

Instead of dipping the paddle neatly into the water to

propel them forward, Dane reversed the paddle and slapped the surface of the lake. Water arced across the front half of the canoe.

"Oi!" Cayden hollered.

"Serves you right."

"For what? Forcing you to admit you like snuggling?" Cayden laughed and returned the watery favour.

"Hey!" Dane splashed again.

"Take that, you super-snuggler, you." Cayden giggled and splashed back, and their cross-purposes sent the canoe careening again.

"Woah!" Dane hollered. "Enough."

Cayden stopped with his paddle across his lap and twisted just enough for Dane to see his full, open face and that vulnerable smile.

Shit.

"Fine. You got me. I slept in your bed. With you. Technically. But I wasn't snuggling. That's not what that was."

"So, why all the cloak and dagger? It's not like I hadn't rolled out the welcome wagon."

Cayden was right. Dane had been the one to reject the invitation. But he didn't have a safe explanation for that. Not without telling Cayden about Alice and, well, everything.

All he could do was shrug. "Didn't want to wake you."

Cayden's eyes shuttered a bit at his non-answer. He turned back around, picked up his paddle, and pulled strong. "Future reference, I like nocturnal nookie. I'm cool with you coming and going. Mostly with the coming. Ha! But there's no need to be so sneaky. Not unless it turns you on." He tilted his head, and his curls moved just enough to shimmer in the morning light. "I mean, we can do magic tricks if you like. I could pull a rabbit out of a hat…"

"Stop."

"No, really. It'll be fun." Cayden's shoulders shook with

silent laughter. "Not sure where we'd get a rabbit since they're banned in Australia. Maybe a science lab. Fucking animal testing. We could adopt an old one. Or do they use rats and gerbils these days? Or cane toads? Don't they hate those fuckers up here in Queensland?"

"Cayden," Dane warned.

"Or you could pull my rabbit out of my hat…" He flashed that wild smile again. "If you get my drift."

Dane got the drift. "Please, never, ever call your cock a rabbit again."

Cayden snorted. "Shit, Dane. Do people know how hilarious you are?"

Dane smiled at the back of Cayden's head and settled back into the familiar, metronomic rhythm of paddling as they canoed closer to The Narrows.

Herons flapped their great wings as they gracefully came in to land. In the distance, the occasional sound of powerboats broke the near silence, before peace again descended. Every time, Dane was brought back to himself and Cayden in a flimsy canoe, surrounded by the enormity of nature.

Cayden seemed entirely at home, but it brought Dane up short. He couldn't help contrasting it to his regular life, which he'd always thought of as big and important and consequential.

As the CFO of Carter Medical Supplies, he was the instigator of change. Every move he made had an actual effect on people's lives.

His choices had consequence.

His efforts saved lives.

Dane knew that wasn't his ego talking. He'd seen the stats.

But suddenly, that world felt comparatively small.

Being out on the water, surrounded by wilderness, paddling up the flowing river, that seeped from the groundwater, that fell from the clouds in the sky, that rose from the oceans, that filled from the rivers, that… yeah, that cyclical world felt big.

Seriously big.

Consequentially big.

"Beautiful, isn't it," Cayden said, quietly.

Dane didn't need to pause to think of the right answer. "Yes."

"Humbling, too."

"Mmm." He wanted to repeat the yes again. But didn't.

It was too much to admit to.

The wild was calming and peaceful and stressful and overwhelming.

He wasn't ready to admit that it also made him feel small.

In the back of their little canoe, he was the navigator, and the keel, and the motor, but that didn't mean he knew where they were going, or where they'd end up. Cayden had thrown his equilibrium way off, and Dane just wasn't sure anymore. Not of himself. Not of anything much at all.

"Everything's where it ought to be," Cayden said in a dreamy, sanguine voice. "Including us. Don't you think?"

No. Yes. I don't know.

All Dane could do was trust in forward momentum, so he dipped his paddle back into the tea-coloured water and pulled.

CHAPTER THIRTY-THREE

CAYDEN

Liberation welled in Cayden's soul.

He'd given Dane stick for presuming to take the rear navigator's seat in the canoe, but Cayden was actually glad to have the reprieve from decision-making—the freedom to simply enjoy the ride.

All he had to do was keep paddling.

Keep going forward.

But it felt significant, as though he was paddling toward some cusp of possibility—toward where he *ought* to be.

"Do you see those pencil-shaped things poking up out of the water, Dane?" Cayden pointed to the mangrove shore, where millions of the things stood proud above the surface of the tidal lake. "Those are pneumatophores. They allow the plant to absorb oxygen." He took a deep breath in, at one with all the living things.

Dane hmm'd, just like he had for every other random factoid that Cayden had thrown the man's way that day.

It took him back to his university days—learning about ecology and habitats and the delicate balance of water catchments. Even back in high school, he'd been passionate about championing places like the Upper Noosa River—lakes, oceans, deserts, reefs—all unique, and all the same, all needing saving, one truth at a time.

And then Lucy disappeared, and that future evaporated.

But there, in the aptly named The Narrows, with all the noise and clutter of regular human life gone, the natural world pressed in—the wild plant species; the birds flying overhead; the insects that dipped in and out of the tannin-stained water, making tiny concentric circles of impact on the glassy surface.

He couldn't not see the challenges to the unique Everglades environment, just as he couldn't not feel the peace and energy it generated in his soul. It sang and screamed to him in equal measure.

Everything was so eerily still and the reflections so clear that it was easy to confuse up from down—water, trees, sky, clouds—all of it mirrored. Even the canoe painted their wash with a wavering red double. And if he turned his head just a little bit more, he could also see Dane's reflection in the water—upright and strong, powering along with sure strokes.

Alone.

Together.

In nature.

Although they were paddling against the current, progress came fast. Soon, they came to the first campsite at Harry's Hut, where multiple boats, canoes, and kayaks crowded the dock.

"Let's just cruise on by. It's not that far to campsite one," Dane said. "Take a break there."

"Slave driver," he joked, but upped his stroke rate. He didn't want to be around all those people. Not yet.

Half an hour later, they saw the short jetty running parallel to the shore at campsite one. A couple of women sat out on camp chairs watching over the river, enjoying a spot of morning tea.

"Looks like the neighbourhood watch," Cayden joked lamely.

When Dane didn't redirect the canoe toward that jetty either, Cayden didn't protest. Not for real.

"You're going to owe me a massage," he called out.

"How do you figure?"

"No stops mean I haven't received the requisite breaks my union demands. Therefore, I deserve compensation."

He heard a soft laugh behind him. "What, the Front Seat Passengers Unite Union?"

"Nope. The Human Motor Union."

"Motor? I'm doing triple the work here—paddling, navigating, and steering. How come you get a massage and I don't?"

"Who says you don't?"

That shut Dane up.

Temporarily.

"Shall I sic Jade the massage ninja on you? You could take my next appointment."

"Is that really her name?"

"She said, 'Hi Dane, I'm Jade. Come on in.' I didn't think to interrogate her further."

"Off your game, eh?"

Dane gave a crack of laughter. "Guess so."

"Jade. It's so stereotypical. How would you like it if I called you Nigel?"

"Why would you do that? I'm not a nerd?"

"See!"

Cayden didn't need to turn his head to know what the man's expression would be—wide smile and a slight crinkle in the skin beside his deep blue eyes.

Everything about the day felt fresh—bubbling with new

possibilities. What would happen if he tried a different tack?

He plunged his paddle back into the water, braced his shoulders, and pulled. "So, I was thinking."

"Danger!"

"Fuck off. I was thinking that instead of asking Jade to work out our new knots, we could give each other a massage."

Dane didn't answer.

He heard the rear paddle dip and knock, dip and knock. The birds twittered and tweeted. The water rushed by.

Still, Dane said nothing.

"Well?" Cayden prompted, listening intently for the man's reply.

"I think that could be arranged," Dane said with a decidedly gravelly voice.

"Excellent." He listened again for Dane's rhythm, leaned forward an extra bit on the next stroke, and ploughed into the water with revitalised intent. His future looked brighter by the minute.

Ten minutes later, campsite two came into view.

Dane swerved toward it, but just as the canoe scooted alongside the jetty, a young couple stepped out of the trees, hand in hand.

Both his and Dane's paddles missed a beat.

"For fuck's sake," he heard Dane mutter.

"We're stopping at campsite three," Cayden said. "Don't care if anyone's there. I've heard the views across the Pacific are amazing from the top of the sand blow."

He heard a rustle of paper.

"I think you mean the Cooloola Sandpatch."

"Patch. Blow. Same diff."

"Not in my world." Dane muttered.

"Ha!" Cayden grinned so hard his cheeks hurt. "Good to know."

CHAPTER THIRTY-FOUR

DANE

Dane grabbed the backpack and caught up with Cayden at the information board at the back of the campground. The simple map of the Great Sandy National Park showed green for bushland, bisected by the blue Upper Noosa River and the larger blue block of the Pacific Ocean further to the east. Between the two watercourses, an island of bright yellow marked the sandy dunes of the Cooloola Sandpatch.

Dane noted their current position and the black-dotted walking track that zigzagged across the map to the patch of yellow.

"Looks simple enough." He pulled the other strap over his left shoulder and jostled the pack to balance its weight across his back.

Cayden was checking his watch.

"Everything okay?" Dane asked.

"It's further than I thought." Cayden pointed at the walking track on the information board. "Twelve kilometres isn't a toddle in the bush. Especially hiking on soft, dry sand."

"Two and a half hours, three if we dawdle."

Cayden nodded. "Bit over, maybe, if we want to check the place out properly." He flashed a smile. "Have a toboggan on the sand."

Dane checked the time. "We'd be pushing it."

Dane didn't want to disappoint Cayden, but they'd need a time machine to hike the path, play in the sand, and return the canoe by late afternoon. "It's a bit of a stretch."

"Yeah." Cayden deflated.

The urge to wrap the man in a hug came with no warning at all—it was weird and wrong and... "Next time," he said, before he could think. As though there was a possibility that in the future they'd return. Together.

He might have been enjoying Cayden's company for the moment, but all the talk of *we* and *us* and *their* and *them* would soon end. Dane knew *their* association was momentary.

Temporary.

Finite.

Which meant he had to be opportunistic—to go for it while he had the chance.

Dane rolled his stiffening shoulders and looked around the clearing.

Gangly paperbark trees with droopy gum leaves cast patchy shade haphazardly throughout the large campground, rubbing up against low grasses and the occasional scrubby bush. A few small tents arranged in a cluster looked shut up tight, but the rest of the sandy campground was deserted. It wasn't private, but, for the moment, they were alone.

He pointed into a smaller side clearing. "There's a shady spot over there. We could have a swim, then Gladioli's picnic, then trade those massages."

Cayden snorted. "Revealing your exhibitionist tendencies now, Dane?"

Dane groaned at the terrible pun. "Can't I be just hungry and sore?"

Cayden just shook his head and quirked a half smile, then strolled back toward the river. "Come on." He curled his arm in an encouraging wave.

"Where are you going?"

"Not just me. *We* are going further upstream. The type of massage I want requires privacy." Cayden sashayed his sweet arse back toward the jetty.

Dane needed no more prompting.

The river there flowed wide, which was a good thing. Dane didn't think he could have spared any attention to paddle around tight corners or watch for submerged logs. Not when he had Cayden's back in view. With each stroke, Dane watched his muscles bunch and relax, bunch and relax.

He was so caught up watching Cayden that Dane didn't notice the small group until someone squealed, "Snake!"

Dane's gaze jerked further upriver, and he mistimed a stroke, knocking his paddle too hard on the side of the canoe.

Two bright orange canoes, each with a young child at the front, an adult at the back, and a mountain of camping gear between, wallowed low in the water.

He did his best not to make eye contact with any of them, but Cayden didn't seem to have read his mind.

"Hey, just leaving?" Cayden pulled his paddle from the water and rested it across his splayed knees, while Dane paddled just enough to keep them even with the shore.

Dane ground his teeth with impatience. What he wouldn't give to take Cayden home to his apartment, where he could have the man entirely to himself. No interruptions.

The thought took him aback.

He'd never taken any man back to his home. None but his closest friends.

"Sacrosanct," the guys called it. Mocking him. As though his friends were any less guarded about their privacy.

"Yeah," the woman said, "pity you two weren't here a bit earlier. We could have had three-a-side soccer."

God, no.

"That's a real shame," Dane said. He knew he sounded about five percent earnest, but he and Cayden had places to be and things to do—chatting with strangers was not on his agenda.

Cayden gave the family a jaunty, "Next time," as though that would ever happen.

Just as Dane thought they were getting away, the littler of the two kids swung his pointer finger at Cayden and hollered. "Snake!"

"It wasn't a snake. It was a goanna," the older kid said. "Tell him, Dad."

"Was not."

"Was too."

"Was!" The kid's scream practically pierced Dane's eardrums.

"Wow!" Cayden interrupted, stopping the kid short. "Did you let it climb you?"

They stared at him, wide-eyed, till the older kid got brave enough to speak. "No."

"But that's what you've gotta do. Otherwise, it'll gobble you up. Isn't that right, Dane? You've gotta let it climb you. Just like a tree." He flung his arms out high and wide, stiff and tall like a tree.

"Careful!" Dane grabbed the sides of the canoe as it careened.

Cayden splashed him in return.

On purpose.

The bastard.

Over their shyness, the kids giggled, lapping up Cayden's attention.

Dane bristled with impatience and a stupid lump in his throat. He'd never be that natural with kids. Not that he cared what children thought of him. Or anyone. Not really. Although he found himself not wanting to disappoint Cayden.

"Don't listen to him," Dane said. "Cayden here is afraid of possums."

"Hey! Possums aren't natural, Dane."

"Oh, really? What are they, then?"

"The devil's spawn," he said, as though it were obvious.

"Ri-ight."

The family's two canoes drifted with the natural flow of the river. As the three canoes slowly crossed paths and separated out again, Cayden waved to the kids and saluted the parents. Then he turned to face forward, dipped his paddle in the water, and stroked.

"Guess the brakes are off now," Cayden said.

"What?" Dane pretended to misunderstand.

"The brush-off," Cayden pressed as they fully rounded the bend where the family had come from and saw campsite four. "Not terribly subtle, are you?"

"I was polite."

"Mm-hmm."

Dane ignored him and took in the promising stillness of the site. All he could he could hear over the rush and gurgle of the river were the cicadas singing their song. "It looks empty."

"Thank you, Gaia." Cayden hopped out as they beached the canoe on the white sand. He hauled the front of the canoe onto the shore and held it steady for Dane to jump out.

Dane didn't need the help, but he leaned on Cayden's

shoulder anyway, enjoying the give of the man's sun-warmed skin and the muscles beneath. He squeezed the spot where Cayden's curls brushed his nape. It earned him a deep groan.

"It's all right," Dane hummed. He knew exactly what Cayden was thinking. "I'm hungry, too."

CHAPTER THIRTY-FIVE

CAYDEN

Everywhere Cayden looked, there was something fascinating to discover. Overhead, he spotted brown-and-white-speckled eastern osprey sailed high on invisible streams of air. Closer, luminescent dragonflies skimmed across the water, river eddies tugged and twisted against the flow, and debris spun and churned on their wild passage downstream.

Cayden floated spreadeagled in the cool water and squinted up through the sparse leaves of the shedding paper-bark gums. Under a foot of water, his tender bits were still pale as a slightly tannin-stained moon, but the rest of his pinkening skin would be sore tonight.

He tilted his head back to look upside down at Dane, still high on the bank, stumbling on the uneven sand as he tried to strip off his shorts.

The guy was usually so put-together, so fucking perfect. A ripple of quiet joy seeded deep in Cayden's chest at the man's demonstrated lack of coordination.

Cayden paddled with his hands, twirling around in the cool water to get a better, fuller look at him. He debated whether to interrupt the strip tease. 'Not' was the easiest answer to that question, but he itched to say something. To tease Dane a little.

Dane's skin had a pink sheen, too. They'd both slathered sunscreen on before they'd set out that morning, but time and sweat had erased its effectiveness.

At first, the cool of the river had soothed the sun's hot sting. The silky water shimmied and shivered in and around his every nook and cranny, washing away the sweat and the heat and the effort of the day. Cayden looked back to the shore, where Dane was stripping down to his very skimpy, very red swimsuit, and every single nerve receptor in Cayden's body woke up and took notice.

Oblivious to Cayden's avid gaze, Dane picked up his shorts, shook out the sand, and hung them over the rustic *Campsite 4* sign. Then he stretched.

"Jesus Christ," Cayden whispered to nobody, "it's like nature porn without the hessian."

Down boy.

Taking his own advice, he jack-knifed his hips deep into the dark water. But he didn't take his eyes off of Dane doing his should-be-illegal yoga moves.

Dane eventually finished and stepped out of the shade to where the sun highlighted the distinct line low on his hips where his shorts had hung while they canoed—pink above and creamy white below.

"Shoulda worn a rashie," Cayden called out.

Dane looked down at himself. Cayden's eyes continued to travel there too—since he'd practically been invited to ogle.

"The way UV reflects off of sand, we'd be lobsters by now if we'd gone to the Sandpatch."

"Sand blow." Cayden smirked.

Dane ignored him. "Without a rashie, you'd be combatting sand-rub, too."

"We, Dane. We'd be combatting sand-rub." He tsked.

"You're not going to get out of our future sand-tobogganing adventures that easily."

"Fantasy adventures, maybe." The water reached to Dane's knees.

"Mm-hmm…It would be that," Cayden teased, purposely skirting around Dane's point.

Dane rolled his eyes, but Cayden could see a little smile lurking there. Happiness.

Dane shivered as the water lapped at his crotch.

It really wasn't fair.

Cayden wanted to lap at Dane's crotch.

"Be brave, Dane. You can do it," he teased.

Dane flashed him the finger. "My mum used to say, 'Get out of the water. It's dangerous to swim on a full stomach.'"

"Ha! My stomach doesn't feel like it's been full for a decade. Maybe two."

"Even after Gladioli's incredible picnic?" Dane rubbed his stomach before it, too, disappeared underwater. "That King Island triple cream brie. Mmm. She definitely stepped it up a notch."

"And the baked beetroot chips," Cayden agreed. "Curious combo, but so good."

"Don't care. It went great with the zucchini fritters and green papaya salad."

"True. The roasted nuts were pretty good, too."

"Mmm-hmm."

"Gotta love a good nut—"

Dane pushed off into a perfect deep dive.

"—or two," Cayden finished saying to the trees and the birds and the insects and the water because Dane was nowhere in sight.

Dane crested a few feet further out into the river, flipped to his back, and floated starfish style.

Cayden did the same. He tilted his head back to take in

the same view of blue sky, the same puffy white clouds, and the same treetops wavering gently on the edge of his peripheral vision. Water filled his ears, and the sounds of the world above warped till all he knew was the light of the sun, the rush of the river, and distinct awareness that Dane was so close they could touch.

He felt warm and natural and loose, the way life ought to be. The tip of his toe touched Dane's—like some kind of upside-down, inside-out, Michelangelo fresco. It felt like a promise of a new normal.

Stupid. He ducked his face under the surface. Because what he and Dane had wasn't the sort of normal he could keep. Nothing about them was a promise. No matter how well they connected, he and Dane were temporary.

Cayden flipped over to look down at the muddy depths. He couldn't see very much, only as far as the light could stream in, but all he was looking for was a shift in perspective—a chance to re-set.

Restless, Cayden tumble-turned, blew a stream of bubbles, then surged up. As he broached the surface, he karate-chopped the water, sending an arc across Dane's uplifted face.

"Oi!" Dane hollered.

Cayden splashed the man again, full in the face, then took off, laughing. A few more metres out into the river, he spun around and tread water.

"What are you, twelve?" Dane slicked the water out of his eyes.

Ignoring him, Cayden sucked in a breath and duck-dived. He locked eyes on Dane's legs where the rays of the sun danced golden on his skin. Then he took a wide, strategic path, deep enough to stay undetected. He swam closer to Dane's arse, then surged up, grabbed his waistband, and yanked down.

The war was officially on.

With the element of surprise on his side, Cayden had the initial upper hand, but Dane's merman dexterity soon evened the field.

In a get-away-not-get-away move, Cayden dove again to grab Dane's ankles and pull him under.

Dane must have known his intent, though, because he let Cayden get close, then wrapped his legs around Cayden's chest and crocodile-rolled him around and around. Soon, they were a tangle of arms and legs, wrapped in a blanket of bubbles, not knowing up from down.

Dizzy, Cayden had no hope of recovery. But Dane must have found purchase on the silty river bottom because Cayden felt a jolt, and they suddenly surged together through the water and burst above the river surface.

A limpet in Dane's arms, Cayden spluttered and sucked in precious fresh air. He felt the rapid surge of Dane's chest against his own and realised that the man wasn't gasping for oxygen at all—he was laughing.

Giddy, Cayden wrapped his legs around Dane's waist and his arms around Dane's neck and went in for the lip-lock kill.

Dane might have won the battle, but, hearing Dane's open laughter, Cayden decided he'd absolutely won the war.

CHAPTER THIRTY-SIX

DANE

The prow of the canoe finally ground into the pebbled shore, and Cayden leaped out.

Not quite as eager, Dane pulled his paddle out of the water and lay it across his lap, arms like jelly.

Painful jelly.

Cayden leaned on the upright paddle. "Come on, Grandpa. Get your butt in gear."

"It's not like they're going to leave without us." If there was a hint of annoyance in Dane's voice, he had good reason. They'd spent far too long at campsite four and had to power back downriver and across the lake without a break to make it back on time. Dane was sore and cranky, and he wasn't above making Cayden pay for it—especially since it was the man's gorgeous skinny-dipping arse that'd delayed them in the first place.

"Maybe not, but do you really want to make someone wait just because you're a lazy arse?"

Lazy? "Need I remind you that I—"

"Navigated, and steered, and paddled. I know. Next time, I'll do the triple, and you can look at all the pretty things from the front. Then you'll realise it's not such a walk in the park."

"No, I won't."

"Yes, you will."

"No, I—" Dane sighed. When had they become twelve again? "Fine. If—"

"When."

He wasn't giving up on that specific qualifier. "*If* we ever come back to the Everglades, you can steer."

"What about the map? I want to navigate, too."

"No."

"No?"

"No."

They stared at each other for a full seven seconds.

Cayden was the first to break. "Fine, keep your bloody map." He blew a huff of hot air up, tousling his curls, then shouldered the backpack and stormed off.

If Dane was to rate the dramatic exit, he'd give it an eight-point-five.

"What would you give yourself, Dane?" he grumbled to himself as he sat alone in the back of the beached canoe, feeling like a bit of an idiot. What did it matter who'd sit in the back when there wouldn't even be a next time? "Three-point two, if you're lucky." His question had been rhetorical, but Dane was nothing if not real with himself.

Dane rolled his neck. The sunburn stung, and his muscles stiffened as they cooled. With a grunt, he hauled himself out of the canoe and into the warm shallows of the sandy lake. He hauled the canoe the rest of the way onto shore, gathered the last of their gear, and then turned to take one last mental image of the lake that glistened silver and blue in the early evening light.

On any other ordinary day, he'd be knocking off work and heading to the gym or the tennis court. After a workout, he'd grab an easy bite for dinner, pour himself a dram or two of Talisker, and sit out on his small balcony overlooking the river. Then he'd take himself off to bed to read a chapter before midnight struck, and the next day would begin…and the next, and the next, and the next.

Rinse and repeat.

That was his rhythm.

His normal.

None of that included canoe picnics, skinny-dipping, or dreamy lakeshore sunsets.

Dane curled his toes into the gritty sand at the edge of the lake.

It all felt so real. Tangible.

Far more real than his regular life.

Hell, after their day out on the water, even *he* felt more tangible.

He was sore, yes, but gone was the numbing exhaustion and the urgent drive to do, run, win.

In its place was a contented sort of tiredness that hummed through every muscle and nerve and bone in his body.

He felt good. Languid.

So good he didn't want it to stop.

Not yet.

Dane's shadow cast far in front of him, stretched thin over the rippling surface of the silvery lake. Sea birds flocked landward to roost. And Venus glimmered in the dark blue bowl of coming night.

He rubbed his hands together, rough and hot where he'd gripped the paddle for endless hours, then spread them out— two five-pointed starfish, floating side by side. Just like he and Cayden had been mere hours ago.

"Dane! Let's go!" Cayden hollered.

He took in the scene one more time and curled his toes

again into the wet sand, then sighed and turned his back on it.

Time to get back to true reality.

A burly, bearded stranger leaned out of the driver side windows of the familiar four-wheel-drive blazoned with the House of Glass Wellness Retreat logo. "Hey, Dane. I'm Tom." The guy slung his arm out the window to shake hands.

"Good to meet you, Tom." Dane took his hand. "I'm surprised not to see Shorty behind the wheel. He was so keen this morning."

"Keen's one word for it. Bit taken with your guy here, isn't he?" Tom chuckled, and Cayden's sunburned cheeks flushed a shade darker of pink. "Nah. Gordon had him doing something else. Secret gardener's business, or whatever. Not my scene. Jump on in, Dane. Let's get this show on the road. If I don't get you guys back in time for dinner, the boss'll shoot me." Tom thumped the steering wheel and ground the gears.

"Good plan." He rounded the vehicle and settled into the back seat.

"Gordon doesn't strike me as violent. Death by kale, maybe." Cayden's chuckle sounded false to Dane's ears. From the way Cayden gripped Tom's seat and leaned forward, the seat belt straining against his chest, Dane figured he must have missed something. What was Cayden fishing for?

Tom's cackle oozed honesty. "God, no. I'm talking about Gladioli. She's the real boss."

"The *real* boss? What do you mean? Is Gordon just a figurehead?"

"What?" Tom asked, puzzled.

Dane reached across to put a restraining hand on Cayden's hammering knee, then ventured a guess. "So, you and Gladioli are married, huh?"

Tom reset the rear-view mirror and beamed a grin at Dane. "Nah, mate. Living in sin. That's us. Gladdie runs the show. I just do her bidding. But, shh…don't tell her I know it. It's a game, see?"

Cayden's tension eased away, and the knee slowed to a shudder, but Dane didn't let go.

"Can't complain, though. Got me two beautiful babies out of it."

"Twins?" Dane asked, surprised. "I've only seen Gladioli with one baby."

"Nah. Grace is a solo-surfer. William was seven last May. He's too busy with friends to hang out at the retreat. Right social butterfly, that one. Hangs out with the circus people, mostly."

"Circus?" Cayden half-perked back to life.

"Yeah. Well, not a real circus. Not one that travels and performs and such. Just a bunch of folks who live in an old circus tent the next valley over. Been there so long they've trained vines to grow all over it. I don't judge, mind, but those folks are queer."

Back straightening reflexively, Dane asked, "They're all gay, or bi, or—?"

"God, no. Wouldn't care about that. But some of those folks are in la-la-land, one duck short of a flock, off their rocker, high in the treetops, if you get my meaning." He twirled a finger in the air. "I just feel bad for the kids. My Willy went for a sleepover with a schoolmate, and he came back with the strangest stories."

"Your willy went—" Cayden started, but Dane stopped him. He knew that voice meant trouble.

"What kind of stories?" he asked.

"Oh, you know…it's just different. All living together in one tent like that. Not much privacy. Luna's all right. She and the kids painted murals on the canvas—landscapes on the walls and an amazing star-scape on the ceiling. You can check it out if you like. It's only about an hour's hike from the retreat." He wavered a finger off to the right of the rough dirt road.

"North of the retreat?" Dane took a guess. He wanted to look at Cayden to see if he was hearing the same prize clue, but what if Tom gave some critical piece of information through his body language? He made do with a squeeze of Cayden's knee and kept his eyes on Tom.

"Sure. Yeah. North-ish." Tom waggled his hand. "I'm not great with directions."

Excellent. He squeezed Cayden's knee again, hoping the man knew how to interpret his message. Then Cayden lay his own hand on top and threaded their fingers together.

Instead of letting Dane relax, it keyed him up even more.

"Anyway. My Willy didn't recognise any of the constellations painted on the ceiling. He's a bit of a sci-fi nerd, so, y'know, he'd know." Tom flashed a smile back over his shoulder. "They're different, for sure, but some people think they're from another solar system. Alien species, they reckon."

Cayden's hand tightened, his threaded fingers curling in toward Dane's palm till they locked together—cog to cog.

"Aliens? Bit of a leap, don't you think, Tom?" Dane scoffed.

Tom shrugged. "They're harmless, so far as I can tell. Friendly, too. A bunch of circus folk work at the retreat since it's a sister community to the House of Glass going way back to when Gordon bought the property. You've probably met some of them."

"Really?" He squeezed Cayden's hand. "Who?"

"Oh, well, you've met Shorty. A couple of the teenagers help Gladdie out in the kitchen, chopping stuff for those crazy drinks you all get so excited about. Gardening and housekeeping. And there's the crafty people. There's a woman who comes to do essential oil therapy. Don't remember her name. She has this voice that puts me to sleep. Gladdie jokes we should record her speaking and play it back as a lullaby at bedtime." He shook his head. "Crazy woman. Why would I listen to another lady's voice while I'm shaking the sheets with her? And I don't mean doing laundry." He waggled his eyebrows.

Dane looked sideways, but Cayden was staring out the passenger window. All Dane could see was the mess of curls on the back of Cayden's head. Alone in his thoughts.

Dane cleared his throat. "Gladioli's quite the woman. We love her food." It was the only response he could think of.

"Too right," Tom said with gusto and stomped on the accelerator—eager to get home to his better half.

CHAPTER THIRTY-SEVEN

DANE

Tom barrelled the four-wheel-drive down the gravel approach to the retreat, under the stone arch, and ground to a halt at the pagoda.

Déjà vu, Dane thought.

The place looked exactly the same as the evening he'd arrived at the retreat, except everything felt different. He felt different. His world felt different. And Cayden's firm grip on his hand sure as hell felt different.

Cayden let go long enough to get out his side and round the vehicle while Dane slid out and groaned as he landed on the gravel. In the space of twenty minutes, all of his muscles had seized up.

Cayden grabbed his elbow.

Dane wasn't sure if it was to hold on or hold him up. Either option was fine by him.

He turned to face Cayden. "Dinner, shower, debrief, sleep," he proposed, then pulled Cayden along the path toward the hub.

Cayden resisted.

"What? No! We have to go to the circus. Right now." He

spun, grabbed Dane by the hand instead, and dragged him the opposite way toward their havens. "We just need shoes and a torch."

"In the dark? It's going to be night soon. Tom said it'd take an hour to walk there, and we don't even know the way."

"We'll ask around. Someone here will know where it is."

"I thought you wanted to stay under the radar?"

"Not much point of that when we've found Lucy."

"Maybe. We've *maybe* found Lucy. We don't know if we have yet," Dane cautioned.

He should have been supporting Cayden's efforts to find his sister. He knew that. But something in Dane resisted. Was he simply being the voice of reason? Was he trying to save Cayden from hurt? Or was he slowing everything down to stave off the inevitable time when Cayden didn't need his help anymore? To put off the time when he no longer had an excuse to stay at the retreat?

That idea was so out of character, Dane didn't even know what to do with it.

Cayden rounded on him. "What are you talking about? You heard Tom. The circus tent is full of people who've been here since Gordon founded the retreat. And there's another artist. Someone who paints murals. What more evidence do you want? In fact, never mind about shoes." He whipped Dane around by the hand and started back in the opposite direction. "Let's go see if we can borrow someone's car. Can't ask Tom. He'll know where we're going. Who's on staff tonight?"

"Cayden." Dane grabbed his hand.

"What?"

Trouble was, he didn't know *what*. He didn't even know his own mind anymore, let alone what Cayden ought to do.

At the hub deck, Cayden shook off Dane's hand and raced up the stairs. He dodged through the crowded dining room, and made straight for Shiloh, the nutritionist, who doled out broth from the enormous steaming vat.

"Sorry. Sorry," Dane apologised to Anna and Lissa and Bernice and Edie as he made his way through the human bottleneck.

"But it's an emergency!" he heard Cayden cry out and arrived in time to see Shiloh do a once-over down Cayden's body.

"Are you hurt?" I don't see any blood. What's the emergency?"

Dane bristled as he sidled up close.

"It's…private." Cayden pinched his mouth shut and side-eyed Dane.

The nutritionist looked between them. Suspicion turned his eyes to slivers. "Are you guys trying to get to the pub? We had a couple do that last time. Totally screwed up their detox. Gordon threatened to throw them out."

"Focus, Shiloh." Cayden planted his fists on the table. "This. Is. An. Emergency. Is there a car we can borrow?"

Dane lightly touched his arm. He wanted to tell him to simmer down. Outrage rarely won arguments.

"I'll have to call Gordon. He's tonight's emergency contact. It's just me and Dwight on site."

"Okay." Cayden sighed. "Great. Let's do that."

"Hang on." Dane pulled him a few feet away, then softened his hold. "Let's just think about this for a minute." He dropped his voice three notches. "Do you really want to answer Gordon's questions tonight?"

"I don't care—"

"Yes, you do. What if these circus people have nothing to do with Lucy? What then? You'll have given away your best asset."

"What asset?" Cayden blinked. "You?"

"Me?" What the hell? "No. Your cover story is your best

asset. What reason could you give Gordon to lend us a car? Best-case scenario, he offers to give us a lift. Then where will we be?"

Cayden's jaw worked. "But she's so close," he whispered, desperation in his eyes.

"I know." Dane guided Cayden further away from prying eyes and ears, across to the far side of the dining room.

Cayden stood, his sunstruck visage rigid in the wide picture window.

Dane stared directly into Cayden's reflected lion eyes. He spoke, low and even, willing the man to hear sense.

"I get why you want to race off and save her, and you should do whatever you think is right. But if you want me there, then here's what I think we should do. Tomorrow morning, we act normal—get up, have breakfast, do whatever. I have a gym session with Fraser, then a massage. It's too late to cancel those without drawing attention. Late morning, we have our second art class. No way out of that. You know Leif will make a fuss if we're not there. Especially you. Then, straight after lunch, we head out." He pointed to the dark night out the window. "If anybody notices us leaving, we say we're going for a walk in the bush. Nobody will question that or want to come with us in the heat of midday. We find the circus tent. And maybe…maybe we find Lucy."

Hearing his sister's name, Cayden's eyes flared fierce and bright, and from the way he worked his jaw, Dane was sure he was grinding his teeth.

Dane turned away from their reflections and stepped closer to the man's side. "If she's not there, then we won't have lost anything. Your cover will still be intact. Nobody will suspect anything, and the investigation can go on."

Dane licked his sunburnt lips, feeling the sting in the cracks. It was only then that he realised he'd pressed his hand to the small of Cayden's back, in full view of everyone.

When had that happened?

He let it drop and stepped a half-centimetre away.

"That's if you want me there," he added. If Cayden didn't want his help, that was up to him. Dane could always find things to do—run the rim, cut a sweat in the gym, plan his escape...

The noise of the crowd pressed in on him, and Dane wanted to tell them all to fuck off.

Finally, Cayden turned so they were face on, then idly ran a knuckle down Dane's abdomen.

Dane couldn't tell if Cayden was aware of the touch or not. He stayed perfectly still, just in case his movement stopped the contact.

Cayden's nostrils flared, and he huffed out a loud breath through is nose. Eventually, though, he nodded. "Yeah. Okay."

Thank fuck.

"Okay. Good. That's good." God, he was an idiot. Dane clapped his hands together like a fucking seal performing a trick, then spun in search of inspiration. Broth! "Let's have a quick mug and get out of here. I can't wait to get out of these clothes."

Cayden snorted.

The amused sound was magic to Dane's ears.

"Come on." He tilted his head Shiloh's way. "Let's go play nice."

Cayden groaned and shoved his hands in his pockets. "Fine. But you owe me."

"I owe you? That's rich."

"Everything okay, boys?" the nutritionist asked.

Cayden stuck his hands in his shorts pockets. "Yeah. Sorry about earlier. Got my wires twisted."

"No worries, mate." Shiloh lifted the lid and released a shitload of steam. "Broth?"

"Sure." Dane grabbed a clean mug from the table and held it out for a serve. "Lots of butter, thanks. It's been a day."

Cayden shuddered. "Just give it to me straight, dude."

"At odds already, lads? Can't have that," came Edie's amused voice.

Dane swivelled, surprised to find the woman so close.

He stepped aside to let her through.

"Good evening, young Shiloh. Two for me, please. Oodles of butter."

"How was your adventure today, Edie?" Dane tried for distraction.

"Gorgeous. We shopped and shopped and shopped some more. Have you two been to the Eumundi Markets? Such a beautiful town. Wonderful local artisans. I bought two divine dresses. See?" She spun around, showing off her rainbow tie-dyed fashion statement. "And I got fed glorious, freeze-whipped nut cream—at least I think that's what he called it. I was a little diverted. Nut cream doesn't sound quite right, though." She turned around and called clear across the room, "Maxine! What did they call that amazing nut cream?"

Jesus. The woman had to be messing with them. "While you think on that, Edie...Cayden, let's go find a spot to sit and sip."

But Cayden was already halfway across the room. Back stiff, knuckles white around the edge of a table.

Pink cheeks turned red hot. Cayden looked spitting angry.

Shit.

What now?

Dane crossed to him in time to hear Cayden muttering over his steaming mug.

"'Let's go canoeing, Cayden,' he says. 'Let's hang out on an isolated river far, far away from a local craft market where your long-lost sister could be selling her art,' he says. Brilliant idea, dude."

"Hey. Dude. It takes two." He plonked his mug down hard, and the shiny yellow globules of melted butter swilled out and onto the table. "And what about you being certain she's joined the circus? Huh?" He wished the snide words back the minute they were out of his mouth. "Jesus. Sorry. I didn't mean that."

The chair scraped loud on the wooden floor as Cayden pulled his chair out to sit down. "Today could have been my chance, Dane. Lucy's chance."

"You don't know that. Not for sure. I assumed it was a farmers' market. And you knew as much as I did when we decided to go canoeing."

"Are you saying it's not your fault?"

"For fuck's sake! It's nobody's fault. We're bumbling along in this together."

"You? Bumble?" Cayden scoffed.

Dane ignored that. "Neither the circus nor the markets will disappear overnight, Cayden."

"Looks hot and heavy in this neck of the woods." Bernice butted in. "How was the canoe adventure, boys?"

Dane looked up at her, stupidly relieved at the interruption. "Sweaty."

"Heaven," Cayden said in the same breath, and Dane did a double-take.

Had he misheard?

"The Everglades were amazing," Cayden added, voice like charcoal, "and Gladioli made an amazing picnic for us. The rest was—"

"Amazing," Dane summed up.

"Sounds…amazing." Bernice cheered them with her broth and drifted out of the firing line.

Wise woman.

Torn between wanting to strangle the man or to wrap him up in a full-body hug and never let go, Dane stalled and sipped the rest of his buttered bone broth.

Heaven?

Where the fuck had that come from?

CHAPTER THIRTY-EIGHT

CAYDEN

Heaven.

The word grated in Cayden's mind like salt in a wound. He closed his eyes and let the torrent of the shower pummel his scalp. Pity it couldn't wash his brain clean at the same time.

The shower stung his sunburn, but he could cope with that. What he couldn't cope with was staying at odds with Dane. Which was ridiculous. He and Dane were a blip on the radar. Whatever happened between them was temporary. His family was forever. He should be thinking of Lucy, and the circus tent, and how they were going to find it.

But Dane was right about waiting overnight. Or, at least, he was right about doing everything they could to stay undetected.

By rushing to Shiloh for help, he'd just about outed his mission. He owed Dane, big time, for pulling him back from that brink.

"I like your haven better than mine. Feels like a treat," he ventured.

Jesus, he was a fool—could he sound even more like a crushing teen?

Cayden ducked his head back under the shower spray.

"Curious," came Dane's muffled voice. "Why's that, do you think?"

Cayden looked back and saw the man leaning against his bathroom sink, brushing his teeth. It was so...domestic. So normal.

Cayden slicked the water from his eyes. Wasn't the answer obvious? "Probably because I'm more likely to find you naked in it." His words were corny, and cheesy, and embarrassing as all get out, but that didn't make them wrong. He turned his back on Dane, closed his eyes, and did his best to turn back time without a fucking TARDIS.

The lukewarm water trailed over his tender skin. It felt like a touch. Like too much. But as he reached for the tap to turn it off, he felt another touch.

Dane's fingers stroked down the right side of his neck.

Such a small touch, but it defeated him. He tilted his head to give Dane whatever space he wanted to roam.

"Does it hurt?" Dane asked, and for a second Cayden thought Dane was still talking about Lucy—about losing her, and taking so long to find her.

Fuck, yes. It hurt.

But then Dane's gentle fingers became a soothing palm, and he realised Dane meant the sunburn. And then Dane closed the gap entirely. He plastered his chest to Cayden's back, smoothed his hands down Cayden's upper arms, and criss-crossed his arms around Cayden's ribs. It was comfort, and affection, and more.

He needed it. Even more than finding Lucy, he needed Dane.

Dane flattened his palms against Cayden's chest and

pressed his lips to the smooth patch of skin behind Cayden's right ear.

"You'll be a lobster before midnight," Dane murmured close. "You sure it doesn't hurt?"

Those lips, that voice, and every-fucking-delicious-thing else.

Cayden's whole body purred with desire.

Dane's chest hair abraded his sensitive, sunburnt skin, but Cayden didn't care one iota. He reached around to grip the back of Dane's thighs.

Stay.

"Stay with me," Cayden said. The intense need took him by surprise. That, more than anything, brought him up short. Other people needed him. Not the other way around.

This wasn't Maslow's Hierarchy of Needs, for fuck's sake.

Shelter, warmth, food…he had all those things.

This was about *want*, pure and simple.

Cayden's breath stuttered.

Dane must have felt him tense because he stilled, and Cayden knew that if he didn't lighten the mood, Dane might leave.

"Stay," he repeated in a lighter tone.

Cayden slipped his hands up a few inches to the hollows at Dane's hips and slowly wriggled his arse encouragingly. Lord, please don't let those feelings end.

Then Dane huffed a laugh that shuddered through Cayden's body, and every skin cell went into overdrive.

"Oh, lord." He squeezed Dane's tight arse cheeks. "Do that again."

Like a true gentleman, Dane complied, and Cayden felt those two perfect hollows deepen.

If things weren't bad-slash-good enough, Dane bit his earlobe tenderly and laved it with his tongue, and Cayden was caught between too much and not enough.

"Such a dirty mind," Dane tut-tutted in his ear, and Cayden could only agree.

"Didn't you know your brain is your biggest erogenous zone?"

"Is that so?"

"Mm-hmm."

"Not your skin?" Dane skimmed across approximately forty-eight percent of his skin in five seconds flat.

The remaining fifty-two percent felt bereft.

"Nope."

"Not your cock?" Dane skimmed that, too. "Feels plenty big to me."

Cayden started to doubt his assertion about the brain because Dane's touch felt fucking fine. But nobody called him stubborn for nothing. "Nope."

"Hmm. Interesting."

"Exact—" He tried to finish his word because proving an argument was one of life's greatest joys, but Dane's hand had firmed, and really, what did it matter which organ was the biggest erogenous zone? He didn't care. Not. One. Whit.

All he cared about was heat and Dane's hand and the building rush of release.

Approximately thirty-seven seconds later, after the last quake left Cayden's body, Cayden turned and dropped to his knees. He refused to feel even remotely embarrassed by coming so swiftly.

It didn't take long for Dane to lose his edge either, and by the time they tumbled out of the shower, boneless, Cayden decided he'd need a horse-pill-sized calcium supplement to be sure his bones would ever stiffen again.

"Stop flushing." Dane softly dabbed the towel over his sunburnt skin. "I can't tell which bits of you are sunburnt and which bits are not, and I don't want to hurt you."

"Can't help it. Autonomic response," he protested, probably flushing even more. "If you're touching me, you'll have to deal with the heat." Cayden threaded his fingers through Dane's hair for purchase as the man crouched and skimmed the towel lower.

Nope. No hope of that flush going away anytime soon.

His skin thrummed wherever Dane touched, which was pretty much everywhere.

The dude had excellent instincts when it came to sex, but the protective way Dane was playing nursemaid surprised him. Not that it should have—Dane owed him nothing, but not once had he left Cayden in the lurch.

Dane pushed at his hip. "Turn around."

Obediently, Cayden unfurled his fingers from the man's thick chocolate waves and turned. His hands clenched at the loss, but the reflection of him and Dane together in the bathroom window almost made up for it.

The man was temptation and tantalisation all wrapped up in one hot package.

"We could test out your shower," Dane offered.

"No. God no. Later. Keep going." His words raised a quirk of a smile on Dane's ridiculously sexy face that bobbed by Cayden's hip.

Dane finished his ministrations with a quick swipe of Cayden's ticklish toes; then he straightened to stand tall over Cayden's shoulder.

"Tease," Cayden said to the mirror, and Dane's eyebrow rose in amused salute.

A challenge if ever he saw one.

Cayden held his hand out for the towel. "My turn."

Dane shook his head. "No need. I air dried."

Cayden's disappointment was short-lived as Dane hung up the towel, took his hand, and led him out of the bathroom.

Without saying a thing, Dane walked to the side of the

bed and sat down, then pulled Cayden to stand between his knees, leaned forward, and pressed a simple kiss to his belly.

Jesus, fuck, the man could romance a flea.

"Ready for that massage?" Free to touch, Cayden ran his fingertips across Dane's strong shoulders, feeling the radiating warmth of sunburn, then sifted up through his damp hair. "Got any aloe vera?"

Dane planted a series of open-mouthed kisses across to his side, firing every nerve as he went. "Nope. You?"

"Nope." Cayden didn't want to let go of Dane's hair in case it made the kisses stop, so he let his eyes do the job of touching every bit of Dane's sun-pink skin, following the line of Dane's spine down to the only pale skin on display— the pale crescent moons of his lean butt-cheeks. "Maybe I could just massage the bits that aren't flaming hot." He bit his lip and tried not to laugh. Seduction was supposed to be serious. Right?

He closed his eyes, curved forward to hide his face in Dane's hair, and nuzzled the kink in the man's natural side part. The imperfection somehow made Dane both slightly less and even more perfect.

Cayden inhaled deep—he sure smelled fucking perfect, too. Cayden's moan of appreciation turned to a groan of pain when Dane's fingernails grazed the raw skin low on his back. He couldn't stop the automatic flinch, either.

"Sorry." Cayden grabbed Dane's fingers and slapped them back to where they'd been. The man's touch set him on fire, anyway. He could deal with a little pain as penance for his levity.

"Why sorry?" Dane again pulled his hands away from the red zone. "I'm the one who hurt you." Before Cayden could whine in protest, Dane slid backward across the bed, swivelled to lie down on his side, and patted the space beside him. "I have a better idea."

Game, Cayden crawled across the wrinkled sheets to line up, lip to lip, dick to dick.

"No, not like that. Flip around."

Oh. God, yes.

They took their time, letting the heat they generated together slowly take over the sun's latent heat. Cayden wasn't sure what he appreciated more—the smell or taste or texture of Dane's silk over steel cock, heavy in his mouth, or the sweet agony of Dane's lips and tongue and throat around his own.

It was impossible to divide his attention, and Cayden left behind any hope of slick coordination as he fell into an endless swarm of sensation. It was like being trapped in a fucking Escher painting, where, instead of endless stairs leading to more stairs, it was cock leading to more cock—no way out. Not that Cayden wanted a way out…

Dane held his hips firm with a hand that Cayden was sure would leave five fingertip-size bruises, while the other hand teased his balls then reached through to tease his perineum with a feather-light touch. His lips and tongue flared wide around Cayden's girth, and he sucked with maddening strength.

Seriously, the man's mouth ought to be trademarked—a fact he'd relay as soon as he didn't have the man's thick cock filling his mouth.

Cayden pulled back far enough to suck in a reedy breath through his nose, swirled his tongue around the head of Dane's cock, eager for a taste, before diving back down. He clenched and released the fist he'd closed around the man's base—freeing Dane's need to thrust.

Cayden moaned, which made Dane jerk deeper, which made Cayden moan louder, which made Dane suck stronger, which made Cayden's balls soar, which made him moan again…and Dane shot off like a rocket, pumping deep into

Cayden's mouth, filling his senses. Control gone, Dane's fingers strayed closer to Cayden's hole. The teasing touch turned insistent and Cayden's head snapped back as he came on Dane's tongue.

"Agh, fuck!"

Dane milked his balls, which made his dick jerk again, but by then Cayden was tapped dry.

Sweaty and satisfied, he licked the last drip of Dane's salty cum off his lip and rolled to lie splayed his back on the sheets.

"Escher-fucking-cock," he muttered to the fan that stirred in a mesmerising spiral overhead.

Another cool shower would be nice, he thought, feeling the fresh sweat dry to crusty salt.

He didn't move an inch.

"Mm." Dane stirred to roll onto his back, too. "Way better than a massage."

Cayden snorted. "Not hard to be better than a fucking lymphatic drainage massage."

The words came out of his mouth, and Cayden was immediately sorry he'd dragged reality back into their blissfully oblivious sex bubble.

But Dane must have seen through his awkwardness because his fingertip flared out on the wrinkled sheet and connected to Cayden's—tip-to-tip.

The move felt somehow more intimate than any other touch they'd shared, and Cayden's heart skipped a beat.

"Anything you do to me is bound to be better than a fucking lymphatic drainage massage," Dane said. "I ought to take you home as my personal masseuse."

CHAPTER THIRTY-NINE

DANE

'Take you home.'

Shit. Where did that come from?

Dane thought he ought to try to distract Cayden from his inadvertent offer of a future together, but he couldn't take his eyes off of the man's lower lip as he licked away the last drop of come.

Dane's lax cock twitched greedily

Twice in one session was hardly his limit, but he felt strangely content to wallow in bed and watch Cayden mouth unspoken words.

"What are you thinking about?" Dane asked.

Cayden's face flamed, sending Dane's curiosity into the stratosphere.

"Wow. Now you have to tell me."

Cayden rolled his eyes. "Maxine's nut-cream."

Dane groaned. "You're such a twelve-year-old."

"I hope not." Cayden's eyes flashed to Dane's cock, the implied 'given what we've just been up to' loud and clear in his upside-down smirk.

It was too much. "Get up here." He tugged at Cayden's wrist.

Instead of complying, as he ought, Cayden rolled off the bed, flicked on Dane's bedside lamp, switched off the main room light, and turned the fan down from evil-thing-possessed to friendly-whirligig speed.

"Why do you keep accusing me of being twelve?" Cayden asked. "I'm only five years younger than you."

Cayden winced a little as his sunburnt skin hit the sheets. He lay down on his side, right-way-up this time, and shuffled closer.

"It's not you."

"It's not you, it's me? Really, Dane?" Cayden fisted his hand under his cheek. "Try harder."

Cayden didn't understand. But how could he? They didn't know each other. "Ask any of my friends. I say that line all the time. Whenever anyone says or does anything immature."

"Immature?" Cayden protested. "When was I immature?"

"Give me a break. You were giggling over nut-cream."

Cayden rolled his eyes. "Fine. It's childish. I get it. But why twelve?" Cayden curled a finger as he asked the question.

Dane grabbed his curling finger. "It's not ironic," he said, glad for the easy rebuttal. He didn't want to tell the truth. He really didn't. Because Dane's reason was private. It had nothing to do with the retreat, with finding Lucy, or with being horny as fuck. He liked the guy, sure, but Dane had no reason to trust Cayden any more than he had four short days ago when he'd sworn to keep Malone and Jet's story and the rest of his personal life to himself.

Dane dropped Cayden's finger and clenched his hand in a fist, close to his chest.

"Our mum died when we were twelve."

Fuck. What the hell, Dane? He pinched his lips together,

tight. But his words were out there now, no take-backs allowed.

"Your mum?"

What was he supposed to say? Yes, my female parent departed this world?

He ground his teeth together, saying nothing.

The silence was deafening. Hell, even the crickets shut up.

Cayden tried again. "What do you mean 'when *we* were twelve'?"

Damn, he'd heard that unfortunate slip, too.

"Nothing."

"Dane." Cayden frowned. His eyes turned the colour of teak in the low light.

Fucking lion eyes.

They saw him. Made him feel like prey.

Dane took a deep breath and forced himself to relax. Then he willed himself to unfurl his fist and spread his hand, palm down, on the cool white sheet in the space between them.

Would it really matter if Cayden knew? It was old news. None of it impacted his current life.

Much.

Just on his pained heart.

Losing his mum to cancer ripped his heart out. He'd recovered. Sort of. He and Alice had found a way forward, together.

Losing his sister? That was like having his heart kicked by steel-toed boots. Was it any wonder he'd put up medieval-style armour? A sort of chastity belt for his heart? Lock it up tight, and throw away the key?

But Cayden just kept looking at him. Patiently waiting for his truth.

Words prickled his tongue—like angry wasps, yammering to get out.

"Fine. I have…had a twin. Alice."

If Cayden picked up on his stumble, he didn't say, just reached out for Dane's pinkie and hooked—his yin to Dane's yang—together.

Only one square inch of their skin touched, but it sent the whole of Dane into a tailspin. Dane didn't know why he accepted it. He wasn't some twelve-year-old kid anymore. He didn't need coddling. But he couldn't look away from that double helix. It felt good. Sweet.

He squeezed back once, then softened the hold and left his finger there—in Cayden's care.

"Mum had breast cancer. It just…took hold. She was so busy taking care of us on her own that she ignored changes." Dane tried to blink away the memory. It didn't work. He rolled onto his back and hooked his free arm across his eyes.

Nothing to see here, folks.

But the words just kept tumbling out. "We went to live with our aunt and uncle. Nice people. Didn't even have to change schools. It was fine." Dane pulled his arm away from his eyes, needing visual confirmation that Cayden believed him. "Perfectly…" *scary, horrible, lonely,* "…fine."

Cayden nodded—not interrupting.

Interrupt! Interrupt! Dane's mind screamed, but that levee was already breached.

"I wouldn't call it a regular childhood, but we were fine. Our aunt and uncle weren't the sort to want children, but they made space for us, and we only needed each other really —Alice and I, I mean. So, we stuck together. Kept going. For a while. But then, Alice wasn't fine. Not anymore." He looked away, but didn't break the soft coddle of their double helix. "And then, one day, she was gone, too."

Dane focused on a beam high under the shadowy A-frame ceiling where a knot in the natural wood spiralled tighter and tighter, darker and darker, till he fancied he might get sucked in—the dense gravity of his very own black hole.

"Alice died?" Cayden asked.

"She…" Dane stopped. Was he really going to tell Cayden what happened to Alice? How she died? How she'd been driven to suicide by journalists macerating her on live television? Did his trust extend that far? "…yeah."

He heard Cayden's sharp inhalation and his own choppier exhalation.

"Does it piss you off?"

He stiffened. "What the fuck kind of question is that?"

Dane tried to wrench his finger from Cayden's hold, but Cayden tightened his grip on Dane's pinkie finger and did a one-shoulder shrug. "I'm pissed at Lucy."

That brought Dane up short. "You are?"

"You bet your arse I am. It's a selfish and misplaced anger. I know that. But I can't stop it. The day Lucy disappeared was my fifteenth birthday. The same day that I planned to come out to my family. I love her, and I miss her, but for every bit of me that wishes she was safe at home, there's an equal part of me that wants to throttle her for derailing my life. All of our lives. Her mysterious absence has affected every single thing, good or bad, that's happened since then. Even you and me." He squeezed Dane's pinkie, then softened the hold. "If not for Lucy, we wouldn't have found each other."

Found? As in, finders, keepers?

Dane's lungs constricted.

What was Cayden implying?

Did he think they had a future together?

Did he want to wind together more than their pinkie fingers?

A cosy fuck was one thing, but keeping each other? That

was about twelve steps beyond the rules of the game they'd agreed to play.

Dane straightened his finger and forced the disconnection. Still uncomfortable, he made a production of rearranging his pillow under his neck. The move bit at his sunburn, but that was easier to take than the tightening bind of shared secrets and misplaced intimacy.

He looked across to his bedside table where *Titus Groan* sat under the glow of the lamp. Thoughts of Alice made him want to flip through to the next chapter and read, just as he'd done every other night. But with Cayden there beside him, he couldn't very well do that.

Could he?

He peered across the puffy white pillows at Cayden's messy curls, gilded in the same warm glow. His eyelashes fanned out across his cheekbones as his eyelids drooped, blinking slowly in a desperate struggle to stay awake.

He considered pushing Cayden out to go sleep in his own bed, in his own haven.

Instead, the words "Go to sleep" tumbled out.

"But you didn't answer me," Cayden muttered, sleepily.

Dane scrambled to recall the question.

"Did losing your sister piss you off?" Cayden asked again.

Dane thought about Alice.

The disease had pissed him off.

Her pain had pissed him off.

The people who'd driven her to quit life had one-hundred percent pissed him off.

But Alice herself?

His Alice?

"Never."

At least that was something he could be sure about.

"Sleep," he said again—a simple word which Cayden took

for permission to re-link their pinkies, inch closer to Dane's side, and nuzzle into his neck.

An open-mouthed kiss landed on his pulse point just below his jaw and sent a rush of hyper-oxygenated blood to Dane's brain.

He waited a few seconds for the flashy lights in his mind to clear—to see what would happen next.

Nothing did.

The world didn't come crashing down.

Life went on.

The night was still, and warm, and calm, and all Dane could feel was the gentle rasp of Cayden's breath as they inhaled and exhaled in synchrony.

He was hot, and sore, and bone-deep exhausted, and the moment should have felt awkward and wrong. Instead, it felt steady and gentle and right, and it wasn't hard to recall old teenage dreams of falling in love with a cute boy and being loved in return.

Perhaps he could play pretend for a while to act out the life his childish heart had imagined before he let reality back in.

So, leaving their linked hands on his chest, right where Cayden had placed them, Dane reached with his other hand to pick up Alice's treasured novel.

One-handed, he opened to his bookmarked place and read of the coming of a miracle.

CHAPTER FORTY

CAYDEN

Cayden put serious thought into linking his pinkie with Dane's again.

He didn't need much—just a smidgen of contact to feel like they were still in this thing together. He doubted anyone else would even notice—given the buzz in the art studio.

Instead, he leaned an inch sideways into Dane and brushed their shoulders together. It took him straight back to the moment they'd woken entwined—sweat-slicked where their bodies met, barely a quark between them, instinctively drawn together in sleep.

Waking beside someone wasn't exactly Cayden's brand of normal, and it had taken him a moment to figure out where he was and why he felt as hot as a rotisserie pig.

Dane hadn't pushed him away. He'd just rolled onto his back and said something in his gravel morning voice. Cayden couldn't recall what Dane had said because his own attention diverted south, evaporating every bit of sense from his head.

Well, from his big head.

His little head still had plenty of ideas—quark-sized and up.

"How'd your lymphatic drainage go this morning, Dane?" Bernice called from across the art studio, drawing Cayden back from memory lane.

"Blissful," Dane answered with a blasé smile.

"Not painful? Your sunburn looks sore."

"No. It was a gentle massage. In fact, I'm not sure if Jade even touched me." He hovered his hands over the top rim of his fired clay pot, demonstrating.

"Did you sleep through it?" Michelle smiled.

"Was it transcendental?" Lissa asked.

"She probably just stroked your aura," Randy weighed in.

"Is that what they're calling it these days?" Edie smirked. "Why, in my day—"

"Young minds, Edie." Maxine stopped her, mid-word.

Edie looked confused. "The boys aren't that young, Maxine."

"Not them," Maxine said, then pointed toward the doorway. "Him."

Everyone turned to see Leif, looking fresh and innocent and far too young to understand the subtext flying around the room.

Leif grinned at the attention and made a beeline to their table. "Hi." He dumped a pile of fresh-picked leaves beside his pot, dropped his backpack on the floor, and lined up his leaves in size and colour order.

"What've you got there, mate?" Dane asked.

"Leaves," Leif said, as though that wasn't obvious.

Dane was clearly about to launch into some other line of questioning when Edie leaned across from the next table. "You lads missed an amazing game of Pictionary last night."

Dane and Cayden said, "Shame," in synchrony.

"Snap!" and "Jinx!" came the return chorus, and Leif yelled, "Pinkie shake!"

Well, fuck. What was a poor dude to do?

Cayden held up his left hand, pinkie outstretched. He didn't have to wait for long for Dane to hook on.

Leif snickered, like it was the funniest thing ever, and hooked his own pinkie into the mix.

Dane smiled.

God—that sucker-punch smile. It killed him. "Think we'll need to keep the little dude around if it'll make you smile like that."

Dane dropped his hand and rubbed his palm on his shorts.

Shit. What had he said? *Keep the little dude?* Had that made Dane uncomfortable? Why? It wasn't like he'd literally keep Leif.

Unless it was the presumptive 'we' that'd bothered him.

That thought brought Cayden down to earth with a thud.

"Good morning, everyone!" Celeste's welcome was all airy Zen and wind chimes. "Everyone settled? Lovely. Today we're going to find our inner bliss."

Dane side-eyed him. "Not a word," he warned.

Celeste paused while the room quietened, then went on in her sing-song voice. "First, I want you to close your eyes and breathe deep. In through your nose and out through your mouth. That's it. Feel the texture and the temperature of the air. In and out. Smell the growth of the rainforest. Taste the moisture on the breeze. Hear the whisper of the wind." Her voice changed direction as she moved about the room. "In…and out. That's it. Today, we are going to tap into the flow of the universe. The feel, the taste, the sound, the smell, and the look of it. Let it swirl around you and through you. In…and out. Be it. Let it be you. Flow with it. Let the energy of it bloom. Boundless. In…and out. See it all around you. Breathe, in…and out…and when you see it…open your eyes."

Cayden obeyed, blinking at the sudden brightness of day.

"Now, with that colour held in your mind, come up and choose your glaze."

Colour.

The single word took Cayden back to Lucy. She was all about colour—paints, pencils, watercolours, hell, even crayons.

As he followed Celeste's direction, he tried to keep Lucy front and centre in his mind. She was his true purpose. Everything else was a distraction. Problem was, Leif and Dane felt truer than any distant memory of his sister—real, and warm, and, in Dane's case, sexy as fuck.

Both intent on glazing their pots, Cayden simply watched them.

Anyone would have thought Dane was painting a complex design, given how much care and attention he gave painting a gradient of icy blues from the bottom to charcoal grey at the top. Each successive ring was a subtly smokier tone—classy and clean.

Leif concentrated hard over his pot, too. His tongue poked out to the left as he painted overlapping feather shapes in every yellow imaginable—canary, lemon, mustard, neon—not the most obvious colour scheme for a four-leaf-clover pot.

"Looks like Big Bird would look if he had four tummies and no head," Cayden said.

Leif and Dane both looked up at him. They couldn't have moved any more alike if they'd practiced their choreography in advance.

"Who's Big Bird?" Leif asked.

"What?" Was the boy serious? What kid didn't know about Big Bird? "Dane, this child is deprived." He was only half-joking.

"Knowing Big Bird is your criterion for privilege?" Dane didn't sound convinced.

"Exactly." Cayden pointed at the yellow pot.

Leif picked up one of his leaves and twirled it. "Birds have feathers, not leaves," he said, as though that solved the riddle. Then he pressed it to the multi-tone yellow glaze covering the outside of his pot. The leaf left a print behind. "See?"

"Impressive," Dane said.

"Okay, so, not Big Bird," Cayden grudgingly conceded.

He didn't need to look to know that Dane was smirking.

"Art is supposed to exercise the imagination." He defended his efforts. Although Cayden didn't know why he bothered. He didn't really care what his pot looked like. Blobs of glaze in various shades of green were about all the attention he could spare on his less-than-perfect, amorphous vessel. What Cayden wanted…no, what he needed was for time to move faster so that he and Dane could get away from the retreat and hike out to the circus.

"Mm-hmm." Dane hummed, not taking his eyes off his own smooth-as-silk glaze.

Cayden took that comment as agreement and declared his pot done.

As every other person in the group finished their glaze, and Celeste directed them to store their pot on the drying shelves, Dane and Cayden remained with Leif while the little dude continued to imprint his leaves painstakingly into the feathery yellow glaze.

"Such a happy colour, Leif. Bet your mum will love that," Celeste said.

Leif shrugged. "I was going to make it grass green, since it's a four-leaf clover, but my aura's yellow today."

Celeste didn't bat an eyelid at the declaration.

Cayden bit his tongue.

"And yours, Dane. It's quite something. Beautiful brush work. Strong colours."

"I was thinking of Antarctica. A winter ocean," Dane said.

Just like his eyes. Cayden shivered, instantly there.

"Yes. During a storm," Celeste agreed. "Lovely work."

Cayden waited for equal kudos from Celeste, but all she said was, "Wonderful effort, Cayden," leaving him and his green pot unfairly wanting.

He looked down at his poor, underappreciated pot, wishing it was already dry so he could give it a consoling pat. "It's all right, pot. I'll love you forever."

Dane snorted. "It's cute—"

"Thanks, Dane. At least someone appreciates true art."

"—in a weird, organic way."

"Organic?" The fuck? He shot Dane a glare, any hint of a happy shiver long gone. He ducked his hand under the table and shot him the bird where Leif couldn't see.

Leif nodded and his grin spread wide. "Yeah. It looks like algae. A great big bloom of it."

"No appreciation for quality." Cayden shook his head.

Celeste ruffled Leif's hair. "On that note. Are you almost done, Leif? Or do you want to keep going and snip the lock on your way out?"

Leif shifted away from her hand, ears burning. "That's okay. Mum's meeting me here, so we can lock up."

"Good boy," she said, which made poor Leif's ears burn even redder. "Don't forget to put your pots up to dry. There's plenty of space on the drying rack. No shenanigans now," she sing-songed. Her skirts and bells swished and chimed as she crossed the studio and disappeared outside.

Glad for the excuse to move, Cayden took his pot up to the drying rack and paced around the room for a bit. He fiddled with the brushes by the sink and the many tins of glaze, then forced himself to sit down again beside Dane. Not that it was a chore to be near him, but Cayden's whole body burned to go, go, go. To seek out Lucy. To finish what he came to the House of Glass to do.

He rubbed at his bare wrist. "What's the time?" he asked Dane.

Cayden really wanted to ask *if it was time yet*—like an impatient kid on a road trip. *Are we there yet? Are we there yet? Are we there yet?*

Dane finished the last brush of blue glaze. "Done," he said, then twisted his wrist. "Lunch starts in fifteen. Looks like Leif's almost done, too. Let's keep him company while he finishes up. Then we can go."

Just his voice made Cayden feel steadier—surer.

Eyes on Leif, Cayden hauled in a deep breath and squared his shoulders, then reached sideways and laid a hand on Dane's thigh. With any luck, Dane would receive his silent thanks.

The way the little dude focused so intently on his art reminded Cayden of his sister. His mind drifted to a long-ago memory of the mural Lucy created for his room out of reams of paper, sticky tape, and poster paint. Just like Leif, Lucy had been so easily lost, for hours and hours, to worlds of colour and imagination.

The memory was so crystal clear that he wasn't a surprise to see her image appear before him—her oh-so familiar face, her long blond hair, her off-centre smile.

"Lucy," he whispered to the apparition.

Then she spoke. "What's shaking, Sprite?"

Leif shoved the trestle table and whipped around. "Mum!" *Mum?*

If the table edge hadn't already punched his gut, seeing her would have had the same effect.

Was she real?

Something gripped the back of his fingers. He looked down to see where Dane pulled Cayden's clawed hand—tense as a steel cable—from his thigh.

"Sorry," he mouthed, but no sound came out.

"Cayden?" Dane's voice was pure question.

Cayden looked back up and across to the entry of the studio where Leif was hugging...

"Cayden?" Dane asked again, a little louder. Loud enough to be heard across the room, to where...

At Dane's voice, Leif's mother looked up. She clenched Leif tight to her chest, and her smile disappeared entirely.

Cayden felt the loss like another punch to his gut.

Was she real?

"Mum!" Leif protested. "You're squishing me."

"Holy shit." Cayden's voice cracked.

"Mum!" Leif wriggled and twisted in her hold.

As though the little dude's movement acted as a release valve for Cayden's body, he stood up on wobbly legs. "Lucy?"

"Hey, hey. Slow down." Dane edged close to his side, flush to his shoulder, a hand flat to his chest. "You'll scare them." Dane spoke low and firm. The voice of reason.

But what did reason have to do anything when he was seeing his sister for the first time in twelve fucking long years?

Nothing.

"Lucy?" His knuckles rapped hard against the tabletop. Bullets from a gun. Sharp with tension.

She didn't respond, just continued staring, her face ghost-white.

"Mum, who's Lucy?"

Cayden dropped his eyes to Leif's face, to his wild blonde hair, to his dash of freckles and quirky smile. How had he not seen the resemblance before? He and Lucy weren't carbon copies of each other, but that expression...how had he not seen the resemblance?

No wonder he'd felt such an instinctive connection.

"Lucy."

"Jesus. Leif's your nephew," Dane blurted, then let go of Cayden to slap a hand across his mouth.

Freed from Dane's calming hold, he took off. He surged out from behind the trestle table and threaded, swift as he could, across the divide. He didn't stop till he had his sister in his arms.

Reflexively, her arms closed around him and squeezed him tight.

CHAPTER FORTY-ONE

CAYDEN

"Who's Lucy, Mum?" Leif asked again, and Lucy's hold on Cayden's upper back lost all of its strength.

Don't let go. Don't let go, Cayden railed inside, but Leif's question wormed its way in.

What did he mean—*who's Lucy*?

Leif wriggled out from between them, and Lucy's grip loosened till it was only him holding them together.

"Holy shit, you have a son?" Cayden's mind finally caught up.

"Cayden, Leif can hear you," Dane cautioned, his voice a quiet rumble.

But Cayden ignored him. *Holy shit* didn't even remotely cover it. What were a few curse words compared to finding his sister and discovering he had a nephew all in one fell swoop?

Cayden didn't think he'd ever be able to let go again, but he needed to see her face. He needed to see her eyes when he asked for the truth because the eyes didn't lie.

He inched back, looking for an explanation. "Lucy?"

Her eyes shied away.

"Lucy?" he pressed.

"I go by Luna now. Have done for, well…" Her words trailed off.

"Twelve years." Bitterness stained his voice.

"Yeah." She let her hands drop away.

Twelve fucking long years of searching for someone who, by all appearances, was doing just fine. Not a single sign of harm. She looked healthy and happy. Alive. Appearances, though, could deceive.

"Are you…okay?"

Cayden hated the hesitancy in his voice and the strain.

He had questions to ask. Difficult questions. Questions and answers that Leif probably shouldn't hear. About that, Dane was right.

He drew Lucy in for a quick just-to-be-sure-she's-real hug, then turned to Dane, who stood by his shoulder, steady and stoic and sure. He could feel the distance widening.

"Could you take Leif to lunch, please? I…we…just need to…" Cayden wagged a finger between him and his sister.

"Talk. Sure." Dane caught Leif's attention. "Come on, let's go see what gastronomic delights Gladioli has in store for us today."

"What's gasto…tri…monic?" Leif tangled with the big word.

"Gastronomic," Dane repeated. "It means food."

"Ooooh," Leif strung out. "Okay," he said, needing no further incentive than food.

"Wait." Lucy brought Leif back to her body with a hand flat to his chest. "Who's he?"

"Dane? He's my…umm." Who was Dane? What was Dane to him? "My…friend."

"Your friend?" she asked.

His nod was a bit manic. "My friend. You can trust him. No question."

"As in your friend?"

"Sure. My…oh. Um." Well, fuck. "I guess. Sort of. Maybe. Um. Yeah." *Way to come out, Cayden.*

He took a quick glance Dane's way to see how that bumble-fuck explanation had gone down, but the man's expression was carefully neutral.

"We won't be far. Find us around the hub when you're ready." His sure, stoic voice oozed reassurance.

Lucy nodded slowly—wide-eyed.

Cayden felt Dane graze the back of his hand. The touch was probably meant to reassure him, but Lucy's eyes dipped to see it, and all Cayden felt was burning awareness.

She squeezed her empty fists tight. "Save a smoothie for me, will you, Sprite?"

Leif seemed to take that as approval, and he tore off at a dead run out of the art studio.

Dane went around Lucy, then turned and gave him a look that he might have meant *be kind*, but which Cayden interpreted to mean *say whatever the fuck you like to your long-lost sister who left you in the lurch twelve years ago and now looks perfectly fine, thank you very much.* She could clench her fists in protest all she liked. No way was he letting Lucy out of his sight—not without answers and maybe, possibly, a microchip in her ear so he never lost her ever again.

He unclenched his jaw long enough to say, "We'll come find you soon," then fully faced his sister.

The minute the art studio door shut behind them, he let loose. "What the fuck, Luce?"

She frowned. "How'd you find me?"

What the hell did that matter? "You just up and left! On that fucking day—"

Breathe, Cayden.

Ugh.

"You left." His heart went right back to that day. His

nerves had been in hyper-drive, anticipating the *I'm gay* discussion to come. Agitated, he'd waited for his mum to fetch Lucy from her room in her share house. But when Mum returned, ashen-faced, all she said was, *She's gone.*

"No reason. No explanation. No word. Just…gone." The fifteen-year-old boy in him wailed, but his twenty-seven-year-old voice was measured. Thank God.

Lucy's gaze didn't quite meet his.

"It wasn't about you, Cayden."

The fuck it was. "No, it was about you fucking off to fuck knows where for fuck knows how long to do fuck knows what."

"Stop!" Lucy looked around.

Was she looking for a way out? A way to leave him in the lurch again?

"No. I will not stop," Cayden spat out, then grabbed her, wrapped her in his arms, and pulled her in tight. His whole body clenched with anger, and pain, and desperate relief. "I fucking will not."

Her arms hung limp at her sides, but he didn't let go.

Her long blond hair stuck to his damp face, but he didn't care.

He inhaled in search of her remembered scent, but found coconut and jasmine and honey where wild rose and vanilla ought to have been.

Perhaps she felt his tension. He didn't know. But she gave an answering tremor in his arms.

"Cayden?" she asked.

He couldn't answer.

She took a shaky breath in and a measured breath out. And then he felt movement.

She raised her forearms and wrapped them lightly around him to settle halfway up his back.

It felt like victory.

"I will not," he whispered in her ear.

He closed his eyes and breathed her in, rocking side to side as though he held a precious baby in his arms instead of his grown-up, renegade sister.

The moment felt tenuous, easily spoiled, but twelve years was a long time to go without answers. He couldn't wait a second longer.

"What was it about, then?"

She spun out of his hold and took a few steps to the sink, where she fussed with the same brushes he'd impatiently fussed with mere minutes ago.

He tracked her every move.

Waiting.

"Do you remember Star Wars Day?" she asked. "You know, May the fourth be with you?"

"What's that got to do with—"

"Remember how Mum was nuts about it?"

"She still is. Present tense." What was Lucy getting at? "What's Star Wars Day got to do with you running away?"

Still not looking him in the eye, she crossed to the other side of the room; her wood-soled shoes clonked sharp on the old plank floors—a staccato beat on a drum. "It has everything to do with everything."

"Everything?" He felt like an idiot, repeating her words, but what other option did she leave him with? He perched his arse on one of the trestle tables, squeezed the edge of the tabletop, and tracked her pacing. "I'm gonna need a bit more than that, Lucy."

She whipped around. "I told you—it's Luna now."

"I heard you." If she thought he'd concede to a name change before he got answers, for fuck's sake, she was dreaming. He didn't care if she thought he was rude. If Lucy had kept her real name, he might have found her years ago. "May the fourth," he reminded her.

She paced back across the room, hands working hard at trying to say something.

"Is that sign language? I don't understand Auslan, Lucy."

The fire in her flashing eyes probably ought to have told him to back away, but he didn't. He couldn't. He needed to bring her to account.

She pinched her lips tight together, then burst out, "I'm not the only sibling you've lost, okay!" She chopped the air with her hands.

What?

"Wait." He slid off the trestle and grabbed her forearm as she paced by. "What the hell are you on about? Another sibling?"

Lucy wrenched away and shook her head. "It's not my secret to tell."

"Bullshit it's not. I need to know." Didn't she understand?

"No. I shouldn't have said anything. It's Mum's secret. She's the one who has to tell the story. Or not. It's her choice."

What the hell? Was he left out of the loop on everything? And when would it be his choice?

"But she told you?" Cayden asked.

"No." She shook her head. "I overhead by accident. But that's not the point."

"Well then, what the fuck is the point?"

Lucy opened her mouth to say something, but from her fierce eyes, Cayden wasn't sure he wanted to hear it.

"The point, brother, was I was keeping my baby, no matter what."

"Your baby? Leif? This is about Leif? I thought you said—"

"And I knew Mum and Dad wouldn't be okay with that." Her step hitched, and she looked off into the distance. "Mum especially."

"Because…?" Was he going to have to play twenty questions to get to the truth?

"Because she's not sorry that she gave her up."

"Her? Who?"

Closing the gap again, Lucy's eyes flashed gold his way. "Keep up, Cayden."

"Whoa." He raised his hands.

She stomped away.

Clearly, Lucy wasn't easily calmed, but Cayden was over her reticence and well out of patience. Never more was he aware of the love-hate tangle he felt in his heart for his sister.

He deserved answers, goddammit.

Now.

"If it had anything to do with you leaving, then you need to tell me."

She strode to the edge of the room again and turned. The noon light blazing through the slatted windows made a halo of Lucy's white-gold hair and cast her face in shadow.

He couldn't see her expression, but he could see her shoulders rise high, then fall.

"You know dominoes?" she asked.

"The game?"

"Yeah, but…" She shook her head. "No, not a game. Real life. Sometimes things just fall, like dominoes, and there's no way to stop them. One thing happens, then the next thing, and the next thing…but until that first one goes, it's so hard to know how they'll fall, or even what will fall. You know? Inevitability. Fate. But none of it happens without a trigger."

Finally, a metaphor he could work with. "And what was your trigger?"

"Clay." She turned to look out the window. "I met Clay."

Details of the research he'd done prior to the retreat spun in Cayden's mind. "Clay Fuller? Gordon's son?"

As though she hadn't heard him, she continued. "I fell

pregnant, and it was so far from what Mum and Dad wanted for me. They'd always been, like, 'You're so smart and creative, Lucy. You'll do amazing things,' which is nice validation and all, but it was like no matter what I did, I'd always disappoint them. And then I got pregnant, and Clay had this other life he wanted to get back to up here—well, not here, here." She pointed to the art studio floor. "But near—"

"Home," he said, naming the place Elise had escaped. "Such a generic word for something so impactful."

Lucy jerked to face him, startled. "How did you know about…?" But she didn't finish that thought either. "I…God… I didn't expect this…to see you like this." She collapsed down into a seat by the window. Looking lost and very much alone.

Cayden desperately wanted to go to her, to collect her in his arms and never let go, but he still needed answers.

"Go on." He hated the coldness in his voice. The distrust. Because the only thing he knew for sure was Lucy had taken herself away. She'd not been kidnapped. She'd not been coerced. She'd chosen to leave. She'd chosen to leave Cayden and not come back.

He stayed silent and waited.

She swallowed. "I just felt like I couldn't have both, like I had to choose. And because Mum had…yeah, anyway…" Her eyes skittered away. "I knew they wouldn't approve. Mum and Dad. But he was persuasive, you know. Clay was. And so I went, thinking I'd make a fabulous new life with him. As soon as I was sorted, I figured I'd get in touch with Mum and Dad…and you…and my friends…and…and everyone would see that I had this amazing thing going and a beautiful baby on the way. They'd see how wonderful Clay was. They'd see I'd made the right choice."

"Having Leif?" Cayden asked. The air felt thick.

"No. Well, yes, in part. All of it, really. But more that I'd chosen to be with him." She broke off. "Only, when I got up north, I realised pretty soon that I wasn't the only one. I wasn't the only woman Clay had convinced to follow him home, *to Home*, and that mine wasn't the only baby. It was… horrible. But, by then, it was too late. It was too late to even think about giving up my baby. It was too late for a lot of things, really. And I…" She swallowed. "…I was ashamed. I'd made a massive mistake and I couldn't face any of you."

"Of course, you could have!" he burst out. "We loved you!"

Past tense or present tense—Cayden wasn't a hundred percent sure.

She interrupted him again. "No, Cayden. I couldn't. Not after Mum and…our sister." She drew in a shuddery breath, eyes glistening. "There was no way back. And the longer I stayed away, the harder it was to see a way back—to fess up." She looked up to the ceiling—covered in thousands of vibrant, painted leaves—and smiled a soft, melancholy smile. "Leif was the reward. I'll never regret him."

Cayden looked up, too, seeing Leif's leaves—evidence of the life that would not have been if not for Lucy's choice.

His mind spun—what if, what if, what if? "What about Clay? And Gordon?" Jesus, how could he have forgotten about Gordon fucking Fuller?

"Poor Gordon."

"Poor Gordon?" She couldn't mean it.

"Out of everyone, Gordon was hurt most of all. He never really approved of how Clay lived his life, but can you imagine finding your own son like that? Dead?" She shuddered. "If Leif ever…no." She shook her head emphatically. "He'll never get into that scene. No substances. Never." This time, there was steel in her voice. "After that, we all packed up and left. Most of us came here with Gordon to make a new home. He was already well into clean living, but needed help to set the retreat up and getting it running. In the early days, we all just did whatever was needed." She waved her hands around, looking everywhere but at him. "Now, we're family."

Family.

That stung. Deep.

"You stayed."

"Yeah."

"Instead of coming home."

"I was home."

He breathed deep, trying to contain his anger, and his hurt, and his…

Yeah, none of that deep-breathing bullshit was going to help.

His shoes slapped as he walked across the room to stand beside Lucy at the window. He leaned up against the opposite side of the window and peered out at the same view—green and bright and so, so alive.

"Is that it, then? The last domino? Or are there more to fall?" He had to ask.

She didn't answer.

"Lucy?"

She sighed and pushed herself up off the seat and clomp, clomp, clomped to the studio door.

Hand on the knob, she turned and said, "Come on. You've got a nephew to meet."

CHAPTER FORTY-TWO

DANE

Leif flicked his toes in the water. The droplets flew out into the sunshine, silent in the cacophony of cicadas.

Concentric ripples waved out on the surface. The refracted light created psychedelic patterns on the pool floor, and Dane couldn't help but be mesmerised by the beautiful light show.

"Da-ane?" Leif rolled the vowel around in his mouth.

"Mm-hmm." He swirled, too—wax on, wax off—and eyed the kid at his side.

Leif bit his lip. "If Mum and Cayden are sister and brother, does that mean Cayden's my uncle?"

He nodded, seeing no problem answering the kid's straightforward question. "Seems that way."

The fact that Leif didn't jump for joy in response wasn't all that surprising. The kid probably needed a bit of time and space to think, to shore up his defences, and to figure out how much of himself he was willing to give. Leif had cottoned to Cayden pretty damn fast. Instant friends. But that didn't mean Leif really knew the guy.

Leif was wise to be cautious rather than risk hurt.

Jesus. Parallel much, Faulks.

"Does that make you my uncle, too?"

"No." God, no.

Absolutely not.

"We're not married."

Dane leaned back, his palms flat on the warm terrace bricks behind him, and stared up at the wide strip of bright blue sky visible between the creamy sailcloth umbrella and the rich green canopy.

He closed his eyes and felt the same bone-deep relaxation creep over him that he'd felt that morning when he'd woken up wrapped around Cayden's warm, giving body.

He hadn't lied to Leif—they weren't together, but they weren't nothing, either.

He raised his gaze to the steam room across the other side of the pool. After Tom's revelations, there'd been no need for their usual steam-room debrief—not in the investigative sense. Dane missed them already.

And after actually finding Lucy, the mission was over. No more investigation. No more need for Cayden to hang about the retreat, pretending to be a detox convert. If he was in Cayden's shoes, he'd check out of his haven by sundown.

Of course, that meant Dane was also officially off the hook.

No more investigation meant no more reason to stay.

He swished his feet in the other direction for a bit, listening to the cicadas' cry, wishing time would slow.

Because the truth was—Dane didn't want it to be over.

He wasn't ready to leave.

Not yet.

The realisation caught him unprepared.

He itched to scroll through his contacts and group chat with the guys back home at Tennyson Bend.

But what would he ask?

Hey, I'm in a bit of a weird situation. I think I was body snatched and replaced with someone who has feelings. What should I do?

Or…

Hey, I'm in a bit of a bind. I'm fucking this guy, and he makes me need…something, but he doesn't need me anymore. What should I do?

The guys would laugh their arses off.

Malone, newly in love, was probably the only one who'd respond with an encouraging, "Go for it." But Malone and Jet had already returned to Tallon Island to complete their volunteer stint, so he was out. Brady was practically a vampire the way he always slept through the day, so he'd be no use. Spencer had shaken off the controversy that shadowed him at the start of the summer of tennis, and finally gotten his chance to compete with a wildcard to the Aussie Open, so Dane was loath to mess up his focus with sappy distractions. That left Lachlan, who Dane already knew would answer with his mainstay question—why the fuck would you ever need anyone?

Why indeed?

Better to stick to helping resolve Cayden's drama, instead of fermenting his own.

Family was a tricky beast. It never made complete sense to outsiders. He could do one last good deed and help the kid make sense of it.

Dane nudged Leif's shoulder, then pointed out a pudgy cloud that hung low in the west. "What do you think? Hippopotamus?"

Leif groaned as if to say *"I'm not a baby, Dane,"* but analysed the cloud anyway because the artist in him couldn't resist.

"Nah. Rhino." He pointed. "See the horn? In a minute it'll become a unicorn."

"Unicorn. Right." Yeah. Dane looked around for more clouds, but, really, what was the point? Finding magical creatures in the sky wasn't going to solve either of their problems.

By silent agreement, they went back to churning the water and watching the cloud slowly stretch in the sky, and Dane wondered if Leif was waiting for it all to make miraculous sense, too.

"For fuck's sake, Cayden. I go by Luna now. You'll confuse everyone if you call me Lucy." Lucy's irate voice came loud and clear from the other side of the hedge between the pool terrace and the hub garden.

"Everyone?" Cayden answered, but something else must have passed between them because he ground out a concession. "Fine. Luna."

"And make sure that gorgeous boyfriend of yours calls me Luna, too."

"He's not my boyfriend."

"Your partner. Whatever."

"No, I mean. We're not together. We just hang. You know? We hardly know each other. Never mind. It's not important."

Not important?

Cayden's summation of their relationship shouldn't have stung. But it did.

Not that they had a relationship.

"Ugh." Dane churned the water a little faster.

"You mean you don't really know him? You asked me to trust someone you hardly know to take care of my son?" Her voice rose. "How could you—"

Dane coughed as loud as he could, and the cicadas crowded back into the sudden human silence.

He saw Cayden's curls over the greenery, like a fluffy

golden cloud on the horizon. They rose to reveal squinting eyes and a wide smile stretched across his face, about as faux as Dane's cough. "Hi, guys." Cayden waved. "Hey, Lucy, look who we found."

Lucy elbowed Cayden out of the way as they came around the end of the hedge, fast-walking to Leif's side.

"What're the odds, eh?" Cayden's eyes skittered around.

Dane didn't move from the pool edge, but he wanted to. He wanted to slide up close to Cayden's side. He just wasn't sure what he wanted to do when he got there—thwack him or hug him. The jury was out on Dane's emotions.

"Sprite? You all right?" Lucy slid her fingers into his tousled hair, as if to make sure he was safe and real.

Dane knew the feeling.

Cayden walked over to stand by Dane's other hip and edged the tips of his thongs out over the water as though tempted to jump in.

Dane knew that feeling, too.

"We found a rhino-corn," Dane said into the awkward silence. He pointed up out to the west, looking for something tangible the kid could rely on. But it had gone.

Nothing but a wisp.

Damn.

Cayden's knee nudged his shoulder. "I believe you."

"It was there—a cross between a rhinoceros and a unicorn. Tell them, Leif."

"Yep. The biggest horn out!"

Cayden snorted, and Dane moved a hand to the top of the man's foot. He ran his fingertips down the grooves between the bones down the length of his foot, feeling for the man's thundering pulse. His fingers drifted over and into the soft, warm arch, and Dane grinned with satisfaction when Cayden peeped. He looked up to see a new streak of pink flash across Cayden's face.

Casual as possible, he asked, "Have you two had lunch? We didn't know how long you'd be, and Leif was hungry, so…"

"Gladdie made her corny coconut fritters, Mum."

"With micro-herb shoots and fermented veggie salad," Dane added, just for Cayden's benefit. "She promised to save a plate for each of you."

"Fermented veg? Mmm. Sounds delicious." Cayden looked more bilious than keen, which wasn't a big surprise. For a man enraptured by nature, he wasn't much into eating it.

"I love those. Thanks, Sprite." Lucy ruffled Leif's hair again, then took a step back, and Dane felt like he'd passed the test.

"Right, then." He let Cayden's foot go and scrambled to his feet. "Let's get you and Lucy fed."

"Luna," she said firmly.

He pasted on a polite smile and held out his hand for her to shake, letting the familiar action ground him. "Good to meet you. I'm Dane Faulks."

She nodded. "Thanks for taking care of my guy."

For a hot second, Dane didn't know which guy she meant. He'd taken care of both of them—in vastly different ways.

Then she gathered Leif to her side.

Leif. Right.

Not Cayden.

"He's a great kid. Must be growing, though. It's a miracle there's any lunch left for the two of you."

"Hey! I left heaps!" Leif protested. "What about Randy? He had five fritters, Mum." He held up his hand, digits spread wide. "Five!"

Given the smiles all around, Dane figured it might be safe to poke the beast. "What about your parents?" he asked. "Have you called them yet?"

"Shit," they both said, looking at him, then at each other.

"Bad word, Mum."

"Sorry, Sprite," she sputtered, cheeks tight, temples flaming.

Cayden couldn't muzzle a half laugh, half groan.

"What's so funny?" Leif asked, all serious and stern.

Lucy-call-me-Luna leaned in to Cayden's side and snorted.

"Mu-um!" Leif crossed his gangly arms.

But the strain had broken, and they were off—over a decade of tension unravelling.

"Jeez," Dane said to Leif, "when the dam breaks, eh?"

The kid had no idea what he meant, but seemed to appreciate having someone sane on his side. He sniffed—all preteen disdain for his oh-so-embarrassing mother.

"Wow. I needed that." Cayden rubbed his eyes. His toothy grin flashed and disappeared as he tried to contain himself.

For an odd moment, Dane thought Cayden had said *I need you,* but Cayden had admitted he didn't think they were anything—they were *not important.* Dane took another step away from the pair. He was glad to see them decompress, but he felt like an interloper on a private party. They were family. And he was not.

Finally calm, Cayden turned to his sister. "Are you ready to call them?"

She shook her head, then stopped. She blew out a big deep breath and nodded once. "Not really, but…" She nervously twirled her hand.

Cayden grabbed it. "I'll be with you."

"Fine. Whatever. Let's just get on with it." She rolled her eyes. Her expression so much like Cayden's, it was uncanny.

Dane took his cue. "They'll probably break the rules and let you two use the office phone. How about if I take Leif up the hill to our havens? Give you two some privacy."

They stared at him—both deer in the headlights.

He almost felt sorry for them.

"I'll take that as a yes. Come on, Leif. Let's go find some possums for your uncle to play with. They're his absolute favourite."

CHAPTER FORTY-THREE

CAYDEN

If he leaned out over the railing of their haven deck far enough, Cayden could just see the fast-moving clouds amassed on the eastern horizon, sending birds into a frenzied flight west ahead of yet another late afternoon storm. "It's like they sense the end of days. Again." He dropped to lie beside Dane on the banana lounge and sighed with relief.

"What a day." Dane stole his thought.

"Yeah. I can't believe she was here all along, right under my nose."

"And Leif, too."

"God, yes. That's a trip." All those years he'd had a nephew, and he didn't know it. What kind of fucked-up shit was that? "You two looked pretty chummy up here."

"He's a cool kid. Dorky, but cool. He'd probably get the shit beat out of him at a regular school."

That didn't sound good. "Even more reason to question her choices."

Dane turned and lifted his eyebrow questioningly. "Harsh."

"But true. I love her. Always will. But now..." Cayden let

that thought drift away. It was hard not to get caught up in the what ifs. In what could have been. He shrugged and stared out at the dense foliage of the rainforest, blurred in the heat and the thickening humidity. "What does that say about me?"

"Says you're a good brother."

He shook his head. "No, it doesn't."

"Says you're human."

He shook his head again, but Cayden couldn't think of a single rebuttal.

"Says you're a good son."

"Ha! You wouldn't say that if you'd heard us on the phone. Straight off, we regressed. Stupid stuff, you know? Like when I used to get annoyed by how our dad always swallowed mid-sentence. Lucy never saw it. Which just bugged me more. So stupid. Then, today, when we had them on speaker-phone, I could hear him stop mid-sentence, and I just knew he was swallowing. God, I could have spit nails. Why do we do that?"

"Get irritated with family?"

"Yes. No." Ugh, what did he mean? "I mean, why do we turn into immature idiots around them?"

"I think that's genetically required. Something about being human." Dane reached across the narrow divide and spread his fingers over Cayden's bare, tented knee. His hand smoothed along Cayden's thigh, idly rubbing the light hairs with his thumb.

It felt good. Warm. As though Dane's simple, soothing touch made every hair follicle lay down its weapon—finally allowed to rest. He wanted to pluck the moment out of all the other shitty moments of the day and hold it safe.

Cayden relaxed a bit into the softness of the banana lounge and let a sliver of tension slip away.

"Before we called Mum and Dad, we talked a bit. And it

was like we were brother and sister again. Like no time had passed and nothing had changed. But then we got on the phone and all that disappeared. She was this whole other person. I don't get it. She refused to tell them about Leif. Nothing about why she left."

"So, it was her choice to leave Melbourne?" Dane asked. "Did something happen between Lucy and your parents? Something that might have made her leave?"

"No." Cayden shook his head vehemently, then slowed. "Well, not knowingly. Ugh. What a fucking mess. All these years. Searching. Tearing our hair out. Not know if she'd run away, or been kidnapped, or worse—left for dead. You hear stories, you know, of people being taken out into the bush and…" he swallowed around a lump in his throat, and his legs flopped flat as they gave out.

Dane's hand fell between them, lax on the banana lounge, pale in the gloom. A shiver prickled Cayden's skin where it had been. Cayden shuffled onto his side to squash the feeling of something absent.

Something lost.

"And yet, here she is. Safe and well. Living an easy, breezy life. With a kid, even. My nephew. Their grandchild, for fuck's sake. And all Lucy could say was, 'I'm happy. I don't need saving.'"

"That's it? No explanation? No hint of why?"

Cayden shook his head and swallowed against the thickness that wouldn't go away. "Not to them, no." He wanted to tell Dane what he knew. But if he started, he wouldn't want to stop. And most of the tale wasn't his to tell, nor his secrets to disclose. As much as he felt closer to Dane than pretty much anyone in his supposed family, he had no business spilling what he knew about his Mum maybe having another baby, or losing a baby, or…*God knows what else.* "Lucy called it the domino effect—one thing leads to another, and another, and so on. The crux of it was her pregnancy with Leif."

"He's a cool kid."

Cayden nodded. "I can't fault her that. But every other decision? I don't know, Dane. All she seems to care about is their life here—living in a tent in this weird-arse place. I just don't get it. Why not tell us where she was? Why not come back? It's not like pregnancy is a hanging offense. She could have come home. We're her family."

Dane tilted his way. "You need more information."

Dane wasn't wrong—he did need more information.

But what truly gutted Cayden was Dane's use of the singular pronoun.

You, not we.

They'd found Lucy. Dane had fulfilled his promise.

Whatever came next was Cayden's problem and Cayden's problem alone.

Dane messed with the backrest on his half of the banana lounge till he was lying almost flat, tucked his hands under his head, and crossed his ankles. "At least she's alive and well. That's what you've wanted all along, right? Now you can get on with your life." The words rolled so easily out of Dane's mouth. As if it was nothing to brush off the mission that had driven Cayden his whole adult life.

His burden.

"I never want to be needed again. Not like that. Not so much that it takes over my life, my job, my fucking everything. It's such a relief to be free."

What would come next?

Fuck knows.

The wind whipped up and rustled the treetops, and the roiling storm clouds pressed overhead.

"Wait, so she and Leif actually live in that circus tent?" Dane asked.

"Yep."

"Wow."

"Yep."

"Stop saying 'yep.'" Dane's grumble made Cayden smile.

Cayden wished he'd not lost the man's touch. A bit of reassurance would have been nice right about then, even if there was nothing real behind it.

Nothing lasting.

Not unless he pressed the issue.

Cayden's pinkie finger crept across the banana lounge, about as stealthy as a tractor.

"Nope." He popped the *p*, just for fun.

Dane literally growled, which was so fucking sexy that Cayden couldn't resist flipping himself over and straddling Dane's thighs. No invitation required.

"Hi," Cayden said, sitting high, smelling a hint of Dane in the ozone.

"Hi," Dane parroted, his voice gravel as thunder.

Dane's warm hands cupped his hips and smoothed around to palpate the swell of his arse.

Cayden rested his hands on Dane's abs. He'd willed himself into the moment, but it wasn't that easy to shut down his vexing thoughts.

"It's just weird, you know, discovering Leif. Did you hear him call me Uncle Cayden?"

Dane nodded. His dark eyes intent.

"All this time, I've had a nephew. It never even entered my mind. I should be happy, knowing he exists, but it just makes me so mad." He rat-a-tat-tatted on Dane's stomach. Not an SOS, but close. "I'll never get to hold him on his first day, or hear his first words, first steps, first whatever. You know?" Could Dane tell how his edges had started to fray?

"First time falling off a bike."

"Exactly." He nodded, inordinately glad that somebody understood.

"First unfortunate swear repeat."

"Ha!" Cayden reared back. The motion rocked his arse back into Dane's hands, and those long fingers slipped between his shirt and shorts, blazing a new trail.

"There's plenty enough time to experience all that with another nephew, or niece. Or son, or daughter." Dane frowned. "If you ever choose that path, I mean."

"True." But Dane had missed the point. "All I'm saying is I ought to have known he existed. It pisses me off that she took knowing him away from me."

"Fair."

"I should be crazy happy to have found them, but I just feel robbed." He leaned forward again, palms skimming Dane's ribs, flicking a glance to see his expression. Fearing judgement. "And don't say 'fair'."

Dane frowned. "Why? What's wrong with that?"

"It's annoying. You're being far too reasonable."

Dane pulled his left hand out from under the band at the back of his shorts and travelled teasingly around to the snap at the front.

Cayden's whole body shuddered, and he pressed firmer against the resistance of Dane's thighs.

"I'd say it's the other way round," Dane said.

That made no sense. "How do you figure?"

"Isn't it obvious?" Dane teased the edge of the cloth. "You keep telling me what you're missing out on while I'm lying here, cock at half-mast, primed for you. Feels pretty unreasonable to me."

"That's not—" But Cayden couldn't finish his argument, let alone remember what it might have been, because Dane's teasing hands had pulled his hips forward to feel the evidence first-hand.

Already in shadow, Dane's eyes darkened even more. "Do you want to keep finding things to complain about? Or do you want to get to the bit where we have wild, sweaty sex?"

Cayden blinked.

What sort of question was that?

"Wild, sweaty sex, please," he answered.

"Good choice."

CHAPTER FORTY-FOUR

CAYDEN

Dane hadn't shaved since he'd arrived at the House of Glass, and the sharp rasp matched the frisson of energy that chased down Cayden's spine to bloom hot and heavy, right under Dane's steady hand.

Cayden tightened his arms around Dane's neck, nearly locking elbows in his efforts to stay close, and Dane did nothing to hinder that cause. Cayden ground down against Dane's proud ridge, never letting up, even when Dane surged up and off the banana lounge.

Cayden fumbled for purchase, tugging at the man's hair and shoulders, dangling in Dane's arms. His dick practically hissed like a snake as he slid down Dane's body until his legs figured out that they were supposed to be keeping him upright.

Pure torture.

"Whurg murv?" he protested around the man's wicked tongue.

Dane laughed, giving him a tiny chance to get his breath back. Sense wasn't so easy to regain.

"We are not having banana-lounge sex," Dane said.

Visions of riding Dane on the banana lounge rushed forth.

"But—"

"No."

Damn.

"Next time."

"No."

Double damn.

They weren't even naked, and he was already hot as a flaming marshmallow. But banana lounge or bed, he didn't really give a shit—hell, he'd be fine with the garden bed, so long as it wasn't a cactus patch. All he cared about was getting Dane's prick in him tout de suite.

"Fine. Have your wicked way."

Please, please, please, have you wicked way with me.

"As though that were up for debate." Dane chuckled again, and his breath blew hot in Cayden's ear. Dane fast-danced them across the deck and into his haven. Dane slid the screen door and curtain shut against bugs and bats and any other night crawlers that might interrupt the proceedings.

"You're so thorough." Cayden followed Dane down as he sat on the side of the bed. Cayden mouthed at his cheekbone, and he felt the man's eyelashes flutter on his nose. He tasted the smooth skin at Dane's temple and ran the tip of his tongue against the grain of his brow.

"I'm not a lollipop."

"Mmm." Cayden licked again. "You're right. More salty than sweet."

One day, he promised himself, he'd learn Dane purely by mouth. Every single, sexy inch of him.

"So, stop licking me."

"No," he said, taking secret joy in repeating Dane's blunt reply.

He planted a wet kiss on Dane's nose, just for shits and

giggles, then pulled up his shirt as he climbed off Dane's lap and began to strip.

Dane didn't let him get far. He tangled his fingers in the front of Cayden's shorts, slipped the button through the hole, then slowly, carefully, ran the zipper open, key by key, over Cayden's straining dick.

It was very distracting.

Cayden stepped closer in between Dane's splayed knees and leaned over his shoulder to pull up the man's top—each revealed vertebra a stepping stone to joy. He skimmed his lips across Dane's wide-winged shoulder blades and closed his eyes against the rush of anticipation.

Curled around each other, he felt Dane's hands around his hips, shoving at his shorts. Wanting skin on skin, Cayden tried to help Dane, but the elastic waistband caught on his ankles and he teetered sideways.

"Hold up." Dane huffed into his hip. He nipped the skin there before pushing Cayden up and away. "Stay there," he said, bracing Cayden upright with his hands and a look that said stop.

Cayden didn't move an inch.

Dane scooted back in the bed, stripping his shorts and boxers as he went, then rolled to grab supplies from his bedside drawer. The fucking tease then spent an inordinate amount of time rearranging the many fluffy pillows to his satisfaction and situated himself back against the headboard.

Cayden didn't wait for more of an invitation.

He followed on his knees and resumed his position across Dane's thighs. Dane's hands also returned to their rightful place—covering his arse-cheeks—and Cayden's sigh turned into a groan turned into a shudder.

His blood raced, but he forced himself to go slow and feel the sensuous pulse of Dane's restless thighs teasing his arse cheeks ever so slightly apart and together, apart and together. It was so hot to watch Dane's gaze travel from where they connected, cock against cock, then up, up, up to lock eyes together.

"Hi," Cayden said.

"Hi yourself."

Each hair follicle fired as Dane's hands smoothed down his thighs, then up again to his hips and around to the concave curve of Cayden's spine. There, his hands parted ways. One went high to pull Cayden's chest closer, while the other drifted down to tease at the top of his crease.

"Kiss me," Cayden demanded.

"You're such a sap."

He collected a drizzle of precum with his fingertip and smoothed the glistening juice across his lower lip. "Kiss me anyway."

Dane complied.

A kiss shouldn't feel that good, Cayden thought.

A kiss like that spelled *crush*—it spelled *my heart trips when you smile at me*, and *let's do it again, and again, and again*, and *if we keep this up, I'm in danger of falling.*

None of that was them.

They weren't comfort, or love, or adoration.

They were need, and convenience, and heat.

But Cayden didn't much care what they were or weren't as Dane pulled him down for another, longer kiss and delved deep.

The node of heat at the base of his spine went fucking nuclear as Dane's heat-seeking fingertip hit the spot.

"Mmm," he groaned, "remind me later to give you a medal for growing such long digits."

"Shh."

One finger became two became three, and Dane matched the assault with soft mouth, firm tongue, and sharp, nipping teeth. Dane's knees folded up behind him, feet braced flat against the sheets, hips bucking with instinctive need.

Cayden couldn't think, let alone coordinate himself to reciprocate with anything but heat and want. When Dane's fingers left him hollow, he gasped on the heady air. "Stop fucking teasing."

Dane bit his neck and sucked hard. The crinkle of foil clued Cayden into the proceedings and staved off any further complaint.

Suited up, Dane guided Cayden to rise and fall onto his blunt head, pressing in with slow, firm insistence.

Cayden squeezed his eyes tight. He forced a shuddering breath out and back in again, trying to relax as the pressure of Dane's rock-hard cock strained his muscular ring.

A moan rumbled deep from Dane's chest, the vibration like a shock wave loosening every cell in Cayden's body. He plummeted, taking Dane's surging cock deep within.

"Holy fuck." He grasped at Dane's shoulders, lungs sawing at the air, balls threatening to erupt already as Dane's solid cock throbbed in his welcome heat.

"Wait," Dane panted.

But he didn't need time.

He didn't need a moment.

He needed to move.

"Now." Cayden braced one hand on the headboard and the other behind Dane's neck. He didn't bother asking what Dane liked, just claimed his mouth and trusted the man was good with a gallop as he rode his gorgeous dick into the proverbial sunset.

Long, selfish minutes later, Cayden lay slumped, half-on, half-off Dane's chest. His heavy breaths battled the thudding heartbeat under his ear.

Thinking it polite, he patted Dane somewhere near his hip. "Good fuck, thanks."

Dane's rumbly chuckle vibrated all the way through him.

Tuned to the same radio signal.

Aligned.

"You're welcome," Dane said, and Cayden couldn't help smiling.

Dane's gentle fingers soothed his spine and the happy-happy-joy-joy twitch of his sensitised rim.

Cayden's fingertips drifted down to where his sticky cum smeared shiny on Dane's skin.

Marked.

He circled Dane's belly button, tempted to stake his claim and say something stupid like, 'you're never allowed to wash ever again,' but Dane wasn't a compliant soul.

The bastard.

Cayden drifted back up again and tucked his thumb beneath where his cheek rested right over Dane's heart. It was a gift to not feel compelled to say anything, or do anything, or be anything special.

He tugged at the hairs closest to Dane's left nipple.

"Hey." Dane brushed his hand away. "Be good."

"Why?" He tugged...again, and Dane brushed him off...again.

"Menace."

He reached for a third time.

Dane growled, grabbed his wrist, and then flipped them both in a spectacularly energetic move that resulted in Cayden lying flat on his back in the middle of the bed, arms outstretched and Dane hovering over him.

Cayden couldn't help grinning at the man's caveman expression.

"So, this is what it's like to be Leonardo da Vinci's Vitruvian Man."

Cayden wriggled his hands, but Dane wasn't letting up, so he tried another tack. "And then the most gorgeous man in the universe lay down on the most fuckable man and stuck his cock in unmentionable places, and all was well with the world."

Dane's eyes narrowed. "Is this your idea of a bedtime story?"

"Shh…and, afterward, the most gorgeous man lay the most fuckable man down in a bed of rose petals and whispered sweet nothings in his ear, because he was so fine."

Dane took over, "Till the most gorgeous man decided the most fuckable man needed to shut up so they could both get some sleep, so they could recharge, wake up, and fuck all over again."

"Such a romantic." Cayden rolled his eyes, not wanting to disappoint. He wasn't about to let on how divine a picture Dane had drawn in his mind.

Dane flopped to his side, making the bed bounce. "You're so easy."

"No," he disagreed, "we're easy together."

A beat later, Cayden realised what he'd said.

Together.

"That's a turnabout." Dane's voice was too measured for Cayden's liking. "You're the one that said, and I quote, 'He's not my boyfriend,' 'We're not together,' 'It's not important.'"

Dane had heard that?

And remembered it word for word?

Damn.

Lights flashed in the awkward silence. Five seconds later, thunder cracked open the sky, shattering the stormy darkness.

Shit. How had they gone so quickly from laughter to lightning?

Cayden thought maybe if he could see through the ceiling, he'd see the Greek Gods looking down on him. Winking.

The bastards.

Before Cayden could formulate a response that wasn't some form of *yes, but...* Dane dislodged him from his lap.

"Which is the truth, really, when it comes down to it," Dane went on. "We might have helped each other out a time or two, but we're not in a relationship. I'll head home soon, and you'll go back to Melbourne—"

"What? Already? Why?"

Dane frowned. "You came to find Lucy. Mission accomplished. Why wouldn't you go home?"

"Oh." He hadn't got that far. "Yeah. I guess. I don't know."

"Why would you stay?" Dane's persistence cut to the bone.

Why, indeed?

Dane was right. They'd partnered up to find Lucy, to get each other off, and to survive the absurdity of the retreat. In that order.

Nothing more.

Nothing less.

Even if...

He rolled onto his back and watched the ceiling fan stir the heavy air.

"Dane?"

"Mmm?"

"Is there any other reason why we might want to stay?" He had to ask.

After a too long beat of silence, Cayden turned his head to search the man's expression. What was Dane thinking? Had Cayden freaked him out? Had Dane even heard the want in Cayden's voice?

"Like what?"

And that said it all.

Cayden rolled to sit up on the side of the mussed bed and planted his feet firm on the cool wooden floor. "Never mind."

The sheets rustled, and he twisted to see Dane roll over

into the heat he'd left behind and pull Cayden's still-warm pillow into his chest with a contented sigh.

Fuck. He could have been that pillow.

"Where are you going?" Dane's voice muffled against the pillow. Then he yawned and snuggled deeper into the warmth and softness of the bed.

"Shower," he answered, but it was already too late. Dane's heavy eyelids had dropped.

Alone, he padded into Dane's bathroom—mirror-image to his own—and cranked the hot water on full blast, stepping in to wash away everything but the memory of Dane's touch.

CHAPTER FORTY-FIVE

DANE

Hours after the wind and the rain had settled into stillness, the crickets had taken over the airwaves, and the stormy grey of afternoon had turned to summer-night black, Dane woke to a timid knock on his glass haven door.

He rubbed the sleep from his eyes. What now?

White torch light danced on the other side of the glass door. It threw just enough light inside for Dane to see Cayden splayed out on his back, with one arm flung back-hand across Dane's chest, his feet twisted in their shoved-down sheets, and a smile on his beautiful face. A naked, sated starfish.

Dane exhaled slowly as he slid out from under Cayden's arm and off the bed and pulled up the sheet to cover him—because nobody else got to see Cayden's fun bits. Not that he had any intrinsic right to them, either.

Is there any other reason why we might want to stay? Cayden's question hung in Dane's mind, flashing like some gaudy neon sign.

No, there was no reason for them to stay together.

Of course not.

Dane had a life to get back to—a satisfying career, a home he loved, and a bunch of friends who'd roast him if they knew he'd ever seen a man, touched a man, wanted a man, and thought *stay*.

Dane would freely admit to wanting the man. Cayden was sexy as sin. But need? No. Dane didn't *need* anyone.

Dane looked back to the bed to make sure Cayden was safely covered. He'd get some distance. Soon.

Another knock sounded, and his sliding door inched open.

Shit.

"Mr. Faulks? Hello."

"Shh!"

Gordon-fucking-Fuller? What the hell did he want?

Dane found his shorts with their other clothes strewn across the floor. He shoved a leg in as he hopped as quiet as he could across to the gleaming head of the torch being used to push the curtain aside.

For fuck's sake! Did nobody understand the concept of privacy?

"So sorry to bother you this late at night, Mr. Faulks. I'm looking for Mr. Spicer. Do you know where he might be? His parents are here."

Cayden's parents?

Holy shit.

Dane pushed the head of the torch to shine down at the floor, planted himself between the interlopers outside and Cayden inside, and thumbed the curtain an inch to the side.

Sure enough, crowded up behind Gordon was a middle-aged, strung-out-looking couple.

The woman rose on her tippy-toes and opened her mouth to speak, but Dane shushed them with a finger to his lips.

"Mr. Faulks?" the man over Gordon's other shoulder started.

"Shh," he repeated, annoyed.

"Sorry," Gordon whispered. "Do you know where Mr. Spicer could be? He's not in his haven."

Well, hell, what was he supposed to say? *He's in my bed sleeping off his third orgasm* wasn't exactly a great way to meet the in-laws.

In-laws? What the ever-loving fuck?

"Umm." He'd struck himself dumb.

"Who is it, Dane?" came Cayden's very sleepy, very audible, very croaky-from-having-a-cock-in-his-throat voice.

"Umm."

"Cayden? Gerry, it's Cayden," the woman said.

"I heard him, Francis," the man said.

"Don't Francis me. What's he doing in there?" She pointed into Dane's haven.

"How am I supposed to know?" the man said.

"Well, go in there and see," she said.

"I can't just go into another man's room," he said.

Was this really happening? Nightmares didn't usually start like this.

Nor dreams.

Cayden's mother huffed.

Dane couldn't stand it anymore. He wasn't about to out Cayden, but his presence in Dane's bed was no longer a mystery. He couldn't very well lie and claim their son wasn't there.

He held up his finger to the three outside. "Just a second." Then he shut the door in their collective faces and let the curtain fall back into place.

Darkness immediately descended.

"So…"

Cayden switched on the lamp on his bedside table and sat up against the headboard.

The sheet pooled at his waist, exposing love bites that stood out red on his still-pink chest, and his hair stood up straight on one side like he'd run cummy fingers through it, which he probably had.

"Holy shit," Cayden said, eyes wide as the sky.

"I know."

"They don't know I'm gay, Dane. I'm out to pretty much everyone else, but not to them." He twisted the sheet in his fingers.

"I know."

"What do I do?"

Dane had no idea. He stood by the door, flat-footed in the dark room, unsure where to start. "How can I help?"

The knocking started up again. Louder this time. "Mr. Faulks?"

Dane shook himself and switched gears. In business, he could do secretive, and he could do subtle. If he put his mind to it, he could do sensitive, too.

Maybe.

For Cayden's sake.

He stepped closer to the side of the bed, cupped Cayden's neck, and planted a quick kiss on the man's succulent lips.

"You go shower. I'll tell them we got to talking and fell asleep. Nothing more to it."

Nothing to see here, folks.

Cayden's lips reached for a second kiss, but Dane was awake to the man's wiles, and he ducked away from temptation.

"Shower," he repeated.

Cayden huffed out a frustrated breath. "I don't see why. Taking a shower would be as much an admission as them seeing us cock-deep in each other."

Dane's snort caught them both by surprise, and he couldn't resist taking another peck. "Nice imagery, but maybe let's not do that in front of the parentals."

The half-smile on Cayden's face felt like a small win.

"You need to wash up before they see you." No way could he let Cayden out to his parents looking as he did. "But then what? What do you want to do?"

Cayden's half-smile fell, and he shrugged. "Face the music, I guess. Hope finding Lucy is enough of a gift for them to forgive me." He climbed out of bed and grabbed his discarded shorts.

"Forgive you? For being gay? That hardly needs an apology." Dane's blood rose at the unjust thought.

"God no. I'd never apologise for that." He shook his t-shirt out before slipping it over his head. "I just mean they'll be hurt that I lied to them."

"It's only a lie of omission. You're an adult; you don't owe them every private thought."

"Yeah." Cayden closed the gap between them and tangled his fingers in Dane's waistband. "But it's still a lie."

Dane ate the word right out of his mouth.

They weren't a thing. They'd already established that. And they wouldn't ever be a thing. But he could be exactly what Cayden needed right then and there.

Because their kiss was no lie.

No lie at all.

The knocking turned to banging on the glass door. Dane broke the lip-lock and looked up to the ceiling for strength.

"It'll be all right, Dane." Cayden patted him on the chest, right over his heart.

That was ridiculous. He ought to be the one consoling Cayden. Not the other way around.

But Cayden was already moving. "They love me…and you're right—I don't owe them everything."

"What do you need from me?"

Cayden shook his head, then seemed to change his mind. He didn't quite meet Dane's eyes as he bit his plump lip and nodded. "Be here when I come back?"

CHAPTER FORTY-SIX

CAYDEN

Cayden twisted his wrist to check his watch, but his arm was bare. "What time is it?" He'd not thought to ask Dane, and the pitch dark of the rainforest on a rain-soaked, moonless night gave no clue.

How long had he and Dane been sleeping? More to the point, how long had they been fucking?

Cayden dragged the sliding door of his haven shut with Gordon well and truly on the other side. When he turned, his mum and dad crowded into his personal space.

"What the hell is going on, son? Were you sleeping in there? With that man? Why?"

"His name's Dane, Dad."

"None of that matters, Gerry. Where's Lucy, honey? I have to see her. Is she here?"

"Sorry, Mum. She's not here."

"What do you mean, she's not here? Where is she, then?"

"She and Leif live nearby."

"Who the hell's Leif? Is that who took her away from us?"

"No. No, Dad. Leif's not...no." Oh, shit. He wasn't supposed to blab about Leif. Never mind that he knew they would love to know they had a grandchild. Lucy had been adamant—they weren't to know her son existed until she told them herself. And he'd stupidly agreed.

"Where is she, honey? Tell us everything. How did you find her? I have to see her."

"I know, Mum. And you will." Geez, what could he say? "It's just…Lucy wants to tell you what happened herself, which is fair enough." He doubted they'd accept that.

He wouldn't.

"How did you get here so fast?" Cayden tried for a diversion.

"It's gone eleven, honey."

"We caught the first flight available. Who was that man, son?" His dad looked genuinely puzzled, and he realized all over again how good he'd been at subterfuge—that he'd effectively been undercover his whole life.

His parents had never questioned his private life. Never asked why he didn't introduce them to women. He'd thought that, maybe, on some level, they'd always known and were just respecting his privacy.

Guess not.

And so, just like when he was a fifteen-year-old kid, he tried to formulate the words.

He'd not been able to do it then. Not with all the other family dramas going on. But at twenty-seven…yeah, Cayden knew it was time to stop hiding from his own truth.

Besides, he'd been looking for a diversion.

This one was a doozy.

"So, yeah, the thing is…Mum, Dad, I'm gay."

It might have just been his lungs that felt like they were suffering from oxygen deprivation, but Cayden would swear that all the air just got sucked out of the room.

His parents just stood there. Silent. Flapping their gums.

Eventually, Mum snapped her mouth shut and rustled up a few words. "Is he—Dane, was it—is he your boyfriend?"

"Dane? My boyfriend?" *Yes, please.* "No. We just, well, you know, got to know each other a bit, while we're both here. Hanging out and…stuff."

He could think of worse euphemisms for fucking.

"At a health retreat?"

"Yeah, Mum. At a health retreat."

"Where you've been gay. With that man?"

"No. Well, yes. But…"

"Which is it, son? Yes or no?"

What was with the third-degree? "Yes, where I've been gay. But no, not just here. I've always been gay. I am always gay. It's not a switch I can turn on and off."

"Do not speak to your mother like that."

"Like what?" Like a grown man who knew his own sexuality and finally felt free to express it?

Except they were right to be sceptical—to question the way he'd presented his truth before—because he had lied. No doubt about that. He'd hid his true self for far longer than Lucy had been gone. And that was on him.

"I'm sorry. Can we just not talk about this tonight? The important thing is that Lucy's safe and well. Tomorrow we can find her—"

His mum clutched her invisible pearls. "What do you mean, *find* her? I thought you knew where she was. Did you already lose her again?"

"Again? I wasn't the one that lost her. Oh, and, by the way, she calls herself Luna now. Like the moon."

Cayden regretted the harsh words the minute they spilled out of his mouth.

"Sorry. What I meant to say was—tomorrow we can go to her home. Or maybe she'll come here. Either way, it's late.

And it's been a day. They'll most likely be fast asleep, and you two must be tired as hell. Do you have somewhere to stay?"

"They?" his dad picked up.

Shit. He'd done it again.

"Nothing. Just. You know. She doesn't exactly live alone." More like with three-dozen other souls, only one of whom was blood related. But Cayden couldn't say anything about that either. *Fucking hell, Luna—see what you've landed me in?*

"I know you need to see that she's okay, but she has good reason to wait. I promise." He held up both hands to stem the inquisition. "She'll be there in the morning."

They looked at each other, communicating silently.

Dad swallowed. "We rented a car from the airport, but, ah...we didn't book a place to..."

"Shit, sorry." Why would they expend energy booking accommodation when their entire focus was on getting to their baby? He got it. "Don't worry about it. You can sleep here."

"Here? But this is your room, honey. Where will you sleep?" she asked.

He didn't bother answering that nugget of a question, just held out his hand and wiggled his fingers at his dad. "Give me your car keys, and I'll go get your luggage."

Dad jingled his keys, but didn't hand them over. "I'll come with you."

Oh, joy—bring on the man-to-man cross-examination.

CHAPTER FORTY-SEVEN

CAYDEN

An agonising hour later, Cayden gave himself a quick towel dry and flicked off the bathroom light, then stumbled through the dark to Dane's bed.

He'd forgotten how bloody dark it got in the rainforest at night.

Cayden felt along the edge of the mattress till he got to the bedside table and switched on the lamp.

"Mhmuph." Dane grumbled and blinked his one visible eye. The rest of his front was intimately acquainted with the sheets. Worst luck.

Not that Dane's hind-half was a struggle to look at.

In the summer heat, all they ever needed was a sheet over them, and it curved around Dane's planes and angles like silk in some Renaissance painting of a lounging Greek God. The only thing missing was a cupid hovering overhead, with a bow and a quiver of golden arrows.

"You okay?" Dane mumbled into his pillow.

No. "Yeah."

God, emotions were so exhausting.

"Wanna talk?" Dane's back muscles flexed as he levered up onto his elbows. Too distracting by half.

Did he want to talk? "Not really." He wanted to lose himself in a good hard fuck, but that wasn't exactly on the cards what with his parents on the other side of the thin, dividing wall.

Failing that, what he wanted was to sleep, and wake up, and for everything to be over...problems sorted...drama done.

Dane eyed him for a few seconds, then flopped back down. "Come back to bed, then." He petted the sheet beside him and tucked his hand back under the pillow. "Sleep."

The sheets on Cayden's side of the bed were still a mess from their earlier acrobatics. He pulled the fitted bottom sheet back over the corner of the mattress and lifted the rucked-up top sheet. As he shook it to loosen the sweaty wrinkles, something flew at his face.

Instinctively, he ducked. "Fuck!"

Memories of attack possums fired adrenaline into his blood, but he stayed perfectly still. His eyes dashed side to side to look for whatever it was that had attacked him.

Down on the floor, a paperback was splayed open, leaves buffeted by the fan. Beside the book lay the sweetest, brightest, least-Dane-looking bookmark imaginable, covered in sparkly rainbows.

Jesus. That's just too cute.

He leaned down to reach for them, and just about face-planted on the floor.

"For fuck's sake, Cayden," Dane grumbled, "what are you doing?"

Oh, man. Dopey Dane was seriously cute.

Cayden sat back up and stroked the book like it was a villain's hairless cat. "Poor booky book, getting slept on by big bad Dane."

Suddenly wide awake, Dane rolled to sit up and grabbed the book. He checked the spine and smoothed the crinkled pages that had folded as it landed, then looked around the bed, brows furrowed.

"Looking for this?" Cayden twizzled the bookmark, turning the tassel into a fan. "I looked everywhere for your unicorn, but couldn't find it."

He snatched the bookmark back and checked it over. "What?"

"You know. Your unicorns—the ones that rode here on their sparkly rainbows."

Dane slid it into the book and laid them both safe and sound on his bedside table.

Cayden's heart twisted at the care Dane took with it. "What's the book?"

"Nothing," Dane replied too quickly.

"It's clearly not nothing. But fine, keep your secrets."

Dane rolled his eyes. "Well, fuck. Now I am awake."

"Oops." Cayden fluffed the pillows and slipped between the straightened sheets, then sighed as he finally lay down. "Go ahead and read. I doubt I'll sleep tonight." He yawned.

"You sure about that?" Dane asked.

"Sure. The light won't bother me."

"No, I meant not sleeping."

He was exhausted. "Too many thoughts whizzing around in my mind. You could read to me. Might help me drift off."

Loving the idea, Cayden turned onto his side and fossicked deeper into his pillow. It smelled of sex.

"Comfy?" Dane asked.

"Mm-hmm." Cayden didn't miss the sarcasm, but he ignored it in favour of watching Dane. He really was beautiful. Especially in the glow of the bedside lamplight. It struck each feature sharp with contrasting light and shadow. He could happily lie there all night, just watching Dane breathe…which wasn't romantic at all. Kinda creepy, actually, if he was being honest.

Dane gave him a long look. Then, seeming to have made a decision, he twisted to pick the book back up from his bedside table.

"Yay!" He said around another jaw-stretching yawn. He'd won the game.

"Menace."

"Uh-huh. What's the book?"

Dane tilted the cover so Cayden could see it.

"Mervyn Peake. Never heard of him. Looks old."

"Like me?"

"You're not old."

"I'm thirty-two. That's five years older than you."

"Pish. That's nothing."

He didn't think Dane was actually going to read, but the man stuffed his pillow higher under his neck, flicked open to a page early in the book, and began to read aloud.

Fully aware he was exhibiting the psychology of an attention-seeking toddler, Cayden slid across the bed, tucked himself under Dane's arm, and lay his head on Dane's warm, bare chest.

Dane paused to reset his hold on the spine of the book, then resumed reading.

Instead of the words that vibrated through Dane's chest, Cayden listened to the solid thwump-thwump-thwump of his heartbeat, and the slower whoosh…whoosh…whoosh of his lungs, and he waited. People always talk when given the time and opportunity to get their thoughts off their chests—even people as stoic as Dane.

Just as Cayden felt himself drift off, the chapter came to an end.

With practiced movements, Dane placed the oh-so-fabulous bookmark in his place, shut the book, and rested it down on the other half of his chest.

Cayden just about went cross-eyed, looking at the creased spine. "Do you want to talk about it?"

His human pillow shifted a bit.

Cayden shifted with him.

"Nothing much to talk about. My sister gave me her library," Dane said, voice rough. "I'm reading through it."

Ah.

Finally.

Cayden tried to recall anything Dane had said about family. If there ever was a trigger word for him, it was *sister*. He itched to ask more questions, but the tightness in Dane's body told Cayden to tread carefully.

He trailed a slow finger in the shadow made by the book. "You don't say much about your life. Your family."

Dane mumbled something that sounded suspiciously like, "None of your business."

But Cayden wasn't about to be put off. "Where do you live? Favourite ice-cream flavour? Most embarrassing moment?"

Six wooshes went by before he got his answers.

"Tennyson Bend. Hazelnut praline. Getting caught jacking off to my mother's Stephan Edberg poster."

Cayden blinked. "Wasn't Stephan Edberg that famous tennis player back in the eighties?"

"Mm-hmm. Mum loved him."

"Oh, God." He buried his forehead in the nook of Dane's pit. When he could school his expression, he lifted to rest his chin back on Dane's chest. "As did you, it would seem."

"Yeah." Dane stared up at the ceiling, but Cayden suspected he wasn't seeing anything but memories. "Nobody else knows that. If you tell, I'll know it was you."

He snorted. "Except for the person who caught you."

Dane didn't comment.

Under the sheet, Cayden curled his right foot around Dane's ankle, drawing Dane's attention, and his gaze.

The deep, dark pain there gutted him. "Alice won't tell."

Oh, fuck—that look; those words.

And suddenly Cayden recalled Dane's story of his sister, who was fine and then not fine.

What happened to her?

How did she die?

Two beats went by...three...then he again repeated the over-worn question.

"Do you want to talk about it?"

Cayden knew it was selfish of him, but he wanted Dane to say no. He'd had enough of pain and worry and drama for one day. He needed the light chocolate mousse version of Dane, rather than the heavy Spanish hot chocolate version.

"No," Dane said, with a great whoosh of air.

"Okay." Cayden leaped on the magic word. Then repeated, "Okay," softer this time, with a barely-there kiss to a space between the man's ribs, right above the thwump of his heart.

The minute he did it, Cayden knew it was too much—too heavy. He had to turn the moment around. For his own sake, even if not for Dane's.

"So..." He drew out the word, hoping Dane would forgive his selfish wit. "Is your love for Stephan Edberg a now-that-you've-told-me-you'll-have-to-kill-me type secret?"

Dane's chest jerked with a surprised burst of laughter. "More like a take-it-to-your-grave type secret. If you don't tell, I won't have to kill."

"Hmm." Cayden pretended to ponder. "A little death would be all right. So long as you make it fun."

Dane groaned. "Terrible."

Cayden snickered. He repurposed his kiss into a tease and

settled back into his rightful place plastered to Dane's side, ignoring the heat and the humidity and the crap of the day.

He lay his arm loose around Dane's ribs and rubbed his cheek against Dane's pec, then closed his eyes—content to just be.

CHAPTER FORTY-EIGHT

DANE

A week in to the retreat, Dane's daily run up to the rim felt like routine, but everything else about the day felt different.

It wasn't waking up half-way underneath Cayden. He was getting used to that.

It was something else inside himself. Some need he couldn't put a finger on.

Resolve the puzzle or run far away? Those seemed to be his options.

Stay or go?

Never had he concurrently wanted such disparate outcomes in equal measure.

Cayden had him spinning. That was for sure. It was a miracle he'd even thought to grab his mobile phone as he'd levered himself out from under Cayden.

Brady's goofy profile pic glowed on Dane's phone screen.

He hesitated a second with his thumb over the call icon.

What would he even say to Brady if he answered?

Hey mate, I met this guy—he makes me want things—no, not that kind of thing—well, yes, that kind of thing—I'm being serious here, mate—I know, I know, I'm never serious about guys—so, what's different about him?

"Fuck knows."

He tapped anyway.

The dial tone rang.

"Mate, how's Noosa fairing?" Brady said.

Dane looked southeast, across the coastal strip, to the shining resort town in the distance. "Not in Noosa."

"You back home then? Carol will have your balls, mate. Two weeks' break, she said. No less."

Dane groaned and leaned his elbows on the rough wooden railing to the platform high on the rim. "She sent me to a fucking health farm, Brady."

Silence never sounded so loud.

"Did you hear me?"

"A health farm...like with chooks and cows and llamas? Do you have to milk goats?" Brady's incredulity came through loud and clear.

"Might as well be. We're fed like herbivores." Which wasn't entirely true, and Dane felt an instant pang at slandering Gladioli's delicious food. Still, the thought of something other than sprouts made his taste buds water. "One of your seared grass-fed steaks wouldn't go astray right about now."

"Preach it, baby."

"Not my style, but yeah. I'd worship at the edge of your barbeque any day, Brady."

"Ha! Yeah. Oh, um, hang on a sec, Dane." His voice muffled.

Was Brady talking to someone else? He was usually alone at dawn.

"Where are you? Is someone there?"

Brady's voice came back, a bit too loud and clear. "Well, of course you love my meat, mate. That's a given. Do you have to wear costumes? I can just imagine you in a Frisian cow onesie, mocking the humans. Wait. Let me get my pencil. I can see it all now. We'll make a mint."

"Slow down. You already have a mint, Mr. I-Got-Rich-On-Lotto."

"Nah. That's different. There's nothing like earning it."

"True." And, despite his friendly tease, he knew it was true. They'd both come from a place of hard luck and each worked their arses off to make bank in their chosen industries. The fact that Brady had gotten a helping hand from a lotto ticket bought on a lark for his twenty-first birthday was irrelevant to anything but what sort of apartment he could buy. The penthouse at Tennyson Bend hadn't come cheap. The rest of his fortune came from diligent, hard work.

"Let me get this straight. Carol sent you to a health farm—"

"More accurately, it's a wellness retreat," Dane interrupted, inexplicably feeling the need to defend the place.

"Okay, to a wellness retreat. Where you're doing what? Chanting? Yoga? Yogic chanting?"

"Neither yoga nor chanting. Though they're likely on offer. So far, it's been lots of green food, amazing massages, and a steam room you'd love." If he was being entirely accurate, he'd add *and a really hot guy*, but his need to spill those beans had vanished in an unexpected wave of special and private and mine.

"You sound like a convert."

To the guy? Yes. To the retreat? "God, no."

"Right, then. So, not that I mind a crack-of-dawn chat, but you don't normally call with no purpose, and it's nearly time for me to crash."

In other words, *state your business Dane, then leave me to my mysterious nocturnal ways.*

But Dane didn't actually know what he wanted to say or what to ask.

"It's nothing. Just had chance mobile phone reception, and you were the only idiot I knew who'd be awake."

Brady snorted. "Piss off. Why not call Carol? Bet she'd love to hear from you at oh-six-something o'clock." And the line went dead.

Brady had meant it in jest, but the idea wasn't terrible. He could do with a reminder of regular life.

Dane skimmed his contacts and tapped on Mrs. Carol Brewster, PA.

He could probably do with a dose of plainly spoken reality from Carol.

Three rings later, she picked up. "You're supposed to be chugging fermented lemongrass right now."

Fermented lemongrass? Hell no. "I prefer fermented grapes."

"Beggars can't be choosers, Dane. And you need it."

"Like a hole in the head."

"Don't give me sass, young man."

"Sass? You sound like someone from America's deep South. Are you rocking on your front porch right now, drinking sweet tea?"

"Don't stereotype. It's small-minded, Dane. And don't try to distract me. I saw your medical results. Any more stress and you'd have keeled over before me."

"You're sixty-four, Carol." The moment he said it, he cringed. "I'm sorry. Clearly, you are a lady of youth and beauty."

"And?"

"Outrageous intelligence."

"Better."

Dane waited because Carol rarely gave single-word answers.

"I'm pleased to hear some pep in your voice."

"Pep?" he repeated. "Are you on something right now?"

She ignored him. "What's your resting heart rate?"

"Seriously?"

"What's your blood pressure?"

"Right now, it's rising."

"Don't be smart. I'm trying to take care of you."

Trying being the operative word.

"Sassy, smart...should I try for saucy, too?" he teased. "I think you're taking the P in PA a bit too seriously, Mrs. Brewster."

She clucked her tongue. "Taking care of you takes care of me and my bank balance, Dane. Purely selfish motivation, I assure you."

He held his tongue about that claim, letting Carol have her fiction.

"Everything going smooth at the office?"

"No. You don't get to question me about work. Everything here is in hand. Nothing to worry about. Nothing for you to do."

"I wasn't worried. I trust you." Sort of.

In fact, he'd not spent a minute thinking of work. Not for days.

"How are you, Dane? Really?" Her voice turned all comfort and care—emotion that deserved a smidgeon of truth in return.

He put a hand over his eyes to shut off the rising rays of dawn and took a proper inventory of himself.

The scramble run to the top of the crater had left him a bundle of grit and sweat. He should be uncomfortable, but he wasn't. Gone was the bone-deep exhaustion, the tension in his neck and shoulders, the weight of his brow. Hell, there were days not too long ago when even his hair follicles had hurt. The only wounds he could complain about that morning were the fingerprint bruises on his biceps where Cayden had clung on tight.

He could probably attribute the bulk of his stress relief to Cayden's excellent ministrations in bed, but Carol didn't need to know that.

Dane stood up tall on the platform and looked over the Pacific. He breathed deep, loving the fresh combination of ocean salt and mountain air. He felt taller, looser, freer. Natural energy coursed through his body.

"I feel good," he said.

Simple and easy.

The gentle sigh on the other end of the line told him Carol had needed that affirmation, and he felt like an arse for leaving her hanging.

"So, the retreat's all right then? It looked so beautiful on the website. You've been sleeping well?"

"Sure, the massages are good, too." Dane closed his eyes and let a montage of all the weird and wonderful treatments he'd endured race through his mind, including the full-body rub Cayden had given him during their marathon bout between the sheets. Cayden spun his wheels, for sure. Just the memory of it had Dane's body waking up and saying go, go, go. Which was, of course, totally inappropriate while talking to Carol.

Ugh.

Dane opened his eyes and stared at the red rising sun on the horizon. The rays blitzed out the sweet memory of Cayden's curls splayed messy on his chest.

"It's not been terrible."

The perspective check surprised him.

"But?" She knew him too well.

But, if he could be such a quick convert to bone broth and share-a-bed cosiness, what other compromises was he making? Would he even fit back into his normal life?

Cayden might've given him something to think about besides his own boring exhaustion. But that distraction was temporary.

"The ginger shots and mud wraps have done their job. I'll be back at work next week." And back to reality.

"No. Two weeks of relaxation. You need to decompress properly. You promised me, Dane."

He hadn't promised that. In fact, he hadn't promised anything at all. Except to help Cayden find his sister, and that one he'd fulfilled.

"I am relaxed. I am decompressed." He leaned up against the platform railing, flipped his wrist to see the second hand on his watch, and held two fingertips to his carotid. "I just ran up the side of a volcano crater. My pulse is sixty-eight beats per minute. Can't get much healthier than that."

Liar.

His pulse was racing.

But it wasn't Carol's business to know his racing pulse was due more to thoughts of Cayden than the challenge of the crater run.

He dropped his fingers. "Gotta go, Carol. Let me know if you need anything."

"But Dane."

"Sorry. Gotta go," he repeated, then tapped end.

He removed his ear pods, dropped them into the purpose-made pocket inside the waistband of his ultra-light running shorts, and took off along the rim track.

CHAPTER FORTY-NINE

CAYDEN

As his dad drove slowly down the winding, potholed drive between massive old-growth trees, Cayden could feel the tension in the car rise.

It was a messed-up situation Cayden didn't know how to resolve.

"What if she runs again, Gerry?" his mum asked.

"Then we'll run after her again," his dad returned.

Fuck that. He wasn't running after his sister again. Not when she'd been so clear that she didn't need or want his help.

When he stepped out of the car, though, and saw Leif playing with a bunch of kids in an orchard beside a giant vegie patch, he knew it wouldn't be possible to switch off the love that had driven him to search for his sister for so many years.

Family was forever.

Whether they needed him, or not.

Still, Cayden stood back and watched from the sidelines as his mum and dad and sister finally came together.

She and Leif were safe. That was all that really mattered.

And, knowing that, Cayden felt free to leave Lucy, or Luna, or whatever the hell she wanted to call herself, to her own devices, and to go live his own fucking life.

Time for him to forge his own path.

Cayden didn't see Dane again until he and Leif escaped the circus craziness, hiked all the way back to the retreat, and begged Gladioli for sustenance.

The ice-cold, ruby-red smoothie she'd whizzed up slaked his thirst, but he couldn't help turning his nose up at the earthy beetroot flavour. Why he hadn't taken advantage of driving out with his folks for a pub lunch, he'd never know.

Then he looked through the hub window and saw Dane sitting alone, eating lunch.

Eating!

"C'mon, little dude. Let's go hassle Dane."

He plonked himself on the bench seat opposite Dane, and Leif slid in after him, to sit wedged together, hip to hip.

Dane was afflicted with the same smoothie, but he had a plate of real food too. If eyes could salivate, Cayden's would be streaming. "Whatcha got there?"

Dane licked a slick of dressing from his bottom lip. "Seared salmon and avocado salad drizzled with lime and crushed sesame seed dressing. Yes, it's as delicious as it looks, and it's all mine."

Evil man.

"Gladioli!" he hollered.

"Don't you think the smoothie's yummy, Uncle Cayden?" Leif sucked so hard on his reusable straw that his cheeks caved in.

"Beetroot has its place, Leif, and that's on Aussie burgers.

Nowhere else. Gladioli!" he hollered again. Where was the wonder-chef?

"You're such a child," Dane said.

"Hey!"

"Hey!"

He and Leif protested at the same time.

"Jinx!" He stuck out his pinkie and Leif shook it with a grin.

If he got anything good out of this family fiasco, it would be his nephew.

Dane shook his head. "I stand by my assessment."

"Feeling the love," he sing-songed, not entirely joking.

"Mm-hmm. How'd they take meeting Leif?" Dane asked.

"Amazed. Especially because he's such a cool little dude."

Leif rolled his eyes. "I'm not little. I'm almost as tall as you, Uncle Cayden."

"In your dreams, little dude."

Thank God for Leif. He'd given his folks something to focus on besides Lucy-call-me-Luna and the weird life the two of them had concocted.

Also, Lucy was noticeably less stressed when Leif was around.

Leif had revelled in the attention. He'd rolled with the idea that he had grandparents, treating them with nearly as much instant familiarity as he had with Cayden and Dane. Which shouldn't have surprised Cayden—the kid was surrounded by dozens of trusted pseudo-uncles, aunts, and cousins.

He hooked his arm around Leif's narrow shoulders for a sideways hug. "This one raced around, showing us every square inch of his mad world, including the amazing murals inside the tent painted by the kids and La Luna Spice." For Leif's sake, Cayden tried to keep all his sarcasm out of his voice.

Lucy had sure doubled up on the hippy-trippy affectation, but he wasn't going to make a thing of it. Not in front of Leif.

"So…?" Dane picked up his smoothie to take a long sip.

"So, it's just you, me, and the little dude. For a couple hours, at least. Let's hassle Gladioli for some proper food, then go steam." He tussled the kid's hair. "What do you say, Uncle Dane?"

Leif beamed.

Dane snorted.

And ruby-red smoothie spattered across the table like blood at a crime scene.

Leif squealed, then fell into a bundle of giggles.

"Ugh." Dane pushed his spattered plate aside.

"D'you want that?" Cayden didn't wait for a reply. He picked up Dane's fork and tucked in to his heavenly seared salmon.

Still giggling, Leif screwed up his nose. "Eww."

"We've shared way more than boy germs," Cayden said around a mouth full.

After lunch, they trundled with their water buckets and towels into the deserted steam room and took up one long bench, Leif sandwiched between them.

Cayden looked across Leif's head to where Dane leaned back against the slick oyster-shell tiles, hands resting on his knees, staring out into the ether, thinking mysterious Dane thoughts.

Was he thinking about their previous few days together? Or was he thinking about the nebulous future apart?

He closed his eyes, acknowledging the emotional exhaustion that had dragged at his heels for years. He'd thought it was all about finding Lucy. He'd thought that once he'd brought her back into the fold, he'd feel light and free. But that hadn't happened.

He'd found Lucy.

He'd brought his family back together.

But something still weighed him down, dragging at him like a suitcase with a dodgy wheel.

For the first time in a long time, Cayden didn't know what to do next. Unlike Dane, who seemed at ease with the established protocol.

Cayden shuffled back into the corner, straightened his legs out along the bench, and watched the man go through the motions.

Whenever Dane made a move dictated by steam-room rules, Leif parroted it—dipping his face-washer into his cool-water bucket and squeezing it over his shoulders and behind his neck. Then, just like Dane, he rested back into captain-of-the-swim-team pose—except Leif's feet didn't quite touch the floor.

Cayden was glad he wasn't the only one getting the favourite-uncle treatment. Dane deserved a little hero-worshipping, too. Hell, they wouldn't have even met Leif, and therefore found Lucy, if Dane hadn't suggested going to the art class. He'd be Cayden's hero forever for that.

The requisite intervals in the steam passed. Once, twice, three times, Dane led them out to cool off under the showers, then back into the steam with buckets of cool water.

The steam gradually did its job settling Cayden's mind, and he simply relaxed and enjoyed the moment.

Into their collective Zen state, the cedar door swooped open, swirling the thick white cloud of steam. First came his mum, followed closely by his dad, and then, after half of the steamy heat had already escaped, his sister came through and shut the door with a thud.

Face pinched, shoulders to her ears, Lucy-call-me-Luna oozed tension.

"Hey, Mum!" Leif waved, excited.

"Hey, Sprite." Lucy made a move toward her son, then stopped when Leif didn't shuffle over to give her space to sit. She did an about-face to find their parents had spread towels along the entire surface of the opposite bench. That left only the adjacent, narrower bench free.

Cayden couldn't help seeing it as symbolic.

It wasn't their fault that she'd excluded herself from the family, but as much as she'd angered him with her *I don't need saving* rejection and *my name isn't Lucy* protestations, his heart hurt at the inadvertent ostracism.

She busied herself arranging her towel and her cool water bucket before sitting. Then she saturated her face-washer and draped it over her face—shutting them all out. Again.

Cayden fidgeted in his seat.

They had to talk. To clear the air. But when Cayden tried to think of what to say, his not-so-Zen brain went blank.

CHAPTER FIFTY

DANE

Dane knew he should hold his tongue. He had no place in their Spicer family tangle. It was bad enough he was with them in that steam room at all, let alone gearing up to spout an opinion. But watching Cayden navigate the situation was painful, and he couldn't not say something. Cayden deserved more than silence for the years he'd devoted to repairing his family.

"Good to officially meet you, Mr. and Mrs. Spicer. I'm Dane." Cayden looked at him like he'd grown a second head, but he could switch on his professional mask anywhere—even in a therapeutic steam room.

Cayden's father jolted off the bench with something of a bewildered smile, reached to shake hands, then returned to his seat, having said not a word.

Cayden's mother came to the rescue. "Very good to meet you, too, Dane. Any friend of Cayden's is a friend of ours." She sent her son a withering look. "Call me Fran, and this is Gerry. Are you from Melbourne, too?"

For fuck's sake. Dane read the curse on Cayden's lips. He wouldn't have caught it, except Dane's attention kept returning to the man like a boomerang. He wrangled his gaze away…straight onto a smirking Luna.

Shit.

Busted.

"No, I live in Brisbane."

"Ah, so, how will you see each other in the future?"

How would they see each other in the future?

He shrugged with a lazy nonchalance that Dane wasn't sure he really felt any more. The only true answer Dane could give was a blunt *we won't* because they lived two thousand kilometres from each other.

Before he could say anything, Cayden landed a bombshell. "I'm thinking of going freelance."

"What?" Fran looked shocked. "But you love your job. And what about Henrietta? You two are so close."

"She might be my boss, but she's also my friend. She'll understand."

Fran's eyes skittered Dane's way. "But…"

Cayden crossed his arms. "I'm sorry, Mum, but what part of the word *gay* do you not understand?"

"Cayden," Gerry warned.

Cayden ignored his father. "Originally, I was thinking Lucy—"

"Luna," Luna said. From her monotone, Dane figured that wasn't the first time she'd tried to reinforce the name change with her brother.

"—would come back to Melbourne—"

"Never."

"—and we'd all get on with our lives. But things are different now. There's Leif to consider." Cayden waved at his sister. "And…" Then he waved at the whole steam room in general.

"Dane?" Luna guessed.

Dane wanted to throttle her.

Cayden flashed him a quick glance across Leif's head, then shied away. "I was thinking more about my work—where I'm headed—career-wise."

"What do you want to do, Cayden?" Gerry asked.

"Well, if I go freelance, I could move around, get more into the environmental science side of journalism, like I originally intended. I could work anywhere in the country. The world even. Be free to come up here to spend time with you and Leif, and…"

"Dane," Luna challenged again.

"Will you stop that?"

A simple *no* got stuck in Dane's throat. And when Cayden's gaze skimmed past Leif, then landed and settled on him, Dane knew he was in deep shit.

They weren't lovers or boyfriends. Hell, they weren't even really friends—they barely knew anything about each other's lives beyond the retreat. Dane shouldn't factor into the man's life and career decisions. Not one iota.

It was too much.

He had to get away from the man.

Fast.

Before he said something he'd regret—something like *yes*, or *stay*, or *be mine*.

Fuck, no.

Dane glanced at the clock on the wall. Five more minutes on their last steam, and then he could escape.

Five minutes of awkward silence.

"Talking about investigations. We ran into Gordon in the car park. Why didn't you tell him you were here to find Lucy?" Fran asked. "He could have helped."

"Luna," Luna muttered.

"Luna. Sorry." Fran's tone left no doubt she hated her daughter's name change. "Don't worry, though, Cayden. Luna explained the whole thing."

"Explained? What did you say?" Cayden asked. Then, after a second, "What did he say?"

Shit. Cayden would be pissed if he'd been outed as an undercover journalist. Facing Gordon after that would not be fun. Or simple.

Dane clenched his hands around the edge of the slick bench, wanting to reach out, but wary too much might be read into his actions.

Rock, meet hard place.

Gerry still looked stunned; Fran puzzled; and Luna...she searched the oyster-shell tile floor as though she was looking for a diamond amongst the oyster pearls. Dane didn't think she found it.

He didn't know them well enough to get a good read. The only thing he could tell for sure was none of the Spicer clan were happy, except perhaps for Leif, who'd taken to humming a discordant song as he slapped his toes on the wet floor to his own beat.

"Well?" Cayden asked.

"Well, what?" Luna crossed her arms.

Cayden pointedly uncrossed his arms.

"Fine. All I said was that you're all family and that you'd come to visit. Simple."

"Not so simple," Cayden disagreed.

"He did seem a bit confused, dear," Fran said.

"Why is it any of his business why we're here, except for the fact that we're all at his retreat?" Gerry asked.

Luna's fists clenched tight in the acute angle of her elbows. "Because it just is, all right? It's...complicated."

Cayden's spine went ramrod straight. "It's not compli-cated at all. He and his son coerced you to leave or...or something and then kept you."

"He who?" asked Gerry.

"Gordon!" Cayden spat out.

"That lovely man?" Fran pointed at the wall in something approximating the direction of the car park, her face a picture of horror. "Lucy, did he kidnap you?"

Luna sat bolt upright. "No! I told you what happened!"

Dane wished he could see Cayden's expression. "I spoke to Elise."

She flung out her arm, finger pointed straight as an arrow to the wall. "That man did nothing wrong."

But Cayden had his back up, too. "Even if he didn't run the cult, he knew about it. He let it happen."

"A cult? What the hell? Who do you take me for?"

"I take you for someone who up and left your family with no explanation. No word. No sign. No nothing. It's been twelve years, Lucy. Twelve." Dane could hear the tight restraint in his clipped voice—the attempt to contain his hurt and his rage.

"That's not…no!" she sputtered.

"Enough, Cayden," Gerry spoke up. "Don't interrogate your sister."

"Don't you want to know where she's been all this time, Mum?"

"Well, yes. Luc-una has already given us some idea. But now is hardly the time. Dane doesn't need to hear all our private business."

"Dane's safe. He knows everything."

That wasn't strictly true, but Dane wasn't about to refute Cayden's word in front of his family. The guy needed bolstering, not tearing down.

"You don't know everything, baby brother."

"You're right, Lucy. Dane only knows what I know. Which isn't ten percent of enough."

"Luna," she said, ignoring the rest, "my name is Luna Spice." Her tone brooked no further debate.

"I'm a Spice, too, right Mum?" Leif said, uncertain.

Cayden whipped around fast, regret at upsetting his nephew clear in his eyes.

"Yes, Sprite. You're a Spice too."

"How does that work?" Dane leaped in, seeing a chance to disrupt the volatile atmosphere. "Most people fantasize about changing their name, but I've never met anyone who actually did it."

"Really?" Fran asked. "I never fantasised about doing that."

"Of course you did, Mum. You weren't born a Spicer," Luna pointed out.

"That's different." Fran cocked her head. "Unless you married a man named Spice."

"Or a woman." All eyes turned back to Dane. "Did you marry a woman named Spice?"

Cayden reached over Leif's head to pat him on the shoulder. "Stop while you're ahead, partner."

"She's not gay, Cayden," Fran protested.

"How do you know, Mum?" Cayden asked. "You didn't know I was gay. How do you know Lucy isn't a lesbian?"

"Because she has Leif."

"Plenty of gay couples have children."

"Does that mean you want kids?" Fran's eyes flashed lightning speed to him again.

Fuck.

Dane glanced back up at the clock on the wall. Hell. Still two minutes to go.

He had to regain control of the conversation. The only way he could think of to do that was by derailing it.

"Are you a spy?" he asked Luna.

"What?" Cayden asked. "Why would you ask her—?"

"A spy." Dane tried his best to keep a straight face. "Either that, or you're in witness protection. Did you have to change your name through Interpol?"

"She's not a spy, Dane."

He raised an exaggerated eyebrow at Cayden. "How do you know? Luna by day, Lucy by night. Maybe she's got other names, too. Lizzie? Louise? Laverne—"

"God, no." Luna wrinkled her nose, looking horrified.

"Linda? Leonor?" Gerry jumped in.

Dane nodded at the quiet man.

"Nope," she protested again, but Dane didn't miss the way her shoulders unclenched.

Mission nearly accomplished.

"Lola? Lexa? Lulu? Liza? Um?" The only other vaguely alliterative name coming to mind was Alice, but that wouldn't do.

Luna bit her lip and uncrossed her arms.

Leif stuck his arm up in the air and Dane pointed at him. "What ya got, Leif?"

"I like Lily."

"Nice one." He high-fived the kid.

Luna hummed, pretending to consider, then nodded, deadly serious. "I could be a Lily."

"Great. Lily Spicy it is."

Leif snickered., "He called you spicy, Mum."

"That makes you spicy, too, little dude." Cayden finally got in on the action, and Dane relaxed back against the hot wall.

"Does not."

"Does too."

"Children." Fran pulled out the mum voice.

They all went dead silent for about five uncomfortable seconds until the now-dubbed Lily snorted, Gerry burst out with a "ha!", and Cayden covered his face, fake-groaning.

Dane didn't miss the small, appreciative smile Cayden snuck his way.

Fran surveyed them all, face serious, then turned her

intent stare directly onto him. Just as Dane didn't think he could take it anymore, she mouthed *thank you.*

He ducked and slicked away the steam that coalesced at the ends of his eyelashes.

It was all too much.

Not caring whatever-the-fuck-time it was, Dane dashed the water out of his bucket across the floor and stood. "Time for a cold shower."

A sad chorus of "No!" echoed off the sparkling tile walls, but Dane didn't let himself be dissuaded. He needed to get out of the heat before someone did something totally irrevocable, said something like—

"Welcome to the family, Dane."

—that.

He strode stiffly through the door and pulled the heavy cedar door shut behind him. He wished he could close his ears as effectively to Fran's disturbing words, or to Luna's misguided follow-up that slipped through the last sliver of a gap as the door shut.

"Good choice, brother."

Jesus.

What the hell kind of family had he gotten himself tangled up in?

CHAPTER FIFTY-ONE

DANE

Dane yanked at the neck of his t-shirt.

The sun had set, but he still needed relief from the sweltering humidity which the gathered crowd on the hub deck only made worse.

Cayden leaned in. "Sign of madness, that is."

"What?"

He mimicked Dane's movement with his own shirt. "Doing the same thing over and over and expecting a different result."

Cayden's family mingled with the other guests, laughing and chatting while Leif, in heaven, zipped around. He dragged over anyone who would listen to meet Granddad, Grandma, and Uncle Cayden, drawing a whole lot of attention to the Spicer clan.

Leif hadn't confused Dane for an honorary uncle—he was safe there—but the family seemed intent on keeping Dane within the fold. They clustered around him, making him wonder if they were trying to shield him or fence him in.

Neither made much sense.

"Why's everyone crowding so close?"

"Safety in numbers, is my guess." Cayden pointed up into the highest corner of the deck's eaves. "Storm's on its way. Didn't you see it massing over the rim? Or did you think they were all huddling around your magnificence?" His lips twitched.

"No," he started, but Cayden was on a roll.

"Ha! Dane the Magnificent! Like WD40, dude. Hub of the wheel."

"I think you're misunderstanding the purpose of WD40."

"Nah. It's perfect. Everything flows around you. Eye of the storm. Centre of the universe. Plug in the—"

"If you say hole, we are no longer friends."

"—tub."

Cayden's laugh drew everyone's attention, and Dane was infinitely glad that nobody could read his mind.

Talk about eye of the storm.

With perfect timing, the first few fat raindrops plonked loud on the corrugated iron roof, and the distinct smell of ozone hit his nose.

"Grandpa!" Leif hollered, high with excitement.

Dane looked to see what else Leif had found to show Gerry. But the kid was pushing his way through the clustered guests, not toward Gerry, but away.

"Oh, hell." Cayden's voice caught.

Dane closed the small gap between them and pressed in to Cayden's shoulder. He looked for danger, but all Dane saw was Gordon running toward the hub. Heavy raindrops splotched his blue linen shirt, and his grin gleamed manically in the gathering darkness. Nobody seemed all that concerned until a real lightning strike streaked across the sky, flaring cold white shards of light across the canopy.

Leif had to struggle against the tide as the other guests

pressed through the narrow doorway into the relative safety of the dining room. "Grandpa!" he yelled as he popped out the other side of the group.

Gordon sped up the few steps from the garden and gathered Leif up into a giant bear hug. It stunned the rest of them into immobility.

"What the ever-loving fuck!" Cayden's voice got carried away by the whipping wind, but Dane was close enough to hear.

He understood Cayden's tension, but they'd already established that Gordon's son was Leif's father. Was it really such a surprise that Leif and Gordon would have a close relationship?

He placed his hand flat to Cayden's back.

Caution.

Calm.

Not that it did much good.

Dane could feel Cayden's thundering heartbeat and the coiled muscles poised for a fight.

"Put me down!" Leif whacked Gordon on the shoulders.

Just as Dane felt Cayden lift onto the balls of his feet, preparing to leap to his nephew's defence, the kid laughed, high and light.

Leif clambered like a monkey around to Gordon's back, his grin showing no sign that he needed saving, while Gordon mock-groaned under the kid's weight.

"For goodness' sake, Leif." Luna tsked. "Get off Grandpa."

Cayden jolted again, but Dane was the only one who noticed.

Another shock of electricity sliced across the sky, catching them all like a still life—mid-motion—followed a half-second later by a gigantic crash of thunder.

The air shuddered.

Then came the sheeting rain.

It pounded the corrugated-iron roof like the beating of a thousand drums, churned every leaf, and drenched everything in sight.

Their small group stepped back from the deck edge, where the gusty wind whipped rain up under the eaves.

"Grandpa?" Gerry repeated Cayden's question, gruff with confusion.

Gordon stood behind the boy, hands on his young shoulders in a blatant claim of kinship.

Gerry turned to his daughter. "Who? How?"

"It's all right, Dad," Luna said.

"No, it's not bloody all right." Cayden broke away from Dane's side.

Dane wanted to trail after him, to step up to his side and lend support—to stand together, strong—just as Gordon was doing for Leif, and Gerry and Fran were doing for each other.

But Cayden wasn't his to protect.

Not your family, Dane had to remind himself.

Not your responsibility.

Not your fight.

Luna stood in no-man's-land, too. Jaw tight.

It was the first time Dane had seen her not step in immediately to protect Leif. That meant she trusted Gordon with her son. It gave Dane pause, and he wanted to pull Cayden back before he could say something irrevocable.

Instead, it was Gordon who spoke. "I wish you could have known him."

"Him? Him who?" Leif flinched at Cayden's harsh tone.

Dane stepped up tight to Cayden's side again, returning his steadying hand to the flat of his back. One wrong move, one wrong word, was all it took for family to disappear.

"Hey." He spoke into Cayden's ear, slow and deep. "Just listen."

The curtain of water thick as fig roots flowed over the gutters and down into the green and the earth. The cacophony grew so loud Dane could barely hear Gordon when he spoke.

"My son, Clay. He was—" Gordon's voice broke, and he dropped his chin to his chest.

"Mum, Dad…you've met Gordon Fuller. He's Clay's father. Leif's grandfather…Leif's other grandfather."

Cayden jerked. "I think we got that, Lucy."

"Hey! Don't snot on me. And my name's Luna. Please use it."

"Mum?" Leif said, hesitantly.

"Don't snot on you?" Cayden laughed, brittle. "What are you, five?"

"Children!" Fran raised her voice.

Keeping one hand on Leif's shoulder, Gordon hooked Luna to his side for a one-armed hug, drawing the battle line across the wooden decking.

Cayden shifted his weight, and Dane noticed the tension in his neck and the bead of moisture at his temple.

Heavy, it rolled, dripped, then caught on one of his blonde lion curls, turning it darker than the rest.

On a scale of one to ten, Dane wondered, how terrible was it that he wanted to stick out his tongue and catch the drip? "Eleven," he said, then clamped his mouth shut when everyone turned his way.

"What was that, dear?" Fran asked.

"Ah…" Dane's mind went blank.

"Dane!" a voice called from the flooding rain, and they all spun to see a giant purple umbrella emerge from the bushes on the other side of the hub garden.

He knew that umbrella.

Red leather pumps poked out from underneath the enveloping purple, picking a careful path between the deepening puddles.

"Bloody hell."

He knew those shoes.

Carol.

CHAPTER FIFTY-TWO

DANE

"Dane!"

"Carol?" He strode across the deck to the top of the slippery stairs. "What are you doing here?"

She stopped, tilted the purple monstrosity back, and looked up at him with a megawatt smile that nearly matched the platinum white glow of her tidy bob.

She flashed the scarlet leather organiser she took everywhere. "Didn't want to barge in on your holiday, but you said this morning to ask if I need anything. I have a couple of documents requiring urgent signatures. Then I'll get out of your hair."

"Signatures?" No way had she driven all the way to the retreat for signatures. "You came to check on me." He shouldn't be surprised. Carol had always taken the P in PA way too far.

"Why on Earth would you think that?" She pulled the umbrella back down over her expression and climbed the step, the purple monstrosity forcing him to the side.

He wanted to say something like *spit it out*, but Dane

knew impatience would do no good. Carol would not be rushed.

Eyes averted, she shook off the rain droplets, folded the umbrella, and clipped the press-stud shut with an emphatic snap. Then she crossed the deck to the tea trolley, plonked her kitchen-sink handbag down, and fossicked around inside.

Leif wandered over. "I like your shoes."

Carol grinned. "Thank you, young man. I like your sandals."

"Carol," Dane warned.

"What? Am I not allowed to appreciate the lad's shoes?"

He felt more than saw Cayden come to his side. "You called Carol this morning?"

Dane nodded, not elaborating because he didn't see how it was any of Cayden's business, except the innocuous words *this morning* triggered a memory—of waking up wrapped around Cayden's warm body—a memory that was supposed to be latched down tight.

Carol shoved up his sleeve and wrapped the blood-pressure cuff tight around his bicep.

"For goodness' sake, I don't need that," Dane protested.

"Nonsense." She slapped his hand away from the Velcro. "Look at you, all wound up tight. I thought this place would be good for you," she muttered with clear displeasure. "Hold still."

Cayden eyed the portable blood pressure machine with interest. "Is there something you want to tell us, Dane?"

"What do you care?" Dane grumped.

"Oh, I care. I mean, there are certain circumstances when it behoves a man to know his limits. You know?" Unfortunately, Carol didn't miss Cayden's cheesy wink, and Dane was suddenly caught between two lightning-bright grins.

"Well, then." She patted his shoulder, obviously reading

more into the situation than was warranted. "That's super fine. Nice job, Dane." She pressed a button on the apparatus, and the cuff tightened.

"Super." Dane looked around for an escape hatch.

Nada.

Damn.

"And, who are you, young man?" Carol asked Cayden.

The bastard cracked an easy laugh and thrust his hand out. "Cayden, my lady."

"Ooh, I like him."

Was it Dane's imagination, or could he actually feel his blood pressure rising?

"These are my parents, Fran and Gerry, and my awesome nephew, Leif." Cayden started the introductions.

Dane tried to step aside to give Cayden space, but the rubber leading to Carol's torture device corralled him close as the cuff squeezed bruise-tight.

Too tight.

"And that's Gordon, the guy who runs the place."

"Owner," Gordon reached to shake Carol's hand. "Gordon Fuller."

The pressure peaked, then the cuff slowly deflated, bleeping loudly with every beat of his too-fast pulse.

"And that's my sister…Luna."

A beat went by, silent except for the thundering storm. Then Luna rushed forward and wrapped Cayden up in her arms. He stumbled back into Dane, who reflexively braced his feet. The rubber cord between cuff and monitor flailed as he brought his arms up to steady them all.

"Hey, it's an Uncle Cayden sandwich," Leif helpfully described them.

Dane gave into the feeling for a moment. Family, friend, lover. Then he stepped away.

Cayden shot him an imploring glance over his shoulder,

but Leif stepped in to take Dane's place in the three-person embrace. Then Fran and Gerry joined in the group hug, leaving Dane and Gordon and Carol on the periphery.

Carol didn't even try to hide her nosy interest.

To stop her from getting tangled in the Spicer web too, Dane asked, "What did you bring for me to sign?"

But Carol paid him absolutely no attention at all.

He extricated himself from the collective hug and waved his hand in front of her face. "Carol?"

"Huh?"

"The documents. What do you need me to sign?"

"Oh, ah." Suddenly all thumbs, Carol tried to unlock the press-stud on her red leather organiser.

He held out his hand and waggled his fingers. "Hand it over."

The first document on the pile was a Carter Medical Supplies Bonus Approval form for five thousand dollars made out to one Mrs. Carol Brewster for—he looked at the fine print—Extraordinary Services.

He whistled.

"Someone must have worked very hard to earn this."

"Indeed." She nodded.

Utter cheek aside, Carol was an amazing assistant. She probably should have earned double, given all the gate-keeping she'd done for him over the years, but company money wasn't his to dish out, and she knew it. So, what was Carol playing at?

He flicked through the next few pages: a memo to all employees advising that a masseuse would be available on a first come, first served basis; a training schedule for new staff that included a meditation hour with fresh sea air at the beginning of every day; and a requisition for bean bags, yoga balls, and...

"What the hell are ankle clamps?"

"They're these things you use to hang upside-down from door-jambs. Very good for increasing oxygenated blood flow to the brain."

"Ri-ight." He stretched out the word.

Did he even want to know?

No.

Besides, none of the papers were real. She'd never have expected him to sign any of them. Which meant Carol, his interfering-is-my-love-language PA, had come to the retreat purely to check up on him.

"Excuse me," Gordon interrupted. "It's a little unorthodox for guests' colleagues to visit during a retreat. Is there anything I can help you with?"

Gordon's disapproval wasn't all that subtle, and while Dane didn't exactly approve of Carol's trumped-up excuse to visit, he didn't appreciate his PA being rebuked, either.

"That's uncalled for. I wouldn't be here without her." That was the literal truth.

His presence at the House of Glass was entirely down to Carol's machinations.

Lucky for Dane, her presence, with faux documents and not-so-faux concern, provided him an inadvertent escape hatch, and Dane was determined to lift the lever and press the proverbial red button.

Her mistake.

His benefit.

Decision made, Dane tucked the papers back into Carol's organiser and snapped it shut. "Really sorry, everyone, but I'm going to have to leave."

Carol spun. "What? No, you don't."

Cayden broke from the group hug. "Now?"

He summoned every ounce of acting skill he possessed. What had Cayden called it? Improv? Carol didn't need to believe him, but Cayden and his family did.

"Yes." He tapped the red leather. "And this can't wait."

"What's happened?" Concern writ large on Cayden's face.

"Sorry. Business."

Cayden swayed back at his blunt, impersonal explanation, and Dane felt even more like a heel.

Carol stepped in. "None of this is crucial, Dane. All I came for are a few signatures."

But her protest fell on deaf ears. The wild swing of emotions on Cayden's face consumed Dane's focus.

The one thing, the only thing that he absolutely knew for sure, was that he cared too much. He had to get out before he got sucked into Cayden's life any deeper.

And really, he'd fulfilled his promise. He'd helped him find Lucy. It was time for Dane to fulfil his original promise to himself—to get the fuck out of the retreat, and back to real life. Back to sanity.

"When will you be back?" Cayden asked.

Relief and regret at the man's ready acceptance shot like hot shards between his ribs.

He ignored everyone else and croaked out, "I won't."

"Dane!" Carol protested. "You don't have to leave."

He ripped at the now-soft Velcro cuff still encircling his bicep. "What was my reading?"

"What?"

"My blood pressure." Dane pointed at the small monitor. "What was my reading?" Not that it mattered if it was high, or low, or wherever the fuck in between. He'd find a way to spin it.

She pressed a few buttons, looking for the last result. "Still not great. Too high."

"Right then, even more reason to leave."

"No, it's not."

"Being here hasn't had the effect you wanted, Carol. If it

had, my blood pressure would be down. It's not. Therefore, this place is not what I need."

Callous logic always won.

Except Dane didn't feel like a winner at all.

And Carol knew him far too well to believe his bullshit.

She stepped up close, side-eyed Cayden, and said quiet enough for Dane's ears only, "Clearly, being here has had one kind of positive effect."

Enough.

He made a firm stop gesture, and Carol snapped her mouth shut.

Given that Carol had witnessed the work-related stress that had prompted his need for a break, he'd forgive Carol her interference regarding his health, but she had no grounds for prying into his love life.

He and Carol had come a long way together, but that was going too far.

Purposely not looking Cayden's way, Dane turned to shake hands with Fran and Gerry, then Luna and Gordon. He tussled Leif's wild hair the way the kid hated, and then, finally, he turned to Cayden.

"Are you coming?" he asked.

Cayden looked stunned by the implied invitation, which shouldn't have been a surprise—it didn't sound anything like a goodbye.

"Back to Brisbane with you?" Cayden asked.

"No, I mean…" What did he mean?

He pointed out into the storm. "To our haven. I have to pack."

Cayden didn't make a sound, just stepped, bare-headed, out into the darkness and the thunder and the rain.

CHAPTER FIFTY-THREE

CAYDEN

Cayden lurched off the hub deck, fuming at Dane for deciding to leave—just like that. Giving Cayden no say. No consultation. As though he was nothing. An after-thought.

Fuck—not even a thought.

He lumbered up the hill. His footsteps felt as heavy as the rumbling thunder, and the rain soaked through his clothes, ran down his spine, and welled in his shoes. It wasn't the sexiest look he'd ever rocked, but that wasn't Cayden's chief concern.

He barrelled straight into the man's haven, not caring that he created a puddle where he stood. Dane collapsed the purple umbrella and entered soon after—dry and cool as a cucumber.

The bastard.

After fucking inviting him all the way up there, through the torrent, Cayden figured he'd get some kind of answer—some promise to return in a couple of days, or to call at the very least. But, no.

Nothing.

While Cayden dripped an inland sea onto the floor,

Dane silently moved around the room. He folded and sorted his belongings, packed his small weekender suitcase with studious care, and didn't say a single fucking word.

Dane safely stowed the classic three-piece pinstripe suit into a zip-away section of the case, then he rolled his still-damp red swim shorts with his sweaty-arse running shorts into a high-absorbency gym towel and packed them neatly into another section.

No cramming used underwear into the corners for our Dane.

Not like a regular person.

No siree.

The whole controlled performance made Cayden broil inside. "Just stop for a second, would you? You're giving me whiplash." He itched to rip each and everything out of Dane's hands.

"I can't. Carol's waiting for me." Dane's eyes remained fixed on his task.

Dane owed him nothing. But it sure would have been nice to be looked at.

To be acknowledged.

To be wanted.

To stick around long enough to figure out if they meshed without the excuse of an investigation to hold them together. A day or two would have been enough. No need to run away yet.

Hell, not even twenty-four hours earlier, they'd lain in bed together, content.

Or so he'd thought.

From the speed Dane was running, it was clear something had spooked the man.

Cayden felt discombobulated—upside down and inside out.

He looked over the room again, searching for traces of his own presence. But there was nothing.

No messed-up sheets.

No damp towels.

No water glass on his side of the bed for easy hydration between bouts of fantastic sex.

No trace at all.

Housekeeping had done their job well.

Too well.

"Guess you won't be taking me home as your personal masseuse after all." Cayden couldn't look at Dane as he heeled off his wet shoes and stripped off his soggy clothes. Each piece fell with a wet slap. "Go on, then. Run away. Don't let me trap you." He didn't wait for Dane's reply—if there ever would be one from the silent arsehole. He just crossed naked to the bathroom, leaving a trail of wet footprints in his wake, and flipped the shower knob to hot.

It didn't take long for steam to rise, and Cayden sighed with relief as the hot water hit his scalp. He didn't bother washing, just stood there and waited for the hot water to purge every wracking need from his body, every inconvenient want from his mind.

Dane wasn't the only one who had a right to choose the trajectory of their fate. It took two to tango, after all.

He slung a towel over his shoulder but didn't bother to cover the goods. Then he leaned on the partition wall between the bathroom and the main room and watched Dane wrestle with the zipper of his suitcase.

Please don't close, please don't close.

"Want some help?" he asked.

Dane's shoulders bunched, and he looked up from under his oh-so-serious eyebrows. "Trying to get rid of me?"

That was hardly fair.

"That's not what's happening here," Cayden said in an

even voice. In no mood to give Dane any largesse, he pointed out what Carol had made blatantly obvious. "You don't have to leave."

Dane increased his efforts with the suitcase, and a flush streaked across his cheekbones. "The mission's over. You don't need me anymore. Time for me to go."

"Need? Maybe not. But that doesn't mean I don't want you to stay." Could he be any clearer than that?

"For what?" Dane asked baldly as his eyes drifted down the full length of Cayden's body. Then he shook his head and looked away. "What about when the retreat ends? What then? There's two thousand kilometres between my home and yours."

Cayden didn't have a good answer for that. Not immediately.

Dane went on. "Our lives are separate, Cayden."

Translation—there's no place for you in my life.

Out of better ideas, and more than ready to take whatever he could in the time he had left, Cayden skimmed a fingertip along the edge of his lip. "BJ for the road?"

He'd half-meant it as a joke, but the second the acronym was out of his mouth, it rushed to the top of his wish list.

Static rushed in his ears and muted the raging storm outside.

A still-life tableau, Dane just stared at him.

Daring rejection for the last time, Cayden took the last few steps between them. He didn't stop till they stood toe-to-toe.

Dane's gaze dropped to his lips and hung there. "A kiss."

Cayden's breath stuttered.

Not a blowjob. Not a fuck. Just a kiss.

It was almost romantic. Which was fucking ridiculous. So much for Dane having a core of chocolate mousse—the man didn't have a sweet bone in his body.

Cayden's eyes dropped too, but they didn't stop at Dane's lips. His eyes skimmed lower. "Are you asking or telling?"

At Dane's extended silence, Cayden looked up again to find Dane's cool ocean eyes blown to winter dark.

"Doing." Dane didn't give Cayden a chance to take a breath before he pounced.

How ought a last kiss be?

Messy?

Bittersweet?

Spectacular?

All the above?

When Dane finally let him get a breath in, Cayden stupidly asked, "So, that'd be a no to the blowjob?"

Dane looked away to the side, face pale and shuttered. "Maybe next time," he said and dropped his hands from where they'd spread across the concave small of Cayden's back.

"What?" Cayden asked.

Since when did they have a next time?

But Dane didn't answer. He picked up his suitcase and briefcase and strode out the door.

"Wait!"

But Dane was gone.

CHAPTER FIFTY-FOUR

DANE

Dane looked out the passenger side window of Carol's old Ford Focus.

The front and rear windscreen wipers womp-womp-womped on high speed, not quite clearing the heavy rain as it fell. The small group huddled under the pagoda looked more like shifting globules of colour and movement than individual people.

Which was a good thing. Dane didn't want to see anyone's expression.

Especially Cayden's.

He pressed his right foot hard on the accelerator, and the engine revved with an impatient need to go, go, go. It was all he could do not to raise his left off the clutch, let the gears engage, and take off up the storm-swamped drive. Alone.

It felt good to feel like he was finally in control of something.

But Carol, being Carol, wouldn't be rushed.

He revved the engine again, skin crawling with the need to get away. He knew he'd be in for an earful, but Dane didn't care if the Spicers, or Gordon, or Randall or Bernice, or Edie or Maxine, or any of the others who'd dared the rain to wave him off judged him a heartless bastard, so long as it got Carol moving.

She finally landed in the passenger seat and dropped her enormous handbag between her feet.

"Get enough intel?" he asked.

His only answer was the tip of the umbrella that nearly took out his left eye as she threw it into the back seat.

When she chose to spare him any attention, her judgmental side-eye said it all. "Well, are we getting out of here or not?"

Permission granted, he went through the motions and took off down the drive.

When Carol reflexively grabbed for the dash, he slowed down a little and spared a morsel of attention to glance in the rear-view mirror. Cayden stood on the edge of the blurred crowd, growing smaller and smaller till his visage was nothing but a golden speck.

Dane took a deep breath and looked forward. The headlights caught on the pelting rain, bright as a meteor shower, and he guided Carol's car along the winding mountain road, deeper into the dark.

"So…your Cayden seems like a nice young man," Carol fished.

"No."

"He's not nice?"

Dane shook his head. "Cayden's not open for discussion."

But Carol's question wouldn't leave him.

What was an appropriate word to describe Cayden? Or to classify their…connection?

Convenient?

Certainly.

Irresistible?

Definitely.

Over?

Categorically.

Dane tightened his fingers on the steering wheel and rolled his neck. The crick-crack of his vertebra echoed loud in his head.

For too long, he stared at the intermittent white lines in the middle of the rain-slick road. Mesmerised as they disappeared beneath the car's bonnet and reappeared red in the taillights—shards of heat vanishing into the darkness behind him.

"He's what?" Carol waved her hand impatiently. Typical Carol—ignoring his obvious wish to leave well enough alone.

"He's nobody."

No. That wasn't right.

Even if they weren't going anywhere, Cayden wasn't nobody. "I don't know. Maybe there's something there." He winced. "Or not. I don't know."

Maybe everything?

Fuck.

"Well, that clears things up," she said, dry as toast.

He didn't want to hear her opinion.

He flicked his pointed finger between them to emphasise his point. "We are not doing this. We're going straight back to Brisbane. You'll drop me off at home. And I'll see you at work on Monday."

"But—"

He ignored her. "I'll get on with my life. You'll get on with yours. And all will be normal."

Nothing was normal.

The minute Dane walked through the door of his apartment, it felt wrong.

The grey colour scheme was too stark. The tile floor was too harsh. The leather furniture was too cold. The granite and glass surfaces were too sterile.

He felt gritty—like he'd need a three-hour shower before he'd be clean enough to touch a thing.

Which was ridiculous. His home was his sanctuary, his true haven.

He fired off a quick message to Brady to let him know he was up for a tennis match-slash-therapy session whenever they could arrange it, then went through the motions of unpacking.

Job done, he poured a dram of Talisker and stepped out onto his balcony to take in his one-eighty view of Brisbane's city lights under the starlit sky. To the east, the new crescent moon threw its cool, reflected light down to glint and scatter on the river that snaked below. As was typical after a summer storm, the city smelled clean and bright. Almost like a new day.

Dane tilted the glass again and let the peaty warmth of the whisky coat his tongue. A dram or two and he could rest. Cool sheets and quiet. Nobody hassling him in bed. Nobody wanting to snuggle.

Bliss.

One glass down, he stepped back into the air conditioning for a refill, but Alice's library caught his eye.

He rounded the black leather L-shaped lounge and stepped closer to her books. Each a part of her heart. If Alice were there, she'd mock him for the strict alphabetical order he kept them in. She'd probably tell him to shake things up a bit. Live a little. Stop trying to control all the things. Especially his love for her, which, he knew, he could never cage in a bookshelf. But where else was he supposed to keep it safe?

He skimmed a fingertip along the dozens of ragged spines

till he reached the glass paperweight that marked the spot of his current read.

The rainbow spiral suspended within the clear glass sphere wasn't exactly subtle.

When he'd first seen it at the Young Designer's Market, he'd dismissed the thing as tacky. But the blatant rainbow swirl drew his eye back, again and again, reminding him of the way-too-obvious, rainbow-sparkle, *welcome-to-the-club* bookmark Alice had given him so many years before. That day, he'd arrived home with the fragile paperweight, slipped *Aesop's Fables* off the shelf, replaced it with the glass paper-weight, and started reading.

Dane shifted to let the white fluorescent light from the kitchen arc through the glass sphere and cast crescent moons in red and green and blue and purple and gold on the white wall behind it. He reached into the space to capture the refracted light in his hand, but his shadow crossed the front of it, shading all the colours but yellow—a single golden moon curled on his palm—a cupid's curl.

"For fuck's sake." Could the universe not hand him a reprieve for at least one night?

Dane shut down all thought.

He reversed direction to the kitchen, placed his empty whisky glass in the sink, and went to brush his teeth. Then stripped and tossed his clothes into the hamper, turned off his main bedroom light, and slipped between the cool cotton sheets.

A visual reconnaissance told him everything was in its place—life as normal.

Since the key to normality was routine—routine environment, routine behaviour, routine thoughts—Dane did what he'd done every night for years. He pulled out Alice's book and read. But when he finished the chapter, switched off his bedside light, and shifted down in the bed to sleep, Dane's body resisted rest.

The natural irregularity of his high-thread-count cotton sheets felt nothing like the soft-bamboo bedding he'd shared with—

"Shit."

He shifted to lie diagonally across the mattress and hiked a knee out to the side for comfort—no space left for Cayden, that was for sure. In fact, there was no space in his life for anything offered at the House of Glass—no buttered bone broth, no chalk-flavoured toothpaste, no pH testing, no getting a boner whenever he entered a steam room, no bonding with trippy kids obsessed with leaves, no helping put other people's families back together, and no snuggling between fucking bamboo sheets.

The trouble wasn't his home. That was his sanctuary.

The trouble, really, was his muscle memory.

Dane's body wanted things.

Cayden-shaped things.

Things that his body thought felt good, and real, and right.

CHAPTER FIFTY-FIVE

DANE

Thwack!

The ball hit his racquet frame and sailed up and over the chain-link fence.

"For fuck's sake, Dane. What the hell's wrong with you?" Lachlan grumped behind him. "At the rate you're going, we'll have no balls left."

"Speak for yourself, mate." Brady held up two bright yellow tennis balls on the opposite side of the net. "Forty-love."

Usually the consummate good sport, Lachlan made no move to slap hands as he and Dane traded receiving positions on their side of the tennis court. Playing two-against-one, it was usually a treat to be on the double's half, but his partner wasn't feeling the love. Not after Dane's deplorable performance on the court.

The guys' irritation couldn't hold a candle to his irritation with himself. From the moment he'd woken in a sweaty mess, humping a pillow, with a fuzzy after-image of dream-Cayden's naked skin glowing under the light of a thousand fucking candles, Dane had known the day would be trouble.

It had only gotten worse from there.

Council works had cut off his favourite river-side run; the local bottle shop had failed to restock his favourite vintage; and his tennis stroke was off—three devilish losses.

Was the universe out to get him? Out to bring him down a peg or two?

The law of threes meant something ought to go right soon. He hoped. But Dane didn't want to tempt fate by explaining to the guys why his game was off. He held his tongue and assumed the position at the net, racket raised, knees bent, eyes focused on the ball.

Ready.

Brady's serve whizzed by his left ear. Dane heard Lachlan's racquet hit it clean. A quarter second later, the ball bit him square in the arse.

"Hey!" He swung around to glare at his partner.

Lachlan looked far too pleased with himself.

"Game!" Brady called from the other side of the net. "Five-love."

"Just doing you a favour, mate. Won't have to run for that one." Lachlan crossed to the other side of the net, collected up the few remaining balls that Dane hadn't sent over the chain-link fence, and stuffed all but one into his floppy shorts pocket.

Brady snickered as they swapped sides, tapping Dane with his racquet head on his abused arse as he passed by. "Hop to it, Dane. One more game and I'll take my winnings."

"You're both fuckers," Dane groused. He rounded the net and assumed the position. The game couldn't be over too soon, but not doing his best wasn't an option.

Brady struck the *thinking man* pose, but he couldn't quite pull off the serious expression. "Mmm... a pint of James Squire will go down perfectly on this fine summer day."

"Oi, don't speak so soon. We may surprise you yet."

Lachlan bounced the ball his requisite seven times, then served.

Dane transferred his weight up onto his toes as the fuzzy yellow ball flicked into his right-side peripheral vision. A classic Lachlan topspin, down the centre line.

Dane braced for the return. He kept his eye on the ball, but it blurred as Brady got his lefty backhand on it, and all Dane could do was grip tight to block the ball as it flew straight for him. No finesse. Nothing but self-preservation. He got his racquet head on it, but the speed of the ball forced his grip to slip, sending it off at a tangent, bare inches over the net, metres away from where Brady crouched, poised for the return.

Winner!

"Fucking finally!" he couldn't help but grunt out.

Lachlan whooped behind him. "Well done, partner. Fifteen-love."

"Fluke." Brady waved them both off, strode to the back of the ad court, and curled his upturned hand in an obnoxious *bring it* gesture.

Dane flipped him the bird.

Lachlan bounced the ball seven times, then served.

A flat slice skimmed by Dane's left ear and skipped out wide to the right. Brady reacted, his left arm fully outstretched, and fired the return ball point-blank into Dane's chest.

At such close range, the ball's momentum pushed him backward, and the hard tennis court did nothing to cradle his fall as his arse, back, and head hit the deck.

Oxygen whooshed out of his lungs, and the world spun.

"Hell!" Brady yelled.

Dane let himself flop, arms and legs splayed out on the hot, hard court—starfish-mode a la Cayden. He closed his eyes against the harsh glare of the summer sun.

Lachlan made it to him first, but Brady wasn't far behind. Both crowded over him.

"Fuck, Dane. Are you okay? Did you hit your head?" Lachlan tapped him on the forehead. "Open your eyes. How many fingers am I holding up?"

"Is he concussed?" Brady lifted Dane's head and shoved something soft underneath.

"D'know. Look at me, Dane," Lachlan tried again.

Dane groaned and muttered, "I hate the universe." Either that, or the universe hated him.

Steeling himself, he blinked open his eyes. He was a bastard. That was a fact. But not so much a bastard that he'd let his friends think he was seriously hurt.

"Thank fuck." Lachlan eased back from his knees onto his heels, and the piercing sun sliced through.

"Ugh." He tented his knees and grabbed the backs of his thighs to pull himself up to sit. The world spun, then righted itself. "It's all right. I'm good. Just a bit winded."

Brady snorted. "Not sure if *good* is the applicable word here."

Dane rubbed the back of his head, where a goose egg was already forming, then pulled his hand away to look at it. No blood. That was a win. "I can play," he insisted.

Brady and Lachlan shared a glance.

"Not sure if *play* is the applicable word either." Brady offered a hand. "How about you go search for those lost balls, then play umpire for the rest of the match? Get your breath back, dude."

"Don't call me dude." He swatted at Brady's hand. He didn't need help standing on his own two feet.

"Fine." Brady held his hands up in surrender. "Maybe quit while you're behind, though, eh?"

"Helpful. Thanks," he said, not at all sarcastic.

"Here." Lachlan handed him his racket. "What's up with your stroke, Dane?"

Brady laughed. "It's not his tennis stroke that's the problem. Our Dane met a guy."

"What? Dane?"

"Bowled him over with a feather, thrown him for a loop, dropped him on his head—"

"I'm right here, you know," he said.

They ignored him.

"Wait. You mean he actually met a guy? For really real? Our Dane?" Lachlan could not have sounded more surprised.

"What's his name again, Dane?" Brady asked.

"You fucker."

"Hmm…nope." Brady shook his head theatrically and held the *thinking man* pose. "That's not it."

Bastard.

"I'm never calling you for advice ever again."

"He called you for advice. Our Dane? Seriously?" Lachlan went from surprised to stunned.

What? He wasn't a robot, for fuck's sake. Was he never allowed to have problems?

"So, Dane's mooning over some guy, and that's why he can't play for shit?"

"I'm not mooning." The rest of the charge he couldn't refute.

Brady, the bastard, was having too much fun to stop. "He's swooning over being rejected."

"I didn't get rejected, for fuck's sake. I just helped a guy out. It wasn't a big deal."

"Ooh, so you did the rejecting, then. Living to regret it, eh?" Brady stuck in the knife and turned it.

"That's so romantic," Lachlan said.

Both Dane and Brady turned to stare at him.

Romantic?

Hell, no.

"Or not." The tips of Lachlan's ears went pink. Looking aside, he slipped a ball from his pocket and bounced it, caught it, bounced it, caught it…

Dane turned back to Brady. "There was no rejection. We met. We fucked. I left. End of story."

"And now you're pining…yearning…" Brady didn't let up. "Wallowing…"

"Nice use of the thesaurus. But no. I'm not pining. I'm not yearning. And only pigs wallow, mate. That's not me." It was just that he'd gotten used to Cayden being around. It made logical sense to feel a little disconcerted by the sudden change.

"Good." Brady nodded. "Glad to hear it."

"Pig swallow?" Lachlan asked. "Why the hell are we talking about pigs?"

Dane's jaw clenched. "Wallow, not swallow."

"How do you know?" Brady wiggled his eyebrows. "Maybe pigs do swallow."

Dear God, with friends like these…

He flicked them both the bird and decided that a search for stray balls wasn't the worst idea in the world. At least he could escape the heat on court. He took off for the far corner, yanked open the wire gate, and slammed it shut behind him. It sounded like shattering glass.

"Don't worry, Dane," Brady called out as Dane made a beeline for the first fuzzy yellow ball he could see. "A bit of lube, and you'll be back on stroke in no time."

Yep. That got the one-fingered salute too.

CHAPTER FIFTY-SIX

CAYDEN

Cayden's leg shot out—to run; to chase; to catch the red taillights that burned.

He woke in a sweat, twisted in the sheets, legs splayed, morning wood undeniable.

With his left eye buried in the soft, downy pillow, he could only just make out the wrinkled sheet on Dane's side of the bed. His heart tripped for a moment with a wild hope that the bastard might have returned during the night, but the ghostly image of those red taillights turned hope to anger.

Deserter.

All over again, he recalled his choice to stay and Dane's choice to go.

Not that Dane owed him anything. Except maybe a blowjob. At the last count, he was at least two up on the man.

Just the thought of Dane's mouth on him turned wood into steel.

He rolled and groaned into the pillow, unable to stop his hips from flexing, rutting into the mattress, the slightest bit of friction from the sheets rousing him to new heights.

"Ugh."

Who needed a hand when he could use Dane's bed to rub one out?

Just as he'd gotten up a good rhythm, taking advantage of the subtle rebound of the mattress against the headboard, a sharp hammering threw him off his stride.

"Gah!" He scrambled to flip over and hide his cranky bits with a pillow all in one quick, ungainly move. The door slid open, and a hand reached in to drag the curtain aside.

A mop handle thrust through the gap, followed by the face of a teen girl, bopping to whatever was playing in her ear pods, oblivious to Cayden lying naked, spread-eagled, stunned into immobility.

Then she looked up.

"Oh. My. God!" The mop and bucket crash-landed with a loud domino of metal on metal on wood. In her attempt to catch the bucket, the girl kicked it, and it skittered across the floor. The sound of it bombarded Cayden's brain until the whole fiasco came to a rattle-crash-thud at the foot of the bed.

Including the girl.

She covered her eyes with one hand, but that did little to hide the blush that stole across her cheeks. "Oh my God! Mr. Faulks, I am so, so, so sorry. I was told you'd left last night." She shouted over the music in her earbuds.

Cayden stayed perfectly, carefully still.

Flashing his dick to a teen was not on his agenda for that day, or any other day. Keeping one hand on his strategically placed pillow, he tapped his ear with the other, trusting she could see him with her spying eye.

She blushed even harder and pulled the pods from her ears.

"I'm not Mr. Faulks. I'm Cayden. Cayden Spicer. My

room's next door." He pointed to the wall between Dane's and his haven.

Her eyes skipped around the room—no doubt taking in his clothes strewn about, the damp towel draped over the wooden chair, and the obviously slept-in bed. He felt a sudden kinship with Goldilocks.

"Dane left last night… Mr. Faulks, that is. And, since my parents are staying in my room, I didn't think it'd be a problem for me to…you know…so I…" He waved his arm around, as if seeing his stuff all over the place would explain the situation.

"Sorry, sir, it's just…" she trailed off too.

Had word not gotten around that he and Luna were brother and sister? Had Gordon not spilled the beans that Dane and Cayden were sleeping in the same haven?

Correction—*had* slept in the same haven. Past tense.

Because everything to do with Dane was past tense.

He'd convinced his parents that it was the practical thing for them to sleep in his room. And he'd sleep in Dane's. Only it hadn't been the true reason.

I slept here because I have a craving for a man that wasn't nixed—still isn't, never will be—because the bastard left me in the lurch with an emotional hard-on the size of Gibraltar.

That reason was truthful, but not something he could say to a teenager.

"Is Mr. Faulks coming back?" she asked.

Her words had his blood humming again, as though asking the question made it possible. But Cayden knew it wasn't.

"I doubt it," he said.

What else could he say?

Fuck knows. Meanwhile, I'm just gonna hang here, naked, in his bed, doing absolutely nothing dodgy at all…nope, nada, nothing.

The awkwardness stepped up a level, until his stomach rumbled with hunger, drawing the girl's attention lower.

Fuck.

What should he do?

What would Goldilocks do?

An image of porridge with a generous swirl of honey popped to mind. Swap the porridge for an egg-and-bacon roll, and he'd be in heaven.

"Breakfast," he said, a little too loudly, nodding like an idiot.

The girl joined him in bobblehead mode. "Right…so…" She firmed her grip on the mop handle, tilting it toward the door in a way that unmistakably invited him to get out so she could do her job.

His toes twitched with his desire to answer the request, but he couldn't go anywhere—not with an audience.

Her eyes snagged on his wriggling toes, splayed wide under the white sheet, and she blushed.

He eyed his clothes on the floor. "If you'll just give me a sec, I'll get out of your way."

"All good." She pointed to the joint wall. "I'll just do next door first."

He nodded.

She nodded.

It was a perfect nod-fest, until, roughly a decade later, the girl seemed to get the drift that if she didn't leave soon, she'd be copping an eyeful of his naked self.

She shoved her ear pod back in, corralled her bucket and mop, and scuttled out the door.

A few seconds later, the girl knocked sharply on his actual haven door and called at the top of her lungs, "Housekeeping!"

Lesson learned.

"A-plus, Spicer," he awarded himself. His dick clearly

knew exactly what it wanted, but his heart hadn't learned a single, healthy, self-preserving thing.

It was time to get himself in order. Time to figure out what he really wanted from life—for the long haul—now that he was free.

Cayden rolled out of bed, planted his feet on the cool, wooden floor, and wished, with every fibre of his being, that he could turn back time.

"Bring it on, Cher."

But the past was gone.

Time to face the future.

Alone.

CHAPTER FIFTY-SEVEN

CAYDEN

When Cayden tucked his head inside the dining room doorway, four faces beamed back.

Mum, and Dad, and Lucy—Luna—and Gordon.

Yeah, treating him like family was going to take a bit of getting used to.

"Shove along, will you?" Cayden didn't give Luna any option. He squeezed his right butt check onto the bench seat beside her to sit in the exact same spot where Dane had sat their first night at the House of Glass.

"Rude," she grumbled.

But his attention wasn't on his sister—it was on the cane chair across the room where he'd sat that same night.

He'd been simmering with suspicion and anger, hiding behind the potted palm, getting poked in the arse by the broken cane, and lusting after a stranger wearing a frown and a three-piece suit.

It felt like eons ago.

Lucy elbowed him, bringing him back to the present.

"What? What did I miss?"

She snorted. "Welcome back, brother. Hope you enjoyed your trip."

"I'm not here for your entertainment, sister," he snapped back, unable to contain his hangry mood.

"That's a shame. What're you here for then?"

Bugger if he knew.

"Breakfast?" He eyed the empty plates on the table, scraped almost clean but showing signs of egg and tomato and… "Is that bacon?" He couldn't keep the accusatory tone from his voice.

What the hell?

"Gladioli!" he hollered, then leaned around Luna to get a better look at the plate in front of GOG. If that man had bacon, Cayden would really flip his lid.

"Cayden!" Mum hush-admonished, then apologised with a can't-take-the-boy-anywhere cringe. "Sorry, Gordon."

Which made him feel like an immature heel for a second, until Luna thwacked him across the chest. "Brat, you've embarrassed Mum."

That was rich. "I've embarrassed Mum? Wow, shocking of me to cause Mum any kind of upset."

Her eyes narrowed, but she said nothing against the low blow.

If it was possible, he felt like even more of a heel.

"You rang?" came a voice from over his shoulder.

"Shit!" He leaped and came down hard on the wooden bench seat, landing with one cheek on and one cheek off. He braced his left leg out wide to stop himself from falling off, which left his bare toes splayed dangerously close to Gladioli's sensible black chef clogs.

"Serves you right." Luna poked him again with her elbow.

He gave up and dragged a seat over from another table, then peered up at Gladioli with a shameless hangdog expression.

She smiled. "What do you fancy, Cayden?"

Oh, God. Were angels singing over his dead body?

Or was he dreaming?

Cayden pinched the skin just above his elbow.

Ouch. Nope, not dreaming.

Was it too much to ask for eggs and bacon and all the caffeine in the land?

He pointed at his dad's plate and smiled his best please-and-thank-you smile. "What they had and a cappucino, please." It wasn't in his detox diet, but surely, they didn't expect him to keep up that farce, did they?

Not anymore.

Gladioli flicked her gaze to Gordon, then back to him. "Be right back." She winked and twirled away to her kitchen.

Her wink really should have clued him in that something fishy was going on, but the prospect of a real, caffeinated cappucino cupped in his hands clouded all rational thought.

Lucy snorted. "Since when did you become a slave to caffeine?"

"Oh, I don't know, Lucy. Probably sometime in the past…" he checked his watch, as though a twelve-hour clock-face could account for so much time passing, "…twelve years or so."

"Cayden," Mum warned.

"The name's Luna." Her jaw tightened. "I thought we'd gotten past all that."

He had.

Sort of.

Mostly.

But he was feeling raw, and it wasn't so easy to sweep away twenty-seven years of habit.

"If it means so much to you—"

"It does."

"—then, fine, I'll call you Luna."

"So gracious of you. Thank you." She pinched out in the faux-British accent they'd used when playing Monopoly on rainy holiday afternoons back when they were both kids.

Hearing it was a trip, taking him back to a time when they'd been close—close enough to tell each other their secrets. Or so he'd thought.

"You're exceedingly welcome." He tried to mimic the same clipped tones, but he was out of practice.

Thankfully, Gladioli returned blissfully fast with a frothy cappuccino in a dark brown earthenware mug.

"Bless the ever-loving Gaia." His shoulders dropped at least twelve inches the minute it landed. He wrapped his hands around the mug and found it surprisingly light and not remotely warm.

He looked to Gladioli. "What's that on top? It doesn't look like chocolate powder."

"Cinnamon is much better for you."

She was probably right, and he wasn't opposed to cinnamon, as a spice, but it just wasn't right to put it on top of a cappuccino.

But coffee was coffee, and detox beggars couldn't be choosers.

He tipped the cup to his mouth to taste...and nothing came out.

No liquid.

No warm milk.

No espresso.

Nothing.

What the hell?

Was it just foam?

He stuck in the teaspoon and scooped out the white foam.

The cinnamon hit his tastebuds immediately, but it took his palate a moment to process the other flavours.

Or should he say flavour, singular?

"What the f—" He looked at Gladioli again, suspicion rising at her twelve-hundred-watt grin. "—fudge is this?"

She giggled.

Giggled!

"That there is a genuine faux-paccino. My very own invention. Full of protein. Do you like it?"

"But it's…it's raw—"

"Egg white. Yep. No big brunch for you, Mister. You're still on detox."

"But…" He looked around at the smears and scraps on the others' plates. Would they think any less of him if he broke down and cried?

"That's four perfectly good organic eggs you've got your sister's chickens to thank for—don't waste 'em."

He didn't know which thing was worse: the faux-paccino or the fact that he had his sister to thank for it.

Certain his gut microcosm was spasming in horror, Cayden pushed the travesty away.

"Weren't you the one telling us how you're so into nature?" Luna challenged.

"Sure—natural coffee beans, natural cows' milk, natural chocolate—what's not to love?" God. If only Dane was there. He'd snigger at Cayden's misfortune, but at least he'd understand.

"Be civil, Cayden," Dad said. "We're guests here."

"Guests, my arse," he muttered under his breath. They had no idea how much he'd paid for the privilege-slash-torture of doing a detox at the House of Glass Wellness Retreat—or, at least, how much he'd have to pay back to the network after he fessed up to Henrietta.

The minute Gladioli was out of range, his dad leaned toward him. "Your mother and I are heading out for a bit this afternoon to sort out a place nearby for us to stay for a while.

We can bring you back a coffee. Is there anything else you want?"

What do I want?

God, such a big question.

He wanted a lot of things.

But the first and last thing that came to mind was the thing that he'd already lost.

"How about chocolate mousse for dessert every day for the rest of my life?"

That wasn't asking for too much.

Was it?

CHAPTER FIFTY-EIGHT

CAYDEN

Cayden swiped clumsily at the corner of his mouth and stretched out of the foetal position. He was very glad he'd thought to lay his side of the banana lounge at a low angle before falling asleep.

"Here," came a deep voice, and Cayden just about leaped out of his skin.

Gordon fucking Fuller.

"Can I help you?" He levered his side of the banana lounge higher.

"Here." Gordon handed him a beer bottle.

"What's this? Beer at a wellness retreat? Has the devil had his wicked way with you?"

"Come on, Cayden. You're not really here for detox."

Fair point.

Dammit.

"But if you're worried for my soul, don't be. It's organic. Locally sourced."

"Oh, well. That's all right then." Cayden tipped the bottle back and...*oh, my God!* He moaned as he slaked his thirst, then gave the most critical critique he could manage, given the circumstance. "It's not...terrible."

Gordon chuckled, then sat down on Dane's side of the banana lounge.

It wasn't right, but since the man owned the bloody banana lounge, Cayden couldn't very well protest. So, he drank his beer in silence and stared out at the great green bowl of the retreat crater.

"I wasn't able to see my son's faults until after he died," Gordon said.

For a conversation starter, it was pretty heavy.

Cayden took another fortifying slog of beer.

"Energetic. Enthusiastic. Generous."

Didn't sound like faults to him. Cayden took another sip of beer and waited.

"Caring. He always said that caring for people isn't about what you can get—it's about what you can give, and he was right. You have that caring instinct, too, Cayden."

"What? No, I don't." He shared nothing with Clay Fuller.

After a minute, though, he realised Gordon was trying to compliment him.

"What makes you think that?" he asked.

"Because of Luna."

Cayden quirked a brow in question.

"It's a rare soul who'll search that long. You're not one to give up on someone you love, Cayden Spicer."

He didn't feel terribly generous or caring right that second. "Stubborn is as stubborn does."

Gordon shrugged. "Clay was also impetuous. Accepting of everyone and everything. Too accepting."

Yeah. Okay. He could see how that could get out of hand. A man had to have some boundaries. And that's where they differed—Cayden rarely accepted anything or anyone at face value. Not after all the dodgy facts he'd had to check either in his professional life or in his search for his sister.

Gordon vaguely waved down at the hub. "Clay called it a found family, and I never thought to question it. Never asked him where he found the people who came to us—the young women. Even some men. Everyone was happy. Or so I thought." He sighed. "Take your sister, for instance."

Oh, yes, let's do that. Let's hear what you have to say about Lucy.

"I didn't know Luna had family. No idea she'd left Melbourne in secret. She never said, or I never asked, or…" He trailed off. "It's a weak excuse."

Cayden agreed, but he didn't say so. Gordon was already doing a pretty good job of falling on his own sword.

"Especially after Clay died." Gordon audibly swallowed. "I should have asked. Not just assumed."

"So, the beer's a peace offering?" It was a cold and cynical question to ask, but Cayden wasn't about to absolve the man so easily. And he wasn't up for a heart-to-heart when his own beating heart already felt so bloody and bruised.

"You'll understand when you have children of your own," Gordon said.

"Not likely." Could the man be any more clueless?

"Being gay or bi or trans or whatever doesn't matter. Not these days." Gordon kept talking, but Cayden barely registered his words about surrogacy and adoption and foster kids who need good homes. Until he found a permanent, loving partner, talk of having kids was pure tease. And he wasn't about to spill his dream future to GOG.

Feeling antsy, Cayden put down the empty bottle on the floor, jumped to his feet, and crossed to the high, triangular A-frame roof at the edge of the deck. Noon had long passed, but the sun was still high in the wide blue sky. The colours of the forest flared pale in the glaring light.

He surveyed the retreat buildings—the silver roofs speckled through the forest and the larger hub at the centre, quiet in the high heat of the day.

Off to the southwest, if he hung far enough out Dane's side of the triangle, he could just make out the roof of the weed cottage. They'd not been back there, nor confronted Gordon about the weed pantry. Cayden didn't suppose he ever would. If Luna and Leif were going to remain part of the House of Glass family, then protecting them meant protecting Gordon, too. He vowed not to say a word.

He let his eyes trail to the east, up the steep slope to the crater rim.

He couldn't help imagining Dane up there, running along the craggy track, serious face dripping with sweat.

The image was like a siren call.

"I've gotta go." He turned back to see Gordon asleep on the banana lounge, beer bottle dangling from his fingers, looking so very human.

Cayden would never forget Gordon's part in Lucy's disappearance, but maybe it was time to forgive—for everyone's sake.

Especially his own.

CHAPTER FIFTY-NINE

CAYDEN

The impulse to follow Dane's ghost like a sexy-as-fuck Pied Piper up the rough path to the rim overrode all rational thought.

"It was beer poisoning, your honour." Cayden panted. "I take no responsibility for my actions whatsoever."

Yeah, like that would pass the truth test.

Cayden grabbed onto the same exposed roots, hauled himself over the same craggy rocks, dripped sweat on the same gravel soil.

Not that walking Dane's path was his goal. Not at all.

Cayden had his own path to ford.

"Which is the whole fucking point." He sucked in hot air.

Step one—get to the rim without dying.

Step two—call Henrietta.

Step three—make a plan.

He fingered his mobile phone in his pocket.

With any luck, Henrietta would be mid-way through her usual Sunday afternoon work preparation session, with a gin and tonic in one hand and the TV control in the other. She'd grump at the interruption. But if he asked her to take off her boss hat for a bit, she'd ignore her well-trained impartiality and offer her very best personal advice on his romantic-slash-life-slash-career woes.

That was the plan.

Of course, he'd first have to fess up that he'd lied to her about the House of Glass, about his true reason for investigating Gordon, and about the tiny fact that for years he'd been using network resources to run a side investigation looking for Lucy.

Worst case, she'd fire him.

That'd blemish his CV, but he was more than ready to quit and go freelance.

Best case, Henrietta would feel so bad for his sad plight that she'd get over his infractions and send him a care package of unlimited hot bacon-and-egg rolls.

"Mmm." Cayden snapped his mouth shut. Never mind the sweat pouring out of every pore, if he salivated any more at the thought of bacon, he'd be at very real risk of dehydration.

Breaking News: Death by Detox

"Good evening. Clive Holstein here with Nancy Bridle for Brisbane Tonight.
"In breaking news, a gorgeous young man in the prime of his life perished this afternoon after attempting escape from a wellness retreat in the wilds of South-East Queensland. Among the contributing factors to the man's demise, Queensland Police listed dehydration, bacon deprivation, and an overactive imagination."
"I think you mean an overactive libido, Clive."
"Apologies, Nancy, indeed I do. Those lost body fluids really do add up."
"A sad way to go, Clive."
"It surely is. In other news..."

A sad way to go, for sure.

Out of breath, fist crammed into a stitch in his side, Cayden finally crested the rim of the crater and collapsed, panting, against the giant granite boulder—the same granite boulder where he and Dane had lain together on their first morning at the retreat and watched the sun fade starlight into daylight.

"Ugh." Enough wallowing already.

Move on, Cayden.

"Literally."

He pushed away from the boulder and scrambled south along the winding rim path to the platform that hung over the precipitous drop to the east.

Cayden leaned against the railing, pulled his phone from his pocket, and scrolled through his frequent contacts.

Best to rip the bandage off quick.

"This'd better be good," Henrietta answered, blunt as ever.

"Hey, Hen. Yeah, so, funny story..."

Ten minutes later, after losing eleven layers of skin from his lying hide and blooming twelve different shades of red, Henrietta neatly summed up the situation.

"So, you used the network's resources for private gain. You've found a sister who I didn't even know existed a week ago. And you're now out and proud. Correct?"

"Correct," he affirmed, "except—"

"Your career needs rescuing?"

"In a way of speaking, however—"

"And you had hot and heavy gay times with 'the sexiest man on the planet'?"

"God, yes...wait, no...ugh! I didn't say..." Backtrack! Backtrack!

His cheeks flamed.

Good thing there wasn't enough internet reception up there to call her via video chat.

"That's what I thought."

Her tone concerned him. Henrietta was slow to anger, but she could hold a mean-arse grudge like nobody's business.

He was prepared to grovel. Not for his job. That he could live without. Trust, though? Their friendship? That he had to fix. "So…which part are you more pissed at?"

"Do you mean which lies?" That was Hen—always getting to the heart of the matter.

"Something like that." It was a weak answer. He knew it.

"Is there a story there at all?" she asked, exasperation clear.

A twenty-tonne boulder lodged in his gut. "No." No way was he taking Lucy's story public. Which meant keeping Gordon and Clay's story secret too. Not that there was much to tell. Not anymore.

"Jesus, Cayden. Do you want me to fire you?"

Was that a trick question? "No?"

She sighed. "Ethically speaking, I can't not—"

"I'll repay the costs of the retreat. I promise. And then I want to go freelance." Just saying it out loud kicked his heart rate up a notch. "Get back into reporting on the environment. Nature documentaries. That sort of thing. Plus, if I'm freelance, I can move around, maybe spend more time with my sister and nephew. After so long apart, I want to be in easy reach, y'know?" The words tumbled out. He wasn't even entirely sure that he meant them—if it was his brain talking or his gut.

Silence. Vast and uncomfortable silence.

Desperate to fill it, he almost told Hen that the 'sexiest man on the planet' would be conveniently near as well, but that was probably pushing her tolerance for his fuck-up too far. Besides, Dane had already made it crystal clear that he wasn't interested in any kind of future together. So, factoring him into his decision was pointless.

"I get it, Cayden. I do. But are you seriously going to leave me in the lurch when I just got you trained up to my exacting specifications? That's brutal."

He knew she was teasing…mostly.

He and Hen were a team. Cayden loved working with her. But he'd only taken the job to aid his obsessive search for Lucy. Not for any genuine interest in news television.

Cayden waited a second to be sure of his heart, then gave the only answer he could.

"Yes. I'm very serious."

CHAPTER SIXTY

DANE

Dane's day was already crappy, and it had barely begun.

"Hey, Dane." Steve didn't bother to knock as he barged into Dane's office. "Can you have a look at this funding proposal for me? I think I lost a digit somewhere. The numbers are off, but I just can't spot the error."

"Logistics is your baby, Steve." Dane deleted another email from the mountain of messages choking his inbox.

"Yeah, but—"

"Excuse me, Steve." Carol pressed through the crowded doorway with two tall, reusable bamboo travel mugs, one designed with a pink and grey-plumed galah, the other with a white-plumed, yellow-crested cockatoo.

Caffeine. Thank God.

"Carol, can you please speak to HR? They've put me on their automatic send list again. I don't need blow-by-blow details on internal budget adjustments to cover parental leave."

"Noted," she said.

Dane nodded with satisfaction, then turned to address

the other minor thorn in his side. He wheeled his executive chair back a few inches, pulled open his top drawer, grabbed his spare scientific calculator, and handed it to Steve.

"Thanks, but that's not exactly what I was looking for."

"If your original data isn't right, I can't help you. Give this a go." He jiggled the calculator, then diverted back to Carol.

"Did Gavin make me the latte I asked for? Three shots." He held up three fingers for emphasis. "If he's replaced my morning coffee with chamomile tea again, we'll be having words. I don't care if it's laced with honey harvested from the lee side of the most remote crevasse on the uninhabited islands off the southern Tasmania coast."

In truth, he'd accept pretty much anything with caffeine.

Even a froufrou caramel mochaccino would be all right.

He wasn't fussy.

Much.

"Tell him yourself." She passed his ridiculous galah travel mug across the desk. "Gavin told me to tell you that, and I quote, 'Unless you've joined the Australian Secret Intelligence Service and can't come down for your own bloody coffee because you need to maintain your secret spy cover, then you need to visit,' end quote. I told him that while he might be the coffee boss, you've got better things to do than listen to him wail on about the origin of his beans."

Dane nodded his approval, then took a hesitant sip, and out rushed creamy, delicious coffee. It hit his tastebuds, then his bloodstream, and then his brain.

"Thank you, Gaia." He moaned. At least one thing was going right. Dane leaned back, let the executive chair take his full weight, and practically inhaled the rich brew.

So, so good.

"Best leave Dane to his poison, Steve. He's been a bear ever since...well, never you mind." Carol shooed Steve out of the office and shut the door on the man's face, then turned to Dane, arms crossed.

Carol meant business.

"What? I gave him a way to help himself. Why aren't you cheering me on?" Defence was sometimes his only offense around the insightful woman. "You're always telling me I need to delegate more."

"Enough already." She returned to the opposite side of his broad desk. "You've been in a funk since you came home. I'm not enduring another day of it. Time to either go deal with it or get over it."

Dane looked up from under his eyebrows. "Is that like the high road or the low road?"

"I'm serious, Dane."

"You don't want me to take the third way? Talk it out? Purge my emotions?"

"God, no. I have no interest in your private life."

"That'd be a first." He mussed through the back of the stationery drawer, searching in the dark for his favourite pen.

Why was everything out of place? He'd only been gone a week, and nobody ought to have been in his office. Nobody except the cleaning service and Carol.

"Have you been in here? I can't find my pen." He pulled the drawer as far out as it'd go and crouched low to see into the shadowy depths.

Nothing.

Nothing was where it ought to be.

And nothing was how it ought to be. Not his work; not his home; hell, not even his tennis game was right. The guys had given him no end of shit for that. His grip and stroke just didn't behave like it usually did.

Stroke.

"Ugh."

Fuck. Could the day get any worse?

One idle word and his treacherous mind took him straight back to all that naked, golden skin, tense with need— Cayden's back, his flank, his shoulder where droplets from wet hair rolled over and under and down, down, down to what Dane really wanted to stroke...

The drawer was far too shallow to fit his head, but he tried anyway since it was the only place he could think to hide his embarrassment.

"You okay, Dane?" Carol asked.

"Of course."

Nothing was okay anymore.

Nothing fit.

And it was all Cayden's fault.

What he needed was a reset. No more lusting. No more imagining. No more playing the *Dane gets sexy with Cayden* movie in his head. Not in his office, not with his friends, and especially not in his bed.

Which reminded him. "Could you please order me a new set of sheets, Carol?"

"Sheets?" Carol asked.

"Yes. King bed. Silk." That wouldn't feel like bamboo.

"Silk?"

"Are you going to repeat every word I say?" He'd go round the bend if that was the case.

Carol cocked a hip. "Please don't say you want them in red. I don't think I can handle that mental image."

"Black will do. Actually, make it charcoal." That'd blend with the rest of his grey-scale home.

"Oh goodie. Want me to buy you some dungeon things while I'm at it? Handcuffs? Whip? A paddle?"

"Don't be ridiculous," he said.

Her joking suggestion took him straight back to the last

time he'd wielded a paddle. He'd sat behind Cayden in their canoe and watched the man's perfect shoulders ebb and flow with the motion of his stroke. Flex and relax; pull and release; in and out.

Carol rapped on the desk with sharp knuckles, wrenching his attention back.

"You can't control everything, Dane, and I don't have the energy to suffer through your love crisis."

Love crisis? "What are you on about?"

Lust? Sure.

Obsession? Maybe.

Love? Fuck, no.

"Enough. You might control most of your life, Dane, but you can't control your heart. Either go get your man, or get over it."

Dane shut the drawer and leaned on his elbows, dropping his forehead into his palms.

Go get your man or get over it. The words rattled around like burrs in his brain.

Nothing that'd happened since he'd left the retreat indicated he was over Cayden.

They'd only known each other for a week, but Dane couldn't stop reliving their time together. Over and over. As though he'd left the retreat behind but taken a ghostly form of Cayden with him. And the ghostly form of Cayden just didn't cut it.

Shit.

Need had overtaken Dane's life.

He needed it to stop.

Somehow, he needed to change it up. Get some perspective. Try to see Cayden for who he really was, instead of the perfect, golden, dream version that visited Dane morning, noon, and night.

It was a problem that he didn't quite know how to

correct.

Go get your man or get over it.

What would happen if he welcomed Cayden in rather than shut him out?

What if he made a neat Cayden-shaped compartment inside his life that he could visit whenever the need struck?

Then, when he'd proven to his libido that the man was nothing special—nothing important—Dane's life could go back to normal.

Could it be that easy?

Only one way to find out, Faulks.

Dane pushed away from the desk. He grabbed his phone, his keys, and his ridiculous coffee mug, then rounded the desk and swiped Carol's cockatoo travel mug from her hand.

"Hey!"

"Two for the road!" He was already halfway down the office corridor before she could catch up.

He shoved his pinkie finger hard into the down button and tapped his foot while the elevator took its own sweet time to drop two measly levels to his floor.

He stepped in and jabbed repeatedly at the P button for the parking basement. The door slid slowly across, but before it could shut, Carol stuck her patent leather shoe in the gap, and the whole thing shuddered to a stop.

"What? I don't have time for this, Carol."

"And I don't have the time or energy to suffer your midlife crisis, Dane." The snap was so unlike her, he did a double-take. Were her eyes glistening?

Mind spinning, Dane didn't trust his reading of her expression any more than he trusted his own chaotic emotions.

"Better make those silk sheets cherry red," he half-joked. At least the colour would camouflage his flaming cheeks.

She pulled her foot back. "Go. I'll reschedule your week."

"A week? No," he protested. But the doors had shut, and the elevator dropped away from everything he thought he knew, everything he could depend on.

CHAPTER SIXTY-ONE

CAYDEN

Hot and sweaty in the noon-day heat, Cayden clambered down from the rocky path to the sharp spit of rock that sliced out into the water at Dolphin Point. From that easternmost point at Noosa Heads, all he could see was ocean, ocean, and more ocean.

He hadn't meant to walk so far around the headland, but the wild crashing waves and the winding trail had drawn him ever on around the next corner, then the next, and the next.

He licked salt spray from his dry lips.

A litre or two of fresh drinking water would have been good, but he'd left his folks' holiday apartment intending to be gone only an hour, tops. No need to haul emergency supplies when all Cayden wanted was a bit of space to figure out a rough plan for his future.

He needed a reset. No doubt about that.

And it should have excited him—to be master of his own fate. Finally.

But the freedom to switch gears was proving to be a heavy burden.

What if he made the wrong choice?

What happened if he chose right, but fucked it up?

What then?

And that wasn't even factoring in his love life—or lack thereof, since Dane had taken himself out of the running.

Short on answers, Cayden had just kept walking. He'd paced along the shore from Little Cove, into the Noosa Heads National Park, all the way to Dolphin Head, searching in vain for certainty.

Seabirds searched the waters, too—fast shocks of white and grey, swooping overhead. Hunting.

"Look!" a tourist behind him cried. "Dolphins!"

Cayden shielded his eyes with his hand and scanned the near horizon.

Sure enough, a pod of dolphins rode the long ocean swell that rounded the point. They played in the water, taking turns to breach the surface, then dive, churning the deep blue waters of the Pacific white.

Normally, the fresh sights, sounds, and smells of the ocean would have inspired Cayden to dream. But, flat and listless after leaving the retreat, he'd not been able to shake off a strange feeling that none of it really mattered—that he'd missed his moment, and that no matter what he did, he'd never get it back.

Which was ridiculous.

All he had to do was start.

But start what? And start where? How?

His phone jangled, discordant in the peace and wilderness of the headland.

He pulled it from his pocket and checked the screen. Ugh. His boss might be one of his best friends, but he wasn't ready to talk to her, let alone decide on his future. Not yet.

"Hey, Hen, it's not really a good time, can you—"

"Don't speak."

He snapped his mouth shut. Yep. He could do that.

"You'll never guess who just called me asking for you."

"Um…" His mind went blank.

"Sheridan Brown."

"*The* Sheridan Brown? You're shitting me?" Jesus Christ. Environmental activist, documentary filmmaker, international superstar—Sheridan Brown could make his career.

"He said 'I want you.'"

"Me?" Cayden's vision blurred at the edges. How was it that the words he'd so wanted to hear from Dane Faulk's mouth came from Sheridan fucking Brown?

"Yes, you."

Hen's voice brought the world back into focus—a world where he'd somehow landed on Sheridan Brown's radar. The thought blew his mind.

"How does he even know my name?"

Hen's annoyed huff blasted through the phone. "Why do you do that, Cayden?"

"Do what?"

"Underestimate your value. If you want to get anywhere in this business, you'll have to kick that by the wayside, tout de suite."

Hmm…suspicion tugged at his gut. "Did you contact him, Hen?"

"Me? Would I do that?"

"It wouldn't be the first time." Until the House of Glass fiasco, he'd not wanted to ruffle too many feathers at the network, which meant he'd rarely stuck his neck out for opportunities, but that hadn't stopped Hen from putting him forward.

"This is legit." She insisted. "I had a call from the network higher-ups asking who took point on the Antarctic expedition preparation story we did last winter. Et voila—opportunity! Sheridan's in late-stage development for a hush-hush newsy wilderness program. Climate science and penguins and such. It's right up your alley. He needs a couple of junior producers to do the legwork, grease the wheels while he lights up the camera with his oh-so-handsome face."

Cayden snorted at her droll tone. "Tell me how you really feel."

"Sheridan's a bastard to work for, but once you're in on a show like that, you're set."

"Wow." What else could he say?

"Don't tell me it's not perfect for you. You're already on location."

"Already on location?" Cayden scanned his two-seventy-degree ocean view. "What do you mean?"

"The network's so piss-drunk happy that Sheridan's come on board that they've agreed to produce the show out of the Gold Coast studios, just so he can be near his grandchildren." She snorted. "Heaven save me from the talent."

Work for Sheridan Brown?

Move to Queensland?

Live near Dane?

Wait, what? Why had that thought popped in? Dane was long gone. A future involving him wasn't even an option.

"It's a done deal, Cayden."

A done deal? That wasn't right.

"You can't just decide things like that for me."

"Seriously, Cayden? This is your dream job. A wish come true. Why aren't you ecstatic?"

She was right. It was perfect. He ought to be thrilled.

"Am I wrong?" she asked.

"No, you're right," he had to admit. "It's a dream come true." He'd be an idiot not to say yes. But the last time he'd let himself dream, Dane had given his wishful heart a harsh backhand in return.

Cayden wasn't eager for a repeat.

"Excellent." Hen swept on, as though he'd agreed. "Look out for the offer in your email. It should come through soon. Meanwhile, enjoy the time with your family, and I'll see you back here next week to train your successor. Big shoes to fill." Then the line went dead.

He looked down at the black screen.

Had that really happened?

CHAPTER SIXTY-TWO

DANE

The retreat seemed weirdly deserted when Dane arrived back at the House of Glass.

He clunked the locks on his car, then stepped through the pagoda.

Cicadas high-hummed en masse, and the noon heat shimmered the air, turning the rainforest into a watercolour wash of greens and browns and the odd tropical flower streak of white or yellow or pink.

The place felt deserted, and it took him a moment to remember that it was Wednesday—excursion day.

Canoe day.

The caveman in Dane wanted to find Cayden, club him over the head, drag him back to his cave—or his sixth-floor, air-conditioned apartment—and keep him long enough to purge the burning need from his system.

Short, sharp, and effective.

Me Dane, you mine.

But he'd left Cayden in the lurch one time already. This time, he'd have to take a more nuanced approach. He'd have to convince Cayden to take a chance.

Dane climbed up the narrow path.

One purpose.

One destination.

The triangular view out from under the A-frame roof; the deck with the yellow-and-white striped banana lounge; the two glass doors of their side-by-side havens—it looked and felt so familiar. And yet so different.

Cayden's sliding glass door sounded like chalk on concrete as Dane slid it open, pushed back the curtain, and stuck his head inside.

"Cayden?"

No sign of the man.

No sign of life at all.

Next, he entered his own haven, finding much the same evidence of his stay—nothing at all.

Dane quickly returned down the hill, past the pagoda, to the garden between the pool terrace and the hub garden. Surely, someone would be around.

"Dane! Is that you?" a female voice called.

He swivelled around.

"Hey, Dane!"

"Bernice?" He reversed his path to peek over the high hedge and saw his old hangman partner floating in the pool on a blow-up swan. She held a carrot in one hand and a dogeared paperback in the other. "You look relaxed."

She grinned. "It's taken me a while to get with the program, but I could get used to this kind of life. What are you doing back? Miss us, did you?"

"Desperately."

"Uh-huh."

"You haven't seen Cayden anywhere, have you?"

"Oh, now I see why you're really here." She shook her head. "He left a couple of days ago. Did you know his sister works here?"

"Yeah." He knew a lot about Cayden. Just not the crucial bit he needed—the man's location.

He huffed out a sigh, but it did nothing to lessen his frustration. "I'm just going to go see…" He hooked his thumb over his shoulder and let his words trail off as he turned and took the path to the hub.

He stuck his head in through the kitchen hatch, but all was quiet. Then he moved on to the rear of the dining room, where the door to the office was half open.

A young woman wearing headphones sat at the computer desk. Her long black ponytail shimmied to a private playlist.

Dane pushed the door fully open and knocked loud. "Excuse me."

She spun around, a hand clapped to her chest, eyes wide.

"Sorry." He raised his hands.

"'S'okay.'" She pulled her headphones off. "Can I help you?"

"I hope so." He looked down at the name badge on her retreat uniform. "Fern. I'm Dane Faulks. I was in haven thirteen, and I'm looking for my neighbour, Cayden Spicer. Any idea where I might find him? He seems to have left the retreat."

"Oh, ah, I'm not really supposed to hand out—"

"Personal information. I know. It's just he left something valuable with me, and I want to return it." The white lie rolled off his tongue. Easy as.

She didn't look convinced.

Damnit.

"He's possibly with his family. Leif promised him a painting, and Luna—"

"You know Luna? Isn't she great?" Her smile blazed.

"Uh…yeah."

"It's Wednesday, so she'll be at the Eumundi Markets." Fern checked her watch. "For at least another hour. Have you got a car? The circus stall's hard to miss. Lots of beautiful, shiny things. See?" Fern held up her wrist, showing off a solid silver cuff inlaid with copper swirls.

"Pretty," Dane offered. He couldn't care less about jewellery, but precious time was ticking away, and he had to keep the woman on side. "Thanks, Fern. One more question."

"Yes?"

"Where's Eumundi?"

―――――

Dane wasn't close enough to see the freckles scattered across Leif's nose, but the kid's messy white-blond curls shone like a beacon.

An older woman teetered on the top rung of a stepladder, reaching for a vivid painting that hung from the wire mesh that lined one of the canvas walls. The three of them laughed together as Leif held the woman's ankles steady, and Luna received the painting.

It looked like they were packing up, which meant Dane had arrived just in time.

He stuck his hands in his pockets and ambled closer. "Want some help?"

"Dane! You're here!" Leif hollered, as though he was afraid Dane wouldn't be able to hear him. No chance of that.

Luna stilled. "You're here." Unlike Leif's, her voice and expression were entirely neutral. Dane couldn't quite get a read on her. Was he welcome? Or not?

Dane stepped a little closer. "It would seem so."

"That's perfect." She gestured to the older woman who'd stepped down from the ladder. "Sabina was going to drop us off at Little Cove, but now that you're here, you can take us. Right, Sprite, let's get this all loaded in the van so Sabina doesn't have to do it all on her own."

Leif beamed, and Dane wondered what, exactly, was the catch.

"What's in Little Cove?" he asked.

"Grandma, and Grandad, and Uncle Cayden, and—"

"Your uncle's in Noosa?" Dane didn't need any further explanation. He barged into their stall, stacked a couple crates, and lifted. "Where to?"

Luna jangled a set of keys in Leif's direction. "Show him where the van is, will you, Sprite?"

Leif took off with one box, and Dane's hands clenched around the corners of the bottom crate as he did his best to keep up through the maze of stalls. Forget beacon. The kid's bouncing curls—so very similar to those on another head—were practically a siren's call. Dane knew exactly how Cayden's hair would feel looped through his fingers—all silk and sun and spice.

His step hitched, and he just about tripped, but Dane caught himself in time.

"Get it together, Faulks." That fantasy needed to go back in the box.

"Come on, Dane." Leif tugged at his shirt.

Shit, he hadn't even noticed the kid come back to him.

"Sorry Leif, lead the way."

It only took another twenty-eight minutes to pack up Sabine's beat-up old van and wave her on her way.

"Nice car." Luna smoothed her fingers along the leather piping of the passenger seat.

Dane shrugged. He tapped the wheel. "He's staying with your parents?"

"Fishing, much?" Luna smirked.

Dane shrugged. No sense playing coy.

He steered out of the parking lot, then followed Luna's directions toward the coast.

"Mum and Dad wanted quality time with all of us. Family,

you know? Besides, Cayden didn't have much choice since Gordon threw him out."

"What?" Dane's head snapped around so fast he inadvertently yanked on the steering wheel and sent the car off onto the gravel verge.

"Dane!"

"Sorry." Course corrected, Dane drove on. He glanced in the rear-view mirror to check on Leif. Cayden would kill him if Dane hurt his family. "Sorry if I scared you, Leif."

"'S'all right. Mum does that all the time."

"Hey!" Luna protested. "What is this, Attack Mum Day?"

"Sorry, Mum."

"Gordon threw Cayden out?" Dane pressed. "Why?"

"What did you expect would happen? He accused Gordon of being a cult leader."

That was rich. "Not exactly. And can you blame him?"

She looked away into the blur of trees.

"Luna?"

She sniffed. "He could have asked me."

"How?" He didn't need to point out that she'd effectively fallen off the face of the earth. Her family had no way of knowing what had happened to her.

Luna shifted in her seat and fiddled with the hem of her shorts.

"What's a cult?" Leif asked into the awkward silence, and they both groaned.

"Nothing to worry about, Sprite."

In the rear-view mirror, Dane saw Leif squint out the side window, looking worried despite Luna's reassurance. Then he cried, "Oh, look! A kangaroo just bounced from behind that tree!"

Dane sighed. Leif seemed to be a resilient soul, but Dane knew all too well that a stoic exterior could cover a lot of hurt. He resolved to be watchful. For Cayden's sake.

Seconds later, they passed a 100 kph road sign.

The vibrations of the rough country road thrummed through Dane's nerves. How much further? He thought maybe he should ask, but Dane wasn't entirely sure he wanted to know. He wasn't about to turn around. Dane was too stubborn for that, but his hazy plan to ensconce the man in his bed long enough to get Cayden out of his head was starting to feel far too real.

"I saw his face when you left the House of Glass," Luna said.

Who? "Cayden? How is he? How did he look?"

"Sad." The lead-weight word came from the back seat.

He looked up to see Leif's reflected eyes—lion eyes—staring straight back at him.

Why? He wanted to ask, but didn't, because he already knew the answer.

Sad. The word unfurled in Dane's mind. If Cayden was unhappy that he'd left, then maybe, just maybe, he'd be open to Dane's proposal.

Hope seeded, Dane floored the accelerator.

CHAPTER SIXTY-THREE

CAYDEN

The world spun.

"Shit." Never would he ever do the Noosa Heads walk in the middle of the day ever again, Cayden resolved.

He'd gotten all the way back to the foreshore at Little Cove before he really lost it, and he had to grab for the nearest object, which turned out to be a beefy dude with a handlebar moustache, tattoos galore, and red polka-dot board shorts. Not your typical combo, he thought.

"Y'right there, mate?" The surfer looked down to his forearm where Cayden still gripped and where they were both getting sprayed from a freshwater shower rose.

"Fuck. Sorry, dude." Cayden let go. "Just, you know…" The words petered out because he really didn't know anything at all.

"Bit dizzy, eh? Get some water into you. Sun's a killer today."

"Sure." Yep. He'd do that…the minute he'd climbed the bazillion stairs back up to the holiday apartment where his folks were gearing up for an afternoon of *special family time*.

"Ugh."

"Come on. Drink." The surfer stepped away from the shower and pushed Cayden so close his sneakers got drenched.

He didn't care—just cupped his hands under the flow and slurped up a few mouthfuls of water, moaning when it hit his parched stomach. Then his brain.

He slurped again and again.

"Good, eh?" The moustache twitched.

"You have no idea." He slurped some more, not caring that he sounded like a fool. Eventually sated, he pulled away and lifted his sweaty shirt to wipe away the drips.

"Thanks, mate," he said. "You're a lifesaver."

"No worries. Take care of that noggin, eh." He tapped his own bronzed forehead.

Cayden threw the guy a quick salute. He took one last look at the amazing view out to the Pacific, then set off across the zebra crossing and up the Little Cove's steep switchback stairs.

Cayden followed the path up between the jumble of older homes and newer holiday apartments. Sweat streamed off of him, and by the time he arrived at Pandanus Street, the world was again spinning.

He leaned up against the nearest trunk on the tree-lined street to take a necessary breather and tilted his head back. The speckled light streamed through the leaves and fluttered in his vision like a wild flight of butterflies.

He closed his eyes and rolled his neck in an effort to reverse the woozy spin.

It didn't work.

Jesus. What he wouldn't give for a beer and a nap.

The thought made him wonder if he'd remembered to ask his dad to buy more beer.

They'd gone through at least a couple of six-packs since he'd opted to crash on their fold-out sofa instead of a yoga mat beside Leif in the circus tent. The little dude was probably better company, but he could do without the three dozen other inhabitants.

Eventually, he got his act together enough to push away from the trunk of the tree, and he dragged his feet the short distance to his parents' holiday apartment building.

Twelve feet away from the entrance, he stopped dead.

A figure stood in the centre of the footpath.

A Dane-shaped figure.

Staring straight at him.

A summer-time mirage?

A consequence of heatstroke?

A figment of his lusty imagination?

Cayden rubbed his untrustworthy eyes.

Nope. Still there.

Walking toward him.

Lips moving.

"Cayden?" the mirage said.

"Holy shit!" It really was Dane.

Cayden's vision wavered. Spots of black flashed around the man's glorious chocolate waves, and the next thing he knew, Dane had caught him high around his ribs.

"Hey, hey. It's okay." That calm, commanding voice.

For just a moment, Cayden let his woozy head drop forward onto Dane's shoulder. Just to rest. No other reason.

Of course, that didn't explain why he caught his thumbs through Dane's belt loops or spread his fingers as wide as they'd go, getting as much traction as possible. Or why he flared his nostrils and inhaled the man's familiar scent, as though it was as needful as water.

He lifted his head just enough to see Dane's Adam's apple bob and a hint of a pulse thrum under his jaw.

Cayden felt that pulse, like electricity, coursing between them.

So, so, so good.

Except…

Memory crashed back in and stirred the hurt up.

He firmed his stance and levered a few inches away from the man's chest. "What the hell are you doing here?"

Dane's gaze skittered away, and the electric tendril between them died.

Could the man not look him dead in the eye?

"Well?" Cayden didn't bother with bullshit politeness. They were well beyond that.

Dane swallowed.

Was the man nervous?

Good.

He fucking ought to be.

"I'm here to ask—" Dane started.

"Boys!"

Dane stiffened.

Fuck. Perfect timing.

Cayden leaned sideways around Dane's rigid shoulder to see his mum. "Yeah?"

"Come out of the sun."

"Give us five minutes," Cayden called over. Simultaneously wanting and not wanting time alone with the bastard.

He felt Dane tug on his sweat-salty shirt. "She's right. Come on. You're swaying on your feet."

"Like five minutes is going to make a difference. I've been out in the sun for hours," he muttered, but followed Dane inside anyway.

Either the dude had that kind of power over him, or it was the heatstroke.

Just inside the apartment, Cayden ducked into the bathroom and shut the door tight, muting everything but the mad rush of his own heart. He grabbed the edge of the porcelain sink with both hands. Shoulders to his ears, he locked his elbows and let his head slump low.

Deep breath, Spicer.

In through the nose.

Out through the mouth.

In through the nose…

…out through the mouth.

What the hell was Dane doing there? Hanging out with his family as though he belonged?

Had Cayden missed a chapter of his own story?

He splashed water on his face, then wrung out a washer and slung it around the back of his neck. If he cooled off his brain a degree or two, the situation might make more sense.

Maybe.

Or he could stop being a chickenshit, leave the bathroom, and demand an answer to his question.

"Lunch!" Mum rapped on the door.

"Be out in a sec," he called back.

When he stepped out of the hallway, Leif leaped up from the end of the sofa bed. "Uncle Cayden!"

"Hey!" Luna hollered from the little kitchenette space in the corner. "Inside voice."

"Wow, Sis. That's a serious mum voice you've got there."

She sent him a scathing look.

"And the look, too. Impressive. Good thing I'm immune. Hey, little dude." He tussled Leif's hair, flopped down beside him on the sofa bed, and did his best to not look for Dane like a heat-seeking missile.

Through the French doors off the side of the main room, the delicious curve of Dane's back looked rigid.

Cayden couldn't look away.

Dammit.

Failure. Utter failure.

"Did you go for a swim?" Leif asked.

"Nope."

"For a hike?"

"Yep."

"Around the head?"

"Yep."

"Wow."

"Yeah, it was pretty cool. And hot. And long. And dry."

"Did you see any koalas?"

"Nope."

"Aw, bad luck."

"Yep."

"Sprite. Enough with the interrogation. Come and sit up."

Leif moaned as though sitting at a table for lunch was torture. Which probably wasn't far from the truth.

Would anyone notice, Cayden wondered, if he closed his eyes and just…opted out?

Just for a minute.

Maybe two.

Between Hen's mind-blowing phone call, the heatstroke, and being close enough to Dane to touch, it'd been a hell of a morning. His mind was shot to shit, and his body wasn't much better. He didn't know if he ought to rest and recharge, spill his news and celebrate, or prepare for fight or flight.

Ice touched his cheekbone, and he flinched. "Shit." Had he actually fallen asleep?

"Hey." His dad stood over him with a glass of iced water that dripped with condensation. "You all right? Caught a bit too much sun, eh?"

"Sorry. Thanks, Dad." He sat up and slugged down half of it in one go, then the rest. Every muscle seized as he stood, feeling about as creaky as the fucking sofa bed.

"Come on. Lunch is on. Your sister brought some kind of savoury pastry to share. Vegetarian, apparently, but it smells good."

It did smell good. In fact, it was a wonder Cayden hadn't noticed the aroma earlier. He'd blacked out for a minute back there.

Must be Dane's fault, Cayden decided. The shock of being near him was probably enough to overwhelm all five senses.

"And your mum made chocolate mousse. Special request." Dad winked.

Chocolate mousse?

For him?

Dad leaned in. "Next time, do you think you could ask for sticky date pudding? She never makes it for me."

"Gerry," Mum warned.

"What?" Dad asked. "Aren't I allowed to have a private conversation with my son?"

"Don't pull that innocent act with me. I hear you."

Dad chuckled and patted Cayden's shoulder, then crossed to the kitchen. He stuck his head in the fridge and rattled around a few bottles. Beside him, Luna stood at the stove with her back to the room, but Cayden could see her cheek lift with the hint of a smile.

One after the other, Cayden looked to each member of his family, and he knew for sure that, finally, he'd fixed what had been broken. His work there was done.

Cayden was finally, officially, free.

The enormous sense of relief he felt had barely had a chance to whoosh from his lungs when the French door clicked and swung open. And there was Dane, looking rumpled and delicious.

As if mesmerised, Cayden tracked Dane as he moved across the room, rounded the dining table, and sat with his back against the wall. With his shirt buttoned to the not quite top and his wavy hair all chocolaty dark and still not trimmed, and, ugh…the man did things to his gut.

And to things lower.

Would it be too obvious if he left the room for a private minute to get himself in order?

Probably.

"Come and sit up, honey." Mum waved him over.

"Beer, Dane?" Dad asked.

"Sure. Thanks, Gerry."

They clinked beers. "So, to what do we owe this visit?" Dad asked.

Dane's gaze flicked over to Cayden, then away. Then he took a long draft of his beer.

Beer.

Just the thought of it pulled him across the room like he was caught in a fucking tractor beam.

Cayden eyed the bottle in Dane's hand.

How dare he come back into Cayden's life, drink his beer, and act all normal? The dick.

Technically, Dane owed him nothing. But Cayden was pissed and hurt, goddammit, and he didn't know what to do with either emotion. Not then. Not in front of his family. Not when everything else in his life felt like it was on a happy upward trajectory.

The whole thing made him feel like a fucking Yo-Yo. Which was just plain irritating.

By the time he crossed to the table, dragged out the chair beside his nephew, and sat, Cayden had taken a firm hold of his balls—metaphorically speaking.

"You didn't answer the question, Dane. What are you doing here? What do you want?"

Does what you want include me? That was his real question.

But Cayden couldn't ask it.

No way.

It was Dane's turn to make an offer and risk the pain of rejection.

Not his.

For a long second, everyone went perfectly still.

"Don't be rude, Cayden." Mum sounded shocked.

Dane held up a hand. "It's okay, Fran."

"No. It's not okay. You're our guest."

Dane nodded to acknowledge Fran's point. "I came to ask Cayden a question." He took a sip from his water glass and said nothing more.

Cayden fingered his cutlery and pondered murder versus manslaughter.

It was justified, your honour.

Lucy placed a bowl of green salad in the middle of the table, then returned from the kitchenette with an enormous flaky pastry pie. "I hope everyone likes asparagus."

"It looks delicious, darling," Mum said. "Thank you."

"Oh, don't thank me. I just stuck it in the oven to warm up." She pulled the quilted mitts off her hands. "Next Wednesday, you'll have to come out to the markets to choose something different. The artisan bakers in the area are amazing." The pastry cracked as she cut through the crisp layers, releasing an incredible aroma.

The happy family domesticity was too much.

Cayden couldn't take it anymore.

"A question?" he prompted Dane.

"Later. I don't want to bother your family with—"

"No. Let's hear it." Ugh. Spicer! Shut it.

"Okay." Dane lay his knife and fork back down on the table and laced his fingers together. "The communications team at Carter Medical Supplies has a temporary opening for a research liaison officer. The man who usually does it is heading off on paternity leave. They found a replacement, but it fell through. I thought you might consider it."

Cayden's chin just about hit the table.

A job? Was the man serious?

"I know it isn't quite what you want to do, but it's steady

for three months, and it'd be a good stopgap position while you get your freelance business up and running, and you know…it'd put you closer to Luna and Leif. Quality time together. And, maybe, if you want, you could…" his eyes strayed sideways, "…stay with me, and we could…well, you know…maybe…" Dane's bumbling words finally came to a stop.

"You're offering me a job?"

Dane nodded. "Yes."

"And to…" How could he say *fuck* in front of his family? "To live with you?"

"To stay with me. Temporarily."

"While I get myself sorted. Yeah, I heard that line."

Dane frowned. "It's not a line. I don't want you to feel stuck. But this is a good opportunity. A stepping stone."

"Dane, I'm not a liaison communication officer, or whatever you called it. I'm a—"

"Journalist. I know. But that's a broad church. You told me yourself that you're really a glorified researcher."

"No, I said I'm a glorified fact-checker."

"Same difference."

"No, it's not the same at all." Cayden put his knife and fork down, hard.

"If we're in the same place, we could be—"

"Boys." Fran interrupted their bickering. "I don't think this is an appropriate time or place for this particular discussion."

"No. I want to hear this. Could be what, Dane? Partners?" The man had rejected a blowjob, for fuck's sake. How did he go from rejecting that to shacking up together? In a matter of days? "I think you've missed about twelve stages of the relationship cycle."

Dane's face shuttered. "That's not what I meant."

Of course, it wasn't. Dane was after a temporary convenience. Someone to scratch his itch. Meet a need. Then discard.

Temporary.

Cayden shuttered his heart against the want for more. "Thanks for the oh-so-kind offer, but I don't need it."

CHAPTER SIXTY-FOUR

CAYDEN

Dane sat stiffly. As though he'd practiced eating with a bloody six-hundred-page book balanced on his obstinate head.

Cayden wanted to poke him.

Roughen up his edges.

Bring back the human that had once curled around him all night long.

"It's not me you want." Cayden tried his level best to keep the hurt from his voice.

"I'm here, aren't I?" Dane said. "I came all this way."

"Oh, you might think you want me, but you don't *want* want me. Want doesn't have an expiry date."

Dane gently placed his knife and fork down in the middle of the plate, aligning them perfectly parallel beside his untouched lunch. Cayden was so caught up watching those long, elegant fingers, he almost didn't catch Dane's softly spoken words.

"What if I need you?"

Well, fuck. That just made it worse. Need was all the things he'd been for his family. Need was obligation and responsibility. Need was all the things Cayden was determined to give up.

His phone jangled in his pocket.

"I'm done being needed." Cayden scraped his chair back with an unforgiving screech on the tile floor. "I can't just tuck myself under your wing, Dane. I need to be in charge of my own life."

And I can't do that while I wait for your temporary axe to fall.

On the third ring, he pulled his phone out. Henrietta.

"I've gotta take this."

He thumbed the screen. "Hey, Hen." He ducked out through the French door that went...nowhere. Shit, no escape. "This isn't exactly a good time."

"No time for that, Cayden. I found out they're talking to one of the network upstarts at the Sydney office, too. Check your emails. You have to decide. Do you want the job or not?"

"I'm sort of in the middle of something, Hen. Does it have to be this second?"

"Now or never."

His gut roiled.

It was like so many choices in his life.

Yes or no?

Give or take?

In or out?

Binary extremes.

"What do you really want?" Hen asked.

Good question.

He hated the urgency, but it was a weird sort of comfort zone, too. Familiar. Like so many other trials—life or death, safe or unsafe, lost or found—extremes with very real ramifications.

But he'd found Lucy safe and very much alive.

Mission accomplished. It was time to put down that sword. Look to other dreams to drive him forward.

He peered out through the sliver-thin gap between buildings to their view of the Pacific Ocean. It gleamed gold and silver and deep cerulean blue, and, from a distance, it looked perfectly still.

No whitecap waves.

No peaks or troughs.

No highs or lows.

Why couldn't life be calm waters and grey tones?

Why did every decision have to feel like all or nothing? Win or lose?

Why couldn't he just flip a coin?

Heads or tails?

Want or need?

Cayden turned to look inside.

Leif was telling some crazy story with wild arm gestures. They laughed. All except Dane. He looked serious. Intense. A deep crease wedged between winter-blue eyes.

What was he thinking?

I need you. Those were Dane's words—not exactly the words Cayden wanted to hear, but want and need weren't true binaries. Just like heads and tails, they were two sides of the same coin. And wasn't it the coin that was counted?

He'd railed against his family's needs, but that didn't mean he didn't love them.

Couldn't need be the basis of love, too?

And why did he even have to consider love?

Why couldn't he just test things out? Trial and error?

What would be the harm in giving the man a chance?

He could take Dane up on his offer—no strings; only pleasure—to come and go as inexorably as the ocean tide.

What was there to be so serious about, anyway?

"Cayden!" Hen yelled in his ear.

"Ah! What the hell, Hen?"

"Don't 'what the hell' me, Cayden Spicer. You've not heard a word I've said, have you?"

"Ah…"

"That's what I thought. Now, put me on speakerphone and check your email. I need your digital signature."

"Bossy," he grumped, but he clicked her to speaker and opened his email. He wasn't about to sign a contract just on her say-so. But he trusted Hen. She'd never steered him wrong. "It's kind of weird that they haven't asked for an interview. Have you read this over?"

"Absolutely. You're already employed by the network, so, technically, it's a transfer. It's a standard associate producer contract. Which is why they approached you through me," she spoke rapid-fire. "Apparently, the plan is to shoot over the winter to take advantage of the dry season up north. Expect to travel. Before that, it's prep work. Normally, they'd do a pilot. To test the waters. But Sheridan demanded all-or-nothing, so the show's guaranteed for at least one season. Instead of a pilot contract, you'll get a three-month probationary period. Do a good job, and it'll stick."

"In other words, I'm being handed the dreamiest of dream jobs, so don't fuck it up?"

"Exactly. You'd be a fool to pass on this one, Cayden. Don't think, just sign. Now."

She was right. It was a no-brainer. He didn't need to think about it. All he had to do was take action.

Cayden hit reply, dashed off his words of acceptance, and then hit send.

"Done." His voice quavered just a little.

"You did it? For really real?"

"Yeah." It felt so good to do something purely for himself.

Hen squealed. "I'm so proud of you. My little—"

"Please don't call me your little boy, Hen. I'm not a green

twenty-one-year-old anymore, fresh out of university. I'm a—"

"A grown man. I know. It's just…" she sighed.

"I know. I love you too. Thank you, Hen. Your faith in me means a lot." Cayden turned to look back through the glass French doors to his family. And to Dane.

Maybe he needed to have a little faith, too. Faith that if he gave Dane a chance, the man might eventually see their connection as special enough to hold onto long-term.

It was a risk, but, maybe…just maybe, it was a risk he was willing to take.

He had the dream job.

Did that mean he could get the dream man, too?

He looked back through the glass at Dane.

Not that Dane was a dream.

Don't lie to yourself, arsehole. Of course, he is.

"I've gotta go, Hen. Thanks again."

"You're welcome. See you next week. I'm dying to hear about all the crazies at the retreat."

"Ha! You got it. See ya."

When Cayden was ready, he opened the door and stepped back inside, drawing not just Dane's gaze, but his whole family's avid attention.

"What did I miss?" he asked.

Leif opened his mouth, probably to regale Cayden with the entire story he'd just told, but Mum quelled him with a touch of her hand. "Everything all right, honey?"

"Yeah, great actually. Seems I have a new job." He grinned.

Dane stiffened and frowned.

"That was fast," Dad said.

"Where?" Luna asked.

"It's not totally official yet."

"But you want it." Dane sounded sure. No question there.

Cayden squeezed the wooden back of the chair. It didn't give. "Yeah. I want it. I want a lot of things."

Leif contorted like a pretzel to look up at him, so Cayden tousled the little dude's hair and pulled out his chair to sit.

"A better offer, huh?" Dane's frown deepened, but he leaned forward, too, as if, like Cayden, he couldn't switch off the desire to inhabit the same space either.

"Where's the job?" Luna asked again.

"I thought you were going to go freelance," Mum said. "Isn't that what he said, Gerry?"

Dad shrugged. "The boy can do what he likes. It's his life."

"Cayden! For goodness' sake! Where's the blasted job?"

"Luna! Inside voice." Mum's parental words brought them all to a dead stop.

"Sorry, Mum." Luna bit her bottom lip. Her eyes went owl-wide, then she let out a snort-laugh and trailed off into a fit of giggles that Leif caught, then Dad, and then Mum, and...

"Jesus. What a shit show." Cayden wished he could mock every single Spicer at the table, but he understood the hilarity for what it was—wholehearted relief.

He rolled his eyes with satisfying exaggeration and felt the muscles between his shoulder blades loosen just a tiny bit more.

Mum eventually settled. Her eyes still smiling, she cleared her throat and asked, "Right, then. Cayden, could you please tell your sister, and the rest of us, where this miraculous new job sprung from?"

"Yeah, where, Uncle Cayden?"

"Not Melbourne, by the sounds of it," Dad weighed in.

"No. Not Melbourne." Cayden nudged Leif with his elbow. "I'd live closer to you and your mum. Would that be cool?"

"Seriously?" Leif grinned and nodded like a bobblehead.

He'd take that as a yes.

"They've based production on the Gold Coast, but," he held up a hand to stop anyone from leaping in, "it's a nation-wide television program, so I'll be spending a significant amount of time out on location. Wherever the stories go, I'll go."

"But it's based up here? In Queensland?" Dane leaned forward till the table foiled his efforts.

Need.

Cayden tried, but he couldn't look away.

"Stay with me." Dane raised a hand, just as Cayden had done. "Wait. Before you answer, just think." His hand dropped to the table. "I don't know the whole job situation, but you're going to need somewhere to live. Right? It'd be practical to stay at my place. No need to rent or buy somewhere else. And we get along all right."

We get along all right?

"You want a velvet tuxedo to go with that magnificently romantic proposal?" Salt filled Cayden's voice. He went to shove his seat back again, but Dane had trapped his hand.

Or so he thought.

He looked down to discover that he'd reached across to Dane, just as Dane had reached across to him.

In the middle of the table, between the pepper and the salt grinders, they'd hooked their pinkies together.

As if by instinct.

It was entirely, horribly, pathetically sweet.

The ocean rushed turbulently in his mind—so loud he barely heard Dane's next words.

"I know you don't need me. I mean, nobody ever really needs anyone, right?" His lips twisted, like the words had to fight their way out. "But what if…" Dane paused and frowned at their fingers, linked so tenuously together. Then his eyes flashed up.

Antarctic winter eyes. Stormy and deep.

"What if I need us?" Dane said.

It hurt to see Dane so unsure of himself—so entirely exposed.

In front of Cayden's family, for fuck's sake.

Need.

He felt the gentle squeeze of Dane's pinkie, and Cayden finally realised that the sort of need Dane was talking about felt different. It wasn't responsibility and obligation. It wasn't a duty. It restricted nothing.

It was necessary—like breathing.

Like life.

Like love.

Flip a coin, Spicer.

He squeezed Dane's pinkie back, because he could, and because he wanted to give his own truth back. The ocean in his mind rushed on in its wild, measured rhythm, scouring with its salt and sand and water, and Cayden felt the stubborn ground he'd stood on finally start to erode.

Dane squeezed his pinkie again. "I want you," he said this time.

Utterly groundless.

Utterly exposed.

And Cayden's world simply crumbled away.

CHAPTER SIXTY-FIVE

DANE

Dane assumed the deck was exactly the same—the same loamy green aroma emanating from the rainforest; the same cool drift of air cycling up the crater side; the same rough wooden railings where he'd practically inhaled Cayden the last time they'd clung together there like a pair of ringtail possums in heat.

Dane assumed it was the same, but, in truth, he wasn't paying much attention. Cayden occupied all his senses—the back-lit tips of his golden eyelashes; the hint of coconut in his hair; the salt-sweat tang on the fine skin at his temple; the catch and release of his sun-cracked lips; and the growly sounds he made in the back of his throat as Dane plundered deep.

Dane hot-stepped them across to the sliding glass door of his haven where, unable to help himself, he pushed Cayden up against the glass and canted his hips forward, flush to Cayden's heat. The door shuddered at the abuse.

Cayden palmed his arse cheeks, kneading, pulling, pressing in rhythmic anticipation of what Dane sure hoped was to come.

All evidence pointed to yes.

Lungs tight, he broke the lip lock to suck in a necessary breath. Cayden mouthed across to his ear, "Get inside."

"I'm trying." Dane couldn't quite contain the whine in his voice because he *was* trying, but the sliding glass door would not cooperate.

"Not in there." Cayden bit Dane's fleshy lobe and tugged, the sensation ripped straight to his groin. "In me."

"God, yes."

Two little words…

In me.

Have me.

Consume me.

Dane had two words, too…

Need you.

Want you.

Crave you.

One arm still tight around Cayden's waist, he leaned sideways and tried the door again.

The thing wouldn't budge.

He eyed the banana lounge reflected in the glass. It wasn't ideal, but…

"I dare you." Cayden's breath ruffled the hairs behind his right ear, and every single one stood up to attention. No erectile dysfunction there. No sirree. "It's *our* haven. If someone comes along and gets an eyeful, it's their own damn fault."

"Don't you care if anyone sees your bare arse?"

Cayden's lips quirked, "Well, technically speaking, I think it'll be your bare arse they'll be seeing. Not mine."

That set off a cascade of images of things to come in Dane's mind.

Privacy be damned.

He abandoned the door, threaded his fingers through

Cayden's hair, and directed the man's mouth back to his where it ought to be. Then he swivelled them both around in a move smoother than Sinatra and fast-danced Cayden to the banana lounge.

He needed Cayden naked and horizontal.

Now.

They hit the cushions.

"Oof."

"Mmph." He tucked his face into the crook of Cayden's neck and bit down on the ligament that sprung up as Cayden stretched, searching for contact.

He shoved a knee between Cayden's legs, spread his left thigh wider, and ground down with heat and pressure and intent.

Cayden squirmed. He humped Dane's leg and scrambled for the tail of Dane's shirt. Beneath it, he found bare skin that he scoured with his fingernails, pulling heat to the surface and a moan from deep in Dane's chest.

"Naked," Cayden insisted.

Dane lifted his hips away just enough to get a hand on his belt buckle and to heel off his shoes. He shed his pants and boxers in quick succession, then took his own sweet time undoing each button of his business shirt, absorbing Cayden's hot, roving gaze as he slowly stripped himself, then returned to help Cayden untangle his shorts from his ankles.

Once he regained his position, Dane guided Cayden's legs to drape over his thighs till they threaded together, tight as a reef knot.

With such a fine view on offer, Dane took his time. He smoothed a hand up the curve of Cayden's upper thigh and hip, thumb spread wide to touch the groove where honey skin met curls, and, higher yet, skimmed the happy trail to where Cayden's hard dick pulsed, dark and angry.

"You're such a sexy fucker. You know that, right?" He ran a thumb from base to crown.

Cayden just hummed in return.

Dane skimmed the head with a fingernail—a tease for them both—then arched over to kiss where a sheeny drop of precum welled.

"Ungh." Cayden's abs bunched, and they both groaned when the reflexive move changed the angle, thrusting his dick firm against Dane's mouth, demanding entry.

But Dane didn't comply.

Broad daylight left little to the imagination. Even less when Cayden hitched his knees high and wide to bare himself fully. The move left Dane in no doubt of what Cayden wanted.

Still, he asked, voice all grit, "You want my cock in you?"

Cayden flashed a half-smile. "I want all of you in me, but your cock'll do for a start."

"Cheeky fucker."

"Promises, promises." Cayden waggled his eyebrows and thrust his hips in rapid succession as if to say *get the fuck on with it* in Morse Code.

"You're such a dork," Dane laughed.

"And yet you love me."

Love.

Cayden's sugar-sweet fluttering eyelashes told Dane he was just joking around, but Dane's breath still hitched in his throat.

Did Cayden love him?

Did he love Cayden?

He had no ready answer except to reach for his discarded pants to find his wallet and the two handy packets inside. Dane ripped the lube open, drizzled a slick onto his fingers, and then applied himself to the serious task of opening Cayden up and taking Cayden apart, bone by bone.

"For fuck's sake, Dane," Cayden writhed, "if you don't get in me now, I'll get in you."

The threat turned Dane's blood to lava.

He must have stilled his ministrations because Cayden planted a foot in the middle of his chest and growled, "What in hell's red arse are you thinking about? You look wrecked."

Wrecked?

More like volcanic.

About to explode.

"One day…" he started, but it didn't really matter what he'd let Cayden do for him one day, when Cayden was already laid out for him. Ripe for the taking.

Dane held Cayden's gaze as he pressed the man's knee up tight to his chest and searched with his fingers for the spot that'd make him...

Growl.

Cayden's grip was a pincer around Dane's bicep. "Get. In. Me. Now."

Fuck.

"As you wish."

He let go of Cayden's foot, but didn't remove the pressure as he grabbed the condom, ripped it open with his teeth, and sheathed himself.

Cayden choked out a laugh. "You've done that before."

Dane didn't answer, just lined up and pushed, slow and steady, feeling Cayden's tight heat open up around him. A warm welcome home.

Cayden breathed through the brief discomfort and urged Dane on.

Dane didn't let up, didn't breathe, didn't stop, not until he was balls deep.

"Dane." Cayden shuddered.

The sound of his name on Cayden's tongue triggered a ragged breath out.

Cayden's ring clenched, squeezing Dane tight as he retreated, till only his crown was gloved in heat. The banana lounge protested as he drove back home, strong and steady, finding a groove.

"Dane."

Cayden's lax lip was there for the taking. He had to bite it.

He reached under Cayden's arse to lift him an inch and curled over.

"Fuck."

Dane swallowed Cayden's harsh curse as he tongued the soft inner flesh of his mouth. Advance and retreat. Advance, retreat.

Cayden growled again at the teasing. He gripped Dane's neck and pulled him down till all Dane knew was teeth and tongue and clinging lips. No barrier at all. Cayden owned his mouth.

Dane hauled air in through his nose and, finally, let loose. Almost frantically, he drove into Cayden. No holds barred.

The banana lounge protested beneath them.

Cayden gasped, then reached for another breathy kiss. "Too much," he said.

But it wasn't. *Never enough*, Dane wanted to say, but that wasn't right either.

"No." He nipped Cayden's lip, absorbing the blissful sigh that Cayden didn't even try to contain. "It'll never be too much."

He slowed his pace and stretched his own legs out long, toes over the edge of the banana lounge, and used his full weight to press deep.

Cayden tightened his hold, chests flush together, so close that Dane had barely enough space to thrust in staccato beats.

He didn't care.

His balls didn't care.

All he needed was friction and heat and the glazed look in Cayden's eyes that said you, me, us, and the answering one in his own that he was sure said yes, yes, yes.

Dane rocked in place, right where Cayden wanted him, and reached to feel where they joined. Taut and hot.

"Dane." Cayden searched for another wet, messy kiss, then bucked with surprise when Dane slipped the tip of his finger inside and stretched his rim. Just enough to—

Cayden threw his head back. Every muscle strained as he flew over the edge. His cock erupted in wild, jerky bursts.

At the mercy of Cayden's wild rhythm, Dane had no control against the fire that bloomed deep within. One full thrust, tunnelled through the pulsing clamp of Cayden's tight hole, was all it took to set Dane off, and he spilled deep inside.

Spent, Dane collapsed. Every single muscle oozed like molten lava.

"Damn," Cayden breathed into his ear. The puff of air tickled, but not even the hairs on the back of Dane's neck had the energy to rise. Not anymore.

"Mm-hmm."

Cayden's ankles unlocked from behind Dane's hips and slowly slid down the backs of Dane's thighs to settle in the nooks of his knees, as though that was where they belonged.

One of Cayden's hands drifted idly up and down the curve of Dane's lower back. The other set up house and home on his arse—palm flat, fingertips curled into his crack.

Dane understood the impulse to possess. He felt the same. But he couldn't inhabit Cayden forever.

"Y'know, that coulda been better," Cayden said, deadpan, as Dane slipped out.

Dane was about to lift his head to ask what the fuck Cayden was on about when he felt the quaking in Cayden's chest.

"Not to be critical or anything, buuuut…"

Dane unthreaded his fingers from the man's curls, determined not to take the bait.

"But?"

Shit.

He planted his hands on either side of Cayden's shoulders and pushed up into a plank.

Cayden's hands chased after him.

Served the man right.

Except Dane felt the sudden loss, too.

Fuck. Would he never get enough of the man?

Dane dropped onto one shoulder, rolled to lie flat on his back, and made quick work of the condom.

Cayden rolled, too, plastering himself along Dane's body with his head on Dane's shoulder and his hand on Dane's chest, just as they'd ended up every other time they'd slept together.

Every. Fucking. Time.

God.

Was that how it would always be?

He slung his arm around Cayden's shoulder. Right where it ought to be, too.

Cayden combed through his sparse chest hair to his right nipple, stirring it to life.

Dane didn't move.

"But?" he asked for the second time, and again felt Cayden's seismic laugh.

Dane swatted him on the arse-cheek. Because he could. And Cayden jerked playfully forward, shoving his junk into Dane's hipbone. It wasn't the worst consequence in the world, and Dane thought about swatting him again.

"Buuut, I think we're going to need to practice a fair bit." Cayden nipped at his shoulder.

"Practice?"

"Mm-hmm." Cayden stretched to lick delicately at his left nipple, then blew on it till it roused—two for two—and a shiver ran all the way to his cock. Cayden must have noticed it twitch too, because his hand drifted south with admirable precision. "Practice does make—"

"Yoo-hoo!"

"Shit!" Cayden stilled, stunned into immobility with one hand wrapped around Dane's firming length.

A rapping sounded on the wooden side of their haven. "Knock, knock."

"Edie," Cayden horror-whispered.

"Dane? Cayden? Yoo-hoo. Anybody home?"

Hearing their names broke the spell.

His adrenaline surging, Dane knocked Cayden's hand away, scrambled off the banana lounge, and grabbed his boxers.

He jammed his feet in and pulled them up.

Cayden just sat there, wide-eyed, cupping his junk.

"It can't be the boys, Edie," came another woman's voice. "They left days ago."

"Shit! That's Maxine," Cayden whisper-shouted and folded the top third of the banana lounge cushion over his lap. "Make them go away."

Dane didn't have the heart to tell Cayden that his ridiculous attempt at modesty screamed *caught in flagrante*.

"Come on." He snatched up Cayden's shorts from the deck and held them out. "Put on your big boy panties."

Cayden blinked. "That's not even funny."

Footsteps sounded on the wooden stairs.

No time. Dane stepped in front of Cayden, doing what he could to guard him from view, then squared his shoulders and turned to face the threat.

"I wonder if it's Dane. Bernice said he came to the hub this morning, looking for Cayden." Edie stepped out from behind the side of the building, then pulled up short when she saw them.

Dane didn't care when Edie shamelessly ogled his half naked body. When he heard a rustle and felt movement behind him, though, he wanted to lash out and blind the woman for seeing what was private, and precious, and his.

Dane felt Cayden's hand touch his right hip, then slide around his abdomen and pull them flush together.

"It's probably just possums," Maxine said, still hidden from view. "Come on, Edie. Let's go back to the hub."

A slow grin spread across Edie's face. "Bonking in the daytime? What self-respecting nocturnal possum does that?" She winked at Dane with more spice than sugar, then herded Maxine back down the stairs. "What was that about liquorice tea? Mm-mm, sounds delicious."

"But, but," Maxine sputtered, "you hate liquorice...and tea."

"Tastes change as we mature, dear."

Dane stood still a beat longer than was probably necessary. By the time he was sure they were alone, Cayden had wrapped his other arm around his waist and hooked his chin over his shoulder.

"Comfy?" Dane asked, with only a slight hint of sarcasm.

"Mm-hmm."

They stood like that for a while, and Dane wondered how warmth and comfort could feel so foreign and yet so right.

Cayden's chin pressed down firmer, and, somehow, Dane knew he was smiling.

"We're going to have to get used to it, you know, if we're going to be together," Cayden said.

That got him turning. "What do you mean, 'if'?"

Cayden's smile turned to a grin. "I mean, *if* we're together, we'll have to practice a hugging." He firmed his hold. "And kissing." He pecked the corner of Dane's mouth. "And groping." He slipped a hand beneath the waistband of Dane's boxers for a squeeze. "And—"

"Fucking."

"Mm-hmm." Cayden's grin turned to pure, wicked sunshine. "Because practice makes—"

"Perfect."

EPILOGUE
DANE

Four weeks later...

"Mmm." Dane felt Cayden's touch right down to his bones, but his kisses were even better. He did his best to keep still and pretended to be asleep as Cayden's lips travelled up the back of his thigh, over his right butt cheek, licked a path up his spine, and finally pressed an open-mouthed kiss over the back of his rib-caged heart.

It was a miracle Cayden didn't comment on how Dane's heart tripped a beat, but Cayden's lips had already progressed north. He pecked kisses up Dane's neck, nipped at the corner of his jaw, and butterfly-kissed Dane's ear with his nose.

"I found a spot," Cayden whispered.

"Mm-hmm."

That he had.

A delicious spot. Except it wasn't enough. Not nearly.

When Cayden tugged his earlobe with his teeth, Dane gave up all pretence of sleep and tried to roll over to catch those delicious lips.

All he wanted was a taste. "Come back to bed."

But Cayden stopped him with a hand planted in the middle of his back and a finger to his lips. "No time for that, Mr. Faulks. We've whiled the day away, and now there's your mate's barbeque to get to."

Dane grumbled something incoherent into the pillow, expressing every wish he ever had that they could stay wrapped around each other in their cherry-red silk sheets.

Cayden snorted, which really wasn't the response Dane was looking for. Instead of snuggling, Cayden reverse-crawled off the end of the bed, cheekily slapping Dane's bare arse as he went.

"Oi!" Dane protested.

He rolled over, eager for retribution, but Cayden just grinned and traipsed out of the bedroom.

Dane drifted, half-asleep, till he heard his man sing-song from down the hall, "Come see."

"Grr..." Left alone in his sea of cherry-red silk, Dane couldn't hold back a deep rumble of discontent. He was caught between wanting Cayden all to himself and wanting to show him off. Twenty-four hours hadn't been nearly long enough to christen his apartment and make it theirs. The last thing he wanted to do was leave their warm bed.

Cayden appeared in the doorway. "Dane, get your arse in gear."

"Fine." He rolled off the bed, nearly taking a tumble off the slippery edge. He hadn't quite gotten used to Carol's unfortunate couple-warming present, but since Cayden liked them, he'd cope.

Showered and dressed, Dane squeezed past Cayden's many boxes stacked along the hallway to the lounge room, where Cayden's stuff was piled high in every corner.

Instead of serenity, his apartment now screamed chaos and colour and Cayden.

It made Dane smile.

He saw a pile of flattened boxes by the balcony door. "Have you been unpacking? How long have you been up?"

"Hours and hours, Sleeping Beauty." He bussed a kiss on Dane's cheek as he breezed past to the bookshelves. "Come see. I found brilliant spots to put our pots."

A knot gripped his stomach. "What the hell, Cayden! You rearranged Alice's library?"

"Isn't it perfect? I had a hard time deciding where to fit Leif's Big Bird, and then I saw Enid Blyton's *The Faraway Tree* right next to *The Secret Garden*. Total classics."

Dane swallowed back the bile and swept his eyes over the collection.

It's okay, Dane, he counselled himself. Cayden hadn't removed or rearranged anything in the precious collection. He'd just added to it.

With more than just his rainbow paperweight lodged between the books, the clear definition between what he'd read and what he hadn't yet read was gone. But the books were still there. Alice was still there. In fact, the bookshelf gave off even more of an Alice vibe after Cayden's input.

Cayden directed his gaze to where Leif's happy, yellow four-leaf-clover, leaf-printed pot sat in the middle of the top left shelf between the two novels that took him straight back to the magic inside. Cayden was right—it was perfect.

If anyone else dared to mess up his most precious possession, he'd have pitched a fit. But with Cayden's breach of that barrier, Dane felt unexpectedly okay. It shouldn't have come as a surprise, but it did. Everything about him and Cayden was unexpected.

Especially how much he fucking loved the guy.

Dane shoved his hands in his pockets and rocked back on his heels, wondering what other magic might come next. Whatever it was, he was ready to accept and enjoy.

Dane shook his head, amazed at the radical shift in his life.

"What?" Cayden asked.

"Nothing. Just." He paused. "You can read any of the books. If you want."

Cayden's expression softened. "Yeah. Yeah, Dane. I want."

Jesus. Talk about hearts and rainbows and fucking unicorns.

Dane swallowed the lump in his throat and diverted his gaze to look for his and Cayden's pots. "What about your…" Dane tried to think of a positive adjective to describe Cayden's travesty of a creation, "…interesting pot."

"Hey, don't bag it! You want me, you've got to accept all of me, including my butt-ugly pot."

"I said it's interesting. Interesting's a good thing."

"Uh-huh. Sure. Anyway, since my pot has a bit more of an angsty vibe, I put it between Salinger's *Catcher in the Rye* and this wild Sappho collection."

Sappho? Oh, God. "Busting to read that, are you?"

"Don't you know it." Cayden threw him a wink. "And yours is between—"

"This should be good." Dane leaned forward to read the titles. "A Georgette Heyer historical romance and Homer's *The Odyssey*? You think I'm stuck in the past? Why those?"

Cayden shrugged. "Well, you're clearly a reformed rake." He gave Dane a meaningful glance. "Emphasis on the reformed. And…and, um…" He turned to the shelf and fiddled with a random book.

"I'm a soldier searching for a way home?" Dane eyed the plain spine of Homer's text. Not much help there. "What does that have to do with me?"

Pink streaked Cayden's cheeks. "Oh, ah…I was thinking more of the siren's call, but, yeah…let's go with that. You've found your way home. Fantastic."

"Siren's call?" he asked, but Cayden had already turned and wound his way through the maze of boxes to the apartment door.

"Come on." Cayden pulled the set of house keys Dane had given him from the hook by the door. "You ready? Don't want to keep your friends waiting. Must make a good impression, and all that." He twirled the keys around a finger, the clink-clank jarring in the quiet room.

Was Cayden nervous?

Dane stepped right up close and took a swift, firm kiss, then pulled just far enough away to look directly into Cayden's eyes.

"They'll love you, y'know."

"How do you know that?" Cayden asked.

Dane thumbed away the frown line that appeared between Cayden's brows, then shrugged and gave the only truth he knew. "How could they not?"

The End

THANK YOU

Thank you for reading *Haven*!

I don't know about you, but I really want to know if Cayden ever opens that beverage stand. Mind you, that's his Plan B...

Plan A is Dane, and true lurve, and copious amounts of hot and heavy...

So, yeah, that's a hard, "hell, no!" to the beverage stand.

If you'd like to support Dane and Cayden and their glorious future together, please consider sharing your thoughts in an honest review.

WANT MORE?

Sign up to my *newsletter*

Visit me at:
www.ptambler.com
facebook.com/PTAmbler
instagram.com/pt_ambler
twitter.com/PtAmbler

Or contact me at:
ptambler@ptambler.com

ABOUT THE AUTHOR

PT Ambler is an Aussie mm romance author who gets a ridiculous amount of joy letting her guys run rampant on the page.

Other fun things include sing-along road trips, zoning out in nature, day dreaming, people-watching in cafes, and coffee…smooth, delicious coffee, covered in shavings of rich, dark chocolate…mmm.

One of these days, she's going to write a novel set in a café about a gorgeous barista, who… (PT drifts away into a caffeine-fuelled daydream).

The Tennyson Bend series features five Aussie friends who don't know they're looking for happily ever after until they stumble upon it, and fall.

Printed in Great Britain
by Amazon